Lyft Faetels
Inner Peace

Volume II of the Lyft Faetels Trilogy

Jeffrey Wood

iUniverse, Inc.
New York   Bloomington

This is a work of fiction. All of the characters, names, incidents, organizations, and dialogue in this novel are either the products of the author's imagination or are used fictitiously.

iUniverse books may be ordered through booksellers or by contacting:

iUniverse
1663 Liberty Drive
Bloomington, IN 47403
www.iuniverse.com
1-800-Authors (1-800-288-4677)

Because of the dynamic nature of the Internet, any Web addresses or links contained in this book may have changed since publication and may no longer be valid. The views expressed in this work are solely those of the author and do not necessarily reflect the views of the publisher, and the publisher hereby disclaims any responsibility for them.

ISBN: 978-0-595-49455-2 (sc)
ISBN: 978-0-595-61109-6 (ebook)
ISBN: 978-0-595-49734-8 (dj)

Printed in the United States of America

iUniverse rev. date: 8/12/2009

To Mom, a lover of literature,

who passed away before she had a

chance to read this.

ACKNOWLEDGMENTS

Many thanks to my wife Barbara, who, during much back-and-forth discussion after relating to her that I wanted to write a novel, suggested the central theme center around a little being who just might happen to have resided in the retaining wall that fronted our previous home. Four years and a trilogy later, Lyft is still flitting around in my mind, waiting on his next adventure.

Kudos go to Kristine Chin, whose previous editorial experience at *Chemical Engineering Progress* magazine proved invaluable in the final edit of this novel. I can only hope she has enough patience left to assist with *Lyft Faetels* and *Lyft Faetels: The Beginning*, waiting in the wings.

My sincere thanks to my sister, Sherry Roberts, whose encouragement along the journey to production helped spur me to the finish line; also to Christine Grady, a savvy Web administrator, who, after reading the manuscript, enthusiastically laid out much of the electronic strategy being employed to help market the book; and to Dov Harrington, whose advice is ongoing in that regard.

Recognition goes to all those cheerleaders who read the initial manuscripts and whose encouragement helped to make this exercise a marketable venture. I can't list you all here, but you know who you are. It's been quite a journey. To you all, I can only hope this final product exceeds your expectations.

FOREWORD

I'm telling you this story because I believe you deserve to read it. I have judged you to be a discerning reader who cares about this habitat we call Earth. If I am correct in my premise, then prepare yourself for a wondrous fantasy.

The name *Lyft Faetels* is a combination of two words from Old English: *Lyft*, meaning air, and *Faetels*, meaning bag, translated into "bag of air or wind." As Lyft's apprentice, I was not privy to all the events in this story. Thus I will tell those parts I didn't witness firsthand as he related them to me. Lyft, let me assure you, is profoundly adept at giving accounts of any escapade in great detail, and someone had to edit his pontifications. Others who were involved in parts of this epic also shared with Lyft or me their versions of some of the events that took place while I was engaged elsewhere. Additionally, there are a few details that Lyft and I pieced together according to what we learned of those who peopled this most recent escapade. These are incorporated as well.

I would like to think that this volume is my small contribution to help rein in the insanity of a world besieged by its own occupants. Although I doubt it will have much effect, I'd like to think I've planted a tiny seed of rationality somewhere within humankind that could keep us from annihilating one another.

As Lyft has now become a part of me, I find him bothering

me at all hours of the night, propelling me onward to ensure his engagement in other efforts to save humanity from itself. I can only hope those who read this novel appreciate his efforts on our behalf.

CHAPTER ONE

I was sitting on the back deck studying a two-page spread in the travel section of the *Times* pertaining to the Pamir Mountains in Tajikistan. Not that I was planning an imminent journey, but the scenery and descriptions were captivating, the author's chronicled exploits notable. They had me transfixed between sips of café au lait and brief pauses to marvel at the beauty of the one-hundred-fifty-foot firs wavering overhead in gentle, balmy spring breezes. I noted that the top of the left tree had changed its appearance, as many small branches had generated in the early spring, filling it out, lending it an air of benevolent watchfulness. At the very top, where previously several spiny spikes had reached to the sky, a perfectly shaped cross had formed that could be seen from the deck below and from no other angle. I was bemused to have been a spectator to its ecclesiastical perfection throughout the year. I would have to ensure less paganish behavior, exhibiting forthwith a more pious attitude in the backyard, as the deck and house had now become officially sanctified.

Memorial Day weekends in the New York City area were normally marked by excessive traffic, crowded airports, and beach openings. The city was generally quiet once the bridge-and-tunnel folk emigrated, but the connecting arteries pre and post were generally clogged, exhibiting a need for continual surgery. Trying to avoid that insanity at every opportunity, I was content in my early Sunday morning quiescence with the paper spread before me on the table, marveling at the author's ascension of the Pamir Knot, when the paper began vibrating.

Oh no, I groaned inwardly. *Not now.*

"Hello, my friend. How've you been? Seems like ages since I was here."

Right, ages. Less than sixty days ago, and here we go again, I thought. "Why, hello, Lyft. And what's made you a stranger over the past two months? Good to see you!"

"Don't be so sanctimonious. I know you're not overjoyed to be interrupted on this beautiful spring morning, but something important's come up, and we need to get moving on it."

Lyft had my full attention, as I knew the serious side of his personality normally evinced a crisis. As he spoke, he materialized atop the chair opposite me, which was unusual, as he normally settled himself unannounced on my left shoulder. I sensed agitation in his demeanor, realizing from his posture that a serious face-to-face discussion was about to ensue. His taloned feet gripped the back rung of the chair as he gently rocked, his large, pure brown eyes centering on me with the impending news.

"We've identified a major problem, and if something is not done immediately to reverse what we think has happened, we are all doomed."

"Pretty strong stuff for seven fifteen on a Sunday morning. What's up?"

"I'll tell you what's up. We have sensed something amiss for some time, but now we feel we understand the dynamics of it."

"Who's 'we,' Kimosabe?"

Lyft leaned forward, talons extended from one large hand, tapping the glass table. "You know, one meaning of that term you just used is 'horse's rear end.' You wouldn't be referring to me as such, now, would you?"

"Absolutely not. Trusted friend is how I see it. Who's 'we?'"

"The 'we' are the Klinque scientists closest to some of the plate activity we've been sensing deep in the Earth's crust. I don't know how much you know about tectonics, but right now, there's more going on within the Earth than there was at its formation."

I stopped midsip. "Whoa!"

"Whoa is right. What has happened is that the spin of the Earth's core has increased, resulting in more volcanism worldwide, which has heated Mother beyond her tolerance level. This is causing tectonic plates around the Earth to expand, leading to severe earthquakes, major shifting of land masses, and a profusion of additional CO_2 in the atmosphere. Armageddon as we know it."

I paused, noting the cackling of a crow somewhere overhead in the morning quiet. "This is serious."

"An understatement if I ever heard one."

"Sorry, but this is hard to get my head around."

All two feet of him rocked on the chair and his eyes widened. He exclaimed, "For us too! Think of discovering it. Along with all that, there will be a marked increase in volcanic pollution in the atmosphere. An increase in the Earth's temperature plus volcanic winters would be a catastrophe. And if the volcanic activity increases, we could have worldwide nuclear winter for God knows how long. Think of the weather fronts generated by such a scenario! It would truly be the end."

I quickly raised both hands in frustration. "Lyft, this is too big for us to handle. How in the world are we going to alert governments around the world to act on this?"

"We're not."

"What do you mean, 'we're not?'"

"Just what I said. By the time the UN got through with debate about plans to deal with the situation, we'd all be fried, or maybe flash frozen. We have a plan. And it began some time ago."

"Who has a plan?"

He wagged a talon. "You ought to know me well enough by now to realize that I always have a plan."

"OK, so now," I said, placing my feet up on another chair, turning at an angle and straightening my paper, "I can get back to the news and relax." I felt him seething. I glanced at him out of the corner of my eye. "I'm on vacation," I ventured.

I considered pointing out that it was supposed to last for two months, but Lyft was nearly apoplectic now.

He thundered, "Punch the time clock, lad, 'cause you're now on it."

My full attention again turned to Lyft gesticulating on the back of the chair, exhibiting a full-blown St. Vitus. I felt it best to not be a smart-ass and to listen to what he had to say, as he was not only my true friend, but my employer as well. I placed the newspaper on the table, subconsciously folding it in the manner in which it had been delivered.

Sitting up and leaning forward, I said, "OK, tell me the plan."

Lyft's silver one-piece suit sparkled in the sunlight. Bejeweled with buttons down the front, it flashed, keeping pace with his temper. His short arms, although in proportion to his body, had prodigious extender talons, which he proceeded to wave in my face. His Tam O'Shanter bobbed, and his large, oval, muddy-colored face wrinkled into several centuries of lines as he exclaimed, "What, do you think you're a union member? I've had no sleep for months working on this, so don't talk to me about vacations. I've left you alone for a reason, as I promised you time off after our last escapade, but this can't wait. This is serious with a capital S!"

Even though I'd been interrupted and had a burning desire to get back to the article on the Pamirs, I decided to leave the paper alone, having the fleeting thought that if I touched it, Lyft's temper might set it afire.

"OK, OK, I get it. Sorry for being flip, but sometimes you bring out the worst in me. I apologize. Just tell me what we're going to do."

"That's better. Here're the basics."

Just then, Barb came out of the house wearing her nightgown and a white terrycloth, pink-trimmed bathrobe and looking bleary eyed. "What's going on out here?" she hissed, her big brown eyes narrowing. "You two are noisier than a one-man band."

As if that weren't enough, Marquis, our miniature apricot poodle, began yelping in the kitchen, his piercing tone echoing off the trees beyond the hedge, his paws scrabbling against the inside of the screen door as he tried to join the party on the deck. Barb quickly went to the door and let him out. He dutifully came to each of us, tail wagging, eyes sparkling, before he ran down the step to the lawn to immediately evacuate his bladder.

From next door, "Christ, I'm trying to sleep, so keep it down out there!"

Lyft piped up, "It's blasphemy to take the Lord's name in vain on the Sabbath, or on any other day, for that matter. And if you look to the top of the fir tree, there you'll see another reason for the neighborhood to practice a little more veneration."

The window slammed from the upper story next door. Barb looked up and covered her mouth with her hand in an apology to whatever deity was looking down upon us, hopefully with great beneficence.

"Why, Lyft, it's a perfect cross. How on earth did that happen?"

"Maybe not on Earth, although it seems to be a natural occurrence, albeit some would say a supernatural occurrence. Either way, who's to doubt it? You know, the cross has a lot of history, most of it not rooted in Christianity. Prior to Christian adoption, it was a pagan symbol for almost all cultures, having various meanings for each."

I interrupted, "Does that mean I can exhibit impious behavior out here, then?"

Lyft pointedly ignored my comment.

Barb said, "Interesting, but not a subject for lecture before morning coffee. Let me get mine, and then I'll join you boys for what I'm sure will be a fascinating dialogue."

As Barb went into the house, Lyft whispered, "Any more irreverent exhibitions from you, and you'll end up in purgatory. I wouldn't be out here in a windstorm if I were you."

She retrieved her coffee, came back out on the deck, and settled in for the explanation. At five foot four with tousled short brown hair and delicate facial features, she looked lovely in the morning light, even without her makeup. Twenty-five years of marriage and two children showed little effect upon her natural beauty.

"OK," said Lyft, his eyes looking directly into Barb's face, "here's what we're up against. The spin of the Earth's core has somehow increased its velocity—we don't know why, and it's difficult to determine how fast, but it has—heating up all the different levels of what constitute the collars surrounding the inner core."

As he paused, Barb and I sat riveted. Even Marquis remained attentive. The chirping of two cardinals in the nearby fir ceased, as if they were listening too. "As you may know, the inner core we feel is solid, made of something like iron, perhaps iron and nickel combined, no one really knows, but we do know it spins at a constant rate, or at least it used to." Lyft's forehead wrinkled. "How do we know? Through exact measurements of seismic events over long periods of time. However, lately, we have detected a marked increase in speed of the spin, and that increase has heated up the outer core surrounding that of the inner, which, in turn, has heated the Earth's mantle, or lithosphere, causing substantial expansion."

Lyft threw his talons in the air and flitted back and forth. "This is tantamount to the end of the Earth as we know it, because all the tectonic plates could expand at once, causing major rifts, excessive volcanic activity, and earthquakes the likes of which no one has ever seen. Tsunamis will circle the Earth, the sky will turn black, nuclear winter will set in for eons, volcanoes not yet formed will spew ash and poison into the air, and it will literally be hell on Earth. Nothing living will survive if something is not done immediately." Placing his arms to his sides in resignation, he said softly, "I'm afraid we are all pretty much doomed if nothing occurs to reverse the course Mother has decided to follow."

Barb said softly, "Suddenly, I don't feel the need for this coffee anymore."

"Me either," I intoned. "But what on earth can be done about such a scenario? How can it be stopped?"

With a glint in his eye, he replied, "You really mean, what *in* Earth. We are working on a cooling mechanism as we speak."

My head snapped up. "You're kidding!"

"I wish this were a kidding matter, but unfortunately, it's not. What we are going to do is cool the Earth through a series of rifts and tunnels. You remember my suit and how it is made? It reflects heat and insulates against cold, depending on the environment. We're going to use the same technology for piping deep into the

Earth, and then we're going to pump liquid nitrogen into tunnels around the outer core in the hopes of slowing down the spin, utilizing the principles of contraction. We're not sure it will work, but it's the best shot we have."

"Won't the pipe melt and the nitrogen heat up as it gets to the outer core?" I queried.

"No. The pipe is being constructed so that it can reflect heat up to ten thousand degrees Fahrenheit; therefore, the nitrogen will remain a liquid. We figure the Earth's core at about seven thousand degrees, so we should be safe dealing with the outer core."

"But how do you transfer the temperature of the liquid nitrogen to the core?"

Lyft had returned to the back of the chair again. "Simple, really. Just like the principle of my suit. We reverse the polarity of the metal, which allows the transfer of cold to hot. The secret is to keep enough liquid nitrogen flowing so that it's not allowed to absorb any heat. This will be the tough part—to produce enough liquid to do the job, and then enough to eventually slow the core while at the same time attempting to keep it from spinning out of control."

"How are you—we, I guess I should say—going to go about constructing the tunnel around the outer core? It's a mammoth project if I ever heard of one."

"Tunnels are under construction already. True, it's the most brutal and the largest construction ever undertaken, but there are many of us, and our engineering skills are superior to anything above the Earth's surface."

"Yes, I remember the liquid metal penguins some time ago. How are they working out, by the way?" I had to admit that the LMPs filtering carbon out of the oceans to the tune of ten tons per day were pretty ingenuous.

"Quite nicely. In fact, they're soon to be constructed worldwide. But that's another issue. So, to continue, since the approximate radius of the outer core is about 2188 miles, we figure the circumference of the circular tunnel needed to surround it should be 13,745 miles, plus or minus three hundred or so." Lyft wrinkled his left forehead as if he were raising an eyebrow, obviously waiting for me to compute the enormity of the task. He had no eyebrows, but slits for air intake, enabling him to equalize any pressure almost instantaneously, and the sight of what looked to be open wounds was somewhat disconcerting. I nodded my head for him to continue.

"The diameter of the tunnels will be about eighteen feet, so maintenance can be done inside them if necessary. There's really no time to lose."

He had my attention as I leaned forward, forearms on the table, hands clasped. "I can see that. So what's our role in this? To convince the various world governments of the magnitude of all we're doing?"

"Actually, no. Your job is to oversee the first project in the Wakhan Corridor, a wild, remote area of Afghanistan otherwise known as the Roof of the World."

"Couldn't you have picked a site a little closer to home, like the San Andreas Fault or something?"

"Nope. Has to start there. Too many earthquakes occur there in a short time, so the area is suspected as being the number-one epicenter event location. It's near where the Indian–Australia plates merge, also encompassing the Java Trench and the Ring of Fire, from which emanated the tsunami that devastated parts of Asia several years ago. You will go to those locations as well. As a matter of fact, you will be traveling the globe, overseeing various projects where the great plates of the Earth meet. I would advise packing your best winter gear first, as much of the Wakhan is fifteen thousand feet or more above sea level. The summers are minimal and the winters brutal, so pack accordingly. I will help you of course."

Barb and I looked at each other, disbelief mirrored in each other's faces.

I queried somewhat sheepishly, "How long am I to be gone?"

"Until the projects are finished."

"That could be years."

"Could be, but won't be. We don't have enough time for it to be years. Our workers have already carved out the first shaft and have begun work on the bottom tunnel around the outer core. We will pretty much have that aspect of construction well in hand by the time you get to the Wakhan. The construction has already been laid out. What you are to do is ensure its continuance on the surface. We'll take care of the subterranean issues. And those issues are huge, by the way. All the sections have to marry up in one circle, and then a filtering system to keep the nitrogen cool must be constructed at the various plate junctures. Look on it as a giant circle with many subloops, all connected, somewhat like your own circulatory system. Someone needs to ensure those operations on the surface are not interrupted while we concentrate on our end below ground."

I heard a bird call to its companions in the stunned silence that followed this pronouncement. How could I respond to instructions like these?

"You know, I'm not at all qualified for this," I finally managed to stammer. "Why don't you get an engineer for this type of work?"

"We already have numerous engineers on the project," Lyft replied without skipping a beat. "I'm interested in your management skills. I need someone to vet our employee roster of over five thousand in the Wakhan, due to some security issues facing us."

"And I have to go to Afghanistan? Why?" I asked, raising my hands in the air. "All I need is a computer. I can do it from here."

"Perhaps, but there are other issues as well. Some of these locales are pretty wild, and in many areas, there is no governmental allegiance, so you can pretty much get my drift here."

I grabbed my coffee mug, toasting it a little too violently in Lyft's direction, spilling the now-cold coffee on the table. "Great. I'll have to sharpen up on my martial art skills."

Sensing my agitation, Lyft took on that kindly look that only he could employ, with his arms spread in supplication, his tone one of empathy and understanding, his eyes wide and moist, absorbing my angst, defusing the moment. "You know, normally, I would never put you in harm's way, but this is different. We are all at risk here, so perhaps it would not be a bad idea to take some basic self-protection course, just in case you need it."

I glanced at Barb who had blanched visibly. She said, "So this is going to be dangerous."

"Yes, it could be. I do not anticipate it, but there is some risk involved. However, we have no choice in that regard, so we best deal with it."

"So when do I leave?"

"One hundred eighty days from today."

"Well, at least that gives me a little time to get used to the idea and to get in shape—not easy for a fifty-year-old, slightly pudgy, balding male."

Lyft raised an eyebrow, or what should have been an eyebrow, intoning, "*Slightly* pudgy?"

Barb giggled. I ignored the thrust and said, "What will you be doing in the meantime?"

"Convincing multiple governments to assign protected status to the areas in which we'll be operating. That will be essential for success."

"Good luck. Some of these 'governments' are nothing more than self-serving dictatorships."

"I realize that. They have their methods, and we have ours. Leave that aspect of the project to me."

"OK then, what's first on the agenda?"

"Get your wills in order."

"Oh, thanks. Any other encouragement?"

"I'm serious," Lyft said, looking pointedly first at Barbara and then back at me. "We'll be going into some unsavory territory. You know I'm pretty savvy in the protection department, but it's best to be prepared. Think of Barb and the children, just in case."

"Well, just so you know, we are pretty buttoned up in that department. Our wills are in order. There's no need to change anything from when we reviewed them several months ago. How about you? Do you have a will?"

"Don't need one."

"That's right." I grinned. "I forgot, you're a card-carrying member."

Lyft, who had long ago explained to me the benefits of the Klinques comprising a truly communist society, remained nonplussed. "I have no assets, no need for them. However, our traditions will suffice to ensure any last wishes are instituted should the inevitable arrive early."

"It's beautiful," I said, ignoring him. "Me working with a communist who pays people off with precious stones, exhibiting the most capitalist philosophy—payola at the highest level for tasks well done. Just like corporate America."

"Harrumph. You can't typify me. In this day and age, it takes any number of philosophies to get the job done. Why do you humans have to have a tag for everything? You have this propensity for placing things in neat little boxes—he's a rightist or leftist, a communist, a fascist; it goes on forever. Philosophically categorizing people leads to misrepresentation and underestimation of their capabilities. Machiavelli had it right. Do what it takes to get the job done, and damn the political labels. I prefer to get the job done, thank you."

"OK, boys," said Barb with inflection. "So this is getting a lot done. Lyft, would the next step, per chance, be to order some major cold-weather gear?"

"Yes, and tropical gear at the same time. There will eventually be some shuttling between the two climates, as the next location will be tropical near the Java Trench. As a matter of fact, most of the work will be done from temperate to tropical climates, with the exception of the Andes Mountains, where the Nazca and South American plates meet. And both of you need to be immunized against nearly everything on Earth. I'll give you a list."

Barb asked, "Why me? I'm not going."

"Oh, you very well may," said Lyft.

Barb and I looked at each other somewhat askance. The dog's ears perked up, indicating that perhaps his radar has picked up an incoming bogie. A truck's rear door compartment shuttered down somewhere nearby, slamming at its conclusion, metal on metal, causing a jay to shriek its displeasure.

"The reason you could be traveling is to understand the nature and magnitude of the project so that when Jeff talks to you remotely, you can understand what's happening on the other end. There's nothing worse than not being able to communicate to the other partner the gravity of a project if one partner can't understand the issues because they haven't been realized first hand. That's number one. A second reason for your occasional travel is that sometimes it takes a woman's sensitivity to break through testosterone-infused ineptitude. I can see where talking sense to locals from another viewpoint will be of value in certain situations that are sure to arise, and we may need your temperate expertise from time to time to explain what we are about. Remember, some of the people we will be dealing with have a thirteenth-century mentality, and they can only see into the next day or into the next growing season at best. So we have the issue of communicating the importance of our mission to them, while at the same time not inundating them with scientific gobbledygook serving only to make them more suspicious. Remember, it's what's not understood that is most dangerous, not what is."

Barb queried, "Isn't language a problem? I'm only fluent in English."

"Not to worry. We will have interpreters where needed—some women and some men, depending on the circumstances."

"What about the home front? The kids, and especially the dog. Marquis needs care and insulin twice a day."

"As for your children, they can take care of themselves. They too will have a mission, to ensure all goes well here. They have their own worries and concerns and will have the added responsibility of ensuring that their mother does not come under undue stress due to her husband being away for an extended period. Cristine and Brad will be fine, trust me. As for Marquis, he will have the best of care, we will see to that. You need not worry about him. Once you explain the salient points of the project to your son and daughter, the significance of the venture will weigh on them to do the required and then some. This is where we all pull together."

"OK then," said Barb. "Time to get busy."

She went into the house, returning in a few minutes with L. L. Bean, Cabela's, and Patagonia catalogs.

"Let's take a look through these and see what we need."

From Lyft, "I like her style: no nonsense, just get to it."

"Well, you should check out this article first," I said to her. "It just so happens it's about the Pamirs near the Wakhan Corridor, and it wouldn't hurt anyone here to read it, as the author just returned from an expedition of climbing the Pamir Knot."

Barb asked, "What's the Pamir Knot?"

"Well," I said, "according to the article, the Wakhan Corridor is a shallow valley between Ishkashim and Qala Panja, bounded by the Pamir Knot. It's a strip of land separating Tajikistan, where the Pamir Mountains are located, from Pakistan and the Hindu Kush. The Pamir Knot is the junction between two sets of mountain ranges: the Big Pamir and the Little Pamir. The Big Pamirs rise two thousand to three thousand feet above the Wakhan, which, don't forget, is already over sixteen thousand feet above sea level in some places. This area is at the eastern end of the corridor and is now part of a wildlife reserve because too many idiots killed off the Marco Polo sheep and those beautiful snow leopards."

I turned to look at the article to confirm the details of my lecture.

"The Wakhan is about one hundred twenty-five miles long, twelve to forty miles wide, and ties into the easternmost ranges of the Hindu Kush and the southeastern-most part of the Pamirs where they join the Karakorams in Pakistan. K2 is in the Karakorams at 28,251 feet, the second highest mountain in the world and perhaps the most lethal, so you can see what type of territory we are entering. The author calls this area one of the most beautiful in the world, and also one of the most dangerous. The article is well worth reading."

Barb said, "OK, you have me interested. That first, catalogs second."

Lyft said, "Well, while you do your homework, I've got things to do, so I'll see you a little bit later after you've settled into your day."

With that, Lyft elevated himself from the chair, floating toward the path leading to the front of the house, humming the Klinque Wassail, probably in anticipation of pending events, and disappeared in a blink. I gazed at the scene, his effortless flight never ceasing to amaze me.

As Barb collected the newspaper and began reading, I sat back, musing on past escapades leading us to a new reality. I thought about my first meeting with Lyft, the unbelievability of it, as he had floated down onto our driveway in front of me last winter after a brutal snowstorm, having winked out of invisibility, appearing out of nowhere.

He'd explained his presence due to the impending planned destruction of the retaining wall holding back the elevated roadway at the head of our property, whose stones were sacred because they imparted invisibility to him and his cohorts, and why *we* could not allow *that* to occur. I thought of the incidents with the local Mafia, the corruption of the contractor bidding on the road expansion project, and then the snowplow accident tearing half the wall apart last winter. Amusingly, I vividly recalled the interview with church officials after Lyft had snatched a boy out of midair who had tumbled off the wall and how he had orchestrated their hasty departure. Most of all, I relished his never-ending historical anecdotes, although I'd never tell him that.

I remembered how astounded I was at his initial presence, yet how readily I accepted it. I figured he was a male by the timbre of his voice, but that was only an assumption at the time. He had no hair that I could see. His face, kindly, wizened, and wrinkled, had large, intelligent eyes, reflecting the moonlight. His ears were rounded, close to his head, with overly large lobes upon which were affixed what looked to be very large diamonds, perhaps four karats or more. His skin had a leathery texture, colored muddy brown. His neck, being essentially nonexistent, was overshadowed by a long, full visage that terminated opposite his upper chest cavity. He looked to me to be somewhat of a cross between an owl and a human, minus feathers. His body was shaped like that of an owl, but his facial features exhibited normal human traits, although he had an overly large head. His body was in proportion, but his hands were huge, each having a large thumb and six digits, talons emanating from all. His dress was simple, difficult to see in the dim light, yet I discerned it was of fine quality, as the sheen sparkled and danced in the effervescent night air. I noted a bejeweled, silver metallic overgarment with precious stones for buttons, coming to his ankles, and then discovered that his feet were unshod. And what feet they were. Thick and muscular, each foot exhibited seven toes with talons extending several inches from the protrusions, grippers more than weapons.

The incredulousness of our first encounter haunts me to this day. There I was, dealing with a being who could wink into invisibility, who flew with seemingly effortless flight, exhibiting the greatest of intellect, when several hours earlier, I could not have envisioned something so alien.

I reflected on his offer to bring me into his organization, which had turned into "us." How our lives had changed since this two-foot whirlwind had inserted himself into our daily routine. Money, along with a secure future, was no longer an issue. Lyft had assured me of that. We had sealed a bargain that the property would remain beyond us in perpetuity, deeded to his dummy corporation in New York should anything happen to Barb and me. So much importance he placed on the preservation of the wall, which now exhibited a new growth of ivy and wisteria. I thought about the children, Crissy and Brad, twenty and eighteen respectively, whether they suspected anything amiss with all the displayed insanity of the past months, but as with many young people, they were pretty much locked into their own worlds, accepting much at face value if it did not directly impact them. I wondered how long Barb and I could keep Lyft's existence from them. Marquis had no issue with Lyft. They had become best of friends, with Lyft occasionally flying him around the front yard, giving the dog the benefit of a cheap thrill.

Lyft's kindness to animals was dampened by his attitude toward humans, however. He generally felt complete disdain for most of our race, which was why his continual historical proselytizing was so important to him. I truly believed that Lyft had a severe case of cognitive dissonance with regard to humanity. He detested our worst attributes, but he realized at the same time that we could all be so much more, while owing his purpose in preserving us all from our own follies. Not that there was only a little self-serving involved with his exploits. Everything he undertook reflected the attitude that he was acting always on behalf of his people, the Klinques, who lived in a subterranean society, of whom, evidently, there were millions.

We had met only Lyft, however, as not many are given the power and authority to operate on the surface. Lyft definitely was the exception with his people. I had even told him once that he should run for elected office, which was met with little humor. He had then gone on an extended diatribe about the entire Klinque political system and into the lineage of all the ruling families over the past several thousand years, which I had felt, at first, to be a complete bore.

However, once he became more animated when he reached his own family, I began to view his society in a different light and attained a new degree of respect for his machinations. Knowing that he could eventually well be in line to rule his kingdom one day had psychologically influenced my relationship with him, although I did not intend to let him know that. As far as our relationship was concerned, it was business as usual. In addition, he related to me that he was approximately one thousand years old, having lived less than half his life. It looked like I was in for a lifetime of rude repartee in a never-ending immersion of historical narratives.

As Barb read about the Wakhan, she exclaimed, "This is where the Oxus River is located. In ancient Greek mythology, it was a defining point between the known world and the unknown. I remember it from the book I have on the Greeks and their gods. I never knew it was in Afghanistan. Huh."

"Keep reading. There's a lot more."

I looked to the top of the fir, seeing the cross wave gently in the breeze. The cardinals seemed busy twittering to each other, perhaps preparing permanent residency. I thought how nice it would be to have more spots of red splashed against the greenery that served as a barrier to the rear communal road.

Barb commented, "This area is really steeped in history. Marco Polo traveled there in the thirteenth century, insuring the Silk Road's reputation as a lucrative trading route. I've never read anything about him, but can you imagine traveling from Italy deep into China back then? What it must have been like?"

"I know. It's amazing really, when you think about it. And that was only one branch of the Silk Road. There were southern branches, offshoots, tributaries if you will, that were operating wherever trade flourished. The whole era is fascinating. It established a major part of world history, as China opened up and then subsequently shut its borders, depending on which dynasty was in power."

"No wonder you and Lyft have a love affair with history."

I smiled at Barb's enthusiasm. I had talked to her often about my love for the discipline, which I shared with Lyft. He and I could philosophize for hours on the past. It helped us to understand what makes us tick, or at least that was the theory.

She continued reading, the gentle breeze ruffling the paper, a glorious, balmy spring day in the offing. She exclaimed, not really realizing she was speaking aloud, "No wonder the Afghans have little respect for Western diplomacy."

I figured she was on to the narrative explaining the "Great Game," or as the Russians had termed it, the "Tournament of Shadows," when the Wakhan became a buffer between Russian and British aspirations for dominance in 1896. It was a compromise between two great powers, separating their territory in a country that had no say about it, Afghanistan. They had never really had the conceptualization of a country until late in this century, with only the beginnings of democracy as we know it being formed today.

For our purposes, what was important is that the Wakhan was now ruled through Afghanistan, a relatively stable area politically, with little there except local small communities struggling with subsistence farming. Geographically, the area was and still is hugely important, as it's the juncture of Western and East–Central Asia. And adding more interest, at the eastern end of the Corridor at the Wakhjir pass through the Hindu Kush, time advances three and a half hours upon entry into China, the sharpest time change anywhere in the world.

I decided to go into the kitchen and give Marquis his breakfast while Barb continued reading the article. I cleaned up the dishes, which I had promised to do the previous evening, and after watching Marquis dive into his dog bowl with satisfaction, I went back out onto the deck. I found Barb ruminating as she gazed into the trees, watching those same cardinals establishing a family while we were potentially disassembling ours.

Barb looked up at me, concern on her face. "What about the general situation in Afghanistan now? Military operations are still going on there, and there are still terrorist incidents. I can't imagine Americans are generally welcomed there by much of the populace."

"True. From what I read, it's still dangerous, especially traveling around the country. Hopefully we won't be doing so much of that. Most military operations are taking place from Kabul down into Kandahar right now. That area of the country is of concern, as remnants of the Taliban and other militant offshoots seem to be hiding in the mountains along the Pakistani border, going back and forth as it suits them. Then there's the general thievery used as a cover to conceal any variety of criminal activity while, at the same time, serving to discredit Americans and add fuel to the fire. There is a lot of rivalry between tribes there, and much in-fighting, with many tribes uniting as it suits their purposes then going back to fighting each other again. One really has to understand the political landscape to operate there and get away with his life."

"I can see that."

"At any rate, I'm glad you're interested, 'cause you know what they say: 'Those who have the most knowledge, win,' or something like that. I'll leave you to it."

I went into the house and got on the Internet to pull up the U.S. Department of State's Consular Information Sheet pertaining to Afghanistan. I noted that a passport and a visa were required to enter the country and thought how interesting it would be explaining our mission to consular officials. Other than terrorist and criminal activity, one of the main security concerns was the five to seven million unexploded landmines and other types of ordinance scattered over the entire country. Random explosions were frequent on and along roads, which were poor and mostly unpaved, although I read with relief that the Wakhan area had never been mined. Highway robbery was literally rampant, and vehicles were poorly maintained and in severe competition with animals and bicycles on the roadways. Potholes were numerous, remaining unfixed in most instances, and there was no enforcement of traffic laws. Few streets were lit at night, adding to the mix of chaos from the criminal element under the cover of darkness, and policing was sporadic, if at all. Healthcare was basically nonexistent, especially where we would be. The information stated unequivocally that

Afghan hospitals should be avoided. Private clinics were operated by unlicensed individuals who had no medical degrees, and there were no agencies to monitor these operations. Phone service depended on satellites, there were no credit card services available, and all financial transactions were done in cash. Airline service was erratic, being generally unsafe. We would be flying into Tajikistan at any rate, so that was a relief.

As I read on, it would have been comical if it weren't so pathetic. To add to the country's misery, it had undergone years of severe drought from which it still had not recovered, so there were chronic food shortages along with a perpetual dearth of potable water. The good news was that we had plenty of water where we were going. The bad news was that it was all the more isolated should the unexpected occur. We were truly going into harm's way.

Aside from all the usual in-country chaos, the most prominent security issue, in my subjective opinion, was the opium smugglers in the Corridor. Most of the opium grown and processed in Afghanistan was accomplished in western Badakhshan province. The Wakhan lay in the northeastern section. However, growers had targeted the populace of the Wakhan farther east for addiction, and it was estimated that up to 28 percent of the population were drug abusers. The dealers were then able to appropriate local lands due to drug debt and use it for further cultivation, bringing the production points closer to the market.

Drug deliveries were made by four-wheel-drive vehicles on a rough road along the border of Tajikistan from Sultan Ishkashim to Sarhad-e Wakhan and then following the Pamir River through low elevations up to the Wakhjir Pass and down into the Chinese province of Xinjiang. For half the year, the road is blocked by snow, and the other half, it remains challenging to navigate its entire length due to landslides and gargantuan potholes. Subsequently, there was a lot of pack-animal traffic in the Corridor, not all of it heading in the same direction. Tajikistan offered even more attractive options for smugglers, as there were many unpatrolled areas along the border that could be crossed on foot.

As it is often a struggle to complete the trek through the Corridor all the way to China, it is easier to use the Tajikistan option, with the route heading north through the Kulma Pass directly over the Tajik–China border. Again, much of the border between Tajikistan and China is flat, so there are many more entry points into China here than farther on in the Wakhan region. Lubricating the greasy wheel, much of the smuggling is done ethnically—that is, Tajiks dealing with Tajiks—albeit in a separate country, making penetration into drug smuggling operations by authorities more difficult. Then there are the border officials at bona fide crossings who continually look the other way, paid well by the smugglers according to local standards, with the graft going up the ladder to ensure uninterrupted transportability.

Reading further, the article stated that, in recent years, the shift from opium to heroin had been dramatic. In 1995, heroin seizures were only 3 percent of all opiates confiscated in Central Asia. In 2001, they accounted for 90 percent, due to higher monetary yield per kilo and a greater punch per hit from the drug. Most smuggling out of the Wakhan centered recently on the border of Tajikistan, as it seems Russia and Europe were a better market for the drugs. Due to the poverty levels of the various ethnicities along all the border regions, there was a fertile ground for recruitment of couriers, even though the activity is abhorred in the Muslim religion.

So not only was the Wakhan area increasing its cultivation of the poppy, but there was also continual drug smuggling traffic from farther west, heading north into Tajikistan, east into China, and south into Pakistan. I was surprised there was no need for traffic lights and a good veterinarian in the Corridor. Clearly our biggest threat was not the climate or disease; it was the ever-prevalent debased human condition. It set me to thinking how to best deal with security issues when it became apparent that Lyft's usual method of financial subjugation would have to be employed. We would have to take along a huge supply of local currency, engaging in our own smuggling operation, which would be a challenge in itself. I whistled out loud at that one.

Just then, I felt the old familiar presence on my shoulder. Although Lyft was not a lightweight, he had the capacity to lessen the load by sucking more air into his apertures, thereby deferentially not dislocating my shoulder every time he required a perch. I often thought how gentlemanly it was of him to retract his talons in these instances so that I could avoid puncture wounds from his repetitive landings. Carrying Lyft around was akin to having an oversize Macaw next to your ear, and a highly verbal one at that.

"Doing some homework, eh?"

I leaned back from the computer, stretching my legs, crossing one ankle over the other, and folding my arms across my chest.

"Yes, and not finding much to like either."

"I heard you whistle to yourself. What was that about?"

"I was thinking of how we were going to get local currency into the area, which we will need for bribes. We'll need several helicopters to transport it all."

Lyft waved his hand, as if annoyed by a gnat. "Bah, not to worry, got it covered. We, I, will take along several bags of precious stones—you know, diamonds, emeralds, rubies, that sort of thing—and convert them near there through our sources. You know, that area is famous for lapis lazuli, and occasionally, diamond finds generate some excitement. But then the realization dawns that they are washed up from upheavals deep within the earth due to earthquake activity, so the excitement dies down quickly. Because of occasional gemological activity in the region, we have been able to find a particularly trusted source there with whom we do business. There should be no problem with the local currency, keeping those we need in a state of fiscal bliss."

I wrinkled my brow. "Drug smuggling would seem to be a worry. How do we deal with that?"

"You're correct; that is a concern—a big one. Payoffs may not work there. All the smugglers will want is more, more, more, until they get it all. So we will have to deal with them by the seat of our pants."

"Very reassuring ..."

Palms up, he lifted his hands. "Well, what would you propose then? After all, it's your race, so you figure out a way to deal with them."

"Very flip. You know what I would do? Take along enough hardware to blow the Wakhan to kingdom come if need be. Drug smugglers mean nothing to me, so what's a few less?"

"Clint Eastwood you ain't."

"Neither are you."

"Most aptly put. Any other ideas, primarily ones that make sense?"

"Yes. Shoot the yaks and two-humped camels the smugglers use for transport of the goods."

He wagged a talon. "Shame on you, resorting to killing defenseless animals. You should know better."

"Well, it was just a thought. You know, it does have the advantage of taking away their livelihood, so to speak ..."

"True enough, but what you are missing is this. These people are inherently poor, and drug smuggling is just another way of making a living. If there were no market for the stuff, then there would be no smugglers, so killing off all the Bactrian Camels and domesticated yaks in Central Asia will do little good. You'd just be making the poverty all that much worse. What is needed is some persuasion that there is a better way of life, and I suggest we show them some opportunities, otherwise nonexistent except for us. Now that's converting a populace."

I raised my arms in exasperation. "How in the hell do we do that?"

"Oh, give it some thought. I'm sure you'll think of a way."

"Thanks for the insight."

"You're most welcome. Now I have some things to take care of, so I'll see you later."

"I love the way you dump on me."

He danced in the air in front of me. "Me too. Before I met you, I had no dumpee, so you have fulfilled a niche in my life that I could not have envisioned prior to your arrival. Talk to Barb. She has great insight into the issues we're facing. You two will figure it out, I'm sure. See you later."

Lyft ascended, finding his way out the front door in invisible mode. The door clicked, leaving me to ruminate on the future challenges facing us.

CHAPTER TWO

As the weeks sped by, interspersed by UPS deliveries and Lyft's continual shuttle diplomacy, the full magnitude of the project we were undertaking began to overwhelm us all, even Lyft. His exhaustion was evident. Sometimes when he perched himself on the back of a chair or on my shoulder, he fell asleep midconversation. Once, he fell, badly cracking his head on the floor, splitting one of the kitchen tiles, which subsequently had to be replaced. Although none the worse for wear due to his thick cranial bone structure, he even admitted to a rude awakening.

I'd been doing a lot of homework in the den when I came across something I thought would interest Barb.

"Here's something interesting about the ETIM," I called out.

"What?" Barb asked with not a little consternation, peeking her head out of the closet. She was organizing the latest of our new gear: hiking boots and numerous boxes of thermals from Cabela's. She was intent on organization, only half listening, articulating grunts of displeasure from time to time over my having thrown the paraphernalia in there helter-skelter. I figured it would all be organized when I packed, but it was obvious my preplanning attributes were at odds with her current temperament. I thought perhaps the conversation could wait as she smacked another box into place.

"Never mind. I'll relate it to you later."

Another grunt and thud emanated from the closet.

The ETIM, Eastern Turkistan Islamic Movement, was centered in the Chinese province of Xinjiang, and as I'd informed Barb over dinner the previous night, the group had aspirations of creating a radical Islamic state in the province. It was comprised of ethnic Uygurs residing in the Uygur Autonomous Region. Founded by Communist China in 1955, the area was originally envisioned for settlement of non-Chinese inhabitants. When the Soviets invaded Afghanistan in 1980, Islamic militancy reawakened with riots and bombings as far east as Beijing, twenty-one hundred miles away. With Xinjiang being approximately the size of Alaska and China's largest province, it would not bode well for the province to become a radical Islamic state, and as I read further, I realized that China had no intention of allowing that to occur. China drove the resistance deep underground with arrests and persecution, flooding the area with development and commercial enterprises, which led to the importation of Han Chinese workers, leading to a great disparity between the two groups. The Han set their clocks to Beijing's time, while the Uygurs utilized the sun, which kept them two hours behind the Han community, and neither enclave had much to do with the other.

I exclaimed again, "You know, you really should read this. It's what we were talking about last night, about the Hans and the Uygurs."

She poked her head out of the closet, her face showing exasperation at my pedantry.

"Why? Are we going to China? How much do I care about somewhere we're not going?"

"We'll be in the region, and as I always like to know what makes things tick, I figured it might be important to know what goes on around us."

"Well, you keep reading and inform me later. Right now I've got work to do cleaning up a pig pen in here."

"Ouch."

"Double ouch for you."

I continued on. Since 1990, China had implemented a crackdown on youths under the age of eighteen practicing Islam in the province. They were not allowed to participate in religious activity, attend madrassas, fast, or wear Islamic head coverings or other religious dress. One could only wonder what happened behind closed doors to Uygurs who were caught practicing Islam after their eighteenth birthdays. Openly, discrimination abounded, from job fairs to religious activity. Suppression was brutal for those who chose nonconformity, with death sentences and executions the penalty for suspected "terrorist activities."

The IMU, Islamic Movement of Uzbekistan, was also prevalent in the area, aspiring to form an Islamic state incorporating parts of Turkey, Kazakhstan, Kyrgyzstan, Pakistan, Afghanistan, and Xinjiang province. It had links to ETIM as well as to the other numerous terrorist factions in the area. All these organizations had proven ties to al Qaeda through training and financial assistance. The ETIM had unsuccessfully tried to attack the U.S. embassy in Kyrgyzstan and had been involved in numerous terrorist plots against U.S. interests in other parts of Central Asia.

I circled on a map near me a place called Kashgar in Xinjiang, 125 miles northeast of the Wakhan–China border. As I read on, it seemed to be the center of Uygur discontent, though, to visit it, one would not discern any dissident activity. Each Sunday, it hosted the world's largest outdoor market, the unplugged eBay of Central Asia, with over one hundred thousand people in attendance, one half the population of the entire city. No doubt the local populace knew they had a good thing going and exhibited their political philosophies only on occasion when so stimulated by outside events. Immigration officers also had little control over the human flow moving in and out of Kashgar each week. Traders from all over Central Asia, and farther, could be identified selling anything and everything from fruits and vegetables to yaks and sheep. Anything one wanted, one could get, for a bargained price.

I got up to open the window, letting in a balmy breeze, and then went into the kitchen for a glass of lemonade, bringing it back to the den, where I stretched for a minute, giving myself a break from the computer. In a few minutes after some refreshing sips, I continued on.

Farther west and directly north of the Wakhan is Tajikistan, the poorest of the Asian Soviet republics, with a per capita gross national product of three hundred seventy dollars. A hotbed of radical Islamic and criminal activity, there were rumors that the country harbored terrorist training camps. Between 40 and 50 percent of the economy was related to narcotics, and skirmishes between smugglers and the Russian military were commonplace, with much of the narcotics traffic being transported through the Wakhan Corridor. Tajikistan had no major cities directly north of the Wakhan, as most of them were in the west of the country, and so from that perspective, the Wakhan was relatively isolated. Tajikistan was rich in oil, natural gas, and, of major concern, uranium, which, if placed in radical hands, was of immediate interest to legitimate governments.

To the south was Pakistan, defined along the southern boundary of the Wakhan by the Durand Line, a 2,250-kilometer border that Afghanistan never recognized. When Britain drew up the boundary, it essentially ceded much of Pashtunland to Afghanistan, splitting families and dividing land previously privately owned by poor farmers, cutting Afghanistan off from the sea. The boundary should have been maintained along the Indus River, which would have solved the problem, but the British thought otherwise in 1947. Due to its history and fundamentally to its geography, the entire border region was a lesson in anarchy. Swapan Dasgupta, author of the "End of the Durand Line," had it right when he typified the area as a stew of criminal enterprise comprised of drugs, smuggling, and fanaticism.

I took a break, standing at the bay window, looking over the idyllic scene just beyond the glass, and thinking of the mélange we were about to enter. I couldn't wait to find out what awaited us on conclusion of the first leg of the journey. Actually, the Wakhan exhibited a peaceful bliss compared to the turmoil of its neighbors. I shuffled over to the built-in cherry bookcase, struggling through the paraphernalia on the shelves to find my atlas, which would give me more of a reference to the geography of the larger area surrounding the Wakhan. Barbara was right. I needed to practice more organization, as I was constantly moving knickknacks from one pile to another in the search of various objects.

Standing while I searched a shelf at eye level, I felt a familiar presence settle onto my shoulder.

"More homework, eh?" Lyft croaked.

"Yes," I replied. "And none of it's good news. What a potpourri over there. If it's not terrorist bombs, it's drug smuggling. If not that, then drug addiction or illegal transport of arms or extortion or terrorist training camps or corruption of officials or outright banditry, or, or, or ..."

"Relax, relax. Let's sit on the couch and talk this over."

We moved to the leather sofa, my favorite spot for rumination, situated under the other bay window in the den. I sat gingerly so as not to propel Lyft through one of the windows out onto the lawn.

He continued. "So what did you expect? Nirvana? Shangri-la in the middle of the mountains like in the movie, *Lost Horizon*?"

"What about the movie? I never heard of it."

Lyft shifted position to the arm of the chair angled toward the couch so that he could properly berate me.

"Ignorant boy," Lyft scoffed.

"Hey, I resent that remark. Just because I haven't heard of a movie, you call me ignorant?"

"Sorry. I guess I'm a little tired, and I get snappy sometimes when I'm worn out. You're right; you're not an ignoramus, just a little uneducated in certain areas."

"Thanks. I'll take that as a compliment so this doesn't escalate any further. So tell me about the movie."

"OK, but I haven't much time, so I'll make it brief."

"What a relief. For once."

Pointing an extended talon at me, he snapped back, "I'll ignore that. At any rate, the movie is from a book written by James Hilton and was produced by Frank Capra in 1937. The plot revolves around a plane crash delivering a group of people to Shangri-la and the mystery of the locale and the secret it contains."

"What's the secret?"

He shrugged. "Read the novel or see the movie. I'm not going to tell."

An eye roll later, I said, "Like I've a lot of time to see a movie now."

"Actually, the movie is rather entertaining, and you just might learn something from it."

He related the scene of the High Lama, played by Sam Jaffe, railing against the misery in those times pertaining to the human condition—a kind of "the more things change, the more things stay the same" type of concept. And yes, we were going into the thick of it, to the crossroads of human insanity. *Welcome to the real world*, I thought.

Lyft concluded, "See the movie; you'll like it. As with most of my commentary, the movie has much to do with the baseness of humans, employing marvelous character studies."

"Thanks for the tip; I will. On another note," I said, ready to switch subjects, the nonengineer in me attempting to formulate the question, "how are you going to build nitrogen-producing facilities at each of the plate juncture locations you have described? Won't that construction take forever?"

"Good question. Actually, we don't have to build production plants at every location. What we are embarking on is a scheme to put recirculators and chillers at many locations, which are easier to construct, cost less money, are extremely efficient, and are less environmentally invasive."

"Guess that answers that question."

"Pretty much. Ever hear of the Cantarell Field near the Yucatán Peninsula?"

"Nope."

"Well, before I begin, I could really use a gin and tonic."

"It's only three in the afternoon—a little early, wouldn't you say?"

Lyft gesticulated skyward with both hands, talons extended, normally an indication that he was serious. "Look, I've been up for hours, so for me, cocktail hour has arrived. Now, if you don't mind, I'd like one with lots of ice and a nicely squeezed lime, if you please."

"You know, that sounds good. I'll have one with you."

"By all means, let's foster a little alcoholism while we're at it."

I ignored the comment, went into the kitchen through the

doorway, did the ministrations, and returned with two gin and tonics. I handed one off to Lyft and resumed my seat.

"Now, where was I?"

"In the Yucatán."

Lyft took a slurp, cutting it short, spitting out that I was a proverbial smart-ass. I agreed and told him to get on with it, otherwise we'd be there all night.

"As I was saying before I was so rudely interrupted, the Cantarell is an oil field run by Petróleos Mexicanos, having the world's largest liquid nitrogen plant used to pump nitrogen into the ground, creating pressure that helps extract oil. As you know, natural gas is a byproduct of oil, and as the gas is burned off, which I could never understand, as it's the biggest waste in the world of relatively clean energy, but I digress ..."

"As usual." I took a sip of my drink.

Lyft aimed a foretalon at me. "Pointedly ignoring you now—I was saying, as the gas is depleted, the pressure on the oil is diminished, and it is harder to get out of the ground with no pressure behind it, so the Mexicans decided to manufacture the pressure when it gave out. Pretty ingenious, actually. The plant has four compressors that are capable of producing three hundred million cubic feet per day and consume fifty-two megawatts of electricity, and they all run on natural gas. Ours will be run on volcanic energy but using the same principles; only ours will be five times the size of the Yucatán plant."

Lyft took a long sip of his drink as I exhaled, trying in my mind to gauge the size of the facility. He continued, relating that the first plant in the Wakhan would be air cooled during the winter, with the nitrogen chilling to somewhere around minus three hundred degrees Fahrenheit. Water from the river would cool it in the summer. The plants were already being constructed under contract with Petróleos Mexicanos, which had more experience than anyone else in this area. Completion was expected within six months.

"Their workers don't much like the climate though," he added with a chuckle.

"Can't blame them either," I replied.

"No, but that's the way it is."

I then asked Lyft about the tunnels and what boring mechanism was being used. He indicated that high-speed tunnel-boring machines with specially devised cutter heads were the workhorses. He related that going to eighteen hundred miles below the surface had its own challenges, mainly not being able to haul the tunnel muck to the surface, so side caverns had to be carved out, which was not too much of a problem, as there seemed to be ample space below ground for storage of excess soil. He gave me a lecture, more than I wanted to know, about how efficient the tunnel-boring machines were at recycling much of the tunnel amalgam, which was being used to coat and seal the tunnels themselves. He ended the lesson with, "It's actually working quite well, if I don't mind saying so."

I could swear he was preening, but the absence of feathers left that in doubt. I quacked, my egalitarianism showing through, "And what about your workers? How are you protecting them from the heat?"

"Trust me, they are well protected. You remember how I described my suit some time ago, how it is made of a combination of fiber and metallurgy, made by our scientists whose workmanship is unsurpassed?"

"Yeah, unsurpassed workmanship and all that," I said, remembering how he'd explained that his clothing had the capacity to reflect or absorb heat as required. "So your workers all have suits like that?"

"Well," he said disparagingly, "you're the one who asked, after all. However, that's the least of our problems. The main problem is the Moho."

"The Moho?"

"Yes, the Moho."

At this point, I couldn't resist. The conversation had lapsed into too serious a mode, so I jumped to my feet and danced, belting out the lines to "I Got My Mojo Working." After several bars, Lyft stamped his talons, yelling, "Enough."

I said, "Wait, there're three more stanzas."

"Those aren't the words, not the ones I know," Lyft yelled. "The ones I know are those Muddy Waters made famous."

"Well," I exclaimed—I had him there. "There was a big stink about this song, for what it's worth, and Muddy Waters tried to steal the song from Preston Foster, who the courts said really wrote it, and Ann Cole recorded *my* version of it, straight from Foster, in 1957, so there."

"Ah, never argue with a blues aficionado. Continue on."

In good form, I did, finishing the song on a grand note.

Lyft, in a calmer mode, said, "Actually, I think I like Cole's version better, more of the bayou in it."

"I agree."

"I'll speak to the Klinque about it. Maybe they'll want to adopt it as their working song as they traverse through the Moho."

"Oh, good one. I'm sure they'll love it."

I had visions of individuals, all who looked like Lyft, two feet high, large oval faces, kind, huge brown eyes, taloned feet and hands, happily swinging pickaxes, singing away. I started to laugh.

"Something amuses you?"

"Yes," I said, jumping off the couch, trotting in place with a grin, and whistling "Off to Work We Go."

"Don't say it," he thundered, hovering above me, ready for a backhand swat. "Time to get back to work."

He then went into lecture mode again, stating that Andrija Mohorovičić had discovered seismic waves changing velocity at the intersection of the Earth's crust and mantle in 1909. The bulk of the Earth, located in the mantle, being very dense, made up of rock such as dunite and peridotite, was loaded with iron and magnesium. Where the waves increased in velocity, the juncture was named the Mohorovičić discontinuity, which was basically where the crust and the mantle of the Earth met. The significance was that there was a delineation of the Earth at this point, defined by its composition pertaining to the seismic wave activity. It was found that the mantle was denser and the waves sped up. When they hit the molten core, they basically dissipated for readability, because they couldn't travel through liquid. He explained that beginning with this area, down through the mantle, was going to be the toughest part of the assignment, and also the longest.

"I can see that. Will this project really work? It sounds like science fiction to me. I can't see anything that we do could make the Earth cooler. It's like using a fly swatter against an army."

"Well," he said hopefully, pacing along the back of the chair, "we think it will work, at least temporarily, until science can get a handle on it and perhaps offer some more permanent solutions." He raised both arms in the air. "Besides, what choice do we have but to try? Sit here and fry like eggs on a skillet? That's not for me."

"Me either."

"Well then."

"Well then, how do you figure on handling the Earth's internal pressure? It must be beyond anyone's tolerance. It must be millions of pounds per square inch."

"Actually, at the deepest we'll be working, it's 33,957,000 pounds per square inch. At the Earth's core, it's 51,450,000 pounds per square inch, so we're lucky we don't have to go too deep," Lyft said with a chuckle.

"How will the Klinques handle it?"

"Easy. We live in the Earth already, as you know, so we already a have degree of tolerance for high-pressure situations. Through repetitive manipulations of our air bladders, we can become as fish in the ocean. The internal pressure equals that in the surrounding environment, so no problem there. Air itself is a little bit of a dilemma, but we think we've solved that by implementing a symmetrical pumping system alongside the liquid nitrogen that will give enough air below to work in relative comfort."

I paused to take in everything Lyft was telling me about the undertaking. I couldn't imagine tunnels strong enough to take that kind of pressure. It seemed they would implode as soon as they were gouged out. I said as much. "How do you ensure the tunnels' integrity with that kind of pressure below? Wouldn't the tunnels implode as soon as they were gouged out?"

"Perhaps the toughest of all the challenges yet. No one, including us, has ever gone much beyond the bottom of the Earth's crust, so this will be a first. However, this was a concern due to the tremendous pressure from all sides on the tunnel walls."

"Was?"

"Yes, was."

I could swear Lyft was preening again. The lack of feathers while he repeated the motions was totally disconcerting, affecting my concentration. It was a force of will to mentally focus on the lecture now.

"What's wrong with you? Why aren't you listening?" Lyft snapped.

I replied, "Well, I've seen birds preen, but nothing like this. It's difficult to listen to you when you preen with no feathers."

"Well, I'm half bird, so what do you expect? Now, listen and learn."

The teacher had scolded the pupil. He continued, straight as an arrow, talons gripping the back of the chair; the material underneath stressed with his exasperation. He related that their chief scientist had invented an alloy that, when mixed with the molten tunnel muck, formed a unique bond able to withstand pressures up to five hundred million pounds per square inch immediately upon the magma hardening, lining the tunnel cylinder. The real challenge was to ensure no cracks or breaks in the tunnel lining. If that were to occur, the whole length of the tunnel would be compromised, so the work was exacting. Using microscopic instrumentation in the examination of the tunnel linings was really taking most of the time for the project, not the actual digging, as would be presumed. However, the project seemed to be moving along nicely, in spite of the pressure differentiation and the need to address it.

I piped up, bowing to His Excellency as I arose to go to the kitchen for more drinks. "No doubt it will move along more quickly now that you've adopted a theme song. Tell the Klinques that they can thank me anytime and that I'm always at their service."

"You really are exasperating, you know that?"

"I learned from the master."

"Yes, yes, another barb, fulfilling your arsenal."

"So let me ask you another question."

"My, but we are full of them today."

"Well, this is a big deal for a layman, so bear with me. Why begin a project like this in an area such as the Wakhan? It's already fourteen or fifteen thousand feet above sea level. It adds two or three miles to the excavation and would seem to make more work. And it seems awfully close to some seismic areas, which I would think are of concern to the tunnels."

"True on both counts, but before I answer, I note empty glasses, which is no doubt why you've taken a vertical stance. I presume more drinks are in the offing, am I not correct?"

"Correct."

I went into the kitchen, made two more gin and tonics, and returned shortly after. He floated in the air in front of me, a twinkle in his eye, either due to the gin or the conversation, as he continued.

"It's seismically active, yes, but it's also remote and will not be a draw for many prying eyes, which is another consideration. For those who do have a curiosity, we have the means to control their relatively small numbers."

I figured he was talking about bribery and said as much. He corrected me, stating that not all things need to be approached from the angle of corruption. He said that employment of the locals was high on the list, but I had too many other questions to go into that specific detail.

"Where else will we be operating?"

"The area around Pulau Simeulue is next on the list."

"Paula Sime-who-eh?"

"Oh, you ignorant boy." Lyft floated into the air off the back of the chair and then settled back down, talons extended. "Not Paula, *Pulau*, pronounced pow-loo. Pulau Simeulue is an island about sixty-five miles from the west coast of Sumatra."

"How do you pronounce the other word?"

"See-meh-*loo*-eh." He fashioned his decidedly human lips around the phraseology. At that point, I centered on his teeth, much like ours, flashing white, all in perfect line. I couldn't remember noticing them to this point, taking things for granted like I sometimes do. I wondered how someone who'd been around as long as Lyft had such a neatly cut pair of choppers. I would have to inquire sometime as to his oral hygiene and see if he could get me a referral to his dentist. Momentarily distracted, I lost my concentration.

Exasperated, Lyft exclaimed, arms in the air, "Can we focus here? What the hell's wrong with you? Already hungover?"

I toasted my drink to the air. "Uh, no. Not even close. Your brilliant smile had me distracted, and I was wondering who does your dental work. I've never noticed your teeth so white before."

"That's because I've had a makeover. We Klinques get them from time to time, as we tend to outlive some of our God-given attributes. Mrs. Faetels was delighted as to how they turned out. Wouldn't you agree?"

He gave me a wide smile, resembling the Ross Ice Shelf.

"Whoa. Beauties," I exclaimed.

"Yes, aren't they though? Now where were we? Oh yes, see-meh-*loo*-eh."

This time, it was my turn to be exasperated. I placed my drink on the coffee table, exclaiming, "Great. The project will be over by the time I learn how to pronounce where I've been."

Lyft raised an eyebrow. "You might not be far off in that."

I ignored the comment. If I sent an arrow back, there was no telling when the salvos would end.

"So why an island in the middle of the most active earthquake zone in the world? The project could be swept away."

He rolled his eyes and said with some irritation, "Please give me more credit than that. Yes, the December '04 earthquake center was not far from Simeulue, and the island suffered significant damage and loss of life."

"My point exactly."

"Let me finish please. However, we will not be on the island; we will be at sea. A floating project if you will. That way, tsunamis won't bother us and, frankly, neither will earthquakes very much. We will be away from the shallows where a tsunami could form, and 95 percent of what we will be doing will be able to fit nicely on some very comfortable U.S. government surplus barges that we have acquired. This project will be a recycler and won't require the infrastructure of the one in the Wakhan."

"So we should be pretty safe there."

"Well ..."

I didn't like the sound of that, and I raised my eyebrows, waiting for him to explain.

"Safe is a relative word. We'll be operating almost on the Java Trench, also known as the Sunda Trench, where the Indian and Eurasian plates meet. It just so happens that the Eurasian plate is the one overriding the other, but that, frankly, is not so relevant. What is relevant is that the subduction rate is between six and seven hundredths of an inch per year, which is pretty quick. So we've had to pick our drilling spot gingerly, as we don't want to get caught in a vice so to speak."

Lyft went on to tell me about the Sumatra Fracture Zone that ran along the spine of the Barisan Mountains on the western side of Sumatra, linked to numerous volcanoes. He said the area was becoming active again, with Samosir Island in the middle of the Pusuk Bukit caldera showing over 1,350 feet of uplift. He related that when the last major eruption occurred seventy-four thousand years ago, the column of ash went into the atmosphere thirty to fifty miles, with ash reaching Asia and the Middle East. Ash was found in the Bay of Bengal, nineteen hundred miles away, and pyroclastic flows covered an area of 27,500 square miles. He concluded, "If things aren't slowed down, this is going to happen again. It's going to happen again someday anyway, but hopefully not while we're there."

"I can only concur with that sentiment, in a big way."

"Just to give you an example, when Toba blew, it was twenty-eight hundred times more powerful than the eruption of Mount St. Helens in 1980."

"Very reassuring. If we're on that barge and it blows, we will never be able to get away from it in time."

"Not true. The winds are primarily from the west, so we have the advantage there, and we have heli-service at our beck and call, so you really need not worry. You are turning into a worrywart, you know."

"Getting old I guess."

"Don't talk to *me* about getting old."

"Too true. I forget."

"Correct, and I have some experience in matters such as these, so perhaps you should leave the worrying to me."

Lyft began pacing on the back of the chair. "It's why I exist. You know, your worries are minimal compared to those of the indigenous populations of some of these islands. Before the tsunami, locals on some islands, such as Pulau Nias, would not even walk the beaches on a windy day, fearing coconuts dropping on them from the tall palms along the beaches. How would you like to walk out of your house and be killed by a falling coconut? Now most of the palms are gone on the western sides of the islands, along with many of those who chose to live near the sea."

I remembered the horror broadcast on TV after the tsunami hit. I intoned, "Very sad."

"Yes, very. I saw the devastation, the bloated bodies, the total destruction, and many more were killed than reported," Lyft said almost reverently, a deep sadness punctuating his speech. "The ones who weren't found make up the tally. It was the worst thing I have seen in your history."

I tried not to conjure the images Lyft was recalling, and I wondered if it were possible that it might occur again.

He must have been reading my mind. I'd have to ask him how he did that. He said, "That is what we are trying to prevent, or at least slow down. But due to the dynamics of the Earth, it is, in actuality, unpreventable. What can be prevented is the huge death toll by getting people away from the shorelines and keeping them in relative safety where they live and work. Plus, better electronic monitoring of the Earth's activities is a must, with the technology available today to implement it worldwide. The will is just not there to do it."

"How many more mega disasters will it take to get governments off their backsides?"

"Who knows? You humans love the act of sacrifice before action, so maybe plenty."

"I hear there are other concerns around Sumatra to be worried about."

"Like what for instance?"

"Like piracy."

"Ah yes, that is an issue, as a matter of fact. I see you've been doing some reading."

"Some. Perhaps not enough."

"Well ..."

"You know, when you begin a sentence that way, it's never to impart good news."

Lyft nodded and then continued, "The Straits of Malacca, between Malaysia and Sumatra, is the most dangerous sea route in the world according to the IMB."

The IMB, International Maritime Bureau, was a reliable source, so I listened carefully as he noted that one-third of all maritime global trade went through the Straits. This, he explained, included all the oil imports for Japan and China. He related that last year, in the early spring, pirates had seized a gas tanker, holding the captain along with the chief engineer for ransom. The incident eventually had been settled, but it showed a certain volatility of the region.

I flailed my arms. "Typically understated."

Now he returned the flail. "What would you have, me running around in hysterics? I don't think so. I'm not particularly worried, because we will have electronic sensors monitoring a nautical mile radius from the barges, and we will be heavily armed just in case. Plus, the Straits are east of Sumatra. We'll be on the west side."

"I like the heavily armed part."

"I figured you would."

"Just because we are west does not mean we won't see any unseemly activity."

"True. And frankly, being heavily armed is a good idea, as some pirates have teamed up with terrorist organizations like Jemaah Islamiah, which can operate anywhere. It's a loose affiliation, each using the other to its own advantages, but the links are there nevertheless. So we will watch activities smacking of terrorism as well. Sometimes it's hard to tell the difference between piracy and outright destructive activity, but in our case, there won't be any differentiation, if you get my meaning."

"You know," I said thoughtfully, "it's too bad these types of people can't be educated as to what's going on. We could use every ally we can get."

Lyft replied, his animation escalating, "You've got a point. But like I said, it's difficult dealing with thirteenth century mentalities. And who's going to teach them? You? Me? The local UN delegation? We've got other things to think about, like defining the rest of the locations and getting on with it. Maybe while we're at it, we could flush a few terrorists down the pipes. Better than saving the world for them. Trouble is, they might clog the machinery."

Toasting my drink to him, I exclaimed, "That would be one way of dealing with them. I like it."

"Don't get too excited. Fire and brimstone is a better touch, leaves less residue."

"Well we are near any number of volcanoes ..."

"Great minds often think alike."

My eyebrows lifted, "You really wouldn't do that, would you?"

"Stay tuned. There's no telling what I might do, especially if I get in a really pissy mood if we ever are attacked."

"I'll be sure to remain on your good side."

Lyft intoned, "No worries there, mate."

"Ah, been down under lately?"

"As a matter of fact, I have. You know that we'll be operating not that far from Australia. I have been concerned with the East Timor–Australia treaty on oil and gas that was just signed. It is called the Treaty on Certain Maritime Arrangements in the Timor Sea. A quaint title, but it got the job done. It sets the maritime boundary between the two countries and stipulates the agreement for sharing oil and gas revenues in the Timor Sea through a project called Greater Sunrise."

I wasn't following. I asked why such a treaty was of concern.

Lyft replied like I was the dumbest kid in class. "Because Australia is the most stable country in the region, and its expanded presence will be guaranteeing our security."

"Wait a minute." I got up, went to a shelf, yanked out an atlas, and thumbed through the pages until I found what I was seeking. "Hah. As I look on the map, Pulau Simeulue is about twenty-four hundred miles as the crow flies from East Timor. What am I missing?"

Lyft pontificated, talon in the air, "What you are missing is the fact that the Australians are already operating gunboats in the Straits of Malacca to help ensure their oil imports. All I suggested at the treaty was for them to swing westward once in a while to check in on us. Of course, some subliminal messaging at the conference also helped ensure the treaty concurrence, so we got two birdies with one rock."

"Um, two birds with one stone, I believe is the expression."

"Same difference."

"You mean to tell me you influenced the outcome of the treaty?"

"Well ... yes."

"How?"

"The same way we did in Cuba in 1962, by preventing you idiots from starting Armageddon. Subliminal messaging through telepathy. Works wonders. You should try it some time."

"Right, mate. I believe you already told me we humans don't have the equipment for that type of thing," I said as I placed the book back in its niche in the bookcase.

"Correct. Just seeing how sharp you are in the memory department."

Plunking myself back onto the couch, I queried, "Hookay, so what's next?"

The resulting activity of my not-too-gentle relocation back into the cushions uplifted tiny granules of dust into the air, illuminating their disorderly dance in the sunlight streaming through the bay window of the den, not the only reflection occurring in the room.

Lyft began, one hand under his chin, striking a thoughtful pose on the back of the opposite chair. "You know, I've been thinking a lot about this project, and what makes sense to me is that we crisscross the Ring of Fire around the Pacific Plate as we girdle the Earth's core. We may get more mileage that way."

The student to the master, "Why, and what's the Ring of Fire?"

"Why, have you had no geology?"

"Nope, not a lick." I took another sip of my drink.

Lyft elevated himself off the chair, slowly circling the room, preparing another lesson for the dunce. "Whoa. You *do* need an education. The Ring of Fire is a giant arc running from New Zealand along eastern Asia, edging along the Aleutians, and then down along North and South America. Here. Bring it up on Google, and it will show you a map."

I stood and walked over to the computer station, sat in the chair, and clicked the keyboard. Sure enough, a colored depiction of the Ring of Fire came up within a couple of entries on the site.

Lyft instructed, pointing a talon at the map as he settled himself onto my shoulder, "You see here? The arc comprises over 75 percent of the world's active and inactive volcanoes. They are located basically where the Pacific Plate jams up against other plates. Included in the Ring are no less than fourteen deep trenches, such as the Sunda Trench, where we'll be soon. The trenches are the subduction zones of the mashing plates."

"Why do we need to orchestrate the project across instead of within the circumference of the Ring?"

"Well, the Pacific Plate seems to be a particularly nasty bugger, as it seems to be responsible for a lot of tearing and grinding lately. I do believe that if we could take something immediately off the plate so to speak, in this case pressure, the whole system of tectonics could be reverse dominoes, taking the strain off the Indian–Australian Plate banging up against the Eurasian Plate and so forth. A ricochet effect in reverse, you might say. You see, we need to keep the plates relatively stable so that all of our work does not get mashed due to plate movement. Crossing the Ring will be faster than following it, so the sooner, the better."

"Seems logical, but how to do it? The plates are, on average, fifty miles thick."

"Don't know yet, but we are working on it. The Klinque agree it's a good strategy, although it would only be a stopgap measure in geologic time. We'd have to be careful, as we would not want to affect the dynamics of the Earth in any way. And it doesn't solve the main problem: the increased spin of the core. Now *that's* a dilemma."

"I'd say."

"What we're hoping is that the project just might cool the Earth enough to reduce the expansion of the plates so they settle down. Time will tell."

Lyft yawned, his exhaustion evident with the pace he'd recently been keeping. "We've been at this quite a while, so enough for one night. I'm tired and need rest. This shuttling between continents is killing me, so I'll say good night. See you on the morrow."

"Good night, Lyft. Sleep well. You deserve it."

"I may sleep for a few days to recharge, so you may not see me for a while—just to let you know …"

"Thanks. I won't worry."

With that, he released the pressure from my shoulder, floated toward the door, humming the Klinque lullaby, and with a click of the screen, became invisible as he made his way to the wall. Who would have thought this two-foot alien creature no one had ever heard of with the most supreme of intellect could have the capacity to control human destiny in devising a plan to salvage the Earth? I shook my head in disbelief. No convention I had managed in my previous life could have ever rivaled the logistics of what we were about to undertake. It was difficult to fathom that I would be spending the next months, perhaps years or even a lifetime, in an attempt to temper Mother Earth, hoping to ensure her continuance.

CHAPTER THREE

All too soon, my time had come for departure. Barb was to remain home on the initial sojourn and come later if necessary. Lyft believed placing her in harm's way should only occur as an absolute necessity. I couldn't have agreed more.

After months of study, ordering supplies, being impaled by vaccination needles, and completing several crash courses on geology and earth dynamics in addition to dealing with the endless bureaucracy of obtaining visas plus communicating with various consulates, I was pretty much set to go.

Direct flights to Dushanbe, Tajikistan, were nonexistent. That meant a transfer at Domodedovo Airport in Moscow on Tajikistan airlines. I figured that with direct flights every day and having heard of no recent air disasters, my chances of surviving the flight were at least marginally acceptable.

I was amazed that I needed visas for airport transfers in various countries. I had to secure one for Russia; Tajikistan, obviously; Afghanistan; Pakistan, in case I needed it; Iran, toughest to obtain; Turkey; Turkmenistan; Uzbekistan; China, specifically Xinjiang Province; and Indonesia and Australia for the second leg of the journey. Anywhere I might end up, I needed a visa. Try telling that to consular officials who viewed most American in-bound travel requests with great suspicion.

Once in Dushanbe, Lyft had arranged helicopter service for

the final leg to the Wakhan, where I had heard construction was proceeding at feverish velocity. I was looking forward to seeing the progress. This sophisticated plant was being erected in record time at a money's-no-object pace and would be almost operational when I arrived.

I had a car service pick me up around two thirty in the afternoon for the six o'clock flight to Moscow, SU 318, which arrived the next day at five after eleven in the morning Moscow time, perfect for the one thirty-five transfer to Tajik Airlines. Figuring the most dangerous part of the trip was the ride into New York (I had almost been killed twice riding with different vendors on my way to and fro on New York expressways), I kept my eyes open during the transfer, which proved to be uneventful. I was traveling lightly, as most articles of necessity had already been shipped and were awaiting the helicopter transfer in Dushanbe. The only luggage I had was a suiter that carried two days of clothing and toiletries in case I was waylaid.

JFK, typically under construction, proved to be a nightmare. Cars were jammed into a convergence of three lanes leading into one, and it seemed the entire world was traveling to Moscow that evening. Once we got closer, after thirty minutes of jockeying into the correct lane for the terminal, that fortunately proved not to be true. Terminal Three housed China, Royal Jordanian, Saudi Arabian, and South Africa Airlines, among others. It had eighteen gates and was a bustling mass of humanity, but not relative to the Moscow fight. As there was no curbside check-in, due to heightened security in respect to the destinations represented at Terminal Three, we all had to wait in line like cattle to check in with luggage and then be completely examined by security. I had forgotten that the UN had just terminated a Mid-East and South African conference in town with many of the delegations leaving that day for their respective countries. If I had been paying attention to the news, I might have selected another travel day, but too late now, so I made an attempt to let patience be a virtue. I was actually irritated because I'd had no lunch yet and was looking forward to a leisurely bite in the lounge with a touch of Red Zinfandel, but with six hundred people in the security line, assuaging my hunger did not look hopeful.

The clump onto my left shoulder momentarily disrupted thoughts of nourishment. I took out my cell phone, pretending I had just received a call, so I could talk to Lyft without arousing any suspicions about someone of questionable sanity talking to an invisible presence in thin air.

Lyft began, only allowing his voice to be heard by me, "How are you? You look well rested having completed the most arduous part of the journey."

"I'm fine. The worst part was once we hit the airport, getting to the terminal, but we managed."

"Yes, my mode of transport definitely has its advantages." I really envied Lyft's ability to fly at great speeds, up to and over the speed of sound when necessary, although it evidently had its disadvantages as well. He prattled on, "However, flying through swarms of mosquitoes leaves something to be desired. They are particularly abundant this year. I find I need a shower several times a day. I've had our engineers design and build special goggles with appropriate self-cleaning lenses so that our flights are less interrupted. We, at this juncture, can't afford to let anything slow us down."

"Yes, I can see that. Is there no way I can piggyback a ride to Dushanbe and avoid all this insanity?"

"Unfortunately, no. The ride would kill you."

"Well, we wouldn't want that."

"No, we wouldn't. However, I may be able to extricate you from this madhouse and get you checked in in a more appropriate manner, as one befitting your stature."

"I take it that was a compliment?"

"Absolutely. Wait here a minute."

"Do I have a choice?"

"Not really."

Lyft left my shoulder, and in a few minutes, a full bird United States Army colonel was eyeing me as he walked across the terminal.

"Mr. Wood?"

"Yes, sir," I replied, forgetting that I was no longer in the military.

"Please come this way. We have a more comfortable method of check-in for you. Here. Let me have your bag."

"Sir, that's really not necessary. I can carry it."

"Wouldn't hear of it. Let's go over around the central counter to the VIP gate. I'd like you to meet Colonel Bashirin, Russian Army, good friend of mine, who will have special care of you during this leg of the journey."

From his black plastic nametag, I was able to discern his name. "Many thanks, Colonel Salvo. I greatly appreciate this."

"My and our pleasure. We know the mission and its potential invaluable service to humanity, so however we can facilitate it is the least we can do on our end."

Salvo towered over me at six foot three, his piercing gray eyes looking directly into mine, his aquiline features reflecting his ancient Roman nobility. He took my bag from my hand, leaving me with my overstuffed shoulder briefcase, and we walked through the terminal with nary a stare to the Aeroflot VIP lounge. He produced a card for the door, inserted it, and opened the door with a slight buzz, revealing a plush reception area with an attractive Russian woman behind the desk.

"How do you do, Mr. Wood?" she queried in perfect English.

"I do well, as I hope you do," I replied.

Colonel Salvo said, "This is Natasha. She will complete arrangements for your check-in and take care of any security regularities. Consider yourself in competent hands."

"Many thanks, Colonel."

I handed my ticket to her, and the colonel placed my bag on the counter, which she took, giving me a luggage sticker in exchange for the ticket, stating to the colonel that check-in was complete.

I asked, "What about security?"

She replied, "Mr. Wood, if we were worried about security, we would have left you in the line with the other sheep, baaing and milling about for position to get through the blasters. I believe Colonel Bashirin is waiting in the lounge for you. Please enjoy yourself."

Colonel Salvo said, "Please come this way. I'll introduce you to my old friend."

"Thank you, sir."

"Jeff, you're not military, so you don't need to 'sir' me. You can call me Basil, after my dad. I'd consider it a privilege."

"Thank you, Colonel, but old habits die hard. It's a matter of respect, as you know."

"I understand."

He led me into the lounge, which was whisper quiet, elegantly appointed with brown leather chairs, black marble cocktail tables, deep red cushioned walls, and a sound system second to none, playing low-key Russian folk songs. In the corner was Colonel Bashirin, sitting on a large, curved leather couch, with a bottle of Stoli and mounds of Russian hors d'oeuvres on the tables in front of him. At our approach, he arose, and Colonel Salvo introduced us.

We shook hands, mine lost in his huge bear paw. Although I rate myself as a moderately virile male, I wondered if my hand would ever recover from the crushing it was receiving. It was all I could do to not yelp in pain as his extender pumped mine up and down, threatening a wrist snap from the torque.

"My great honor to have you here as our guest. Please, be seated and have a snack. I understand you missed your afternoon luncheon today."

I wondered how he knew that. Just as I took my seat, Lyft settled again onto my shoulder.

"I know what you're thinking—subliminal messaging, remember? Now, eat."

I gazed at Bashirin, who was shorter than Salvo, about my height, five foot eleven or so. But what power he projected! Gray crew cut in the old flattop style, twinkling jet blue eyes, a face like a prize fighter, resembling a Russian bear with a pushed-in snout, his uniform straining against the rippling bulk beneath, this was not someone with whom I would feel comfortable in any kind of altercation. Side by side, the two made quite a contrast, the overheads reflecting off Salvo's closely shaven pate, while Bashirin's seem to absorb the light.

The varied array of hors d'oeuvres looked to be excellent,

everything from smoked salmon with condiments to platters of venison steaks. Colonel Bashirin explained some of his favorite recipes on the table to me in great detail.

On the other table were the desserts. The good colonel elaborated, pointing out his favorites; the mini chocolate pancakes with vodka–cherry sauce, Ukrainian honey cakes and prianiki honey biscuits.

"Oh, boy. Take a look at this," exhaled Lyft whose eyes were always larger than his stomach. "Should we begin with dessert first or save it for last? What a decision … and the vodka. Let's have a smack of that to get this celebration started."

I groaned inwardly, sensing imminent disaster. I could see myself taking care of an invisible inebriated member of the Klinque in front of two commanding officers. I could see attempting to get him onto the plane, and subsequently listening to him rail about being kidnapped while carping that the mode of transport provided for him was too slow, as he had better things to do than sit on an airplane for nine hours, and "would you mind very much opening the airlock door and letting me out so I can get the hell out of here?" I could see it all, and it took my appetite away.

"Gentlemen, would you excuse me a minute? I need to use the men's room."

"Certainly," they replied in unison. "It's around and over to the left, behind the bar," Colonel Bashirin said.

"Thanks. I'll be right back."

I got up and walked over to the restroom, with Lyft still attached, no doubt sensing we needed a brief conversation. We read each other's minds that way, somehow knowing when the one needed to speak to the other.

Luckily there were no other patrons in the men's room.

Lyft appeared in the mirror, floating near my head, shimmering in all his emerald-like finery, while I placed my hands on the peach-colored marble counter containing three sinks. The three beige stall doors were open, as if attempting to listen in on the ensuing theatrics. The swirled tan marble floor, the immaculate thick white hand towels etched with Russian emblems, and the soft brown velvet plush walls all gave the room an air of sanctity.

I exclaimed, "Lyft, I didn't know you were going to be here. And I know how you are around food and drink, especially this kind of food and drink. I can't have a scene here. These officers are of some importance, and I need you to behave yourself."

Lyft extended a talon quickly, just missing my nose. "What? Lecturing me? Who do you think you are? What's wrong with a little bon voyage party in the afternoon? You're a real killjoy, you know that?"

I raised both eyebrows, looking at him in the mirror. "Yeah? Remember the brewpub fest in Bryant Park last year? If it hadn't been for Barb and me, you'd still be there."

"There may be some truth to that, but I was on vacation at the time, so you can't fault me there. I'm not on vacation this time, so you can't fault me here either. I know what I'm about, I just hope you can handle your vodka."

"I don't drink vodka straight."

"Wanna bet?"

I straightened up. He wasn't the only one who disliked dictation. "Why should I have to drink it if I don't feel like it? I saw some nice red Zin on the table to the right of Colonel Bashirin. Why wouldn't that suffice?"

He raised both arms now in frustration, exasperated with the dolt. "Because it would be an insult to Bashirin to not partake of the innumerable toasts that are inevitable at a Russian banquet. The red Zin is for dessert, at any rate."

I practically yelled, "This isn't a banquet; it's a lunch."

"Tell that to them. You've got two and a half hours to boarding. If anybody's concerned, it's me for you. You'll be well primed by flight time, especially if you survive the main courses and get into the Zin. That ought to be a pretty picture."

I bowed my head. "Oooh, boy."

"'Oooh, boy' is right. Now get out there, and do your duty. I'll slurp and munch incognito to take some of the pressure off you. Don't say I never did you a favor."

"Fair enough."

I left the men's room and made my way back to the tables. The vodka remained untouched, waiting for the first toast. I had hoped that the drinking had commenced so there'd be less for me, but the two colonels were obviously waiting for the lightweight to return to kick off the party. Bashirin was first, as he grabbed the Jewel of Russia, known as the drink of the czars. I thought the bottle most impressive, depicting a hand-painted scene of a snarling wolf with gold onion domes in the background against a backdrop of snowcapped mountains. I was afraid the ice and water in the bucket would hurt the artistry, but Bashirin seemed unfazed. The tall shot glasses were also hand painted, scrolled with various Russian designs that I could not fathom. Bashirin poured three glasses and said, "Here's to success. May we all live in peace and harmony, and may Mother Earth reign supreme forever."

"Here, here," Colonel Salvo said.

"Here, here," I echoed.

"Strovia."

"Strovia," Salvo and I replied in unison.

We raised and touched our glasses, and in one gulp, the first round was complete.

Lyft whispered, "Strovia, baloney. Where's mine?"

"Colonel Bashirin, I wonder if I could ask a favor of you? To comrades lost and no longer with us, could we set up a fourth glass in commemoration? In that manner, they could drink with us as we honor them."

"An excellent idea. No trouble at all. I like this boy."

From Lyft, "Well done."

The colonel set up a fourth glass and hailed "strovia" again, "To comrades lost but not forgotten," as we drained another shot. He began to apply some smoked salmon to some bread, and Colonel Salvo began digging into the food as well. I noticed, as the others were preoccupied, the full shot glass rapidly lift off the table, tip up, drain, and be placed back on the table in what seemed like a millisecond. A light belch in my ear confirmed Lyft's first libation.

Bashirin motioned me to take some food, which sounded like a capital idea at that point, as I was feeling a small buzz and a spreading warmth from the inside out. I sensed a presence around the table and noticed some pelmini missing along with some venison steaks and smoked meat. Then a couple of honey cakes and chocolate pancakes disappeared along with some pickled eggs and herring. I began to chuckle at the opportunistic selection vanishing under our noses, wondering how the hell Lyft could eat in such a manner and still have a functioning digestive system. Bashirin noticed my humor and gave me a quizzical look.

I had to think fast, not at first realizing that I'd been caught in reverie. "I was just ruminating on a humorous incident and couldn't help but think of the situation."

"By all means," piped in Bashirin, "let us in on it."

"Well, it has to do with two priests concerned with a boy who fell off a wall in front of my house. The youngster felt he'd been saved by an angel who had broken his fall and set him down feet first from a twenty-three foot height."

I went on to explain that eventually the two priests came to the house for an interview, and somehow while situated in my living room, simultaneously had hallucinations that the seventh angel was in the house, the one who threw Satan into the pit, telling them to mend their ways. They subsequently ran from the house out into the driveway screaming, bolting from the property, never to be seen again. I related that they ended up somewhere in Central or South America, having retaken their vows of poverty, eventually doing what they were supposed to be doing, which was helping those less fortunate, instead of investigating purported miracles. However, I related that the scene had stuck in my mind, and that sometimes I could still see their faces as they reacted to what must have literally been the fear of God. I ended with, "And "I'll never forget it."

From my shoulder, "Nor will I. I thought I bordered on sublime divine that day. I actually did the Church a service. From what I know about them to date, they have entire villages under their care and have saved countless lives through intersession between various rebel groups and the central government. I was most angelic that day."

Bashirin noted the empty fourth shot glass. "A good story. The next toast will be to priests everywhere. Hey, our boy can drink. He's one ahead of us, Colonel. Time to fill up again."

This was not going as planned. However, I took my medicine like a good patient.

"Strovia. To priests everywhere."

In unison, "Strovia," as we knocked back another one.

This time, Lyft, sensing a little of my distress, left the shot glass full but went back to the pickled eggs. I could only hope they didn't convert to methane prior to departure, as his emissions could endanger the preflight warm-up. Several more smoked meats disappeared from the platters, as well as a number of Siberian cookies. It was going to be a long night.

We kept at it, telling stories, stuffing ourselves with the wonderful display of culinary delights, finally getting to the desserts after a bottle and a half of vodka. Lyft had imbibed several more shots while almost simultaneously ensuring the fourth glass remained full, pouring quickly while the two colonels were busy with the buffet. In spite of the drinking rate, he did his duty in stemming the red tide. Bashirin popped the cork on a delightful red Zin, Murphy Goode Snake Eyes, which tipped the alcohol scale at over 15 percent, a blockbuster by any measure. I had stopped thinking about how they could know my preferences, as it seemed Lyft had that angle covered. Bashirin poured the wine and gave the usual toast, and we all had a sip.

"My God, you Americans have perfected this Zinfandel. What an outstanding wine."

With all the vodka we had consumed, I'm surprised we could taste anything at all. However, it did go exceptionally well with the sweets, almost like a port. I was beginning to feel downright uncomfortable, having eaten and drunk too much, but could not resist the pull of the Zin. We chatted about the mission, the progress of the plant in the Wakhan, and the chance of success of the whole venture. It was agreed that the plan could work, barring any radical unforeseen circumstances like death or permanent injury, which really boosted my security level. Eventually, the announcement came over the sound system in the lounge that it was time to think about getting to the plane—if I could remember what departure gate had been designated.

We all stood, and the two colonels seemed straight as ramrods as I weaved slightly, catching myself on the arm of the couch. They noted my distress and laughed, with me embarrassed because I'd been one-upped by those whose tolerance was far greater than mine.

Bashirin said, "Don't worry. We took it easy on you. Normally, during a light snack like that, we have three times that amount to drink, and that's just to prime us. The party before the party, so to speak. Ha ha!"

"Colonel, I don't think I'd survive long in your culture, but I do like the way you celebrate life. Now, I think I'll go and pass out in an airplane seat. Thank you for your exceptional hospitality and your friendship. I hope to see you again soon. I feel as if I have made a lifelong friend."

"You have. I feel the same. We will expect great things from you in the Wakhan. And you'll see me sooner than you think. I'll be with you there. Call on me anytime I can be of service."

With that, he shook my hand in his great paw, simultaneously pressing a business card into my hand. I looked at it and placed it in my pocket. He already had my particulars, so I did not reciprocate.

Lyft slurringly whispered, "Don't lose the card. You may have need of it again someday."

I would make sure to secure it.

The three (four) of us crossed the lounge, with some difficulty on my end, exiting and making our way to the gate through a back passageway.

Lyft sloshed into my ear, "This is where I get off. I can't ride in such an outmoded manner of transport. I'll be flying in tomorrow, provided my headache isn't too severe."

"You're not coming with me?" I queried out loud.

Bashirin replied, "Not on this trip. I'll be flying a military jet tomorrow. Sorry. From here, you're on your own, although we'll have guides all along the route to get you to Dushanbe. From there, you fall under U.S. military control, but we'll be working closely together, so not to worry. I suggest you try to sleep. You'll be very comfortable, as you've first class accommodations, with seats that fold down into beds. Have a nightcap and relax. You'll be in Moscow before you know it."

"Right. Just what I need, a nightcap," I laughed.

Realizing I had almost made a major faux pas by talking to Lyft out loud, I decided to attempt more cognizance of my speech as I hailed goodbyes.

Bashirin and Salvo gave great guffaws as I shook their hands. I then proceeded to enter the Jetway with a buzz in my ears and a spin in my head. Lyft said he'd see me tomorrow, and I felt his weight levitating, leaving my shoulder slightly sore where he had been gripping me with his talons while swaying half-inebriated in the effort to not fall and crack his head as we swayed in opposite directions. I made a mental note that he should trim those things so I could avoid permanent puncture wounds.

I made my way to my seat with some guidance from the flight attendant who evidently took pity on me. I woke up a couple of hours later under a soft blanket albeit with a nasty headache. I groped around in my carryall, found the Advil, took four of them, and eventually went back to sleep. It wasn't the way I had envisioned beginning the journey, but then again, it did avoid the interminable security-line wait.

The plane landed in Moscow on time. Even if it hadn't, who cared? I slept through the night, refreshed and ready to go upon landing. Maybe there was something to the consumption of vodka for a good night's sleep. I thought it had more to do with the Advil, myself.

We landed at Sheremetyevo, which is located northwest of the city. I thought how interesting it was going to be making my way to Domodedovo Airport, southeast of the city, a direct diagonal as the crow flies, since I knew virtually nothing of the geography, local customs, and nightmarish traffic patterns of Moscow. I had heard that hailing a local taxi was tantamount to giving away one's bank account, and I could see myself taking a public bus or, worse yet, the metro, where none of the signs were in English.

The stewardess, who had kindly ensured I was covered the previous evening, came to my seat and said there would be a gentleman waiting for me in baggage claim with all entry procedures arranged. She gave me instructions to navigate the terminal, which was not particularly large, and saw the relief on my face that I had a minder. She told me not to worry, that they were proficient at this sort of thing, and that I would be met with VIP treatment throughout the journey.

She evidently was much more than a flight attendant. I felt it inappropriate to question her as to her real identity, so I thanked her very much, rose from my seat, gathered my weighty shoulder briefcase from the overhead, exited the plane into the Jetway, and then made my way into the terminal. I followed her directions, which were perfect, finding a gentleman crisply dressed in a chauffeur's uniform and holding a sign with my name on it near the baggage carousel for the luggage from JFK. I signaled, walking over to him.

"Mr. Wood?"

"Yes, sir, I'm Mr. Wood. Thank you for meeting me."

"It is my pleasure," he said in perfect English. "Please come with me. Your bag has been collected, so we'll be on our way."

"I didn't think the bags were even off the plane yet. You folks are quick, I'll say that."

"Your bag was tagged VIP, so it came off immediately on specialized transport straight to me. And you are correct; the other bags are not off yet, and it will probably take at least forty-five minutes for the airline to do so. Baggage handlers these days, you know."

"Ah, yes. I see you have some of the same issues as do we back home." We walked quickly through the terminal area, not so different from most, bustling with people, corridors lined with shops and eateries. "Nice to know the problem is universal, not just with the labor unions."

"Yes, more to do with human nature than with unions. When is your flight out of Domodedovo?"

"One thirty-five, so we have some time, I gather."

"Yes, some, but it will take a good hour and a half through Moscow traffic to get there, so we'll eat some time up doing that. Ah, here we are," he said, stopping short at a large, black Lincoln sedan. He popped open the trunk with a click. "Landing at eleven thirty in the morning is a good time to transfer, as it is between rush hours, so we may be lucky," he said, tossing my suiter in and shutting the door. "Let us see."

He opened the rear door, and I clambered in; then he made his way around the car to the driver's seat, and we were off. We headed toward Moscow on Leningradsky Prospekt to the Garden Ring, where we headed south, going by the Moscow Zoo, and the famous Gorky Park. We then turned directly south on Lusinovskaya and then east to Andropova, which ran due south to Domodedovo. I was following a map and, at the same time, seeing in real time the various routes we were taking, realizing that the way Moscow was laid out actually made some sense.

As with many cities in Europe, the city grid followed a circular pattern. With the Kremlin in the middle, encircled by the first ring, or that of the Boulevard, and then the Garden Ring, I noticed that the roads paralleled many beautiful parks and ponds interspersed by pedestrian walkways and playgrounds. Evidently there used to be major gardens along the Garden Ring, but they had been supplanted by the needs of modernization, giving way to ten lanes of traffic. Tretye Koltso, or the Third Ring, was built outside the Garden Ring to ease traffic, and the final ring is the outer ring, or MKAD, which is like our Beltway 495 around the city of Washington. Living inside the Garden Ring in Moscow is most desirous, as it still encompasses the beauty of the city, means less commuting time, and is relatively safe. As with most cities in the world, Moscow was growing exponentially, with traffic a never-ending nightmare.

However, again figuring that the person servicing me was more than he appeared, when we became stalled in heavy traffic, he flashed his lights in the grill, pulled to the breakdown lane, and expertly skirted the bottleneck until clear road was again evident. Being the beneficiary of these illegal maneuvers, I was not about to question his methodology, so I sat back and relaxed, enjoying the stunning scenery.

We arrived at Domodedovo in an hour and ten minutes, well under the normal two-hour travel time. Since the highway police ignored our machinations, I figured they must know something I did not, probably a tag on the license plate or some other identifying insignia that led them to turn their heads in the opposite direction when we passed.

Domodedovo was more modern than Sheremetyevo. My driver escorted me to the executive lounge, which was as nice as any in the world. The receptionist spoke passable English as she told me to make myself comfortable in one of the corner booths, where there were aperitifs and more Russian hors d'oeuvres displayed. What I really needed was something to alleviate the searing heartburn I had developed, so I popped a Pepcid AC and settled into the booth, resigned to another force-feeding so that someone could harvest my liver.

The hors d'oeuvres were excellent, much like the others of the previous evening, with the aperitifs featuring a more eclectic fare, such as Aperol, an Italian sweet orange liqueur, and Pernod, from a liqueur called a pastis, something like ouzo, with a licorice flavor. Pernod packs a wallop at 40 percent alcohol and is the successor of absinthe, which was responsible for several generations of brain damage in France, as it contained a toxic oil from wormwood out of which it was made. Henri Pernod invented the drink of same name to save his fellow Frenchmen from further mental addling, producing a drink of much lower alcohol and toxicity. Unfortunately, although it was outlawed in 1915, many Frenchmen continued to illegally drink absinthe, as its alcoholic properties were highly addicting.

Pimm's No. 1 was of interest, it being a gin-based liqueur of fruit juices and spices. James Pimm, an oyster bar owner, invented it in 1859. It is said that only six people in the world know the original recipe. As a testament to English taste, there was a container of fresh lemonade beside the bottle for use as a mixer. I merged the two, took a quaff, thinking, *How delicious is this!* I could only hope the all-knowing six never traveled in the same car or plane together.

As I finished the offerings, the receptionist came to the table to inform me my flight was ready for boarding. She led me to the Jetway, bid me goodbye, and turned back toward the lounge. Aeroflot no more, now it was Tajikistan Airlines. I could only hope their maintenance was up to par. I settled into the first-class section, not really looking forward to the next leg of the journey, comprised of approximately seventeen hundred miles. We would be heading southeast, crossing over a good portion of Russia, through Kazakhstan, over a small part of Uzbekistan, and then to Dushanbe in Tajikistan, about a three-hour flight. With only one runway at Dushanbe, I could only hope there were no flights attempting to land in the opposite direction.

I must have been more exhausted than I realized, as I immediately fell asleep upon take off, awaking with a start when the plane bumped down onto the runway.

Not a bad way to travel: sleep through it, I mused. *I'll have to try that more often.*

When I flew on my own, I couldn't sleep in coach. Maybe a first-class ticket was worth it after all. I'd have to think about that.

I exited the plane, and unlike the other airports, there was no VIP lounge in the terminal this time in which to relax. There were two duty-free shops inside the terminal, not a large building, perhaps seventy-five yards long, along with a coffee shop at either end. The three-story building was undergoing major renovation, as some areas on the ground level were gutted, with wires hanging from the ceilings and workers scurrying about with demolition carts full of plaster and piping—an airport in transition, struggling to serve an overburdened air system.

A young man of Asian descent met me in the gate area, told me he was acting on orders of Colonel Bashirin, and asked if I would come with him, please. We exited the building whereupon we entered another low-roofed structure that had a staircase leading down under the tarmac. We went through a series of steel doors through a maze of corridors that eventually led to a leather-padded door studded with brass. My young companion pulled out a card and slid it into a slot, tripping a solenoid that opened the door. We entered into a room fit for the czars, decorated in red velvet and gold, with original artwork on the walls of Cossacks galloping on steaming horses across frozen lakes engaged in a cavalry charge. I was led to a table, again laden with the usual, and I thought, *My God, don't these people do anything but eat and drink? It must be*

*the winters. They need to pack it on like bears to ensure warmth for
the cold season.*

My young minder said, "Colonel Bashirin will join you within
the hour. In the meantime, relax and enjoy. Your luggage is in good
hands, so nothing to worry about."

"How can the good colonel arrive so quickly? I left him in New
York not hours ago."

"Military jets are quite a bit faster. He'll be arriving shortly."

"Thanks. I'm looking forward to seeing him again."

"Yes, there's been a slight change to the itinerary, which he will
explain. Good day."

"Good day, and thank you for your attention."

"It has been my pleasure."

I looked over the offerings at the table, deciding against more
food and drink, at least of the alcoholic variety. Perhaps my hosts
had anticipated that I was becoming sated, as I saw some American
Coca Cola on ice, which was exactly what I had in mind. I poured
myself a glass and opened up my file to study the upcoming final
destination: the Wakhan Corridor. I wondered what the slight jag
in the itinerary was but felt, so far, that I was in capable hands, so
I decided not to worry about it.

I became immersed in the file, studying biodiversity in the
Wakhan. Prior to 1998, there were no regulations regarding
conservation or husbanding of resources. Abdul Wajid Adil of the
World Bank established a program to educate the local population
to protect its resources, teaching that once the resources ran
out, people would have to leave, as they would have ruined their
own livelihoods. All seventeen mammalian species known in
the Wakhan were threatened with outright extinction due to
overhunting. Snow leopard, brown bear, ibex, Marco Polo sheep,
and urial were among those in harm's way.

People thought these resources were inexhaustible, but Mr.
Adil persuaded them otherwise. Through education, the animals
have rebounded to a degree, although there is still a great deal of
poaching from Pakistani transients and also from the indigenous
drug traffickers.

The animals weren't the only sufferers. Poverty was rampant, people shared small spaces, allowing respiratory diseases to fester, and there was no health clinic in all of the Wakhan, little energy production, and sparse fuel for heating and cooking. No wonder people relied on the drug trade for survival.

While so absorbed, Colonel Bashirin entered the room with a hearty greeting. He came over to the table and gave me a bear hug, pounding me on the back, seeming as genuinely happy to see me as I was to see him.

I asked, "How did you arrive here almost at the same time as me? And I've been traveling for a full day."

"Military jet out of Cuba, straight here, not going through Moscow. In spite of the Cubans bleeding the Kremlin dry, the country's location does serve some purpose. Other than that, Castro's pretty much a royal pain. I don't see the relationship lasting much longer, especially if he expires pretty soon, which would not be soon enough, frankly. Probably one of our biggest mistakes was our alliance with him years ago. Since that was ratified, the relationship has been nothing other than a hollow, sucking sound on the teat of the treasury. I compare the relationship to one of your Hollywood ex-wives, continually going to court suing for more alimony. He even has a nickname around the Kremlin, not for publication of course—our X. How's that for Western influence?"

We both guffawed over that one. "Now that's a perspective I hadn't figured on."

"Once you get to know us, we're not that different from you. Except that maybe we eat and drink a little more."

"Yes, I'm finding that out."

We had a seat and dug in again, although I took small bites.

"So, Colonel, from here we head directly into the Wakhan?"

"That was the original plan, but since Dushanbe is relatively small and does not have facilities to service military aircraft, we'll take a military Russian transport to Kulyab, where we will helicopter over to the Wakhan. Our base in Kulyab is more rustic, shall we say, but it has better maintenance capabilities."

"Where's Kulyab? I'm not familiar with that city."

"Directly southeast," he said, spreading a map in front of me and pointing to a small dot not far from the Afghan border.

"Ah yes, I see it now. What, about one hundred miles to the border?"

"Exactly. However, as you note, the Wakhan is still a considerable distance east."

"Nearly four hundred miles, I'd say."

"Pretty much correct."

"So tell me about Kulyab. I know nothing about it."

"Actually, I'm ashamed to say there's not much to tell." Bashirin drained a shot he'd poured for himself, looking rather dreary as he laid out the details. "Population slightly under a million, depends mainly on agriculture, especially cotton, for subsistence, with some heavy industry such as the aluminum plant, and 80 percent of the people live in poverty. The civil war in the 1990s ruined much infrastructure, especially the water system. Number one is to rebuild a functioning water supply. Unfortunately, as the city is close to the Afghan border, drug smuggling and addiction is a big headache. The poverty level is astounding, at five to seven U.S. dollars per month per capita, so there's not much to turn to except illicit activities in many areas. One area of progress, though, is salt mining. The area has unlimited reserves of salt. At some point, you may very well see the famous Kulyab salt domes, which look like mountains covered in snow."

"Poverty seems to be the major concern almost everywhere I travel lately."

"Unfortunately it's more the have-nots than the haves in general throughout the world. We in our countries are very lucky, wouldn't you say?"

"Yes, we are. Perhaps we should send some of our spoiled youth to some of these areas to teach them just how lucky they are."

"An excellent idea. Let's get a plane-load now," he said, guffawing.

"So, Colonel, why the itinerary change?" I queried through a mouthful of food.

"Well, it seems a large piece of equipment for the Wakhan plant needs to be hauled over to the site, and your organization decided to utilize the services of a U.S. military heavy-lift helicopter called a Pave Low. It can externally carry nine thousand kilos, is armored plated, carries three 7.62 mm miniguns, transports thirty-eight troops, and can go just about anywhere and do just about anything with its terrain-avoidance radar and forward-looking infrared sensors. The piece of equipment was fabricated at the Kulyab plant, so it needs to be moved over to the Wakhan immediately on our arrival."

"I see. And how to get to Kulyab?"

"We'll be traveling on a rather unique air vessel, the An-124 Condor Long Range Heavy Transport Aircraft, somewhat comparable to your Lockheed Martin C-5 Galaxy. In typical Russian fashion, however, ours can carry more and does not need a paved runway because of the multilegged landing gear. I won't bore you with its other capabilities. Suffice it to say that the plane measures up, as you say in the West, an extremely capable aircraft. I remember it delivering a locomotive and a yacht that was over eighty of your feet long. So it should be able to deliver us, no problem," he said laughingly. "And by the way, we will have some troops with us for security, just in case. Kulyab has lately seen some nasty incursions of drug smuggling."

"Ah, the ubiquitous smugglers. Where would the world be without them?"

Bashirin slammed his tumbler on the table. "Better off, that's where we'd be. I've lost good men to those fawking *sukiny deti*. It makes me want to puke my guts into the gutter. I hate those bastards."

Toasting, I exclaimed, "That makes two of us, the scourge of the world. They should be shot on sight."

Bashirin's large frame leaned forward as he slapped his thigh, chortling, "Can I let you in on a little secret? They are. Sometimes, when our intelligence lets us know who and where they are, we surprise them in our helicopters and have a little target practice. We try as much as possible to avoid hurting the animals, so that makes it an interesting exercise in sniper practice from the air."

I raised my eyebrows. "Kind of a Wild West mentality, don't you think?"

"Baahh. If we arrested them and took them in, they'd be out in a week. Our system is getting to be more like yours every day. And to what end? Both of our countries are awash in drugs of all kinds. Mine is being ruined by cartels and organized crime. It is a major source of income in Russia and its 'provinces' getting worse daily, with overdoses common on the streets of Moscow. You know, it used to be Russians and their vodka. Now it's Russians and their drug of choice. So don't go left on me now, boy."

I agreed, thinking perhaps this was not the best time for an ideological discussion on the subject.

"Good man," he crowed.

"By the way, Colonel, what does 'sukiny deti' mean?"

"Sons of bitches. Wonderful expression."

"Ah, I'll remember that."

"I'd better see how arrangements for our flight are progressing. I will return shortly. Please enjoy the offerings at your disposal."

"Thank you, Colonel. See you soon."

He rose from the table, exiting the lounge as the door shut behind him with a resounding, very heavy Russian metallic clank. Just then, a familiar presence settled on my shoulder.

"How'd you get in here?"

"Do you really need to ask?"

"Guess not. How are you?"

"Fine. I felt compelled to drop in briefly to see how you were doing, and I can see from the looks of things that you seem to be doing exceptionally well. Have they wined and dined you like this at every stop?"

"Yes," I hissed. "And I've just about had enough of it. I don't want to be rude, but these people eat and drink like there's no tomorrow. They never stop."

"I know," exclaimed Lyft. "That's what I love about them. Mind if I join in? I'm starved. Haven't eaten for several hours. High-altitude flying uses up a lot of calories, you know."

"Be my guest, and do me proud, my friend. The more you eat, the more Colonel Bashirin thinks I've partaken of his hospitality, so have at it."

Lyft ascended, and the slurping started. Several beers disappeared along with half a side of salmon, a bowl of pickled white fish, an assortment of bread tidbits, one platter of smoked meat, a half dozen pork sausages, innumerable slices of smoked ham, five shots of vodka, three Russian cakes, and a half dozen cookies, followed by a deafening belch. He perched once more in the same spot, somewhat heavier than a few minutes before, weaving slightly, making me fear again for his safety.

"I'm kind of schleepy now. Perhaps there is a place I could lie down?" he belched.

"Take your pick." I gestured around the empty lounge. "Why not take that one over there, the soft velvet one with the high back. That way, if your invisibility diminishes due to your intake of alcohol, no one will see you."

"Very funny. You know very well that doesn't happen. And I'm perfectly cogent, just a little tired, that's all."

"This reminds me of a biblical quote I learned as a young man about gluttony. I believe it goes like this: 'For the drunkard and the glutton shall come to poverty; and drowsiness shall clothe a man in rags.' Proverbs twenty-three, verse twenty-one."

"Think you're pretty schmart, don't you? Well, try this on for size: 'Seest thou a man diligent in his business? He shall stand before kings.' Proverbs twenty-two, verse twenty-nine,[1] so there. And I do stand before kings. As a matter of fact, I'll be one myself someday. And I'm pretty diligent, if I do schay scho myself."

"Not at this rate, you'll never make it. Although you are diligent; I'll give you that."

"Baaaah. Go quote more scripture. You know what Shakespeare said."

"No, what *did* he say?"

"He said it oh so well: 'The devil can cite Scripture for his purpose,' The Merchant of Venice,[2] oh, don't you know? You do it pretty well for yours. Now I'm going to sleep, as the next few months may not see any. Good night."

It was just as well, because I saw Colonel Bashirin making his way across the lounge.

I felt Lyft rise and heard a soft plop onto the couch next to ours and then an immediate soft buzzing as his labors caught up with him. Bashirin came over to the table and with a toothy grin said,

1   The Holy Bible, Revised Standard Version (Thomas Nelson & Sons, 1953)
2   Act 1, Scene 3, Line 99

"Well, we're pretty much set to go. My God, you were hungry. Look at this table. You pretty good Russian. We may have to adopt you," he chortled.

"Yes, I guess I had more of an appetite than I anticipated," I acquiesced, quickly changing the subject. "Shall we go?"

"But of course," Bashirin replied, palms raised upward near his sides. "We will be ready for takeoff by the time we get to the gate. Understand, this is not a commercial flight, so we leave when I say, not when the airline schedule says. So not to worry about missing the flight. We go when I give word."

"Got it. I'm ready any time you are."

"My God, I like this boy," he bellowed. "We make vodka-drinking Russian out of you yet." I felt like saying nyet in rhyme, but I kept my mouth shut, thinking that luckily I had not had enough liquor to influence that muse. We made our way through the labyrinth and out of the building to the tarmac, where the huge plane awaited us. It was a monster of an airship. I could only hope I wouldn't get lost in it.

The plane had been modified with a lounge, not dissimilar to the one we had just left. Sure enough, it was stocked with the traditional fare, including more vodka, beer, and sodas. Except this time, there was an outstanding selection of single malts. I wondered if anyone over here ever performed their duties without the influence of alcohol. When I saw the spread, I felt relieved that Lyft was comatose elsewhere, as he would have been uncontrollable in his present state.

Colonel Bashirin said, "It looks like we may be delayed for about forty-five minutes. We are waiting on that piece of equipment we need to take to Kulyab. I thought you might like to sample this excellent selection of single malts while we wait, or do you prefer blends?"

"No, single malts are perfect, thank you."

"Yes, I agree. Here. Try this Lagavulin 21. Outstanding."

I would much rather have had a Turley Vineyards red Zin, but one could not be rude, so sample I did. "It truly is," I agreed quite honestly. I sipped it very slowly, as I don't drink much single malt, it being powerful stuff. In addition, there were some single malts on the side table completely unknown to me. I scanned the table and made note of a few. There was Arberg, Lord of Isles 25 from Silay, and a bottle boasting Banff 1976 from Speyside. And I couldn't help but notice a malt labeled Secret Stills 50 Year Old in an emerald green bottle with thick, black lettering, distilled in sherry casks on the Isle of Skye, no doubt by Talisker, as it was the only distillery on the island. Others were there as well, but I stopped counting at the first sip.

Just as I was about to ask how Bashirin had acquired these uncommonly expensive lubricants, in walked what I deemed to be two Russian princesses in black leather and Lycra outfits and heels. They were truly magnificent creatures, one bedecked in pearls, the other in diamonds, nearly identical as they slinked over to the table and sat down, one next to me, the other next to Bashirin. Both were blond, each with hair coiffed in well-manicured buns.

Bashirin chuckled. "Now the party is complete. May I introduce you to the twins, Natalia and Alexa Blanschenko? Natalia is seated next to you, quite comfortably I might add."

"My pleasure, Mr. Wood. I have heard so much about you. I am honored."

She held out her hand, which I took in mine, and as she withdrew it, her nails traced my palm and then proceeded along my fingertips.

Uh-oh, I thought. *This is dangerous territory. Watch the single malt.*

Bashirin grinned. "Girls, we have a little feast prepared. Please help yourselves. There is vodka, beer, soft drinks, and an excellent selection of single malts. I declare the party begun."

Bashirin dug into the smoked wild boar platter, relishing the black bread, onions, and horseradish he added to it. With all the smoked meat I had seen in the past twenty-four hours, I wondered at the extinction rate of certain species. A shot of vodka here, another mouth stuffing there, a beer here, a cake there, topped by a single malt until my good friend loosened the pants to his uniform.

"Music," he bellowed. "We must have music. What's a party without it? I'll tell you, there is no party without it."

The lounge minions must have heard him, as the booming base kicked in to "Hot Stuff," by Donna Summers. Somewhat dated, but evidently it did the trick. Bashirin rose from the couch, as did Alexa, and they bounced to the rhythm on their way to the dance floor, where Bashirin cut a reasonable swath to 1980s disco. I was enjoying the spectacle when Natalia turned to me and queried, "Would you like to dance? It would be my pleasure."

"You know, Natalia, no offense intended, but the only person I dance with is my wife. I made her that promise long ago, and I have kept it ever since. Please don't be offended; it has nothing to do with you. It all has to do with me."

"I'm not offended at all. It makes you all that much more attractive, trust me. One does not run across honest men much these days."

This was not where I wanted the conversation to go.

"So tell me, Natalia, are you a true Russian?"

"Yes, Moscow. I work for Russian Army, when they need me."

"What exactly do you do?"

"Modeling, you know, at tradeshows and a little of this and a little of that. You know how it is."

I knew all right.

The dance progressed, with Bashirin shedding his coat, then his tie. The great bear of a man was sweating profusely, probably from the quarts of alcohol he had consumed. Another tune came on, but they had had enough, so they came to the table, he laughing, she giggling.

"Come, you two. We have much more comfortable quarters behind the lounge. It's playtime."

"Colonel, may I be forgiven if I remain here? Not to be awkward, but I would feel much more comfortable surrounded by this excellent cuisine and most rare of single malts."

"Ah, a man with a conscience. I knew there was something I liked about you. Of course you can stay, but as the girls work for me, you won't mind if Natalia joins us?"

"Be my guest. Just don't have a heart attack."

He roared over that one.

"Ah, you Americans, always with the one-liners. I love you guys. Come girls; we have work to do."

He lapsed into hilarity over that one as well, leading the girls to the rear, where they disappeared behind a paneled door.

Whew. Now for some time to myself, I thought.

Having finished the Lagavulin, I decided to sample the Macallan 50 against it, before my palate became inoperative. I poured an ounce into the single malt glass, smelling the peat on the waft rising around the rim. This was something special. I took a sip, truly startled by its smoothness.

I said out loud, "Well, now. Once they seen St. Louis, there's no goin' back to the farm."

"Like that single malt, do you?"

I jumped in my seat, spilling the scotch on my pants.

"Damn it, Lyft. How long have you been there?"

"Long enough to know I don't have to report you to Barbara."

"What are you, my chaperone?"

"I smelled food, so I thought I'd drop by, even if it was a rather unpropitious moment."

"How could you smell food from the airport lounge in the bowels of the terminal?"

"I couldn't. I left there some time ago, with a smashing headache, I might add. That single malt might be just the thing for a cure methinks."

"Have at it, but don't blame me for the consequences."

"Have I yet? No, so let me sample this one. Oh my, this is superb. These Russians are getting rather sophisticated."

"Yes, in more ways than one. Say, Lyft, do you feel that? Kind of like a rocking motion?"

"No, but then again, I can't say I'm at 100 percent efficiency over here, so perhaps the plane is rocking a little. Why do you ask?"

"Oh, no reason. I thought maybe I was getting a little tipsy, not really wanting affirmation. Probably loading cargo in the belly of the plane."

"Um, most likely. I say, this single malt is pure Nirvana. I wonder where he ever obtained a Macallan 50. Perhaps I don't want to know."

I said, "Perhaps you don't. I've been reading a lot about our Eastern brethren. Smuggling in Russia is at an all-time high, controlled by organized crime syndicates. You name it, from tea and sugar to nuclear material, even major military aviation—if you have the money and the will, there is a way. It's best not to inquire about our Macallan 50, might open up a can of snakes."

Lyft said from an opposite seat, "Can of worms; you mean can of worms."

"No, I mean can of snakes. Take it for what it's worth."

Lyft said, "OK. So when do we leave for Kulyab? Seems like this stop's taking forever."

I replied, "I presume when the good colonel is through with his playmates. I could swear the plane is rocking."

"Wishful thinking on your part. This may take a while. Russians have prodigious appetites, extending well beyond the culinary arts. Might as well sit back and enjoy. Here. Have another scotch. You spilled yours. Naughty boy, wasting good Macallan."

I looked around from my chair, gazing through the plane window onto the tarmac, wondering at the delay. The lounge walls of the plane were padded in burgundy velvet, the carpet was a plush tan Berber, rotating leather chairs surrounded the parquet dance floor of the finest quality, the marble tables with rounded edges were loaded with condiments. Everything seemed devoid of sharp angles, probably designed so that drunken guests and crews did minimal damage to themselves when fully inebriated.

I retorted, spinning in my chair, "Right. If you'd announce yourself once in a while instead of scaring holy living hell out of me when you arrive, it would save a potential disaster of your discovery. One of these days, you're going to forget that I'm not omniscient, and then there'll be trouble. You'll arrive in a crowd of people, startle me, and make me do something stupid that I can't explain, and then there'll be hell to pay. I'll say, 'Oh, my invisible friend just arrived. He does that often without warning. He normally sits on my left shoulder, harangues me with historical anecdotes, saves the world on occasion, and—oh yes, by the way, I work for him through a dummy corporation set up in New York. He's one of the most intelligent beings I have ever met, and—oh yes, he has a colossal appetite, so your buffet and liquor is about to disappear.'"

"Thank you for the last part, the part about being intelligent, I mean. You really do care, don't you?"

"Baah, you're impossible."

"True. That's why you're drawn to me. You know, I don't let any of my other employees talk to me that way."

"I'm surprised they talk to you at all."

"Well, in actuality, they don't. It's done through intermediaries. You are one of the select few, probably because I enjoy the sparring and the repartee so much."

Lyft uplifted for a second, giving the seat a twirl, and then settled himself onto the backrest, spinning like a kid on an amusement park ride. I wondered how the centrifugal force would interact with the scotch.

He continued, his voice near and distant as he spun around, "I don't really get much of that in the Klinque. They are way too serious, always on the lookout to ensure you humans don't screw things up. As if they could prevent it."

I was slightly disconcerted, talking to his frontal and dorsal sides simultaneously, but I replied anyway. "The problem with you folks is that you're always in a reactive mode. You can't interact with us, so you'll always have cleanup duty—not really a good way to monitor activities that could bring us all down. Who knows? Perhaps this Earth spinning thing is the result of some idiotic human activity that could have been prevented if somehow you were better able to monitor what goes on up here. Must be hard to do situated as you are deep in the Earth's mantle. Cell phones don't even work properly up here. I can only imagine what your communications are down there."

I pointed to one of the monitors embedded in the wall displaying CNN Headline News on mute, and he said, "You have a point. But don't forget, there are quite a few of us who are invisible. As you know, we are tasked with the monitoring, reporting, and initiation of action, as with the current situation, so we make a valiant attempt to ensure you don't kill us all. It's difficult sometimes, however. You humans are so enigmatic, so brutal, so inhuman, that oftentimes when we choose one course of action, it must be reversed before its implementation due to your fickle natures."

He stopped the chair by elevating again, grabbing it by the arm, whereupon he settled into it, his taloned feet jutting out from the seat in my direction, another distraction. I couldn't help but wonder if he did these things on purpose just to jolt my concentration. I'd never seen the bottoms of his feet—they looked like old, cracked parchment, lines running through them like rivers on a relief map.

I focused. "Well, we do have our issues, that's for sure. I'm not sure if we're more complicated now, or if we were more so eons ago. Court intrigue in ancient Egypt, the Borgias in Italy, the French court prior to the revolution, you name it, it was complicated then, and it's complicated now. It's the nature of the species. You're lucky you have no such complications in your world."

He rammed a talon in my direction. "We do, and it's you."

"Another barb hits its mark."

"I am rather good at that."

Lyft preened, another disconcerting movement. He continued, "On another note, I've come up with what I deem to be a rather esoteric name for our project."

"Oh? And what's that?"

"Abzu."

"Abzu?"

"Yes, Abzu. Abzu was the river that supposedly surrounded the Earth in Sumerian mythology. In Babylonian mythology, it was known as Apsu, the freshwater god, having existed from the beginning of time, married to Tiamat, goddess of saltwater. When they had children, they made a hash of it, and their rotten kids turned into swampland."

He gave a great chuckle over that one.

"Very funny."

He raised his arms. "Have you no patience for a little humorous embellishment?"

"None."

"Harrumph. No sense of humor."

"Nope." I took a sip of scotch.

"As I was saying, I prefer the Sumerian version, as it fits my need to identify the project. It's succinct, descriptive, and to the point."

I raised an arm to the air. "Who's to argue?"

"True. No one really. So Abzu it is. We'll name it the Abzu Scientific Nonnuclear Supercooling Subterranean Crucible."

I rolled my eyes nearly out of their sockets. Sarcastically, I intoned, "Descriptive I get. Succinct and to the point, I don't think so."

Lyft's eyes widened in innocent query, "You don't appreciate my nomenclature?"

"Not at all. How about The Abzu Project? What's wrong with that?"

Lyft looked thoughtful. "Not very empirical sounding ..."

I set my scotch down and raised my arms in some frustration. "So? Who cares about the other stuff? Only you. This thing does not need a grandiose title."

"Perhaps you're correct. I'll take it under advisement."

"Sure. Have the council vote on it. That should take several days if they're anything like us," I retorted somewhat too sarcastically.

"I don't need the council for this."

Imperiously, I added, "Then I guess you'll take it under your own advisement. Let me know what you come up with."

I poured another scotch, this time the Suntory. It was similar to the Macallan, but not quite as peaty, perhaps a little smoother. I thought, *We'd better get this show on the road before I get nice and plowed. The scotch is too good to waste, but if I drink it all, I'll be in no shape to do anything once we get to Kulyab. And if Lyft has any more, he might fly into the side of K-2.*

Now it was my turn to have a spin in the chair. I said as I twirled, "Hey, Lyft, you don't suppose this is a plot by our Russian friends to leave us indisposed so that they can take over the project and reignite the cold war, do you?"

"My friend, the cold war is over. And no, I trust these folks implicitly."

"Well, you never know ..."

"Do you know what you just did?"

"No, do tell."

"You just practiced an aposiopesis."

I stopped spinning, making a feeble attempt at concentration, the scotch having gone to my head. "A what?"

"An aposiopesis."

I slurred slightly, "It sounds like surgery."

"Actually, it's an incomplete sentence, deliberately not completed for rhetorical effect."

"And how is that incomparable bit of knowledge going to benefit me in the future?"

"I just thought you'd like a definition pertaining to some of your practiced use of language, that's all. Most people embellishing their conversation through emphatic idiomatic expressions have no idea as to the definition and reasoning behind their rationale. Now you do, at least in a microcosmic sense."

"In other words, I have much left to learn in this regard."

"That you do. Understanding the nuances of language is an infinite exercise, but a fascinating one."

Just then, Colonel Bashirin appeared in the doorway from the anteroom, slightly disheveled, but evidently none the worse for wear. Lyft had blinked into invisibility.

"Ah, these Moscow women. What angels of mercy they are."

Angels of mercenary would be more like it, I thought.

"What would we do without them? The world would be a darker place. Well, enough poetry. On to Kulyab and then to the belly of the beast. Let's get underway. Finish your scotch, which I see you have found to your liking, and we'll be off."

I couldn't very well tell him that Lyft had consumed half of it, so I drained my glass, keeping thoughts of Lyft's strangulation to myself. He whispered in my ear, "I appreciate the sacrifices you make to keep me incognito. In this case, not such a burden, although, trust me, there will be others that will weigh heavily. Now, put a smile on, be pleasant, and keep me to yourself. I'll see you in Kulyab."

I stood, slightly rocky, gave Bashirin a meaty grin, and followed him to the passenger section of the plane. In less than fifteen minutes, we were airborne, south to Kulyab, closer to the Afghan border.

Chapter Four

The flight was uneventful, the best kind in my estimation. Kulyab was pretty much a dismal place, population just short of a million souls, all of whom seemed mired in poverty. Upon landing, the thought running through my mind was "drab," in part due to its rhyming functionality. The airbase had been built by the Russians in the early 1990s, seemingly with some American presence scattered about. I would have to inquire about that. Our equipment was already loaded onto the Pave Low. The only delay in its departure was us.

We boarded the helicopter, featuring an American crew, along with twelve American and twelve Russian commandos. Talk about a joint exercise. Colonel Bashirin related that Colonel Salvo would soon join us when we arrived in the Wakhan and that, for purposes of clarity, the language of the mission would be in English, although his comrades were fluent in any number of languages. I could tell he was looking forward to seeing his good friend once again.

The transport took off with a roar, and soon we were jostling along at 150 mph. The top speed at sea level of the MH-53J Pave Low III was 165 mph, but due to the load we were carrying underneath, our speed was diminished and would be further as we climbed over higher terrain. At less than top speed, I figured about a two-hour flight, give or take a few minutes. The commandos were checking their equipment, with one each on the 7.62 mm miniguns. Colonel

Bashirin motioned me to the rear, where he suggested I change into more appropriate garb. Lyft had briefed me on what to wear, so I changed quickly into my winter gear, as the temperature was rapidly dropping. I yelled to Bashirin, "Why the miniguns?"

"Smugglers taking potshots."

I relaxed slightly, realizing that we had some protection.

The province of Badakhshan on a map looks like a closed left fist with an outstretched thumb extending to the right, the thumb representing the Wakhan region. We were currently flying over the fist, with the starboard doors seemingly more of a concern, as I was told that any shots taken would most likely emanate from smugglers heading north. I wasn't so sure of the rationale, but I had to acquiesce, as it was not really my mission. Mine had not yet really begun. Theirs was to get me to my destination alive. I took it for granted that they knew what they were about.

Bashirin had suggested earlier that I utilize a headset so that I would be included in the crew's communications. Suddenly, the pilot barked, "Incoming," into the headset, and the gunners stiffened at their positions. The guns were connected to radar-seeking devices on platforms that could be extended beyond the sides of the helicopter for better angle of fire if necessary. Both gunners had deployed, checking the radar, when sure enough, the starboard gun gave a burst. Then the port gun, firing under the helicopter, echoed the first. I heard the one in the front break out as well, although I was not sure of the nomenclature of that weapon.

Bashirin gave me a wink and said, "RPGs, two of them, fired at us. The miniguns, at five thousand rounds per minute, took them out before the package arrived. Now, to deal with the perpetrators."

Even with a load slung underneath it, the helicopter proved surprisingly agile. It swung around to face the four mujahideen crouching among the rocks, preparing to sight in on us. I held my breath as one lifted another launcher onto his shoulder. It was as if, for a moment, time held still, and I could zoom in; I was amazed at the hatred I imagined I could see in the man's eyes. *Why?* I found myself wanting to ask him. We were of no harm to them. They simply saw us as those who were outside their faith—infidels—the current invaders to be driven out of their land. Their twelfth century mentality had permanently locked them into an endless cycle of repressive paranoia, perpetually transcending into violence, the status quo of tribal governance their only goal.

Suddenly, the realization that the man was about to pull a real trigger jolted me back into the present. I wasn't just reading about this. I gasped and took a step back, just as the helicopter's minigunners burst two short loads from the gun platforms. The shots kicked up dust, and when it cleared away, I was looking at four bodies strewn awkwardly, one lying halfway down a hillside in the shale. Intrigued by my lack of remorse, I noted only with pleasure that the men had had no animals with them.

The helicopter swerved back on course, the corpses receding into the distance. All I could see was sand and shale as I thought about the futility of preaching democracy to a populace fueled by reactionary fanaticism such as we'd just seen, nothing more than an excuse to create chaos. It would be as foreign to the people as would a movement to convert them to Christianity.

There is an old adage that things happen when they are ready to happen. I had no doubt the United States had done the right thing by waging war, driving the Taliban out of the country. I did have my doubts about the type of government we were attempting to install, with many of the southern and border tribes feeling disenfranchised. I also realized that I did not have a viable solution. But one thing I did know: this country had a long way to go to establish any type of democratic government, as a populace has to be ready to accept such a radical change. The only way it can do so is through a rational decision-making process, a process promulgated through education. Not only did Afghanistan have no health system, it had no educational system.

So here we were, delving into a radical fundamentalist patriarchal society, where woman were considered less than chattel, where, in Badakhshan, the poorest of the Afghan provinces, the mortality rate for women in childbirth nationally hovered at sixty-five hundred per one hundred thousand babies born, and where 75 percent of all infants born in the province die in their first few months. Male children are preferred. Female children are often used as barter to satisfy tribal feuds. It is rare to find an unmarried girl over the age of eighteen. If so, she would be defective in some way, unacceptable in "social" settings. Many girls are married before the age of twelve, have no recourse for abuse, are normally malnourished, and are ill prepared for the rigors of childbirth and matronly duties. I have often thought a society that treats its women as partners in its success will exhibit an enlightened, stable culture. Not this one. This one had miles to go before it slept.

I motioned to Bashirin. "Aren't we going to land?"

"No, biggest mistake we could make. We are more vulnerable on the ground than in the air. Either their comrades will find them, or the wolves will first. Either way, we continue onward."

I remembered stories of Russian helicopter pilots making the mistake of landing to investigate incidents during their Afghan war, only to be ambushed on the ground by forces in the hills and then hacked to death by both women and men with Afghan swords. The heads were then wrapped in skins and substituted for dead calves in the ancient game of Buzkashi, a contest on horseback whereby the first dead calf pitched across a goal line determined the team winner. The game could last as long as a week, normally resulting in broken bones and head injuries. Buzkashi literally means "goat killing," although in some quarters in the 1980s, it meant "pilot down." The more I thought about it, the more I was thankful to have remained aloft.

We flew over Faizabad, the provincial capital, heading to Shar-e-Buzurg. I recalled reading that, in April 2004, Shar-e-Buzurg, which wasn't that far from the Wakhan entrance and happened to be on a major drug running route for caravans headed north to Central Asia, had been the battleground for two local warlords. They had utilized heavy artillery, mortars, and vehicle-mounted rocket launchers. Civilians caught in the crossfire were injured and killed along with some of the warring parties.

Even though there still was a contingent of two hundred NATO troops in Faizabad, they did not intercede in regional disputes. They did not feel ironing out grievances between warlords to be their mission. Nazeer Mohammad, known as Nazeermad, was the commander of influence in the Faizabad area, having wielded power for over ten years. Even the provincial governor held no power, having little say in the governance of the town and province. Nazeermad, pretty much autonomous, sported four wives, had been married eleven times in the past fifteen years, continually divorced one wife and married a new one via forced marriage every three years. Most of the government was run by supporters of Nazeermad. His grip on political office remained so strong that Badakhshan Province was one of the few unable to be subjugated by the Taliban.

On top of that, the province was the number three poppy production area in Afghanistan, which accounted for the proliferation of heavy weapons and the well-armed local militias. Petty crime was rampant, as the warlords, concerned with their own area of control, production, and distribution, left opportunistic windows open for lesser thieves and malcontents, ignoring the concerns of the honest civilian population. The farmers and traders, those at the bottom of this food chain, had been left as carrion, feasted on by these warlords who deemed them to be the residue of their own society. An amalgam of the worst of the human condition, it would seem to be a hopeless situation.

Yet hope there was. If Lyft could vent hope, then so could I. I was anxious to hear more of it upon arrival at the site.

We eventually made our way into the Wakhan area, although with a distance to travel. To the north were the Pamirs, to the south the Karakorams. We were flying over the very heart of the Hindu Kush, so very romanticized in Kipling's *The Man Who Would Be King*.

I could see why Kipling had fallen in love with the area. The scenery was starkly spectacular, albeit not fit for human habitation. The scrub pine struggling to gain footholds in rock crevices, gnarled and bent away from the prevailing winds, contrasted with the treeless mountains on either side of the valley, their rugged outcroppings continuously spitting shale to the valleys below. The Wakhan grasslands waved in the breeze, cut through by freezing rivers fed by snowmelt, and the barren dirt of the mountains leading to their snow lines lent the area a surreal aura. It was a land of sharp contrasts, harsh, with howling never-ending winds, which were said to have driven men mad in the nineteenth century.

But inhabited it was anyway, meagerly. It was difficult for me to fathom why people would want to make an attempt at scratching out a living where there was little means of subsistence.

And then I thought about the poppy. What better place to raise it than in an area where its production and the resulting end product were never subject to scrutiny by a unified authority? It was like the company store, exhibiting the means of cultivation, production, manufacture, and distribution owned lock, stock, and barrel by the very organization that, in essence, was supposed to put such a self-sustaining cartel out of business, but instead promulgated it, fed off it, and expanded production until the province became number one on the bestseller list. The warlords' mantra was to effectuate a world awash in heroin. They were succeeding due to the insipidness of the propensity for humans to destroy themselves.

Many being Muslims, they left it to the infidels to carry the monkey, although they were not above selling their product to their fellows if pressed. After all, they were businessmen first, criminals second. Even though the dollar yield for heroin was greater, opium in the Wakhan was the drug of preference, probably because it was more affordable. Tobacco paper was cheaper and more readily available, as was the opium itself. The basic difference between the two drugs is that opium is a naturally occurring substance, whereas heroin is a result of synthesis from morphine, a byproduct of raw opium.

Little did C. R. Alder Wright know of the havoc he would create when he first stumbled on heroin through experimentation in 1874 at St. Mary's Hospital Medical School in London. He was initially trying to find a nonaddictive alternative to highly addictive morphine. After bringing acetic anhydride to a boil with morphine, presto, he had his miracle drug. Heinrich Dreser of Bayer in Elberfeld, Germany, in 1898, actually named the drug, which, in those days, was accepted as a morphine substitute and cough medicine for children. It meant "heroic treatment" from the German word *heroisch*. If he only knew. However, some good came out of the discovery. Acetic anhydride is the main ingredient in aspirin, which Dreser discovered, and it became an instant success for the Bayer Company. Unfortunately, Bayer also imported heroin legally into the United States until it was outlawed in 1914 when the country realized it had an abundance of addicts as the byproduct of the wonder drug. Dreser turned into the ultimate oxymoron. It was rumored that he became addicted to heroin, which eventually caused a cerebral hemorrhage. He did not know then that if he had taken aspirin as a preventive, he may have been able to avoid the stroke that killed him, or at least, perhaps, he could have prolonged his life. So we had the English and the Germans to blame for the original importation of heroin.

As I was musing on the history of heroin, I realized we were about thirty minutes from our destination. We were approaching the small town of Langar, the only point of civilization left in the Wakhan from there to the China border. Our destination was equidistant almost directly north of Zimistani Dawan Su and south of Qara Jelga, basically in the middle of nowhere, about twelve miles or so from the Wakhjir Pass into China. I could begin to see the site as we approached, realizing that Lyft had chosen well. The plant was located on a relatively flat plain, elevated between two narrow valleys, no doubt so that the wind could be harnessed in the cooling mechanism of the plant. It also made landing large helicopters easier than on a mountainside. As the helicopter approached, I was amazed at the scale of the construction site and how much had been accomplished. We soon arrived at the landing pad, gently discarding our underslung burden onto a giant flatbed truck. Our delivery was soon carted away, allowing us to then land in a designated zone, as there were numerous flights in and out of the area day and night.

Once on the ground, Colonel Bashirin led me to quarters where all the luxuries of home awaited. Fifty four-story cinderblock units of fifty living areas per floor had been built back-to-back on each level, with insulation sufficient for temperatures exceeding minus one hundred degrees Fahrenheit. They were also soundproofed due to the constant whining of the wind. Each had one bedroom with a small den, kitchen, living room, and full bath, comprising one thousand square feet of living space. I unpacked my gear, set up the laptop, organized the files, and sent an e-mail home via satellite while settling in to wait for instructions from Lyft.

I didn't have to wait long. There was a gentle rapping on the door. I opened it to a breeze and a presence. He materialized, gently floating in the air in front of me.

"Good to see you," he intoned.

"It's good to see you too, finally. Please do come in. When do I see the plant?"

"Oh, you *are* an eager beaver. Aren't you worn out from your trip?"

"Not really. We had a stimulating experience on the way over in the chopper, and that woke me up. The crew dispatched four mujahideen."

"Ahh yes, I was meaning to tell you about them, but more pressing matters took hold."

"Would have been nice if you'd taken an extra second to tell me that they occasionally take potshots at anything that moves," I said, plopping into a utilitarian but comfortable brown faux-leather minisofa that faced a small fireplace.

Lyft, playful now, flew to the end of the wooden mantel looked on by a tastefully framed Matisse print, where he hooked a talon around a brass ring inserted into the wood on its underside. There were any number of such rings around the house, placed by the builders so that equipment could be conveniently hung via snaps and extricated quickly in case of emergency. Lyft's immediate emergency was to hang upside down, swinging back and forth from the end of the mantel while he garbled, reminding me of a metronome at a piano recital.

He croaked, "Well, what difference would it have made? You were riding with the best of the best. They informed you, didn't they? And in good time, no? So what's to worry about? Nothing. And they were dispatched with aplomb, were they not?"

"Yes, they were. Expeditiously, I might add."

"You see? No worries."

I said softly, "Does it bother you that four human beings were just killed less than an hour ago?"

Lyft stopped swinging, changing feet. "No, it doesn't. Does it bother you?"

"Not really. They deserved what they got. I do worry about the animals that get caught in the crossfire, though. That does bother me, frankly."

"Me too. I trust you voiced an opinion on that to Bashirin?"

"Not really. He tried his best to be accommodating under difficult circumstances, but luckily the issue didn't come up. There were no animals in sight."

"Bashirin's a good man. Under this new era of cooperation, he works for the United States as well as for Russia. I'll bet you didn't know that, did you?"

"I had no idea. How does that work?"

Lyft extricated himself from his reverse perch. He flew gently to the back of the left green-cushioned carved chair angled toward the sofa, settling himself on its sculpted backrest. I noted withdrawn talons to avoid scratching the wood. As they were reproductions of Georgian design, I wasn't worried about the antique value, just appearances, a psychological remnant of my New England upbringing.

He continued, "He's one of very few who have that status. He draws two paychecks, basically double his normal salary, although the Russian component is not that great, but we made up for it, trust me. He is a true warrior, has great compassion, is loyal beyond doubt, and has a razor-sharp mind. Word has it that he truly likes you. You have made a great friend who would gladly give his life for you."

"I'm flattered. I really am. I've done nothing to merit such acclaim."

"You are who you are. That's good enough for him."

"So where is the good colonel staying?"

"In his own dacha, just like yours. We are all equal in that regard here. We can't afford to play the status game, too busy with too much to do. He understands that, as does everyone here. If I can be graphic, we have no time for such bullshit. Here they call it yak shit, all the same."

"Graphic you are," I responded, thinking that Bashirin was most likely pleased with the amenities of a loaded refrigerator and cupboards and, most of all, the fully stocked bar. Though I was certain that the accommodations were nothing like Bashirin was accustomed to, the dachas were actually quite tasteful. The tans, browns, and greens along with the utilitarian features for housing equipment had definitely been employed with the male species in mind. The only thing missing was the domesticating touch of a woman, but that was not going to happen, at least not for me.

I said, "You know, sometimes you surprise me. You can be so erudite, and then you can roll around in the barnyard."

Lyft did a quick spin. The only thing missing was the hay. "Who cares, as long as it gets the job done? Do you know the derivation of 'bullshit?'"

"Nope, but I'm sure you're going to tell me."

"Correct. Some think the word is derived from the papal edicts, called bulls, from the bulla, or seal, on the documents, with the convenience of an appendage of an appropriate sort added for emphasis. I disagree with that assessment. I believe it is derived from a word in old French, *boule*, which means fraud or deceit or perhaps trickery, or nonsense. Again, America took liberty with the original meaning, adding the latter descriptive phrase for emphasis to make a compound word, claiming the term as its own around 1915. It became very popular by World War II and, forgive me, remained stuck to the wall, so to speak. Some other wordsmiths have attributed its usage to the fact that many thought feces from bulls, being relatively useless, at some point wound up in a drunk's vocabulary and subsequently was incorporated into daily speech, but I doubt it. Normally there's a true derivation for this type of expression. I believe my version, thank you very much."

I got up from my chair, crossed the living room into the kitchen, and retrieved an iced tea from the refrigerator. I poured out two glasses, returned to my seat, and offered one to Lyft on the way by.

"Thank you. I was getting rather thirsty. All this lecturing dries me out." He wrapped his talons around the glass, tilted it, and took a long sip.

"But no one really knows how it got started, do they?"

"Couldn't prove it in a court of law, no."

"I think I like the drunk's vocabulary explanation. Sort of has a poetry about it. Although, with your affinity for bashing the Church, I'm surprised you didn't opt for the antipapist version."

A talon in my direction. "Now let us not be discriminatory. I basically rail against all organized religions, except the one I spoke to you about a long time ago, Baha'i, remember? The Catholic Church just happens to be the most obvious target, as it's most prominent in 'recent' history. However, as for the derivation of the term at hand, you can suit yourself. What you should be proud of is that it's a true American euphony."

I took a sip of my tea. "What on earth is a euphony?"

"Words formed that are acoustically pleasing to the ear. You know, when something is euphonic."

"You think the word bullshit is euphonic?"

"I think it has a harmonious poetry about it, especially if you think of *boule*, which seems to have a little more emphasis on the 'ou' instead of the 'u.' You know, when you round your lips around the vowels a little bit, the lilt of the word changes dramatically. In German, it's even better. The word for bullshit is *schwachsinn*. Now doesn't that have a ring?" Lyft gave a little fly around on the word *ring*.

I raised my glass. "As in *das ist doch schwachsinn!*"

"Oh, go to the head of the class!" Lyft exclaimed, almost spilling his tea.

"I had a boss who spoke German, and this is one of the phrases he taught me."

"Slang, but oh so appropriate for 'That's utter bullshit.' I'd have it no other way. Kudos to you, my good friend. Did you know that *schwachsinn* also means idiocy and any other variety of mental deficiency?"

"No, I didn't. Somehow you always have to one-up me."

"That's what it takes to be educated. Through education emanates humility."

I rolled my eyes. "Yes, oh sage one."

"Well, you have to admit that I do have a few years on you."

"Approximately a thousand, give or take."

"Yes, giving or taking a century here or there."

"What's a few hundred years when you're talking a millennium?"

"Right." More tea sipped on both parts.

"Well, what's on the docket for tomorrow?"

"I'll show you around, get you acclimated, and introduce you to much of the crew, and then we'll outline your responsibilities. We are pretty much up and running, so there's not much for you to do with the exception of organizing some security issues."

I quacked, "How do you propose to introduce me when you are to remain invisible?"

"Good point. Colonel Salvo will be here, obviously along with Bashirin, and they will take charge of the agenda as I have outlined it. Their orders explicitly detail how you are to be handled."

I toasted, "I sound like the newest hot commodity."

Lyft exclaimed, both arms in the air, the tea dangerously sloshing in the glass, "But you are. After all, you are a civilian with military propensities. They love you."

"Glad to hear it," I chuckled sarcastically.

"At any rate, I'll leave you to your own devices for the evening. I'm off to attend to other matters. I'll see you on the morrow. Thank you for the tea."

He handed me his glass as he floated in the air. I arose, seeing him to the door.

"Good night, Lyft."

"Good night, my friend. Sleep well."

"You too."

He manipulated the door, humming a soft melody as he exited. I wondered if it were contentment or put on for my benefit to help instill calm in a tortuous ocean of doubt about whether we could possibly be successful in our venture. I could not think of failure; the consequences of it were too dire to contemplate. No one seemed inordinately worried about project failure; rather, all exhibited a true can-do attitude. I decided to do the same. I prepared for bed, not really knowing or caring what time it actually was. I just knew that I was suddenly bone tired and needed a full night of uninterrupted sleep. I lay my head down, tumbling immediately into a dreamless black abyss that did not release its hold until morning.

CHAPTER FIVE

I remembered Lyft saying that our first plant was to be a super nitrogen producer, but I really had no idea as to its size until I looked at it from the distance of my dwelling. It was mammoth. It sprawled over approximately three hundred acres, appearing to my untrained eye to be over 50 percent complete. What lay underneath in the subterranean portion, I had no idea. Bashirin and Salvo had arrived promptly at nine in the morning, somehow knowing that I needed every bit of the twelve hours of sleep I had blissfully accumulated. We were headed toward the plant, which was protected by two concentric chain-link fences, fifty feet apart, both topped by razor concertina wire. On the perimeter of the outer fence were warnings in various languages pertaining to landmines situated between the fences. Lyft wasn't kidding about taking security seriously. I wondered how the overly abundant resident marmot population dealt with the issue. Since the average male marmot in the area weighed approximately ten pounds, with the female normally weighing less, I presumed that, once in a while, there were male population explosions unrelated to breeding habits, as the average landmine is set off by approximately ten pounds of pressure. I made a mental note to only ask Lyft about the issue, not wanting to make a complete fool of myself.

At the road entrance to the plant were two raised fifty-caliber machine gun bunkers, each attached to the fence opening. As the weather was temperate, the gun emplacements were located on top of the flat cement pyramids. In winter, they were inside. I was surprised to see what I thought were Wakhi tribesmen manning the posts. Another question for Lyft. They checked our credentials, waving us through the checkpoint, clicking their heels smartly while snapping a salute to the two colonels who promptly returned them. So far, I was duly impressed with the security arrangements.

As we approached the plant, the enormity of the quest became apparent. I had no idea what I was really viewing. It was all a jumble of pipes, compressors, storage tanks, and service vehicles intermixed with more pipes that had more U-turns than Route 100 in Yonkers. I had never encountered such a mishmash of construction so unexplainable in laymen's terms. Gazing upon the scene reinforced my college decision to become a liberal arts major. However, my fortunate circumstance was to help ensure its security, not ensure its actual operation. For that, I was thankful.

Suddenly, I felt a familiar presence clump down onto my left shoulder. Having anticipated his arrival, I wore a left-handed hunting coat underneath my overcoat, which had the advantage of extra leather padding on the shoulder around the approximate area where Lyft's talons continually punctured me.

At least I'll be more protected in the front, I mused. *The back I'll have to work on.*

"Good morning," I heard whispered in my ear.

Having little recourse, I kept my mouth shut.

Lyft was evidently in a playful mood.

"What? No good morning?" he quipped. "How rude. And did we have a good night's sleep? I've been up for hours, checking gauges and running tests while you were happily ensconced in dreamland. Suffice it to say, last night was your only full night of sleep for a while. I can't do all the work here, you know. And I've no one to talk to, so you'll just have to keep me company a lot of the time from now on."

Now we came to the crux of it, probably the real reason I was recruited for the mission. The light dawned. I would have to suffer through his pedantry, his capricious nature, and his insane hours in order to mollify his anguished, lonely soul. Perhaps there was a way I could volunteer for tunnel duty, a more tolerable task at three times the assigned depth.

The plant site resembled an anthill under siege. Five thousand workers were crawling over the entire structure, those on the ground performing maintenance, those above securing the maze of pipes and electrical circuits. Giant double-walled vessels hundreds of feet high, called Dewars after their inventor, lined one area of the plant. I supposed those were the holding tanks for the liquid nitrogen before it was to be pumped into the tunnels. They looked like fat, giant rocket ships.

I saw the tunnel entrances. I could only imagine the activity below. Both colonels introduced me to any number of foremen whose names eluded me as soon as the introductions were completed. Most were foreign, the majority Mexican. I had always exhibited a mental block pertaining to the Spanish language. I attributed my passing the course in college to my soccer coach, who was also my Spanish teacher.

It was explained to me that the plant was nearly operable. It would be finished before the tunnel system was complete, which was taking longer than anticipated. I would have to ask Lyft how the tunnel workers interacted with the others. That would be an interesting conversation.

Initially, earthquakes were feared, but sections of the plant had been built on giant coils, so unless the ground actually opened up beneath it, the plant was designed to withstand a 9.0 Richter event. Landslides were common due to earthquakes, but the plant was on a plateau with no sharp peaks nearby, so that concern had been alleviated. What was of concern were the wandering nomadic and drug caravans, which were major pests and needed some control. The previous week, two RPGs had been fired from a neighboring hilltop, and the culprits had disappeared, it was thought, into a cave system in an adjoining valley. It turned out the fools had fired out of range, with the rounds landing about one hundred yards short of the entrance. Then again, perhaps they were smarter than we thought they were, as probably they were gauging the distance purposely for mortars or light artillery. At any rate, the incident needed attention, topping the priority list for security concerns. As

I had seen a full-blown exhibition of the insanity of some of the local dissidents, I was not particularly surprised at the incident.

Colonel Salvo gestured with one arm sweeping toward the facility. "So, how do you like the plant?"

"Impressive, and large, very large."

"Yes, it's that all right. Say, how'd you like to go hunting?"

"I assume for human prey?"

"Correct."

Colonel Bashirin said, "It will be a joint operation, as previously in the helicopter on the way over. As a matter of fact, we'll use a light helicopter for bait. These idiots can't refuse a shot at it. They know from experience that it's a spotter helicopter, so they always hope to bring it down before it can radio their position for a heavier gunship to move in. When they do, we put Thor's hammer on them."

"I like the analogy," I said loudly as I looked at the activity on the helipad some five hundred yards distant, seeing another bird take off against the shale of a mountain. If I hadn't been looking closely, I might have missed the chopper, as its camouflage blended perfectly against the jumbled stone in the background.

We walked away from the main plant on the road leading to the dacha area, away from the din of pounding ball-peen hammers and the continual shouts of the construction crews.

"We leave at first light. Let's go to your dacha and discuss what you will need. I assume you are proficient in using the Kalashnikov and/or the M-16?"

Between rumbles of trucks on the road, I replied loudly, "Yes, sir. Had extensive training during the past three months. More with the M-16 than with the AK."

"Good man. Let's go get you outfitted. Hanging around here is like watching Afghan grass grow, even slower than regular grass on Steppes in USSR," Bashirin guffawed. "Now we begin to have some fun."

We walked back to my dacha, where the colonels proceeded to ensure I had everything I needed for tomorrow's safari. I sensed Lyft's presence, but he said nothing. When an item was missing, Bashirin radioed in on his walkie as to what was needed, and it arrived with an immediacy denoting the seriousness of the mission: pistol belt with four ammo clip pouches holding five clips each of thirty rounds; two canteens; special cold-weather gear for high-altitude operations, including special sheer Thinsulate gloves for weapons operation; special-op mountain boots, high on the calf to help ensure against sprains and broken bones; and a standard U.S. Army–issue M-16 sporting an extra clip. Salvo related that it was the same one I had sighted in back home. I looked the rifle over, took it apart, examined its components, and then pieced it back together again in less than three minutes. Bashirin and Salvo looked at each other.

"Impressive. But can you hit anything with it?" Bashirin joked.

Good naturedly, I quipped, "Got any of them there Afghan groundhogs you want eliminated 'round hea? Show 'em to me, and we'll have an early lunch."

Laughs all around as I felt the familiar presence on my shoulder. No laughing there, however. No sense of humor, evidently, either.

Colonel Salvo said, "OK, looks like you are set for tomorrow. We leave at dawn. We rise at 0400 for preflight checks and leave by 0500. We use the Pave Low for the initial flight in, and then we walk the next several miles. No sense in alerting the critters before their breakfast. If we're lucky, we'll surprise them during morning prayers. If not, they'll already be on their way. We'll still find them; it just won't be as easy. We think we know where they are holed up, so we'd like to catch them in their lair, perhaps getting an arms cache in the process. See you in the AM."

At their departure, Lyft materialized, perching himself on the back of a kitchen chair. He had a look of some concern on that unique oval countenance, his large brown eyes boring into mine.

"OK, out with it. What's bugging you this time?"

"When I signed you up for this gig, this wasn't what I had in mind. *They* are supposed to engage in combat operations, not you. You are to stay here and deal with any security issues on-site."

I raised my arms in some frustration. "What security issues? You've pretty much got it covered if you ask me. And, my very good friend, this matter does concern an issue on-site. If you'll remember, some idiots fired those RPGs from, frankly, not too far away. They only missed by a hundred yards. So in the colonels' minds, they see nothing amiss in pursuing the subject with me in tow. I'm actually quite proud I was invited."

"Actually, you were impressive in taking the gun down and reassembling it. Where did you learn that?"

"Some things one teaches oneself. I figured the exercise might be useful some day. I was right in that assumption."

I went over to the rifle where I'd left it on the couch, picked it up, and took aim at an imaginary target.

"They asked a question. 'Can you hit anything with it?'" I held the rifle in one hand, pointing to the mechanisms over the bolt with the other.

"Yes, I can. Part of the equation is the windage and elevation, which I adjusted back home. Those components are essential if one is to be an accurate shot. I do hope, however, that I really don't have to use it. I would rather not have that embedded memory for the rest of my life."

Lyft leaned over to look upon my instruction for once. Then he said protectively, "Well, hopefully you won't have to. I plan to tag along to help ensure you don't."

I looked up. "Haven't you better things to do?"

Arms in the air, talons extended, he exclaimed, "What, and miss all the action? I think not."

I took aim with the rifle again. "Hah. Is this going to be anything like New Rochelle?"

The previous year, he had cleaned out the local city mafia through a spectacular display of bodies thrown through windows onto the roofs of cars, pistols discharging and a transformer exploding, placing several streets into darkness. We later found out that a state trooper was forced into temporary psychiatric treatment who swore he had followed a BMW at over one hundred miles per hour on I-95 with no driver in the car.

I laughingly inquired, "Do you plan to employ similar tactics?"

"A true tactician never reveals his game plan. Let's just say we'll play it by ear."

"Ho, this ought to be good. Morning can't come soon enough," I exclaimed as I placed the rifle back in its case.

I spent the rest of the day doing paperwork, going over the timetables for the plant interaction with the subterranean activity below, the day caught between napping and intermittent bouts of worry as to how tomorrow's excursion would play out. I had never been in actual combat. The thoughts of "measuring up" played through my mind continually. Here I was, fifty-year-old civilian, volunteering to go into harm's way in one of the most rugged areas of the world in an altitude higher than I'd ever been. I could only hope I did not contract altitude sickness or worse, forcing a medevac mission back to the base. At seven thirty that evening, I took two Benadryl and fell into a dreamless sleep by eight fifteen.

I awoke without the aid of an alarm at three forty-five to multiple rotor activity on the helipad. As I lay for the final few minutes in bed, I heard the front door softly open and close. My constant companion drifted into the room, entirely visible as he perched himself on the footboard of my bed.

"Good morning."

"Good morning," I croaked weakly. "Although I'm a little buzzed from the Benadryl I took last night, so no philosophical discussions please."

"I didn't intend any, unless of course you happened to be in the mood; then I'm always game."

"Not this morning, thank you."

Lyft queried, "Did we have a little sinus problem last night?"

"No, we had a physiological problem called getting to sleep before combat."

"Oh, you've never been in combat have you?"

"No, I haven't, and I'm not sure I'm prepared for it."

"At least you're honest."

"Unfortunately, to a fault."

"Look on it this way: it's an honor for you to have been invited. I guarantee our two colonels would not have extended an invitation to anyone else outside the clique."

I propped myself up on one elbow, my open hand against the side of my head. "Oh, I'm honored all right. I get the significance of it. I have to tell you this openly. I'm afraid I won't measure up, you know, do something totally asinine that will be a complete embarrassment, humiliating me forever. I'm really not trained for this."

Lyft raised his arms to hip level. "You'll be fine, trust me on this. First off, I'm not going to let anything happen to you. Second, our two good friends and company don't know that I'm along." He exclaimed, "This is going to be some hayride."

"Ooh, boy."

"Ooh, boy is right. Now, get out of bed. We've got work to do."

Reassured, I arose, performed my morning ministrations, collected my gear, checked to ensure I had forgotten nothing, and then made my way out to the helipad with Lyft on my shoulder, where there was a bustle of activity. It was close to four forty-five. Salvo and Bashirn were inside the Pave Low performing last-minute checks. The troops were gathered in a loose formation to the side, gear ready, as the smaller spotter chopper, called a Loach, readied for its mission on the other side of the landing zone. Egg shaped, small, and nimble, the Loach, or as some affectionately called it, the Egg, was deceptive in its looks, as it had a nasty sting, carrying a 7.62 minigun and a forty millimeter grenade launcher. It could carry a pilot, observer, and four passengers. This one had been modified to accommodate no passengers, opting instead for more ammunition for the minigun.

Bashirin's voice suddenly crackled over a loud speaker, startling me.

"Five minutes to departure. Load up."

Lyft held on, almost toppling off my shoulder.

"Calm down," he whispered. "This is going to be fun. Remember, we have the element of surprise. This'll be one for the scrapbooks for the grand kids. Relax."

We climbed into the helicopter, settled in, and went through a one-minute gear check with Colonel Salvo, and then he spoke to Bashirin via his walkie, which, in turn, prompted our departure. I turned to one of the American troops, Gary Willis.

"Does this helicopter have loudspeakers attached to it? Almost scared the hell out of me when Bashirin's voice boomed a minute ago."

Gary laughed. "Yeah, there's a speaker on each side, state-of-the-art sound system, mainly used for phys-ops. Comes in handy once in a while, especially during civil disturbances or when you want to play God."

I chuckled to myself, knowing Lyft would love to get his "hands" on the microphone. Although, having seen him in action, I realized that when he wanted to project his voice, he needed no amplification.

Our journey would not be far, less than ten miles up into the foothills of the Karakorams. Although it was close to autumn, the air was balmy that morning, which was, to me, a warning sign that it could turn at any moment. The weather was notorious at this time of year during the transition of the seasons. Raging storms dumping inches of rain on lower elevations in minutes materialized out of nowhere, with the precipitation swirling to a blinding snow during precipitous temperature drops. Instant waterfalls cascaded over outcroppings, turning dry gullies into violent torrents, and the sheer wind caromed off the mountains and rushed through valleys, flattening helicopters into scrap heaps without warning. Hopefully the weather would hold for our purposes.

We headed southwest, with the sun just peeking over the ranges to our rear. It would be a while before the valleys were lit. Shortly, we arrived at the landing zone several valleys away from our destination. The helicopter was unloaded quickly, vulnerable as it was to machine gun fire from the hills. Bashirin had brought another pilot to ferry the helicopter back to the main base, on call for the operation in case we needed air support. The idea was to first find the lair on foot so as not to alarm the occupants with rattling rotor blades overhead, allowing them to melt into the hillsides. The next step would be to employ the Loach as bait to ensure we would not be attacking a hapless band of nomads. Bashirin and Salvo figured that if an RPG round came whooshing out of a cave, then the lessees were fair game. I had to agree, although if I hadn't, it would have made damn little difference. Some things are better kept to oneself.

Colonel Salvo briefed us all, stating that we were still approximately four miles from the expected area. As distances in this topographical area were deceptive, I figured we could be anywhere from three to ten miles away, but again, I kept my thoughts to myself. Either way, it was going to be an arduous trek. I was secure with the physical aspect of what I hoped to be a brief sojourn, as I had been running three to five miles a day for the past six months in the hopes of losing some weight. When Lyft had originally informed me of the itinerary for the next six months, I became much more serious in my exertions, running the final mile of each morning under seven minutes.

The rest of our small company had been operating in the region for well over three months, seemingly acclimated to the altitude. I was not so sure, although I currently had no symptoms. As we were only at six thousand feet at the moment, it was not yet of concern. However, I remembered being in Colorado once, when I had contracted a serious case of mountain sickness at seven thousand feet. One of the keys to keeping mountain sickness at bay is to refrain from alcohol or any drugs that contribute to dehydration. I was running a small convention for my organization, ignorant of the golden rules pertaining to personal watchfulness in high altitudes, subsequently drinking at receptions, social hours, and dinners, not realizing I was literally making myself ill. I had to leave a day early, as I thought I was contracting pneumonia. The condition cleared within an hour in the pressurized atmosphere of the plane. It was a lesson well learned.

The most sensible way to avoid mountain sickness is to acclimatize properly. That means adjusting to certain altitudes over a period of time. No one reacts the same to this phenomenon, but a general rule is twenty-four hours for every fifteen hundred to three thousand feet. A more rapid ascent can bring on acute mountain sickness, resulting in a mild swelling of the brain tissue due to hypoxic stress—that is, being unable process enough oxygen in the bloodstream. The symptoms are those of a raucous hangover or worse with more severe stages of mountain sickness, which I hoped to avoid.

We all had plenty to drink, which is an absolute necessity in high altitudes due to evaporation of moisture from the body, about which most individuals uneducated in high altitude operations are unaware. Drinking clear fluids ensures excessive urination of the same, essential to monitoring one's health in such situations. Colonel Salvo looked us over, handed us each a roll of sticky tape, used to secure any rattling object either to another or to the uniform itself. Sounds carried in thin air at high altitudes. He then threw the excess into the chopper, whirled his hand overhead, signaling the crew to take off, which they did in whisper-quiet mode, making their way back to the pad at the plant site. He inspected each of us, satisfied that we were taped down, as we made our way into formation for the beginning of the hike. I was next to last in the second squad of ten men each. Bashirin had the lead squad, Salvo the rear. Off we went at their command, in search of elusive quarry.

All this time, Lyft had been very quiet. However, as we progressed into the first valley, I heard him clear his throat, which probably meant an imminent history lesson. Sure enough, it began, with me at the severe disadvantage of being unable to retort.

"You know, I've been thinking a lot about war, about what we are engaged in this era, where it could lead, how your country is dealing with it, the ramifications of it in actuality. Many campaigns throughout history have made the classic mistake of underestimating the enemy. One of the most famous examples is the Germans turning back after the siege of Stalingrad in World War II. There are many others—Napoleon in the invasion of Russia, the Russians recently right here in Afghanistan, the Romans overextending the boundaries of their empire; it goes on and on. It's incredible that the same mistakes keep repeating themselves, but they do. Obviously this has something to do with the short-term memory of humanity, of lessons not being handed down for cultural assimilation, either that or sheer idiocy. I prefer the latter, for your information."

I really wish I could have engaged him, but that was impossible, so I just listened as he prattled on.

"The British, throughout their era of Victorian colonization, epitomized the sheer arrogance of colonialism, continuously exhibited by their military frontal assaults in numerous campaigns. One of the most humiliating was their loss to Maori warriors in New Zealand during the Battle of Puketakauere in the Taranaki War in June of 1860—June 27, to be exact."

I could have kicked him here. He was always so damned exact with the minutiae.

"Really feel like giving me a swift kick on that one, eh? I know you so well."

He really did.

"As I was saying before you interrupted me with thoughts of goal posting, the Maori primarily fought a defensive war against the British, and this battle was no different. The Maori, masters at deception, dug two fortifications, leading the British to believe that the first, on Onukukaitara Hill, was the primary, when really the one on Puketakauere was the true fortified position. When the British frontally attacked the decoy, they were caught in a crossfire ambush, losing thirty with thirty-four wounded. The Maori lost five. Due to Maori tactics throughout the war, the British never did win a decisive battle, eventually electing to a truce unsatisfactory to both parties, even today.

"Losing that battle was due to inordinate ignorance. Treatises on warfare have survived and been studied by the world's greatest strategists for centuries. I do believe the British read none of them. The most famous treatise on war, as you no doubt know, is Sun Tzu's *The Art of War*, written approximately twenty-four hundred years ago. He had it just right in Chapter Three: 'If you know the enemy and know yourself, you need not fear the result of a hundred battles. If you know yourself but not know the enemy, for every victory gained you will also suffer a defeat. If you know neither the enemy nor yourself, you will succumb in every battle.'"[3]

I wondered where this was going.

"Wondering where I'm going with this, eh? Stay with me."

3   Sun Tzu, *On The Art of War.* Lionel L. Giles, translator (Oriental Book Section, British Museum, 1910)

How did he do that?

"Master Sun also said, 'Hence to fight and conquer in all your battles is not supreme excellence; supreme excellence consists in breaking the enemy's resistance without fighting.'[4]

"So where I'm going with this is, perhaps on our little mission here we do not have to engage in actual combat. Perhaps there is a better way of persuading our hosts of a more civilized method of communication. We shall see."

I really wished I could communicate with him somehow, to find out what he had in mind. But that was not to be.

"I understand your need to communicate with me, but you really don't need to. I know you well enough to know what you're thinking. 'What does he mean? How's it going to work if there's not actual combat to root the bastards out?' Blah, blah … relax. Anything I do will enhance the mission, not detract from it, trust me. So be patient and observe."

We were coming into the second valley with no signs of any human activity. High up on a slope, however, I spotted a snow leopard slinking toward prey I could not discern. Suddenly, he charged, successful in the hunt, his great tail sweeping behind. I had heard that snow leopards used their tails for balance. Now I understood why, operating as they did on 40 percent grades, always charging downward in the advantage. Their tails, often as long as their bodies, swept from side to side, balancing their movements, which were twisting and violent. Seeing the leopard hunt from an elevation reminded me that we were doing the reverse, hunting on the upslope, not the perfect scenario. Seeing the magnificent animal, however, was not bad news, as he wouldn't be here if there was any human activity in the nearby valley.

We traversed the valley floor, having walked for about ninety minutes. We had covered two to three miles, having slowly climbed to an elevation of about eighty-five hundred feet. The colonels, mindful of altitude sickness, were proceeding cautiously. To evacuate anyone now would be to end the mission. The third valley turned out not to be so idyllic. It was huge, several miles across, surrounded by steep jagged rocky upthrusts covered in shale, pockmarked by black dots, that Willis told me were caves in the mountainsides

---

4   Ibid, Line 2

about thirty-five hundred feet above. Even though the area had specifically been scouted in advance at a distance, actually being there and looking up at the quarry was disconcerting. Intelligence had missed the two caves on the right, concentrating instead on the left mountain range. I could see how that could happen. It all depended on the time of day one was looking up into the hillsides relative to the angle of the sun. When they surveyed the valley, I guessed the area in question must have been in shadow. Since the caves were outlined in the direct morning sunlight, the small ones were visible as large, black dots on the mountainside.

The point of the exercise hinged on the element of surprise. However, it would be slow going to get to them in totally exposed postures. I could not see how this was going to work. It would be like the British frontal assault in the Taranaki War all over again.

The colonels called their squads together in a war council behind cover, expressing dissatisfaction with the situation, not even wanting to call the Loach in as bait. The area between the two mountains offered perfect fields of fire simultaneously directed onto a helicopter such as the Pave Low. Maneuverability would be difficult in a crossfire from fifty-caliber in-place machine guns, the mujahideens' weapon of choice for downing choppers at that altitude. The question now was how to deal with the unexpected.

Suddenly, Lyft ascended from my shoulder, saying, "Stay here. I'll be back in a little while."

As I was a little distance from the group, I asked, "Where are you going? You can't leave now; we may need you."

"You trust me, don't you? Then do as I ask. Stay here and watch the fun. Zero in on that first cave on the right in a few minutes."

Salvo approached me, saying, "We'll have to scrub the mission. We didn't count on the right-hand caves. It's too dangerous. We'll have to set up shop above them behind the peaks, taking opposite shots directly into the caves, irrespective of what's in there. Let's get our gear together. We'll take a quick breather and then head back to the LZ."

Suddenly, a giant, billowing flame erupted from the mouth of the first cave. There was a commotion, discernable even from where we were situated, of what I guessed to be Arabic curses amid much yelling and panic. Mujahideen poured out of the cave, scrambling to get away from the explosion, firing guns at each other in the attempt to ward off the cursed beast that had descended upon them. I could hear Lyft's voice clearly over the din, first in Urdu, then in Pashto, yelling that he was Iblis, Satan in the Islamic religion, with the mujahideen screaming, *"Aduw Allah,"* meaning "enemy of God." Many *Al-Ghaibs* were screeched, meaning "a thing unseen" in Arabic. Then a second flame shot out of cave number two with a giant roar, shaking the entire valley. The troops looked up in awe, speechless. For once, I had the intelligence, was all knowing, but not yet omnipresent. I would have to ask Lyft how to achieve that status.

Lyft had evidently found their ammunition storage, as the explosions became multiple, now with much popping and sputtering, which would be the small arms ammunition. I could only hope he did not engage a stray round. Thinking that their comrades were under siege, the caves on the left side of the mountain range opened fire with everything they had. The tracer rounds arced over the valley from their fifty calibers as they fired high to get the range, but accuracy at that distance was questionable. It was several miles across from mountain to mountain, although the fifty caliber had been known to fire at a distance of over four miles. We could see fighters on the right waving frantically to those on the left to cease fire. One man tied a white something onto his rifle, frantically swishing it back and forth indicating truce, but one of the rounds from his comrades across the valley tore him from the mountainside, sending him to the shale several hundred feet below.

As there were only two caves to the right, Lyft evidently had it in mind to give the same treatment to those on the left, satisfying his propensity for political moderation. The mountainside was now quiet, with the exception of shouted exclamations of Iblis and *Aduw Allah* from the shell-shocked mujahideen now milling around outside their lairs. As before, only above us, suddenly came a clamor resembling banshees screaming for prey. Men scurried from the openings as before, except double the number. Then a series of explosions rocked the valley floor, sending shards of shale and large boulders tumbling down the incline. All five caves were lit like Roman candles accidentally set off in a tent, with tracer bullets popping, ninety-millimeter rounds exploding, mortar shells propelling themselves into the interior cave walls, and AK rounds snapping like firecrackers during a celebration of the Fourth. What a carnival. The only thing missing was a calliope.

Lyft had evidently found some rope as, before our eyes (some more disbelieving than mine), the mujahedeen on the left were marching, tied in tandem, toward the valley floor. Lyft would later explain that as he tied them up, he had continuously assured them he was the true Iblis, and if they did not obey his commands, he would return and throw them off the mountain. He repeated the process on the right. Then, as both lines marched, he explained that they would be greeted in the valley by a multinational force. He harangued them all the way down, explaining his presence and why the Abzu Project was so important as we watched, some of us open mouthed, following the progress of the men tailed by five mountain mules on the right and two yaks on the left. By the time the men on both sides of the valley reached us, they were thoroughly indoctrinated, all realizing they had found new careers.

The soldiers stood in awe, not believing what they were seeing. The two colonels were chuckling, evidently knowing something of what had occurred but still amazed at the rapidity of what had just transpired. Evidently they knew about Lyft and the Klinques, but had never seen him or his cohorts. All of a sudden, in a voice that shook the valley itself, Lyft boomed in Urdu and then in Pashto, just for effect, "I am Iblis. You belong to me. You will now pay for your sins. Allah has sent me to correct your ways. You have fallen astray, adopting a false Islam. These people are here to help save the world, and you will help them. If you do not, you will suffer the pains of hell itself. Do you understand me?"

In chorus, "Yes, Master."

"You will wait here for further instruction."

Our troops were stunned by the authoritative unidentifiable bass rendition of student discipline.

Lyft fluttered onto my shoulder, told me to take the colonels behind a rock outcropping, where he would make himself visible so that they could be appeased in the realization that they had not contracted mountain sickness. I did as he asked, and he revealed himself, latched onto my shoulder.

Bashirin was the first to comment. "Holy Mother of God. I had heard rumors, but this is unbelievable. You really do exist."

From Salvo, "What a secret weapon. We could really use you, my friend."

From Lyft, "You just did."

From Bashirin, "How long has he been perched up there like that?"

From me, "Oh, about a year and a half now."

"What? You mean he's been on this expedition all along? Why didn't you say anything?"

"Please, Colonel, how would I have presented it to you? 'Oh, Colonel Bashirin, by the way, I have a traveling companion with me who's invisible, about two feet high, kind of owl-like.'" Here Lyft gave me a grip that almost made me yelp. "'Has talons for hands and feet, who flies at the speed of sound, is highly intelligent ...'"

From Lyft, "Thank you."

From me, "You're welcome ... 'sits on my left shoulder, discourses continually on historical anecdotes, and is also my closest friend.' How would that have gone over?"

Lyft gave me a gentle squeeze on the closest friend part.

"Yes, I see your point. But we have much to discuss, much to learn, much to talk over. Think of the possibilities ..."

"Enough," hissed Lyft. "I'm not a commodity to be bandied about like a ping-pong ball. You now know I exist, and that's enough for now. Both of you have top-secret clearances. This falls under that category, so I need not say more about it. As for your men, I will not be showing myself to them. I am revealing myself to you out of deference to your employers, who are good men all. I also know you two can be trusted and am counting on that for the duration not only of the Abzu Project, but for life. Successful continuance of essential missions on behalf of Mother Earth is contingent upon the secret of my invisibility. If word got out, my fellows and I would be rendered ineffective. We would become circus sideshows. So it is in the best interest of all to contain this secret, bottle it up, leave it be."

The colonels both agreed.

Lyft replied, "Good. Now we need to get back to the landing zone. One chopper won't hold us all, so we'll need another to get everyone back. Plus, the animals need to be taken care of. They can't be left here. I trust there's a method of transport for them?"

Salvo said there was. They would lash the animals under the Pave Lows in slings used for sensitive equipment.

"I leave it to you both to deal with that. I need to get back to the plant and do some real work. Ha ha."

As the colonels chuckled, Lyft rendered himself into invisibility, disengaging from my shoulder. Salvo said to me, "I had a feeling there was something special about you; I sensed it. You're no ordinary civilian. And that little guy, what a whirlwind. You two must make quite a pair."

From Lyft in thin air, "We certainly do. This is only the beginning of this journey. Wait until you see where we're going. And, if Jeff is in a good mood, he may tell you a bit about where we've been. But enough, I'm off to lower elevations."

We felt a wind go by us as Lyft departed.

From Bashirin, "Does he do that often, talk right out of the air? Must scare hell out of you …"

"Yup, it does. He likes to do it without warning, just to see how I react. Normally, it's always the same: totally pisses me off."

Both colonels laughed. Salvo said, "Well, we'd best be moving. We'll get Charley to speak to them in Urdu so they know what to expect and also tell them they won't be harmed, as long as they cooperate. We need to tell the men something. I'm damned if I know what."

I said, "We could use the old altitude sickness trick, but somehow I don't think that will go over. Why not tell them it's a new Army phys-ops program? Voiceovers beamed through ultrahigh frequencies. The explosions were due to a new microwave program aimed at embedded infrastructures, which, in the experimentation phase, worked quite well, as they saw. I think you can sell that one."

Colonel Salvo said, "Not bad for an impromptu explanation. I like it. Yes, I think I can sell that. Thanks."

"You're most welcome."

"Let's get going. We need to get back before dusk."

"You know, Lyft's already there. I envy him that benefit."

"Convenient way to travel, that's for sure. I'll brief the troops, and then we best be on our way."

We made our way back to the formation, where the dejected prisoners stood motionless, waiting for the wrath of Iblis to descend upon them. Colonel Salvo yelled to his troops, "Now men, listen up," as he promptly and succinctly dictated his summary of events. He was brilliant, I'll say that. He even had *me* convinced. A few of the men mumbled that they didn't buy it, with a retort from the colonel to offer a more plausible explanation. None could, so they seemed to be satisfied for the moment. Charley instructed the prisoners in Urdu and Pashto as to what they could expect, with some lightening up when they knew Iblis was no longer among them. We began the long trek back to the LZ. I was going to sleep well that night.

Chapter Six

Back at the dacha, Lyft was in a conversant mood as he related the details of his exploits thirty-five hundred feet above the valley. All had returned safely, including the animals, which were quite a sight slung under the Pave Lows, protesting vehemently as the helicopters gently settled them down onto the landing pad. I had come to understand over the past eighteen months to readily expect the unexpected pertaining to Lyft's adventures. I had become unflappable relative to the diversity of his many actions, which seemed, at times, to transcend the boundaries of rational thought. We were currently engaged in the ultimate dichotomy of moods, he animatedly wanting to relate the details of the most recent military campaign in minute detail whilst I just wanted to fall between the sheets and sleep for twelve hours. Every cell in my body was bleating for oxygen, for inactivity, for replenishment, for Lyft to go away. I was in the process of putting equipment and clothes in order in the bedroom closet and was just about to turn down the bed.

"So why don't you pour me a drink? This is cause for celebration," he boomed, flitting to and fro, the pinnacle of energy.

"Because if I do, you'll stay longer."

He raised his arms quickly, exclaiming, "What an affront. Denying the war hero a celebratory libation. I've never heard of such a thing."

I looked at him, still animatedly flying about the room. "Hah. War hero. You call that little skirmish a war?"

"Admittedly, rather short, but yes, in a manner of speaking. I'll have you know I've been in some real wars, so I do know the difference. But this little exercise took some strategizing. I didn't see anyone else coming up with a game plan, except to withdraw in the face of a little adversity. Any military action that requires strategy to execute and then uses that actionable strategy to accomplish the mission successfully is tantamount to definition of the word 'war.'"

"From Sun Tzu?"

"No, from Lyft Faetels."

"Ah, a Faetelism."

"Very funny. You know, I could smack you sometimes."

"And vice versa. I want to go to bed."

Now in my boxers and T-shirt, I quickly turned down the covers and crawled under the sheets, propping three pillows behind me, arms spread, hands behind my head.

"Not until you hear me out."

He flitted over to the footboard, where he centered himself staring directly at me, his gaze acting as a cordon to ensure sleep remained at bay.

I whined, "Why can't this wait until tomorrow?"

"I've got a big day tomorrow. Part of the plant is coming on line."

Exasperated, I retorted, pointing at him, "So now we're down to it. This is all about you, and to hell with me who's totally exhausted and needs rest. But *no*, you don't care if I have a high-altitude heart attack. You forget that I don't have those internal air bladders that automatically regulate atmospheric pressure. I have to acclimatize the old-fashioned, hard way."

Somewhat plaintively, he mewled, "It's only seven forty-five. You can spare me another forty-five minutes, can't you? It's not like you have to get up at four again, you know. You can sleep in tomorrow."

I yawned, the force of it causing a fine expectorant to cascade onto the sheet in front of me, not being propelled quite far enough to hit Lyft.

"I plan to, and with no interruption, I might add."

Arms up, palms upraised, he said, "I promise to let you rest if you just indulge me tonight."

"Prattle on."

"As I was saying, I became Iblis to get them out of the caves along with the animals. In the process, I think I may have corrected their thinking to bring them back to the true path of Islam. Two birds with one stone, really. In a microcosmic sense, I'm rather proud of that."

He preened visibly on the footboard of the bed.

I propped myself up on one arm. I said, "You know, you remind me of a rather pedantic eighteenth century English character by the name of Alexander Cruden, affectionately known in England as Alexander the Corrector. His real claim to fame was his concordance to the Bible, finished in 1737. It was a monumental task. He presented it to the Queen of England who died ten days later. Perhaps the concordance fell on her. At any rate, old Alexander, thinking he was going to get rich from his labors, soon realized that the concordance was not to be a bestseller. Imagine putting a majority of one's working hours into a project, only to have it ignored by the general public, thinking all along of riches and fame and then coming to the fact that no one really gives a damn. Well, Alexander popped a few screws over that one and was committed. After a time, he was pronounced well enough to be on his own, taking up various posts, including that of 'corrector,' a self-appointed position that, in effect, was supposed to correct the morals of the nation, especially blaspheming, and to ensure proper observance of the Sabbath. As he felt God had called upon him to undertake this task, he petitioned parliament to officially sanctify his office, but to no avail. His eccentricities, accentuated by constant rejection, led him to begin carrying a sponge to erase odious graffiti around London.

"After several more treatises and years of 'correcting,' he appropriately died while praying in his dwelling in 1770, but not before dispensing two more editions of the concordance to the king for eight hundred pounds, a princely sum in those days. He finally realized his dream, making money from his excessive labors, even though it probably helped to kill him."

Lyft's eyes rolled in his head as he asked, "So what's the moral of this ridiculous historical anecdote?"

"That you are the corrector. The only thing lacking on your person is the sponge. Ha, ha, ha."

I lay back on the pillows, unable to curtail my laughter.

Lyft replied drolly, "Very amusing. However, when you really think about it, what's wrong with a little correction? Even though a ruse, it worked in this instance. And approximately forty people, five mules, and two yaks are going to have a better life for it, although admittedly unrealized as of yet. As a matter of fact, maybe I'll adopt a new title if and when I'm ratified as King of the Klinque: Lyft the Corrector. I kind of like it, has a nice lilt."

I propped my hands under my head again. "You know, if I were you, I might keep that one under wraps. Old Alexander was looked on as a fairly unbalanced individual, and although regarded with some affection, he is still viewed that way today. You wouldn't want to be relegated to history in the same way, now would you? Lyft the Conqueror or Lyft the Benevolent I could see, but Lyft The Corrector? I think not."

"What are you, my publicist?"

"Well, someone has to protect you from yourself."

Lyft imperiously replied, "All right. In that case, I shall assume the mantle of corrector as my *nom de guerre*. You know, correcting is what I do best. My goal is to correct the course of humanity so you all don't destroy yourselves along with us in the process. However, there's not enough of me to go around, so I relish my small victories where I find them."

"I understand. So would Alexander. It's too bad he's not here today. You two could have joined forces, calling it the League of Correction, sponging away humanity's detritus, leaving the slate squeaky clean for your own social admonishments." I made a sweep in the air, as if cleaning off humanity's blackboard. "You know, Lyft, you can't change humanity. Humanity is humanity. As pernicious as the human race is, as well as every other adjective you can think of to describe it, the word 'human' denotes and defines our lot. It's in the nature of the beast. It can't be changed. Certain small segments maybe, like a group of jihadists intent on self-destruction, but all of humanity? Give it a rest."

"Now wait a minute. You're wrong about this. Look at the world's great religions. Some of them emanated from a single idea. What about that for change?"

"You yourself said 99.99 percent of them are bunk, so where're you going with this tack?"

"I never said they were bunk; I just said they were all based on something else from previous times. That's not the point. The point is, an idea is able to change the way in which humanity views itself in relation to its place in the cosmos. If a single thought can be that powerful, there is hope."

I retorted, "The great religions of the world are responsible for more misery than most of the secular wars that have occurred throughout history. So what if one of them began from a single thought? That single thought did nothing but propagate the antithesis of what was supposed to have been produced."

I was fired up now, sitting up in bed. This was something I'd thought on long and hard. I continued animatedly, hands in the air, "Humanity has a great knack for perverting its most cherished institutions into shams. It's like a rumor that gets started in seventh grade. By the time it reaches the last kid in class, it's unrecognizable from the original. That's what humanity does to noble ideas."

Lyft piped, "What a cynic."

"Yes, especially when I'm dead tired." I lay back on the pillows. "When are you going to leave me alone so I can get to sleep? I wasn't counting on you cavorting around on my footboard tonight, engaging me in a heavily philosophical discussion as to the merits of the human condition. I need some rest, otherwise you'll be carting me off the mountain tomorrow like we did those yaks earlier today. That ought to be a sight, Wood underslung on a Pave Low, medevaced to a hospital, God knows how far away."

Lyft chuckled. "We could tack a banner onto you, like they do with planes flying over the beach with advertisements, saying you are Iblis and that all below should repent or else you'll be dropped into their midst to create havoc and turmoil."

"Your humor eludes me at this hour." I pulled out one of the pillows, placing it over my head as I turned on my side. My speech muffled, "Now leave, or I'll call Salvo and Bashirin. Then you can entertain them all night."

"All right, all right, I'll go. We'll continue our discussion tomorrow."

I yelled from under the pillow, "No, we won't. I've had enough of it. Plus, we never come to a conclusion about anything in our interchanges anyway. Like most philosophical discussions, useless."

"Oh, you *are* tired. I'll leave you now. Sleep well. Here's a little something to soothe you."

I peeked out from under the pillow, wondering what abuse was to follow now. I saw Lyft floating above the bed as he waved his arm over me and then exited the dacha. I immediately fell into a sound ten-hour sleep, totally refreshed by the next morning.

With my mood considerably lightened, I exited the apartment around ten in the morning, heading to the plant. Lyft immediately settled onto my shoulder, exhibiting a rather chipper attitude. We were on the side of the road, heavily populated by military and construction vehicles, with cement mixers prevalent, going to and fro from the loading site to their dumping grounds, providing fodder for foundations and walls to segregate various pieces of heavy equipment.

"So, have a restful night?"

"Yes, thank you, extremely so. What's that thing you do, you know, like the waving of a magic wand, that gives such a joyful night's rest? Something you learned from your fairy godmother?"

"Hilarious, although not far removed from that, actually. Since, as you know, we sometimes have to work ridiculously long hours, sometimes weeks at a time with no sleep, on your behalf, mind you, we've had to adapt to conditions that would appall most humans. So there are a number of 'spells' we have concocted to enable us to survive such conditions. One of those is that for a restful sleep. Not only restful, but accelerated. In your case last night, it was a two for one scenario. For every hour of sleep obtained, you received two. However, last night was tame. We can do a lot better than that. Certain gestures by us with a few incantations, and we can work it up to a 1:24 ratio. Very handy, as you can discern. Right now, the Klinques below work a week at a time with no sleep, get a couple of hours off, and then immediately go back to the tunnels. We could normally do two or three weeks, but the stress of the environment cuts into that, so a week at a time is enough."

He explained that there were ten thousand individuals currently involved with digging on permanent rotating shifts. He added that they were coming along nicely, with the first tunnel due to be linked to the Sumatra site within the next month.

He continued, "We really are making rapid progress, which delights me and should delight you, by the way."

"Oh, it does, trust me. I don't want to see the Earth torn apart any more than you do. But tell me something, back to the arm waving. How do you do it?"

"What do you mean, 'how do you do it?' I just do, that's all."

"What mechanism allows your use of magic to place spells?"

Approaching the plant now, we noted the beehive of activity—workers crawling among pipes, pieces of equipment on chains overhead, foremen directing their placement, the clanging and booming of construction deafening. Whining drills punctuated the air, nail guns staccatoed, trucks roared forward, others electronically beeped their warnings as they reversed—a cacophony echoing off the mountains.

"Some things are just built in. You know we have telepathic powers. It's all part of the same machine. I can't really tell you the physiology of it; it's just there. Kind of like how you reason. You don't question how your mind actually works as you worry a problem to death or figure out some grandiose scheme. It's intuitive; you just do it, that's all. Same for me, although I will admit the fringe benefits that come out of it are extraordinarily useful."

"I'll say. I feel like a million bucks this morning, ready to take on the world."

"That was the general idea. The little spell I used on you last night is generally reserved for cranky children who need rest and don't know it."

"Thanks a lot. Are you insinuating something here?"

"A little. You know, you were a little nasty last night."

"I get that way when I'm dead tired."

"I rest my case."

"Yeah, the difference between me and one of your Klinque kids is that they didn't have Grandpa dancing on their footboard, keeping them awake by telling them war stories all night. So I rest *my* case."

"Touché. Glad to see you're back among the living."

We made our way onto a level, grassy surface not far from some Quonset huts, five hundred feet or so below the elevation of the plant, where I looked out across the entire Wakhan. The long grass in the distance rippled in waves, contrasting against the immovable snow-capped mountains in the distance. The brilliant sun reflected a valley floor alive, a pale yellow and green ocean, its never-ending swells keeping rhythm with the wind.

Away from the din, I queried, "So what's up today?"

"I want you to come to class."

"What does that mean?"

"I established a class for the Muslims we rounded up yesterday. You didn't think the corrector's duties were terminated just by yesterday's actions, did you? There's no end to the correcting mechanism. I was even able to scrounge a sponge from the supply post to erase the blackboard. I thought a sponge a most appropriate tool, don't you?"

I laughed. "Lyft, you are beyond the pale. So what are we teaching our Muslim brothers this morning?"

"First, about the plant; they need to know it's not a threat. In order to have them absorb that fact, they need to know the seriousness of the situation and what we are trying to do here, for all of us. Then we're going to teach them to read and write. Once they become more acclimated to our customs—our way of life, if you will—then we will offer them jobs."

"Jobs?"

"Yes, jobs. We need locals here who are on our side to oversee certain operations."

"You had this planned all along, similar to the Romans who conquered others and then left administration of the provinces in local hands."

"Correct, except that I don't always foresee fortuitous events like those of yesterday."

"You really are an opportunist, but I see your point."

"Thank you. I think it worked out rather nicely. Beats going out into the shale recruiting with a sandwich board."

I looked out on the beauty of the scene, some billowing cumulus clouds now beginning to tumble up over the distant mountains. "That it does. So who's the teacher?"

"One of Salvo's men will instruct in Urdu. We found out that Pashto really isn't necessary, although it's native to two of the men. Urdu is acceptable, as all understand it, even if a word or two eludes some of them. If so, he also knows Pashto to fill in, so no problem."

"Did you tell Salvo directly what you wanted to do with this class thing?"

"As a matter of fact, I did. Since he knows of my existence, what's the harm? Direct communication is much easier. And if I worked through you, it's a little problematic for a civilian instructing a military person of his stature, don't you think? I thought I'd save you from that situation. I'd rather build good fences than put holes in them."

"Right. So where's class?"

"Right over here."

We entered a Quonset hut, where Captain Greer was in the process of drawing a simple diagram of the globe, depicting Xs for the locations of the various plants that would either supply or recycle liquid nitrogen to the tunnel systems. Everyone turned when we entered, some with trepidation, as they evidently associated me with Iblis. Greer told them to relax, that I was a civilian helping with the project, ensuring the security of the facility. Lyft, of course, was invisible. Greer introduced me, giving them some of my background, which seemed to visibly reduce the tension in the room. I said good morning, welcoming them, explaining that we meant them no harm, that we had something to show them so that they would understand why we were there. I gave Greer a few minutes to translate. I then told them the importance of the project, calling it Abzu, which some of them recognized, and why the Earth was threatened. Greer once again translated. I'm not sure they could accept all I related, but it looked to me as if my first impression was having some effect. I saw inquisitiveness in their eyes, which, to me, was a good sign. I bid them good day, telling them that their animals were being cared for, hoping they enjoyed the class. I saw one or two nod, so that was another good sign. I left the building with Lyft on my shoulder.

"Good show," he quacked. "Couldn't have done it better myself."

"Good thing you didn't do it yourself. All hell would have broken loose."

"Too true. Would have been fun though. I rather like the role of Iblis. Iblis the Corrector. Now that has a rather nice parlance to it, don't you think?"

"Yes, indeed, kind of a poetry to it. I do believe you've found your true calling. It's only taken you several hundred years to find yourself. I'm flattered to have been part of it."

"You really are the proverbial wiseass."

"From you, I'll take that as a compliment."

We walked back to the grassy area overlooking the valley. It looked as if a storm was brewing in the distant mountains, as the clouds had gone from puffy white to bruised thunderheads.

"So what's next on today's agenda?"

"Security issues. I brought you along on this jaunt for just that reason."

"Looks to me as if you've already covered that angle. I can't really see that there's anything more I can bring to the party."

"Actually, there's quite a bit more. None of these people working at this plant has had an in-depth security check done. Guess who's going to do it?"

A bolt of lightning flashed over a distant mountain peak. "That would be me, I fathom."

"You fathom correctly. You know that computer in your dacha? Well, you're going to be very busy on it from now on. Each and every worker needs to have an extensive security check done on him, much more than the cursory one a Mexican plant normally employs. Mexico's basically a neutral country, so their security is pretty lax on issues such as this. Also, their immigration laws are pretty liberal, so we need to know who's among us here, as America is sponsoring a healthy portion of this project."

"OK, gotcha. I'll get to work on it today. How many employees did you say are here?"

"Approximately five thousand. You only need to worry about foreign workers, particularly any emanating from Mexico. That leaves about four thousand, give or take."

I whistled. "That's a lot of files. No wonder you need help."

"Exactly. Yesterday's exercise was trivial compared to this. You've got a lot of important work ahead of you. FYI, we think something's a little smelly in the cheese heap, but we're not sure what it is. Too much cheese of the same variety to differentiate, if you get my drift."

Clouds were beginning to pile up in the Wakhan now, the storm currently venting its fury among the peaks in the distance.

"Got it." I pointed across the valley. "Looks like we may be in for it. Any names for me?"

"Unfortunately, no."

"Then how did you determine that there was an odor?"

"Call it a sixth sense. I start to tingle when things are amiss. I've been tingling for about two weeks now. I'd like it to stop. It's a very unpleasant sensation. Almost like the shingles, however, not quite as severe."

"If you are tingling, that's good enough for me. I'll try to find a remedy."

"That would be most kind of you. I'm afraid if the tingling doesn't stop, I'll build up an electrostatic charge within my suit, possibly igniting the fuel source for the plant site. We wouldn't want that, now would we?"

"No, and if we don't get out of here, it may happen sooner than later. I believe we are in for a real doozy, coming across the valley there."

Lyft agreed, so we began walking rapidly back to the dachas.

I said laughingly, "You know, it would be interesting to see you as a shooting star, shot heavenward, taking your place among the great constellations. We could call the new star system The Collector, as it would have a tendency to draw in other stars because of its benevolent size, keeping them in its gravitational field."

"And do you know you have an imagination that is dangerous? Where do you come up with this stuff?"

"Your very presence seemingly activates the thought process."

"You really are a little nuts, you know that?"

"Barbara says the same thing."

"She's right."

"Well, on that note, I guess I'll get to work. You'll be the first to know if I find anything."

"Of course, I'll be the first to know. Who else would you tell first?"

"Just an expression. My, didn't we get enough sleep last night?"

"Some of us put in an honest day's work around here."

"Ouch. Double ouch, as you even lulled me to sleep. Tonight you ought to wave your arm over yourself. I think you need it."

"Very funny. Now get on the computer and compute. I need to get to Sumatra to ensure operations are underway there as planned. Then I need to check on the other sites along the pipeline. I'll be back in a few days."

"Yes, boss. You've established the other sites?"

"Many of them, yes."

"So, is it a secret, or are you going to tell me?"

We had reached my unit, so I opened the door just as the deluge sweeping across the valley caught up to us.

"Good timing, by the way. I wasn't in the mood for a midday shower. The locations are midway between the Bougainville Trench and the Kermadec Trench, then over to the Peru–Chile Trench. The only other major plant to be built in all this is in South America. All the others will be recyclers. Then we head east along the Scotia Plate to where the Mid-Atlantic Ridge intersects the Antarctic Plate, and then to the intersections of the African Plate, the Antarctic Plate, and the Indian–Australian Plate, and then connect it all up at Pulau Simeulue. Now you see why Simeulue is so important."

"Where are all these locations? This whole things sounds more like an aquatic project than one on land."

Lyft released the pressure on my shoulder, fluttering into visibility, hovering in front of my face.

"Correct. We've had to reevaluate sites due to the subterranean pipeline route. Look on a map. Better yet, Google it; you'll have a better feel for some of the geography. I'm too busy to give you that lesson right now. We may have to build another plant as well near the Mid-Atlantic Ridge on a giant platform. That's under consideration but not in the works yet. So you can see I've a lot to do. This one has to be finished first for the other one to begin, because there aren't enough workers in this industry to go around. And by the way, we have another rather nasty issue that has just arisen."

"Oh? And what's that?"

"Do you know where one of the largest calderas and the potential for the next great eruption is?"

"Don't tell me. Right where you're headed: Sumatra."

"Not even close. Right in your own backyard. Yellowstone."

"Yellowstone? You're kidding."

Lyft began flitting back and forth. I felt like I was at a tennis match.

"I wish I were. It's a little-known fact that Yellowstone sits on top of a giant caldera, the Norris Geyser Basin, where the ground temperature is two hundred degrees Fahrenheit one inch below the surface. It is one of the world's greatest super volcanoes. The caldera has bulged over five inches since 1996. We have just determined that in the past three months alone, it's added an inch a month. Clearly there's some frenetic underground activity going on. The last eruption was about about 620,000 to 640,000 years ago years ago. Yellowstone's cycle is about every six hundred thousand years, so we are overdue. If it blows, it will be twenty-five hundred times more powerful than Mount St. Helens in 1980. At the bottom of

Yellowstone Lake, there is a bulge over one hundred feet high. The surface temperature of the lake is eighty-eight degrees and rising. Dead fish are in the lake and streams, and all the vegetation is dying in the vicinity of the basin, which is twenty-eight miles long and seven miles wide. If Yellowstone goes up, North America will be covered in three feet of ash, the sun will dim, agriculture along with much plant life will be wiped out, and there will be a two-year nuclear winter worldwide. Your very civilization will cease to exist as you know it. It will make the Tambora eruption on Indonesia's Sumbawa Island in 1815 look miniscule in comparison, not so much because it will be larger, but because there is so much more at stake. Then, Tambora killed about eighty-eight thousand people. If Yellowstone goes up, it will be in the tens of millions. We may not have much time, which is why I need to get moving to the different sites."

No wonder he was agitated. So was I. Raising my arms in alarm, I shouted, "Why don't we know more about this? It's in our own domain, for God's sake."

"Evidently no one wants to sound the alarm, as it could be another one hundred thousand years before anything happens. But I don't think so. I think it's imminent. We need to do something fast to take the pressure off the geology of the area. You don't have much time either, so get to it. I'll see you later."

He pulled the door and exited. When I went to my computer, there was an e-mail waiting from Lyft, stating that the employee file had been sent, residing on a shared drive. I went into it, perusing approximately four thousand names, last known addresses, phone numbers, names of next of kin, and so on. This was going to be a task, even more so knowing full well some of the names were undoubtedly aliases. With each file was a JPEG picture, which was fortunate. If I could not come up with a known individual to match the name, perhaps a downloaded picture would lead to an identity. What a bore. I'd rather be traipsing through the valleys as bait for terrorists.

I looked at a map of the Ring of Fire on the Web, and sure enough, all the trenches were outlined. I understood the plan. The pipeline completed the circle at Simeulue. I believe I understood why the linkup could not be at the main plant in the Wakhan. The nitrogen could only be pumped in one direction, and linking it up there would confuse the pumping mechanism, forcing the nitrogen to be pumped against itself. Rather brilliant of the little guy, I thought.

Never in the history of humanity had such a task been undertaken. And it was in jeopardy because of a medieval mindset. We would have to bore deep to find the termite in the wood. Like all insects, they always left a trail. We just had to be smart enough to find it.

CHAPTER SEVEN

Lyft wasn't kidding when he said he needed to move quickly. He was gone substantially longer than the few days he had promised. He had toured all the sites in spite of the obstacles with personnel, arranged for the giant platform's construction through intermediaries as well as its transport to the Mid-Atlantic Ridge area, and had solidified plans for the connections and eventual linkage of the giant pipeline at Simeulue. The platform was to be four times the size of the Hibernia platform off the coast of Newfoundland. It would be the largest sea-drilling platform in the world, which meant over two hundred fifty feet off the ocean's surface, weighing in at over four million tons, devoid of the weight of the giant liquid nitrogen plant to be constructed on top of it. It would be a floater, versus being anchored, due to the violent storms blowing up from the Antarctic. Constructed with giant serrated outer edges, the first defenses against iceberg impact, it would sport a crew of twenty-five individuals at computer consoles just to keep it stable as it operated. It had the capacity to be permanently anchored, but Lyft and company preferred the floating option, as they felt it gave them more flexibility in the main plant's operations.

While I was pecking away at my computer keyboard, Lyft was involved in a particularly nasty situation at Pulau Simeulue, he later related. With the large barges in place and the nitrogen regeneration apparatus almost operational, evidently word got around that there were some easy pickings to be had off Simeulue. One day, several supposed fishing trawlers along with four supercharged speedboats approached the barges. Knowing full well that the flotilla meant the ultimate harm, Lyft employed computer code red in his invisible mode, having all battle stations manned. There were eight fifty-caliber machine guns on board and numerous Javelin antiarmor missiles that could be fired from stationary stands or from the shoulder.

Once the code red was activated, the naval commander took over the military operations. When a rocket launcher was fired from the second speedboat from about a half-mile away, two Javelins opened up. The offending boat's missile went awry, as it was not computer guided, errant because of choppy seas. However, with a range of a mile and a half and an automatic self-guidance system, the Javelins did not have the same problem, blowing the first and second speedboats out of the water. When the missiles were away, the operators were free to load others immediately, as the missile systems gave the command to fire only after they zeroed in on the target. The missiles weren't guided after launch, a marked improvement over the older generation of fiber-optic–guided or laser beam missiles, leaving the operators free immediately after discharge.

Once the pirates saw the barges had teeth, they backed off. But not far enough for Lyft. He decided to give them a personal greeting. He flew out to the largest trawler, ripped off the four fifty-caliber machine guns mounted on the decks, and threw them overboard. He then took all the automatic rifles, grenade launchers, RPGs, and all the small arms, doing the same. One panicked crew member had a pistol, which Lyft later admittedly told me he had missed, who began firing wildly in all directions, hitting two of his own crew, killing one. Lyft threw him overboard too. Lyft then proceeded to harangue each crew member in his native tongue that he was an angel of their particular worshipped deity and that if they didn't have one then they'd better obtain one hastily. One crew member jumped overboard, hoping for salvation in the form of a pluck from the ocean by his comrades. However, the comrades were so confused by the actions onboard the trawler, they didn't dare approach. Viewing the bedlam through field glasses, they could not believe the mayhem created by a seemingly invisible force. Lyft then disabled the engine so that it would only operate in forward and reverse slow modes, to give the crew time to think about their new religions. He then told them he would be watching them in the future and that if they were unable to mend their ways, he would return with five hundred such angels to do it for them. He went back to the barges after directing the trawler in a straight line back out to the open sea. The other boats followed, coming alongside the first, shutting off its engine, and taking it in tow.

As Lyft had no one to talk to near Simeulue, he decided to fly back to the Wakhan to relate his exploits. He'd been gone about ten days when suddenly he rattled the door and then perched himself on my kitchen stool while I was eating a sandwich and sipping a Pilsner Urquell. He related in exquisite detail the recent escapade as I sat rapt, not daring to interrupt him in his breathless explication. He finally concluded with, "And that's that."

"Well, I guess it is. So why not Iblis this time?"

"Iblis would not have worked, too many nonbelievers in the crowd, many not even Muslim. So I took the opposite tack. Seemed to work pretty well."

"What explanation did you give to the barge crew upon your return?"

"None. None needed."

"Didn't they see anything through their binoculars?"

"Too far away. The boats had backed way off by then, out of range of the Javelins. They could see the boats but none of the detail, so no explanation required. Good thing too. They don't even know I exist, so how would I explain it anyway? However, I do have to talk to you about something. The cheese heap is getting riper."

"In what way?"

"Someone had inside information about the Simeulue project. I don't buy these boats showing up by chance. And if someone has information about Simeulue, they could have it about the other sites as well. Have you found anything while I've been committing savagery on behalf of humanity, putting myself in harm's way, risking life and limb on your behalf?"

I put my hand to my head to emphasize the large headache Lyft was beginning to impart to me. "Oh, brother, can you wax any more melodramatic? You love to mix it up, so don't try that tack with me. My only wish is that I could have been with you, because this job you've given me is boring me to death. Tedious isn't the word. And to answer your question, I've found nothing. I've been through approximately a thousand records since you left with nothing amiss."

"That's about one hundred records a day—not bad with the extensive checks you have to do. At least you haven't been loafing while I've been doing battle with the dregs of the Earth. However, don't you agree that my safe return demands a liquid offering of some sort?"

"In the middle of the day while on duty with this stuff, one beer for lunch is enough for me, as I might miss something. However, feel free to pour yourself anything you like. I will be with you in spirit, so to speak."

Lyft went to the cabinet, pulled out the vodka, poured himself about five fingers and a dash of tonic, and then threw in half a sliced lime into a tumbler.

I queried, "How do you manipulate all that with those long, curved talons you have?"

"They're retractable. You knew that, didn't you?"

"Yeah, but never really thought about it, I guess. I seem to learn something new about you every day."

"When I need 'em, they're there, and when I don't, they're not extended. Pretty handy, so to speak," he chuckled.

"I can see that," I said, peering closer at the ends of his appendages from which only the ends of the talons I was so used to seeing were protruding. *Interesting*, I thought. "They don't totally disappear, so typing on a computer must be tough."

"I manage. Just takes some getting used to."

"So I wish I could tell you it's been really exciting here since you left, but that would be a lie. Status quo, which may be a good thing."

"Well, buck up. Nothing stays the same forever. Once you find out who's stinking up the cheese pile, I guarantee there'll be some action, so keep at it. And by the way, I heartily approve of you forgoing this celebratory drink with me. You've more important work to do. I understand how boring it is, but you're the only one I can trust around the site to perform the function. Bashirin can't do it, either can Salvo. They have other duties to administer. So you're it. It's an important task, so don't get discouraged."

"I'm not. I'm just bored. I'll survive. But thanks for the pep talk just the same. Now let me get back to it."

"OK if I sip and watch you work?"

"Be my guest. But I have to concentrate, so the less conversation, the better."

"Huh. Guess you told me. But I understand, so I'll just look over this paperwork I brought with me pertaining to the other sites while you peck away."

I got up from the table, crossed the room, and sat down at the console beginning the tedious search once more.

After several hours, I went over to the kitchen to get a Coke. I needed a break. Something was bothering me about a computer record I saw, but I could not get my mind wrapped around the nettlesome aspect needling me. I poured the Coke over some ice in a tumbler, grabbed the jar of cashews from the counter, and went back to the computer. There was his picture. He looked Mexican, but then again, maybe not. His features were different from the others I had studied. Then it hit me. His features were more Indonesian than Mexican. I thought, *This could be a sleeper. Let's see what we can find on this guy.*

Lyft had fallen asleep on the leather couch, flat on his back, his hands folded gently on his chest, his feet sticking straight up in the air. His buzzing was practically lulling me to sleep as well.

I turned my attention to the machine and brought up all the information on the gentleman whose name was Ramón Rodriguez.

Innocuous enough, I thought.

As I had begun at the end of the alphabet, being a nontraditionalist, I was lucky to have stumbled on this character so quickly. The more I looked at him, the more he did not look like a Ramón Rodriguez. His essential information seemed to match his credentials—born in the right place, immigrated legally, et cetera. However, his features kept bothering me. I did not believe him to be a native Mexican. If not, then he could not have immigrated into Mexico unless directly sponsored by a company. Once a company was interested, the company takes it upon itself to approach the immigration officials in Mexico City to obtain the necessary work permit authorization. In addition, an FM-3, a one-year document permitting residence in Mexico, must be issued and renewed yearly. If one was issued, perhaps it was to this individual under another name. So I sent the picture to my friend Hector who worked in immigration in Mexico City, asking him if he could identify the picture as being a non-Mexican immigrant.

While I waited, I turned on ESPN to see how the baseball playoffs were progressing. It looked like another classic matchup between the Red Sox and the Yankees was in the offing for the next several weeks. Hopefully it would not be a four-game blowout.

Between the droning of the television and the buzz saw on the couch, I was having difficulty staying awake. It had been about two hours since I sent my request to Hector, when suddenly my computer notified me of incoming e-mail with the appropriate sound of a two-thousand-pound whistling bomb exploding on impact. I got up and went to the machine, noticing an urgent e-mail from Hector. I opened it to his statement emphasizing that this individual was not who he said he was. His name was Ali Sastroamidjojo; he had immigrated into Mexico two years ago to work at the nitrogen plant in the Cantarell Field in the Yucatán Peninsula, and he was from Semarang on the north side of Java. He had evidently bribed an officer in the local immigration department to change his name and identity to his current status to obtain the job in the Wakhan. Here was the kicker in the message: he had known affiliations with Jemaah Islamiah, an al Qaeda affiliate operating in Indonesia and Malaysia. The Mexican authorities had been on alert for him during the past year, but little did they know, he was in Afghanistan. Now two plus two equaled four. This was too good to be true. I yelled for Lyft to wake up. Upon doing so, he yelped, flew up into the air, and then landed on the floor with a resounding thud of body and cracking of head.

"What the hell's wrong with you?" he bellowed. "Can't you have a little more civility than to frighten me half to death out of a sound sleep? I was having a dream about Mrs. Faetels, I'll have you know, of hearth and home. What tranquility. Then you go and stick a hot poker in it. I ought to wreck this place."

"Now don't go doing that. I think I've found our man."

Lyft calmed down immediately. "Really? Let's see."

He fluttered over to the machine. "I believe you're right. I wonder what the chances are that there are more than one. Probably not great, as the process of getting in here is somewhat complicated. But we'll have to check. Rather, *you'll* have to check. By the way, how'd you find him so quickly?"

"Thanks for that. I figured as much. Trust me, the search isn't over until it's over. To answer your question, I began at the end of the alphabet. Why? No reason. I just felt like it, to alleviate the monotony. At any rate, you have to admit this is one of them. If there are more, I'll find them. Somehow, I don't think so. The question is, what now? If we expose him too soon and there are more, we'll take the chance of losing the rest of them. But if we don't act soon, we may be putting the plant and other sites in jeopardy. So what to do?"

"Leave it to me. I may be able to save you a considerable amount of work. Let me do some snooping. Maybe we can expose the others in that manner, if there are any more. You know, I can be rather surreptitious if required, so either way, it works to our benefit. We identify others, or we prove he's working alone. Oh, this ought to be fun. I was getting a little bored here after several hours of inactivity. Let's get to it."

"You mean, *you* get to it. You're on your own on this one."

"True. Wish me well as I again defy all odds, thrusting myself into the maw of battle."

"You really are something, you know that? You're worse than the corniest melodrama of a Greek tragedy. How Mrs. Faetels copes, I'll never know."

"Harrumph. I've nothing more to say then. I'm off to uncover nefarious doings."

"Oh, brother."

"You know, there have been spies throughout history whose exploits have been responsible for major historical events, with even beneficent governments spying on each other. I plan to uncover the greatest subterfuge of all, one that could potentially save the Earth. Another sleeper in the woodpile, so to speak. So don't 'oh, brother' me."

"C'mon, aren't you being a little melodramatic?"

At this, Lyft flew around the room in a frenzy. He eventually settled down onto the back of the sofa.

"How can you say such a thing?" he bellowed. "What if this project isn't finished? We might have a major event take place, like Yellowstone, for example, that could have been prevented if we'd brought the project in on time. Say this idiot succeeds in blowing up a site or two. What happens if we miss our schedule and subsequently a conflagration occurs that shuts down half the globe? And you think I'm being melodramatic? I think not."

"Perhaps it's your delivery."

"Bah ... I have to get to work."

"Good idea. I've lots of files left to get through. See you later."

He exited the apartment on a quest to make history. I went back to my computer.

I should have learned that to doubt Lyft is tantamount to subversion. He tailed Sastroamidjojo night and day for two weeks. It was propitious we found the sleeper when we did, as his awakening seemed timely. Lyft later related that he even sneaked into Sastroamidjojo's quarters, where he slept perched on the metal-runged bed footboard while Ali slept, so he at least had a chance to recharge from time to time. Lyft eventually uncovered over twenty Semtex charges Ali had placed in various locations around the plant, ready for detonation, complete with detonating cords, clips, and boosters. He had disarmed them by inserting fake cord in place, so as not to alarm the saboteur, or 'tuers, and scare them off. His goal, as mine, was to catch those responsible, not only in the Wakhan, but in relation to the other sites as well. We figured we would bring down the network now that it was obvious a full-blown conspiracy had been exposed. The issue was what if the terrorists decided to blow up the plant, and nothing happened? Lyft and I were engaged in that conversation.

I asked, as he helped himself to a Pilsner Urquell in my refrigerator, "So what to do now? We need to move it before they decide to blow the plant."

"Maybe not."

"Why 'maybe not?'"

"Well, think about it for a minute," he belched, and then went on, "If this jerk is the type we think he is, he's committed, right?"

"Right …"

"So if he's committed, he is probably prepared to go up with the plant, which means if he tries to blow it up and then nothing happens, he'll try to investigate what went awry. No doubt he'll slither around after dark. Then we nail him with the aid of night goggles. And trust me, he will try, when he gets a phone call."

"Sounds risky to me. Why do we have to wait for the phone call? We know who he is. Why don't we just pick him up and torture him for the rest of the information?"

"You've been a civilian too long, you know that? Things aren't that simple, especially with these guys. He might not reveal anything except a lot of disinformation. If he gets the call, Bashirin and Salvo can trace it easily, especially here in the Wakhan, where there's little interference. Then we'll have hard proof. We can even triangulate the area the call emanated from and, with a little luck, nail the sukiny deti."

"Aaah, more bilingual exhibitionism."

"Yes, I'm becoming more Russian every day under Bashirin's influence. However, he still outpaces me in the appetite department."

"You know, it's too bad there's not a way to restrict Semtex access to terrorists. It's become a royal pain in the ass to legitimate authorities to deal with this stuff."

Lyft noted that, back in the good old days when the Czech

government was "communist"—here he threw his talons in the air framing the quote (I tried not to laugh), as I knew from past discussions he was noting that the Czech version of communism was not the true version practiced in his society—the Czechs had exported over nine hundred tons of the play dough to Libya and another thousand tons to places like Syria, North Korea, Iraq, and Iran. The estimate was over forty thousand tons worldwide out of legitimate governmental authority. Then these governments would down sell it to organizations like the IRA, which had been using Semtex for years. He concluded with, "What a nice, lovely stew this has produced."

"Yes, I can see that. Nasty stuff."

"Even more so because it's odorless. You know how sensitive a dog's nose is? Well, dogs can't detect this plastique. It does not show up on x-ray machines, and so far it has eluded detection at any number of security points throughout the world."

I queried, "Why is it called Semtex? The U.S. version is C-4."

Lyft pontificated, floating in front of me, clutching his beer, "You are correct there. It is named after the village of Semtin, not so far from where this wonderful libation is brewed," he glowed, holding the bottle aloft, "in what then was known as East Bohemia. Stanislav Brebera invented it for the North Vietnamese as the answer to the American C-4 being heavily used in Vietnam at the time. Brebera reminds me of Alexander the Corrector. He worked all his life, basically penniless and scorned for his brilliance, ending his career teaching in a nondescript university. Brebera is still alive, a bitter man knowing his invention has gone astray."

I drew my forefinger under my eye. "I'll make sure to shed a tear for him."

Lyft slugged down a quaff. "Actually, it's a wonderful invention. What happened to it was not his fault. It was through concerted efforts of a paranoid Czech government that the control of Semtex became unmanageable. It's so easy to attribute the exigencies of history to scapegoats such as Brebera. As for Semtex, we use it quite a bit in the excavations below. It's very versatile, requiring no special care in the heat and pressure. And it only takes a minimal amount for our use."

Now it was my turn to pontificate. "A prime example of good versus evil: Semtex located throughout the plant for its destruction, and Semtex being used to help save civilization. I can't think of a clearer dichotomy."

"I'll turn you into a true historian yet."

"So what to do now?"

"Wait for a phone call."

"How do you know it hasn't already come through?"

"Bashirin's on it, and it won't happen during the day. Too many people around. He does have to cover himself by working his shift, you know."

"Does he go on nightshift?"

"Yes, but there's a full crew on nights as well, so we don't think he'd get the call while he's working on day shift, but at night in his quarters, while he's alone. He's not even supposed to have a cell phone here. That alone is against regs."

I looked up at Lyft who seemed to be closer to the ceiling. Perhaps it was the carbonation in the beer. "Now you tell me."

"That doesn't apply to us. Someone has to have communication with the outside world, and we're it. But not the workers. They have a central communications area in which to correspond with their families, either via phone or e-mail, admittedly monitored, but we have no choice in that regard."

"He could use that system utilizing coded messages."

"True, but we don't think so. All workers know we monitor communications. I don't think he'll take that risk. We know he has a cell phone; we've monitored the signal. He's only used it once. He caught us off guard that time. He won't again."

Lyft belched, dropping a foot or so in elevation. I said, "Excuse you," and he retorted that he needed no excuse. I said, "OK then, I guess we sit and wait—something I hate doing, but it looks like we've no choice. So on that note, since you seem to be enjoying that beer to the fullest, I'll join you for one."

I got up from the computer table, went to the refrigerator, and grabbed a beer. Lyft was right behind me, talons extended, hooking onto another one, ever the opportunist. I felt like locking him in the cooler.

As we opened our beers, I cracked, "Have you no manners? At least you could ask."

"Su casa es mi casa."

"Well, yes, it certainly is beginning to seem that way."

"True communists share everything, especially beer." Deflecting any more criticism, he got back to business. "By the way, how're you coming on the list?"

"I'm in the Ps—getting there. So far, nothing else found. Really boring work."

"Quit bitching. You're saving the world, remember that."

Just then, there was knock on the door. Lyft instantly dematerialized. I went across the room, opening up to find my two favorite colonels standing there, asking if they could pay a visit. I let them in, employing two hearty handshakes, gratified in their company. Lyft materialized, floating in air, bottle in hand, which had never been invisible, just unnoticed. They both cried out, not anticipating the whirlwind specter to instantaneously appear, suspended in their midst.

Bashirin chortled, "Christ, that takes some getting used to."

Salvo yelled, "Damn it, give a man a little warning, eh?"

I yelled, "Lyft, how impolite."

Lyft bellowed, "Sukiny deti," as we all broke into hilarity, guffawing around the room.

Bashirin exclaimed, "I'm thirsty. What do you have for a man on the verge of dehydration?"

I piped, "Vodka in the freezer, beer in the fridge, wine on the side table. Take your pick."

"Aaah, as it's only about eleven in the morning, I'll have the light stuff now for an eye-opener and the rougher stuff later," he chuckled.

He reached into the freezer, pulling out the vodka, offering it all around, but getting no takers.

"In that case, since I must drink alone, do you have any tomato juice and spices with which to make a proper Bloody Mary?"

"Horse radish, lemons, and tomato juice in the fridge, Worcestershire and Tabasco in the cupboard, salt and pepper on the counter," I said.

"Brilliant," he bellowed to no one in particular.

Colonel Salvo chimed in, "I'll just have a beer. This nutcase will drink himself to death."

Bashirin, busy with his ministrations over his drink, let loose with a "Bah," continuing to swirl the ice in the mixture he had just concocted. I decided to make myself one as well. Then we took places around the coffee table, all settling in, each with his respective poison.

"So," Salvo began, "Lyft, tell us of some of your exploits and how you came to be in the company of this reprobate."

"Aaah, a long story, but one filled with hope relative to human insanity. This 'reprobate,' as you call him, I know, affectionately, is perhaps mankind's greatest hope. He is one of the few we have encountered who really gets it, who is intelligent enough to understand the world's ignominies yet have the fortitude to help me deal with them. He can also keep his mouth shut, which is perhaps the greatest attribute of all. And, gentlemen, I know you two can as well, otherwise I would not have shown myself to you. So to make what could be a long story short, I appeared in front of Jeff because I needed his help. He lives on a particular plot of land that has a retaining wall twenty-three feet high, running across the front of his property. This wall is made of special stones called sarcens. The stones, especially when bonded together, have unimaginable properties, like rendering us invisible when we brush against them on our way to save you heathens from your own destruction. The village in which Jeff resides decided to widen the road and, in the process, destroy the wall, replacing it with an ugly cement slab. No one wants to pay for expert stonework these days, mind you. So I petitioned dear Mr. Wood to approach the village and fight the initiative, with my help of course. And we won, but not without some complicated human interference."

Salvo queried, "OK, but how did the stones get into the wall?"

"We brought them up the Hudson River as ballast in Viking ships in the tenth century."

"But there was no road there then. How did you happen to place them in that exact location?"

"Back then, superstitions were rampant, so it was easy to get them moved. Just a few ooga boogas, and the persuasion was complete. However, you are correct; there was no road there. There was not even a village there at that time. We needed to get them away from the Indians along the Hudson, who were contemplating using them for their own purposes, so we moved them inland to a location that had a hill on one side and a valley on the other. For many years, the stones graced the side of a hill, the same hill that Jeff's house currently faces. But as time went on, one side of the hill was cut into for a road. We could have opted for the stones to stay where they were, but it would have been ludicrous for them to appear on the hillside above the road when they should in actuality have been retaining the wall below the road. So the stones were moved and cemented into place where they are today."

Salvo leaned in toward Lyft, rapt with attention, nodding slowly and sipping his beer.

"How did you get them to their current location without anyone knowing what you were about?"

"I'll say this, you're very detailed."

Lyft looked quite businesslike now, standing on the walled partition separating the kitchen from the dining area, as if sagely addressing an audience at a press conference. But I knew he was loving the opportunity to explain how he'd masterfully manipulated the placement of the stones over the years. He cleared his throat. "We have what you call subliminal messaging, somewhat akin to mental telepathy. The village elders eventually agreed that having stones upon a hillside with no purpose was an exercise in futility, so with a little mental prodding, they moved them to a functional location, admittedly to our benefit. We bribed the local stone mason via night notes with rubies, stones of a more precious nature were not necessary at the time, to mold the stones in a certain way and cement them into the wall so that each one touched the other behind the cement. This made a most powerful rune. We could remain invisible for much longer durations due to the concentrated power of the connectivity of the sarcens. The mason eventually became the richest man in the village. He was forced to move because of inquiries into his finances, eventually becoming a famous personage in Pennsylvania."

Salvo looked impressed, and he sat up straight. "May I ask who?"

"You're not going to believe it," Lyft replied, all nonchalance, "but it was Benjamin Franklin."

"No, I don't believe it." Salvo took a dreg from his bottle, clearly a bit disenchanted with this seemingly unbelievable revelation.

"Why not? I was there, don't forget."

Salvo looked up at the sage. "How old are you, anyway?"

"A thousand years, give or take a hundred or so."

I began to shake with laughter, as Salvo almost fell out of his chair. Bashirin's hair seemed to have stood up a little straighter. Salvo croaked, "And you say it was Ben Franklin, one of our most revered historical figures, who built your wall and then moved on?"

Nonplussed, Lyft evenly replied, "Correct."

Salvo exclaimed, "I never knew he lived in New York."

Lyft, not missing a beat, continued, "Kind of a sad story really. His brother persecuted him in Boston, sibling rivalry I suppose, and forced him to flee his post at *The New England Courant*, Boston's first real newspaper. Josiah, Ben's father, had him apprenticed to his brother, James, who started the publication when Ben was fifteen years of age. As can happen even nowadays, the Franklins as newspaper owners ran afoul of the authorities, Puritan preachers in Boston, by not supporting inoculation against smallpox. They felt it helped spread the disease rather than prevent it. James wound up in jail, as he mocked the clergy during a debate. Ben ran the paper for him, which went totally unappreciated, during his incarceration. Upon his release, James humiliated Ben, beating him, evidently out of jealously that the paper could run without him. Ben ran away in 1723, even though it was illegal, as he was an apprentice. He arrived in New York, hoping to find work as a printer. He was unsuccessful and out of funds. He settled in what is now Briarcliff Manor for a year, doing stone masonry in order to save enough money to get to Philadelphia. He built the wall in question, was shrewd enough to realize stonework was not relative to his life's potential, and subsequently moved on, and with a heady sum of money in those days, I might add. His genius was doing well at anything he attempted. The wall held up for almost three hundred years before it needed major work, and then only due to a freak winter accident in the year 2000. I have always appreciated his outstanding work ethic along with his attention to detail."

Salvo, seemingly convinced now but still in the stage of revelation, marveled, "Huh. You learn something new every day."

"Too true. As sad as it is that he had to run away from his brother, Franklin had an innate toughness. By 1729, he owned his own paper, the *Pennsylvania Gazette*. The rest is pretty much history."

"So in essence, you gave Franklin his start."

"You could say that. However, he had a powerful intellect. If we hadn't interceded, someone else probably would have. So we don't feel we did anything out of the ordinary in his case."

"So," Bashirin intoned, "interesting story. Getting back to the present, however, it is my pleasure to announce that all the locations where there are explosives have been neutralized, and no more have been found. We have one of my most trusted men monitoring the airwaves for cell phone usage."

I asked, "What if the signal doesn't come verbally over a cell phone? What if it comes in another manner, like a two-ring signal or whatever? How do we know you can get a fix on something like that?"

"Good question," Bashirin replied. "However, as with all things, there is an upside and a downside. We are counting on contact with his comrades, as he feels he will never see them again. Perhaps also with his family. That would be an extra stroke of luck. We'll see."

"This is important enough to take the risk," Lyft piped in. "We need to nip this in the bud here because of his affiliation with Jemaah Islamiah around Sumatra. He's too wired in for us to bring him down now."

"Agreed," said Bashirn, with Salvo nodding in agreement.

From Lyft, "So we wait."

"So we wait," Bashirin piped in. "But waiting doesn't have to mean a waste of time. We can always wait and drink. Ha ha."

Salvo looked askance at Bashirin. "I'm surprised you're not dead yet from noncombat-related injuries."

Bashirin retorted, "Baah. You Americans. Too puritanical in your own right. This is a way of life in my country. It alleviates the sorrows of empires past and what could have been, indeed, what *should* have been. We Russians are our own worst enemies. You only need to look at the past three hundred years to discern what I say is true. We were fighting and killing each other long before your Constitution was signed." Bashirin looked down into his drink, contrite now. "We're still doing it today, except in a less organized, more anarchic fashion. Now it's gang warfare, organized cartels, the government authority ceding its discipline to paranoid fiefdoms composed of drug lords, smugglers, extortionists, prostitution rings. You name it, and there's an island fortress with a wall around it, opening up when it's convenient to do business with a neighbor, closing down and firing at will at the very same neighbor when irritated. In greater Moscow alone, there are nights when there are a hundred murders, too many for *Pravda* to follow. The papers now only report the sensational cases. You see, we Russians yearn for empire, for greatness, for international recognition as a great power, and we'll gladly kill each other to attain it. It's in our psyche as a people. What we fail to recognize is the methodology as to how to obtain our national aspirations. So instead, we turn ourselves to a medieval mentality in the meantime, ruining further what could have been a great nation."

There was a lull, so I said, "Sounds to me like you need a benevolent dictator to pull the country together, along the lines of Lucius Quinctius Cincinnatus."

Bashirin asked, "And who is that?"

It was my turn for a little historical pontification. "Cincinnatus was a consul in Rome around 460 BC. He was a simple farmer and had no political aspirations. Evidently having impressed the Roman Senate, they petitioned him to assume the title of dictator to keep the city of Rome from falling to the Aequians and the Volsci, tribes that were menacing the city at the time. Even though it was planting time, and he feared for his crops and near starvation of his family, he did as requested, defeating the tribes and placing Rome in a secure position. He immediately resigned his authority to resume his familial duties after the military campaign, and within sixteen days, the governance of Rome was back to operating as a republic. Cincinnato, Italy, and Cincinnati, Ohio, were named after him. Our George Washington was often referred to as a latter day Cincinnatus, as he too did not seek political power after the American Revolution. He did serve two terms in office as president of the country, somewhat reluctantly, but he gave it up to permanently retire, believing any more political aspiration was equitable to being king."

"Wouldn't work in Russia." Bashirin rose to his feet, heading back to the freezer. The flint in his eyes as he met my gaze reminded me of the pure strength of this bear of a man. "Too much corruption," Bashirn replied matter-of-factly as he refilled his tumbler.

"Baloney, if you don't mind me saying so. You think ancient Rome was any worse? It was one of the most corrupt governments on the planet. You think the intrigue was any less then than it is now? Think again. All you need is the right person to pull it all together, one who cares more for the country than for what comes with the position to run it. Something for you to think about."

The decision in his own mind made, he replied quickly, "Something for someone else to think about. I plan to come to the West when my stint is over. I like you guys over here."

I retorted, not wanting to give this one up, "Like I said, something for you to think about. We might like you guys over there a lot more if we had a stable partner we could deal with."

Lyft piped up as he toasted to the skies, "Yes, and a stable supply of vodka would then be ensured worldwide."

We all laughed at that one.

Just then, Bashirin's walkie-talkie crackled, saying we should come to the front gate of the complex, as there was a considerable commotion taking place. We all jumped up, leaving drinks in place, scrambling into Salvo's Jeep parked in front of my apartment. We could see the entrance from our position, although it was hard to discern what was happening due to the dust kicked up, evidently by a circus of animals.

We arrived to find bedlam, a seemingly endless train of braying animals, rattling pots and pans, and people shouting and gesticulating in what we perceived to be a Kyrgyz caravan. Unruly children were running around, overloaded supply wagons pulled by protesting yaks ground to a halt, with the women shouting in the children's direction and gesticulating toward the men at the front of the gate, whom I guessed to be the tribal elders. A man I assumed to be the group's leader was yelling at the security guards, evidently to let them into the compound, with the guards holding up their hands, denying entry. Salvo spoke quickly into his walkie-talkie to get an interpreter to the front gate pronto, and in a few minutes, Captain Charles "Charley" Thomas arrived with two lieutenants. He began in Pashto, then Urdu, and then back to Pashto, as it seemed to suffice. We gathered around Charley and the leader to discern what had brought the wagon train to our doorstep.

Charley reported that the train had been attacked by drug traffickers. Jafar, the leader's name, was seeking sanctuary, as they had been able to fend off the first attack but were unsure about a second. He explained to Charley that this was his family, including cousins three times removed, and that he was responsible for all of them, as they looked to him for leadership due to his help in repelling the Soviet invasion in the early 1990s. Bashirin asked through Charley if he was mujahideen. He shook his head violently, telling Charley he had given that up when the Soviets departed the country. Now his responsibilities outweighed any political aspirations. He had turned to trading and farming for subsistence, but it had been a bad year, too much drought, and he had little to trade now. That is why he desperately needed sanctuary. If the traffickers took what little they had left, they would be destitute and could well starve.

I felt sorry for the lot of them. I supposed they were telling the truth, and even if they weren't, it was a pathetic existence. Who could blame them if they trafficked in drugs? My personal supposition was that they did when there was no other alternative. Sometimes there was no other way to scrabble out a living in these desolate valleys.

Bashirin and Salvo along with Charley had a council to the side. Soon they joined us, with Charley taking the lead.

"You can stay here, but not inside the compound. We will explain why later. Right now, you can set up camp in the field over there, where you will be protected day and night. We will feed your people. When you feel it safe to move on, you will be free to go as you wish."

Jafar bowed, shook hands with all of us, and then turned to his people to tell them what had transpired. A great shout of glee boomed off the hillsides. The train moved forward and to the left, away from the helipad area and into a field of grass about one hundred feet below the elevation of the plant and several hundred yards from the perimeter. Bashirin and Salvo went into the compound to orchestrate the mess duties, which were not particularly complicated for forty to fifty people. Later that afternoon, a portable field mess unit was established. Soon traditional Afghan meals were being served, consisting of lamb kabobs, fresh vegetables, and pilau, rice flavored with lamb broth. Slabs of Afghan bread accompanied the meal. There were two tandoors, clay ovens, in the mess area for cooking the bread. Dessert consisted of fresh fruit, with green tea as the closer.

Jafar sought out Captain Thomas after the meal, thanking him profusely on behalf of his people for the fine meal and the generosity of the two colonels. He asked if we would like to join his group for some entertainment. Of course, we accepted. The instrumentation pulled from wagons and from the donkeys' backs was an interesting array. There were dholaks, which looked like large conga drums, made out of jeldis wood with goatskin heads. Then one of the men fingered a rabab, an instrument with a long neck and a gourd-shaped end, with a face of goatskin and frets of gut. It had mother-of-pearl inlays with eighteen strings of different variety and was played with a plectrum, something akin to a guitar pick. There were three dhambouras, stringed instruments that look like guitars with side holes cut out of them. Two men brought out surnais, which looked like flutes. Each had seven finger holes on the front and a thumb hole on the reverse.

Upon seeing the instruments, I realized that these were no Taliban. The Taliban I knew from reports disliked music and entertainment of any sort. They had made it a point to seek out and destroy musical instruments during their short reign, feeling that musical entertainment took away from focus on religious teachings, subsequently undermining their inordinately strict theocracy. The women joined around the fire, beginning with a clapping beat, with the men keeping rhythm on the dholaks as Jafar began the story. The women chanted to the background beat as Jafar and others began the tale.

It was epic, a universal theme about two lovers, Ali and Ari, whose families did not approve of their union. There was no dowry, thus no family alliance, so they were on their own, outcasts, with no one to even marry them. They roamed the regions of the Hindu Kush, subsisting on handouts, living in squalor, depending on the girl's extraordinary voice for a living. They went from village to village, campfire to campfire, where she sang folk songs for meals, until she became quite renowned throughout northern Afghanistan. But still, no one allowed them sanctuary, as they were not husband and wife, until one fortuitous day, after a brutal storm caromed off the Pamirs and descended into the valleys of the Wakhan. The rivers raged, and from the ravine of one of the tributaries of the Little Pamir came a cry for help.

When Ali went to investigate, he found a small boy clinging to a pine log wedged between two boulders, shivering and frightened, a third of the way out into the river. Thinking he could save the boy by swimming out to him, he waded into the froth, soon realizing when he was knee deep that the current was too strong. He turned back, with the boy thinking he was being forsaken, when Ali's companion arrived. She immediately saw the situation and began singing to the boy in her operatic voice, telling him to be calm, that they would soon have him around a warm campfire. She kept singing as Ali went to their only mule, coaxed it to the river's edge, and tied his only rope around its belly as he tied the other end around his own, giving instructions to Ari that the mule should hold its ground by digging in its front quarters as he fought the current to get the boy. He hoped the mule was in a good mood that day and that he liked the song Ari was about to sing to him.

Ari and Ali took a long look at each other, and Ali asked if she was ready. She replied yes, she was ready, and so she began to sing, but not just any song. This was the sweetest, most poignant melody that had ever crossed her lips. The mule's ears perked up, his feet dug in, and his hindquarters lowered, seemingly knowing exactly what was expected of him. Ali waded into the current above the boy's entrapment as the water began to sweep him to the boy's location. He banged somewhat rudely into the log with a thump, but he hung on, knowing that if he missed his target, he would have to perform his acrobatics again, and he did not know if he would have the strength. The water was like ice from the snowmelt, sapping his energy and robbing him of reserve. It was now or never.

All the while, Ari kept singing that beautiful song of love and courage to the mule, who hadn't budged an inch. When Ali reached the boy, he explained that they were going to get wet, even immersed, and that the boy should not panic. They would be going against the current, but the mule would haul them ashore. So if they went underwater, and they were sure to, the boy should take a deep breath first and not be afraid. He said he was ready, that he wanted to go home. Ali tied the boy around his middle, told the boy to hang onto him by clamping both arms around his neck, and then he encircled himself once with the rope, in addition doubling a loop around one wrist and then the other, settling himself into the river. Immediately, the current tore at them, and the rope snapped taut. Ari sang a crescendo, and the mule began backing up. Ali and the boy both went under, with Ali yelling for the boy to take a deep breath. The mule dug in, and in a few minutes, they were dragged sputtering and coughing to the shallows by the heroic animal.

As Ali was extricating himself and the boy from the rope, some tribesman appeared on the upper bank, gesticulating and yelling. They did not seem threatening. In fact, they seemed overjoyed. They ran to the edge of the river, yelling and praising Allah, exclaiming that it was a miracle that the boy was found alive. They immediately realized what had occurred, yelling for some warm blankets and hot green tea. A fire was made, a change of clothes was offered to the wet river rats, and a celebration was had. They explained that the boy was the son of Mahmood, the most powerful tribal leader in Northern Afghanistan, and that he would be there shortly to thank Ali and Ari and the mule, who it seems had no name.

Sure enough, he shortly arrived on a magnificent white steed with a long mane blowing in the breeze. His son ran to him, giving him a great hug, explaining excitedly what had occurred, how the mule had held its ground against the raging current and the manner in which Ari had coaxed the mule into action with her beautiful song. Mahmood was mightily impressed, and he hugged Ali and bowed to Ari as a gesture of thanksgiving. He insisted that they come to his village, about five miles distant, to partake of his hospitality and anything else they wished. Ali said he just wished to be warm, which impressed Mahmood, realizing that this couple was simple in their desires and required nothing in return for their heroism. Ari went to the mule and gave him a fresh carrot, which he delightedly chomped, readying him for their journey. Mahmood was also impressed with this act of kindness, realizing his good fortune in having these strangers come upon his only son instead of a band of thieves demanding ransom or worse.

Mahmood insisted that his guests ride at the head of the column. The trip was not arduous, although Ali and the boy were shivering during the ride in spite of the blankets wrapped around them. Mahmood sent a rider ahead to alert the village of their arrival and their great good fortune. He had instructed that a hut be superheated and ready upon arrival for his frozen guests. When they arrived, Mahmood took Ali and the boy to the structure, which was heated to about one hundred degrees, and told them to take off any remaining wet clothes and put on cotton wraps until they were warm enough to join around the large bonfire that had been lit. In that heat, it did not take long to thaw, and in less than thirty minutes, they joined the throng around the campfire.

They arrived to a great huzzah and celebratory atmosphere. Freshly killed lambs were on spits, stews were simmering, vegetables were cooking, flat bread was piled on tables, dates and sweets were trayed on side tables for dessert, with the women swatting at errant children who thought life too short to wait for dessert.

Ali had explained to Mahmood on the journey what had transpired and how they happened to be near the river. He told him of their past, their hardships, and their love for each other and that they were unmarried but hoped to be someday. Mahmood was mightily impressed with Ali and Ari's humbleness, realizing that Ali had put his life in danger on behalf of his son. He was also impressed with the mule's behavior, asking Ari how could an animal know what to do in such a circumstance. Ari replied that the mule was part of their small family, that it shared their joys and hardships, always responding appropriately to kindness with some sort of sixth sense, knowing that it was in good, kind hands. She felt that the mule responded because of the manner in which it was treated. Mahmood asked the name of the mule, and Ari said it had none. Mahmood said they should change that.

"From now on," he said, "this noble animal's name shall be Alparsian, meaning 'courageous lion' in Turkish. This is a most honorable name."

Ari and Ali were delighted, as was the mule, who let out a loud bray in approval. Mahmood told the two they could stay as long as they liked. Then he rose, motioning for them to join him as he headed toward his home. It was time to rectify their past.

He invited them to sit in his comfortable surroundings, which, to them, seemed like the ultimate in luxury but, in actuality, were simple furnishings for a simple lifestyle. He said he had no repayment that would suffice for the rescue of his son, but that they had been done a great injustice. He invited them to join the village, to permanently reside there, and then he gave them the greatest gift of all. He said he would be honored to officiate at their marriage ceremony on a date of their choosing.

They both flushed, not knowing how to reply, when Ali stammered, "But there is no dowry, nothing of value to be transferred to unite the family. We are penniless, not even able to produce wedding clothes. It will be a dismal wedding day, I fear."

Mahmood said soothingly, "Your troubles are over. Let us worry about the details; you worry about you two. I bequeath the dowry, so consider that issue closed. We will build you a fine house, and you will have the finest of wedding clothes for your day. Just give us time to make them. Ha ha."

And so they were married and settled into village life. Ali through the years eventually rose to second in command. The son he rescued turned into a first-class leader, whom Ali served throughout the rest of his days.

It was a first-rate story with a perfect accompaniment of music and rhythm. When it wound down, with great accolades from all, I motioned Captain Thomas over and had a sidebar with him. He motioned to one of his men who clambered into a Jeep and drove to the apartment complex where I lived. He soon came back with some sheaves of paper in hand.

I asked Jafar with a wink via Charley to gather the children around; anyone under the age of twelve would do. I had in my hand some excerpts from *Alice in Wonderland*, which I had told Charley's aide to take off the Internet in my dacha. As the children somewhat shyly gathered around me, I could only hope Alice translated half as well in Pashto as it did in English. I slowly told the children who Lewis Carroll was, when he lived, and that he was English and a fine writer. That he had written a wonderful fantasy story of a little girl who had accidentally arrived in another world, not quite knowing how she got there. She encountered all sorts of fantastic characters, one of which was the famous caterpillar who could talk. I asked how many knew what a caterpillar was, and all raised their hands. Then I asked how many thought a caterpillar could really talk, and none raised their hands. So I told them that the caterpillar made Alice recite a poem, which went like this:

> "You are old Father William," the young man said,
> "And your hair has become very white;
> And yet you incessantly stand on your head—
> Do you think, at your age, it is right?"

Evidently, Charley's translation was on target as the children all giggled, many attempting to stand on their heads, with some falling over, which prompted more hilarity. Continuing on, I related,

> "In my youth," Father William replied to his son,
> "I feared it might injure the brain;
> But now that I'm perfectly sure I have none,
> Why, I do it again and again."

That one broke up the party, with much hooting and hollering, with more of the children trying to stand on their heads, all unsuccessfully. Jafar was laughing, as was everyone else around the fire. When all had settled down, I continued,

"You are old," said the youth, "as I mentioned before,
And have grown most uncommonly fat;
Yet you turned a back somersault at the door—
Pray, what is the reason for that?"

Much laughter and attempts at back somersaulting, all again unsuccessful, turning into shoulder rolls instead. The children were now getting quite dirty, but no one seemed to mind.

"In my youth," said the sage, as he shook his grey locks,
"I kept all my limbs very supple
By the use of this ointment—one shilling the box—
Allow me to sell you a couple?"

Not too much understanding of this one, so all remained relatively quiet, with the exception of some chuckles from the men.

"You are old," said the youth, "and your jaws are too weak
For anything tougher than suet;
Yet you finished the goose, with the bones and the beak—
Pray, how did you manage to do it?"

Great guffaws went up on this one, with the younger children pretending to be geese while the older ones chased them down, attempting to devour them. It took a while for the screaming to die down, as the older children took delight in terrorizing their younger siblings. I eventually continued,

"In my youth," said his father, "I took to the law,
And argued each case with my wife;
And the muscular strength, which it gave to my jaw,
Has lasted the rest of my life."

The men roared on that one, with the children giggling, not

really understanding the context. They would have to wait a few years.

"You are old," said the youth, "one would hardly suppose
    That your eye was as steady as ever;
  Yet you balanced an eel on the end of your nose—
    What made you so awfully clever?"

More hilarity from the children as they ran to get wooden spoons and tried to balance them on their noses. Eels were evidently in short commodity. When they eventually quieted themselves, I dug in for the finale.

"I have answered three questions, and that is enough,"
    Said his father, "don't give yourself airs!
  Do you think I can listen all day to such stuff?
    Be off, or I'll kick you downstairs!"[5]

As Charley ended the translation, he made a kick-swooping motion simulating an attempt at extra points through the uprights. The children rolled over, clutching their stomachs from the sweet pains of laughter. I thought his embellishment an excellent ending to a pleasant evening, or so I thought, but the look on Bashirin's face said otherwise as he listened to his walkie-talkie. I felt the familiar clump onto my shoulder, knowing full well that two simultaneous occurrences harbingered a long night. Bashirin finished his conversation on the walkie, came over to consult briefly with Salvo, and then headed toward me. He exhibited a wry look on his face, relating to a cat and canary, as he motioned me away from the fire to the background.

"We have contact," Bashirin whispered to me. "Unfortunately for our boy, he can't say the same, as when he got the word, the flipped switch did nothing. Is Lyft nearby?"

"Right here," he squawked into Bashirin's face.

"Son of a bitch, I should have known better. Next time, I won't ask. Christ but that's disconcerting."

---

5   The Hunting of the Snark and Other Poems and Verses. Lewis Carroll.
(Harper & Brothers, 1903)

"Isn't it though?" I piped up.

"Your own fault," said Lyft indignantly. "You should know by now that I'm omnipresent."

"And a deity complex to boot," I added. "You know, you're turning into the company curmudgeon. We should have a name plate made up for your desk that says so."

Bashirin chuckled at that one.

"I don't have a desk. I'm too busy."

I ignored Lyft. We walked away from the assemblage toward Bashirin's Jeep. Illuminated by the fires, Jafar's group was in animated discussion, I assumed about the hospitality of the evening and their good fortune in stumbling onto a kindness that hadn't been seen in quite a while.

I said softly, "Colonel, what's the course of action?"

"We wait for the bastard to make his move. Sure enough, the call came from a family member. We traced it to Belawan, the port city of Medan in Northern Sumatra. We even know the address, and from that, we will obtain a name. I believe the thing to do is to work that angle simultaneously with this one."

I ruminated on this for a second or two. "But," I said, "won't he know when he discovers the fuses have been altered?"

"Sure enough, and then we place him in lockdown. But he may not know we are working on his family. That's our ace in the hole. We use the family angle to eventually get more information from him. Knowing we are jeopardizing his family will make him crack. It's one thing for them to martyr themselves, but to martyr their families is another matter."

I said to the air, "Lyft, are you in agreement with this course of action?"

The air quacked back, "Absolutely. I couldn't have planned it better myself."

I said, "From you, that's quite a compliment."

"I am capable of giving them when merited, you know."

I queried, "Colonel, do you think there are any more here in league with this guy?"

"I don't believe so. We have no evidence of that, but we'll probably find out tonight when he goes investigating the various locations of the explosives. If there is anyone else involved, he'll request help to check them all out."

"So he'll be watched all night?"

"And the next night and the next, however long it takes to flush our partridge."

We arrived at Bashirin's Jeep. He offered me a ride, but as my dacha was relatively close to his, I told him I'd rather walk, hoping to get the kinks out from sitting around the fire too long. He said good night, clambered into the vehicle, and roared off. Lyft had alighted on my shoulder, but I sensed something amiss.

I asked, "So what gives? You're a little cranky tonight."

"Well, can you blame me? I've been working the whole night while you've been partying. Someone has to keep this show on track."

"Oh, now we're down to it. The great martyr has spoken. Just because you have to remain invisible, you feel uninvited to the party. Feeling a little sorry for ourselves, are we? Well, you get to party enough. Or is something else bothering you?"

"You know I love children."

"Ah, so that's it. Can't interact with the kids. Well now, that's one I can understand. They were a delight tonight. Such unbridled innocence."

"Yes, that's why I'm drawn to them. Adults don't exhibit the same traits. Children represent all of what could be in the world before their characters become polluted by their elders. But as we all know and understand, I can't interact with them, because their innocence in tattling on me is their undoing, or rather, would be mine."

"Understood. Perhaps we could manufacture an epic tale of Lyft Faetels. At least you could participate unobserved. How would that be?"

"I would like that. It's probably the closest I could come to concrete interaction. Please work on that."

"OK, but for another night. So, Lyft, does that mean you can back off, you know, take a break, quit scurrying around in constant motion and perhaps get some much-needed rest? Let someone else do the worrying for a change?"

"I'm not sure your tone is concern or derision, but it would be nice all the same to take a break. Thank you for the suggestion. I will bunk in Colonel Bashirin's dacha, as his hospitality is somewhat more accommodating than yours lately."

"Ouch."

"Yes, and let that be a lesson to you."

"I should warn him about your snoring. I should tell him about the last time someone woke you from a sound sleep, when you fell off the couch and cracked your head, not that it hurt you any."

"Oh, you're flip. The rack would be too mild a torture for you. I shall have to think up some new methods to plague you as I fall asleep into idyllic oblivion under the auspices of Colonel Bashirin."

"I'll bet you to be in a foul mood in the morning due to an excess of vodka. But don't say I didn't tell you so."

"I'm perfectly capable of taking care of myself, thank you. With that, I'll say good night."

"Good night. I'll look forward to a blissful evening of uninterrupted rest."

"Harrumph."

I looked back on the entourage now some distance away, outlined by the fires, watching the children still running after each other, trying to "kick each other downstairs." I smiled to myself, thinking the evening a success. I anticipated a postmidnight visit from Lyft, no matter what he said his plans were. I was wrong. It would be a while until I saw him again.

CHAPTER EIGHT

Belawan, Sumatra

Belawan is a gritty place, a bustling port on the Deli River twelve miles from Medan, the capital city of North Sumatra province. Medan is the largest city in Sumatra and the third largest in Indonesia, with two and a half million people. It is known for the profusion of its motorized becaks, or tricycle rickshaws, that have been banned in Taiwan and Bangkok due to excessive traffic congestion. Belawan and Medan do not have the same restrictions, and noise from the small motors on the vehicles can be overwhelming during rush hours. Some would say it's always rush hour and that they can tell no difference at any hour of the day in the decibel levels of cacophony, along with the fistfights promoted by the territorial imperatives of the drivers intermixed with the street hawkers selling everything from raw fish to newly minted tobacco.

Into this mélange flew Lyft in an attempt to seek out the family of Ali Sastroamidjojo. He and Bashirin had cooked up a scheme, whereby Lyft would unobtrusively "live" amongst the family, provided he could find their address, to root out the core of the terrorist connection, hopefully shutting it down once and for all.

Easier said than done, thought Lyft as he sought out the

address Bashirin had given him. "What the hell?" Lyft exclaimed to himself.

The address, he'd discovered, was in the middle of the Deli River. The satellite must have wobbled due to sunspots when it sent the information.

What Lyft didn't know was that the address was correct. He invisibly set himself down on the top of a large container vessel, above the captain's bridge, as befitting his station, to think about the situation as to how to find the real address, when he noticed a Thai fishing trawler moving up river toward Lama Village. Lyft briefly thought about the number of Belawanese fisherman who had been displaced by the illegal fishing activities of other nations. Now twenty thousand inhabitants of the village depended on their livelihoods by ironically supplying the illegal trawlers with supplies to hunt and deplete their own waters. As sorry a tale as it was, Lyft realized that he had not come to the port to solve that problem. Then, while ruminating how to solve his own, it hit him, almost staggering him, making him weave on the bridge support.

"Of course. The address most probably *is* correct. The signal came from a boat. Hah. That must be what occurred. OK, if so, then what vessel? This could be a knotty problem." Lyft laughed at his own pun. *I'll have to make a few inquiries*, he thought.

From the main port frontage, side streets emanated, many featuring teahouses, other types of unadvertised houses, illegal bars catering to foreign workers and crews, along with some surprisingly good restaurants. Lyft decided to disguise himself while making his inquiries. He found a version of a thrift shop, where he "borrowed" a number of items that he felt would be adequate for his purposes. He tied a do-rag around his head, concealing his elaborate ears, pulled a longshoreman's cap over his head, changed his complexion with some motor oil pilfered from the docks, pulled on a pair of oversized steel-toed black work boots, pulled on a long, rather greasy coat he had smeared with some alley garbage he had found, which had extra long sleeves to hide his talons, one pocket stuffed with U.S. twenties and the other with one hundreds, looked at himself in a shop window, and pronounced himself adequately made over to accomplish the task. He flew to one of the illegal bars he had earlier perused for his purpose, set himself down on the sidewalk, puffed himself up to a height of just under five feet, the maximum expansion his air bladders could tolerate, and sauntered into the bar. Not very populated at eleven in the morning, there were a few patrons at the bar and some in the corners, chatting, eating an early lunch. Lyft went to the bar and ordered a beer. The bartender did a double take, clearly thinking Lyft to be one of the uglier patrons he had ever served, but then went about his business. Lyft figured by the bartender's looks that he was Minangkabau, but perhaps not from Aceh, so he growled in Bahasa, the official language of Indonesia, "Where can I find the family of Ali Sastroamidjojo?"

The bartender looked closely at him. "Who wants to know?" he replied.

"A friend, with good news."

The bartender replied, "I don't recall anyone by that name ever being in here. Don't know any Ali Sastroamidjojo or anyone associated with him."

Lyft couldn't tell if the bartender was lying, so he took a twenty out of his pocket, placing it gingerly on the bar so his talons didn't show.

"Does that help your memory any?" queried Lyft.

"Nope. If I don't know the guy, I don't know the guy. Try down the street, The Blue Lady. The bartender's been there for a million years running the joint. And do yourself a favor, would you? Get yourself cleaned up. You're disgusting. You stink."

"Thanks for the advice. Keep the twenty," Lyft said sarcastically.

"Yeah, thanks. I'll have it fumigated before I put it in the cash drawer."

Lyft casually extricated himself off the bar stool, exiting the building as the other patrons waved their hands in front of their faces in an effort to get some fresh air.

Perhaps I overdid it on the more odious elements of my disguise, thought Lyft. He realized that, on the plus side, the answers would come quicker in an effort to get rid of him, so he decided to see what the new address held.

He made his way to The Blue Lady, a bar much dingier than the first, with a much less affluent clientele than the previous location, a description kind to the patrons. Lyft wondered why it was called The Blue Lady, a title he hoped wasn't derived from spousal abuse. He would have to inquire.

This bar was full, which he thought unusual for this time of day. There were tables full of every conceivable despicable character, weapons bristling in full sight, with numerous women amongst the clientele, some sitting on laps and some sauntering their wares. Lyft looked around, figuring he had found the right spot, although he wondered if the first bartender sent him here to get rid of him in finality. He wondered how, in a predominantly Muslim country, this sort of establishment flourished, and then he immediately realized how stupid a thought it was. Bribery was as rampant here as anywhere, so he had just answered his own question.

He made his way to the bar, repeating his question to the bartender whose face was covered in scars, with one particularly nasty one running from under his left ear, along his upper lip, under his nose, and to the right corner of his mouth. He was shiny bald and heavily tanned, with gold hoops in both ears, and he had forearms with enough power to crush a derrick.

Must have been some knife fight, thought Lyft. *I wonder how the other guy fared.*

Lyft repeated his request.

The bartender looked at him, growling, "Who wants to know?"

Lyft thought, *That must be a standard reply around here.* He replied, "A friend with good news."

"OK, friend with good news, you can do better than that. We don't like strangers snooping around asking questions about our people, so let's try this again. Like I said, who wants to know?"

Bingo, thought Lyft. He said, "Lyft Faetels wants to know, that's who."

Lyft produced a twenty and placed it quickly on the bar. The bartender glanced down at it, basically ignoring the gesture.

"Lyft Faetels? What the hell kind of name is that?"

Uh-oh, thought Lyft. *Here it comes, the pissing contest.* He hissed with an edge to his voice, "That's my name. Who are you to question it?"

Thinking he needed more bait, Lyft pulled out a hundred, placing it on the bar, looking the bartender directly in the eyes. A few patrons gravitated over to the empty stools on either side of Lyft. He seemed to have the bartender's attention now, but he noted eye contact with one particular patron and then with others in the crowd sauntering toward his location. The mirror behind the bar provided him with an advantage, although it appeared the customers didn't care if their movements were noted.

Lyft said in a low voice, "I have a message from Ali to his family, an important message that can only be delivered in person. Now, are you going to help me or not?"

Lyft produced two more twenties from his pocket, adding to the pile on the bar. The gentleman on Lyft's left leaned toward him and whispered, "Seems like those pockets of yours could use an emptying. Why don't you do us all a favor and turn them inside out?"

Lyft looked in his grinning face, devoid of upper and lower front teeth, heavy crow's-feet around cruel, gray eyes, do-rag on a bald head, one eye wandering toward the bartender, a greasy, olive green T-shirt over a body rippling with muscle and said, "OK, asshole, something tells me you won't listen, but here it is. You make one move toward me, and I'll turn you inside out. You'll wish you never woke up today. So back off. You've been warned."

Lyft turned back toward the bartender. "So?" he queried in a loud voice.

The bartender said, "You've got guts, I'll give you that much."

Lyft noted a sudden movement to his left, sighing as he morphed into invisibility, "Don't say I didn't tell you so."

Everyone whose attention had turned to the scene at the bar were perplexed, seeing an empty stool in place of Lyft's presence. Unbeknownst to most in the bar, Lyft had seen the flick of a switchblade to his left, so he decided to deal decisively with the situation. He figured the immediacy of a knife between the ribs overruled the consequences of his invisibility and action. He lifted the do-rag man off the floor, propelling him into the mirror behind the bar at nearly supersonic speed. The impact shattered the glass explosively, showering the bar and beyond. Do-rag, his head acting like the business end of a lethal projectile, accelerated through the wall, with half his body protruding through the structure into the den of promiscuity next door. He looked like a newly minted trophy on the opposite wall, straight from the taxidermist. The girls next door ran for their lives out into the street, screaming that a murder had been committed. The bar patrons gawking at the carnage had the reverse view. The force of the impact had ripped do-rag's pants halfway down his legs, exposing his hairy derriere to the crowd.

Lyft chortled, yelling, "Didn't your mother ever tell you it's impolite to turn your bare backside to others in public?"

He then violently pushed the man through the opening, propelling him across the room next door, where he ended up face down on a pool table, unconscious, blood pouring from his head, staining the felt as the eight ball spun into the far right corner pocket.

"Game over," pronounced Lyft.

He flew back through the hole into The Blue Lady, from which some had fled, but where others were just standing, stunned, encased by their own inertia, their synapses unable to process and transmit the scene from their eyes to their minds. Lyft picked up the bartender, sat him on the bar facing the devastation, invisibly floating in front of him, and bellowed, "Now, where can I find the family of Ali Sastroamidjojo? I'm not going to ask again."

The bartender, wide-eyed and shaking, said in a quavering voice, "Go to Lama Village, up the river. There you will sometimes find the Sastroamidjojo family on a fishing vessel. You'll know the boat by its low beam and the words 'Lotus Blossom' on the stern."

"You know, this all could have been avoided if you'd given me the information I needed earlier, you stupid donkey. Have fun cleaning it up."

Lyft grabbed the money off the bar as he exited, stashed his disguise in an alley garbage can, and then zipped out of the port in invisible mode for a dip in the ocean in his regular garments to partake of a much needed bath. He returned, much refreshed, heading to Lama Village, about twenty-two miles from Belawan.

He cruised at a low altitude, where, sure enough, he saw numerous foreign trawlers plying up and down the river, interspersed with a few native ones. He soon came to a cluster of junks, trawlers, and other assorted vessels tied up to quays along the riverbank, framed by shanty huts bordering muddy, garbage-strewn alleys. He floated behind the trawler line, trying to discern their individual names, when finally he saw the *Lotus Blossom* toward the end of the line at its own small dock. He looked it over, realizing that, relative to the neighboring village squalor, this was a four-star floating resort. An overall picture of doting maintenance typified its highly polished teak decks, shiny hardware, fresh paint, and properly stowed gear. In relation to every other vessel in the village, this was a thoroughbred among mutts.

Bingo, he thought. *U.S. aid dollars at work.*

He saw no immediate signs of habitation on the vessel, so he descended, making his way into the main cabin. The engine controls were impressive. He wondered about the horsepower. He flew out to the back deck, noting no one near, and then lifted the engine compartment doors, astounded at finding twin enamel-blue Mermaid Mirage II 325 horsepower diesel engines. He noted that they were turbo-charged, 7.5 liters with six cylinders each, state of the art for maximum power and minimal maintenance for operation in remote areas.

He thought, *Whoever put this baby together knew exactly what they were doing.*

He gingerly let down the compartment doors in place, noting two tarpaulins left and right on the deck, evidently covering some machinery. He peeled one of them off and found a newly minted Suzuki DF250, the newest outboard offering from Suzuki in its class. At two hundred fifty horsepower with a V-6, four-stroke engine featuring multipoint digital fuel injection, this was some additional horsepower. Lyft peeked under the other tarpaulin, finding its identical twin. He thought these engines were not used for additional power on this vessel; rather, they must be for another purpose. There was no way to mount them and probably no need on this boat, which had enough power of its own. He figured they could be used for hit-and-run operations on the high seas, being mounted onto innocent-looking vessels hydraulically by the crew, and then hoisted back onto the deck post-operations.

Ingenious, I'll say that, thought Lyft.

He looked at the hydraulic net minders to port and starboard, realizing that his supposition was correct. The hydraulics could easily be converted to simple hoisting operations and then converted back again to dispel inquiries by any inspecting authority. Lyft wondered how many times the Australians had been duped on this vessel during inspections in the Straits of Malacca. Perhaps they only hit it once, registering it in their databases, approving it, and then leaving it alone so that it could ply its trade unimpeded.

Lyft thought, *That will soon change.*

He put the tarps back in place and then flew back into the wheelhouse. He looked around at the sophisticated array of electronics, seeing an Icom IC M602 VHF marine radio that had remote control microphones for three intercom points onboard; a twenty-two-watt hailer with a built-in foghorn and continual watch on emergency channel seventy along with an array of other features; a Furuno 1944CNT Color NavNet vx2 radar network, good out to sixty-four nautical miles; tied into that was a Northstar 6000i, a state-of-the-art global positioning navigational system good to within six feet, featuring a fifteen-inch screen with 640-by-480 resolution. In addition to this smorgasbord in front of the pilot's seat, there was a Garmin GPSMAP 168 BST Fishfinder/Chartplotter. Lyft harrumphed at that, wondering if any fish had ever been displayed on the unit. Probably a cover, since there already was a GPS unit onboard sufficient to service the U.S. Navy.

Lyft sensed someone on the dock, so he flew out of the cabin onto the wheelhouse roof. There were two well-dressed men of Indonesian descent, one in a beige shirt and the other in maroon, walking toward the vessel. Lyft thought, *No poor fisherman these. If I could only dress so well. Pure Armani.*

Each had on expensive pleated gabardine slacks, spiffy new boat shoes, and silk short-sleeve shirts. Lyft noted four other rougher-looking fellows following on shore. They too soon made their way to the "trawler." Lyft guessed correctly that they were locals hired on as crew. Then a truck with a large depiction of a fish on its side rolled up to the end of the quay.

Interesting, thought Lyft.

The four crewmen walked off the boat to the location of the truck while two other individuals climbed out of the cab. All met in the rear of the truck, where two unlatched the rear tailgate, hoisting themselves up to the shipping level using ropes and step placements at the bottom of the gate. They maneuvered as many as twelve large rectangular wooden crates to the edge of the truck's loading platform and then used a hydraulic lift to lower the cargo two crates at a time.

Uh-oh, thought Lyft. *Not good if those are what I think they are.*

He flew closer so that he could discern the writing on the crates. He saw the word "Javelin" inscribed on the top.

Oh boy, antitank missiles. This'll be interesting. Won't Salvo have fun running down that connection, he thought.

Lyft flew back to his perch on top of the wheelhouse.

The four crewmen began to lug the crates down the quay to the boat, two men to a crate, where they stowed them in what appeared to be custom-made compartments carved into the decks. Each time two were placed side by side in the deck, the men displaced fishing nets and gear, which they subsequently stowed on top of the crates. The hinged doors were then put back in place, the only sign of their being there a heavy-duty brass O-ring lying in a groove flush with the deck.

Slick, thought Lyft. *If these guys would put as much effort into making an honest living, they'd be millionaires ten times over within the space of a year. But then again, what a stupid thought. They have no concept of honesty, bred as they were out of the slums of Jakarta or wherever. What a problem this world faces. Maybe good and evil really is a divine creation, a testament to the human condition.*

While Lyft philosophized, the last of the crates was loaded. Then Lyft was fascinated to see a small spring-loaded brass plate on each door pop up as the crew hit a button hidden in the starboard and port rails wherever a deck door was located. The crew each then took a key, inserted it into the keyhole now exposed under each plate, and locked the doors into the deck with a simple deadbolt. They then, by hand, forced the plates back into the doors flush with the wood, which reactivated the springs that opened them. Lyft was amazed at the detail of subterfuge entailed in the boat's construction. He couldn't wait until the Australian Navy appropriated it, but first he had to find out its mission. He would have to be careful not to employ his usual method, which was to cry havoc and let loose. He would have to preserve this vessel at all costs. Too many connections and threads into the network would be lost if the boat were destroyed.

Lyft figured that the action would be centered in the Straits. He was correct. As the crew was leaving the boat, beige shirt ordered in Bahasa, "Be here at 0900 a week from today. We sail at 1000, so don't be late. We go to Georgetown."

Lyft exclaimed in his head, *Georgetown? That's across the Straits in West Malaysia. What the hell is in Georgetown?*

As they departed, Lyft decided to remain in place, hoping to learn more detail about impending events. He was rewarded for his patience when he heard the radio fire up. He flew into the wheelhouse to ensure his hearing wasn't interrupted by the noise of river traffic, hovering nearly over the machine, which began emitting instructions. As he listened, the short hairs on the back of his neck rose. Three miles from the port of Georgetown, the boat was to meet two other smaller boats of disguised junk origin design, where the two engines under the tarps on deck would be hoisted into place on their respective covered transoms, along with six Javelins each, to be set up and placed strategically on their decks for use against two liquefied natural gas super tankers moored offshore from Georgetown. Lyft could not fathom why the tankers would be stationary there. He thought perhaps the captains had lapses in judgment mooring their time bombs at the head of the Malacca Straits. He figured that they were on their way to the liquefied natural gas complex at Bintulu, Sarawak, in Malaysia, which meant they had to go around Singapore across the Java Sea to Malaysia proper, a treacherous route on any day, but to let the crew on shore for R & R in Georgetown was crazy. These guys were too complacent, even if they had 'round the clock security on patrol around the vessels. Some of the best food in the

West Malay peninsula was in Georgetown, no doubt influencing the poor decision.

Lyft thought about the consequences of a successful attack on these vessels. The new liquefied natural gas super tankers held approximately eight and a half million cubic feet divided into five large cargo holds, the equivalent of six billion cubic feet of normal natural gas. The size of these tankers was enormous. They were a quarter mile wide, almost half a mile long, and a quarter mile high. Even though *liquefied* natural gas is not flammable, no one really knew what could happen if six Javelin antitank missiles were fired into the hulls. On contact with air, liquefied natural gas converts to natural gas and becomes flammable at a certain air-to-gas ratio. When the final missile was fired, perhaps enough would have been converted to allow a fireball that would consume half the Malacca Straits. Lyft did not want to put this scientific experiment to the test. He wondered how the perpetrators planned for their escape if a fireball ensued, and then almost slapped himself as to why he even posed the question.

The radio transmission terminated, with Lyft thinking he had to find access to a cell phone somewhere. He noticed them on the belts of the two individuals he was shadowing, but he could not get access to them. Just then, maroon shirt's cell phone rang. He unclipped it, spoke briefly, listened, replied, and then set it on the console near the ship's radio. Lyft figured he did not replace it in his belt because he was expecting other calls momentarily. Outside on shore at the head of the quay, a commotion began taking place. The truck had arrived again, with the four crew now walking down the dock, gesticulating as they jumped up and down. They were animatedly complaining that their contact had stiffed them, telling them they would be paid at the termination of the exercise. That was not their understanding. They were to be paid half on delivery of the cargo and the rest after the mission was completed. They bitterly complained that they had obligations that were due and that they depended on the money to settle those debts. Both vessel commanders walked out onto the dock, maroon shirt having forgotten his cell phone near the pilot's seat.

Bravo, how fortuitous, thought Lyft.

He grabbed the cell phone, flew at light speed to two hundred feet above the vessel, quickly dialed Salvo's number, and then explained the situation rapidly to him. As the United States was not welcome to patrol in the Straits, Lyft told Salvo to relay the message to the Australian authorities, which Salvo said he would do immediately. Lyft also told Salvo to find out the controlling country in charge of the tankers' dispositions.

While talking, Lyft kept an eye on the activity on the dock. He saw one of the men walk back to the boat and return with a bundle of cash, which he distributed to the four crew. Placated, they walked back to the truck, clambered back in, reversed it, and then drove off down the road. The two men then began walking back to the boat. Lyft signed off, deleted the call to Salvo, and quickly flew back into the wheelhouse, where he placed the phone back in its exact position. He thought he could do little more here, so he decided to vacate his perch, thinking he could learn more by following the truck back to its origin. He was hoping the four crew would go back to wreak vengeance on the contact who had welshed on them. He flew down the road, where he caught up with the vehicle, which had to move slowly due to potholes and the sundry animal life meandering in the roadway. The truck eventually made its way to the outskirts of central Belawan, where it stopped at a warehouse. Lyft could only hope this was the point of contact. His hunch turned into reality when the four crew jumped out, took weighted teak ax handles from the back of the truck, and then walked through a door on the side of the building. He flew down and followed them in before the last crew member could shut the door. He didn't want the contact killed before he could glean any information from him. The crew made their way toward a glassed-in office, where an attractive female sat doing paper work.

Damn, thought Lyft. *The main contact's not here.*

The woman looked up, alarm in her face, as the crew approached. One of the crew lifted his ax handle, swinging it like a baseball bat, smashing the glass door to gain entry to the lock below the glass inset. The woman screamed. Lyft instantly realized that she was the contact and that the men were about to show no mercy. He quickly flew over to one of them, snatched the handle out of his grip, and then proceeded to clock each of them on the skull, rendering them unconscious.

The woman, totally perplexed, ran out of her office to her car, slamming the warehouse door, and started her Mercedes, flooring the gas pedal, sending a spray of mud and debris in the car's wake. Lyft followed closely as she bolted through central Belawan to the driveway of a sumptuous estate in the hills above the city. There, an electronic gate let her up a long cobbled driveway to a magnificent palatial mansion, complete with armed guards, Dobermans, maids, butlers, pool boys, sycophants, and camp followers. She jerked the car to a stop and ran inside the back entrance to the house.

Now this is getting interesting, thought Lyft. *I wonder what's on the menu for lunch. All this activity has stimulated my appetite.*

Lyft noted the scurrying near the giant kidney-shaped pool, where a large buffet table was being set off to the side under some palm trees. Tumbled tile all around led to various archways, some into the main house and others into gardens, with the largest leading through an arch into the double-gated parking courtyard carefully laid out in a cobblestone motif, just rough enough that ladies in high heels risked broken ankles.

Lyft noted armed guards on the parapets above the main courtyard, more from the road to the estate walls, as well as a system of heavy electronic surveillance throughout and beyond the villa. He could only hope that his good luck in finding this place led to more than unveiling the delusions of a paranoid corporate magnate. That later, food first, as Lyft was a true believer in the hierarchical pyramid of biological needs.

He swooped down a little closer to the buffet display, eyeing the various assortments. He figured lunch was soon in the offing, as the buffet set was almost complete, along with the guests' tables just then receiving ice water. Ever the opportunist when confronted with such an array, Lyft descended, gobbling as fast as he could along the entire line of the food service, some thirty feet. He sampled some broiled ostrich, several Kansas City strips, some baked garlic minced lamb, several different seafood salads, two unshelled broiled lobsters, numerous shellfish on the half shell with their assorted sauces, clams casino, oysters Rockefeller, along with various vegetables and some tossed green salads, one of which included his favorite—fresh raw spinach. As he was about to make his first reverse back down the buffet line, he spied a mound of jumbo shrimp over ice in one corner on an isolated table. In the throes of his gluttony, he had almost missed what he considered to be one of the main events of the party.

"Now this needs some of my attention, methinks."

He began at the top so that the whole pile didn't tumble from lack of support. In seconds, the ice at the top of the heap began to show through. As Lyft made his way down the mound, it began to look like the Matterhorn, bleeding snow from the top exposing the darker soil and rock midway down to the base. When he could, he slopped shrimp into the cocktail sauce that was embedded in the ice left and right of the mound. Suddenly, one of the headwaiters inspecting the buffet began gesticulating, yelling that the food line had been raided. Service personnel ran up to the table, confirming his suspicion. They looked upon a scene of carnage where some of the meat had slopped off the trays onto the table, staining the cloth, the stains spreading from the gravy drippings as they dim-wittedly gazed on the destruction. A plate of broiled lobster had disappeared, the salad platters where in disarray, and much of the shellfish was missing. Fortunately for Lyft, they hadn't discovered the pillaging at the shrimp heap yet, so he was able to keep assuaging his gluttony unimpeded.

Everyone was yelling, "Who could have done this?" and "How could this happen? There was no one here."

The headwaiter arrived on the scene, yelling at the waiters and waitresses that this was their fault, how could they have let this occur, was no one watching over the buffet line? It was obvious that all feared for their jobs. He quickly quieted everyone down, snapped out instructions as to what repairs could be implemented, and then sat determinedly on a stool in front of the buffet line to oversee the ministrations to the food array. A small scream from the shrimp table meant that Lyft's activity rendering Tai shrimp extinct had been found out. He went to the back of the mound, where, unobserved, another sizable portion of the display found its way into his pockets. Sated now, he floated over the buffet line, impressed with the command performance of the staff. He noted new tablecloths, not changed, but merely laid over the others in exact positions as the waiters manipulated the food while the cloths were laid. New plates of food replaced those previously ravaged, and in no time, the buffet line exhibited perfection. The shrimp was replaced, with those servicing the table muttering that the place was haunted, that perhaps they should find employment elsewhere. Being in a somewhat playful mood, Lyft gobbled down the rest of his shrimp, placing the tails in his pocket. He had decided that the headwaiter was an ogre who showed his staff little respect. Lyft thought there was a semblance of Hitler in the waiter's appearance and demeanor. The only thing missing was the abbreviated mustache.

He floated down behind him, noting that the waiter's collar was open with his tie undone, as there was some time left to the commencement of the event. Lyft ensured no one was looking, that all were busy, and then took the tails, yanked the waiter's collar open, and dumped them down his back. The headwaiter screamed, yelling that he had been violated, looking around wildly, unable to comprehend who had played such a deceitful act. There were no other personnel near him, so his perplexity exponentially increased as he whirled like a dervish, attempting to get at the tails, which scratched mightily beneath his waiter's coat and shirt. As some of them had been covered in lemon-infused cocktail sauce, the slimy nature of the tails along with their prickly consistency was no doubt maddening. He walked across the courtyard, nervous ticks plaguing him as he tried to reach around for the tails, some of which had slipped into his beltline. Swearing and irrational, violent motions were the norm as he jerked his way across the yard through the archway, the rest of the staff looking on the scene, averting their eyes but, Lyft noted, happy in the thought of the waiter's discomfort.

As the staff went about their duties, Lyft saw that there were two bars set up, one at each end of the patio. He also was cognizant of the near bar's vacancy. The far bar was occupied by a bartender taking inventory to ensure he hadn't missed any of his clientele's favorite libations. Always one to recognize an opportunity, Lyft floated behind the unoccupied bar, piling several bottled beers into his expandable pockets after opening them via the opener tacked to the bar table leg, keeping the bottle caps. He then floated up to about thirty feet in the trees overhanging the patio, where he gulped down the beers. He placed the empty bottles back in his pockets, and then zoomed to the bar once more, placing the caps onto the bottles and then squeezing the empties back into the ice.

Let's see what happens when he finds those, thought Lyft.

Thoroughly satisfied now, he floated over the buffet in anticipation of the commencement of the luncheon.

The headwaiter returned, newly minted, attempting to stride across the patio with an authoritative air, as if nothing had occurred. However, his surreptitious glances out of darting eyes seeking sniggers from the staff told Lyft that his paranoia was in its finality of the third trimester, waiting on the right moment for delivery. Just the right push, and the headwaiter would blossom into a raving psychotic.

As Lyft was thinking what evil he could perpetrate upon the waiter, the guests began arriving into the patio. In spite of the humid heat, the ladies were dressed in long, shimmering silk gowns with slits, strappy high heels, jewelry the envy of the British crown, and small cocktail purses with long chains slung over shoulders so that both hands were free to indulge in food and drink. They were arm-in-arm with husbands already perspiring profusely in black tie and cummerbund. The host and hostess had taken positions at one end of the patio, where the receiving line was already being formed.

Huh, thought Lyft. *I wonder who the greeters are.* He recognized her from the warehouse, but that told him little about the couple's identity. It was time for a little investigative work.

Lyft dropped down closer, hovering over the couple who pleasantly greeted their guests. Out of the corner of his eye, he saw the bartender who had been raided gesturing to the headwaiter. The waiter silently strode over to the bar's location, where the bartender was gesturing behind his station, pointing to the empty beer bottles encased in ice. He picked one up, displaying it to the headwaiter who grabbed his arm, motioned him downward, and convinced him to hide it back in the ice along with the others. The waiter placed his hand on his forehead, as if suffering from a severe migraine, Mount Kerinci ready to blow. Lyft chuckled to himself, wondering if this were the proverbial straw, but the waiter recovered, conversing briefly with the bartender, telling him to keep a sharp eye on the staff.

Those non-Muslims who were through the receiving line began making their way toward the bars, where fruit punch seemed more in order than hard cocktails, at least with the ladies. Some of the men ordered beer as well as the usual array of hard-liquor drinks. Lyft noticed that the food remained untouched out of deference to the host and hostess, who had not yet completed their reception duties. Finally, the last guests made their way through the line. The host and hostess walked arm in arm to a position in front of the buffet table as the headwaiter helped gather the guests around them. The wait staff swished fans slowly over the food offerings to keep the flies at bay. The host, dressed in a pale yellow tux and pale green cummerbund with a pale yellow bow tie against a starched white shirt, looked over his audience with benevolence. His very pale yellow and white, very expensive Armani slip-ons scraped slightly on the cobbles as he shifted his considerable weight. He began, "Dear guests, thank you for taking time out of your busy schedules to join me on this beautiful but rather warm, humid day."

He received some ah, yeses at the end of that sentence.

"For those of you who don't know me, I am Ali Sastroamidjojo—Senior, I might add, as some of you may have made acquaintance with my son, Ali Junior. Right now, he's abroad on family business, but we are sure he will be returning soon. And this is my lovely wife, Licia, to whom I have been married for thirty years."

Lyft thought they made a unique pair. Ali's rotund figure against that of his diminutive wife; his porcine face dripping into his shirt collar; his corpulent hands that had never seen a day of manual labor, swollen from the heat, making them look like puss balls ready to burst; and his slicked down, black hair, combed to the right with too much hair gel, making him look like a slimy pig in a barnyard with a toupee, shuffling back and forth at the trough, as his undersized feet oscillated on the expensive tile. Licia, by contrast, was the epitome of Hollywood attractiveness. She had on an expensive long, sliver, slinky, metallic dress, exhibiting a perfect figure for her five foot six inch frame, along with silver-strapped open-toe high heels. Her exquisitely coiffed medium-length, jet-black hair, her deep brown, almond-shaped eyes, and her gorgeous features were quite a contrast to the behemoth standing beside her. Lyft thought he must have stolen her from a museum, as a beauty like this would never have acquiesced to a lifetime of servitude with this prehistoric mammoth. Then again, there was always greed, so perhaps it was a legitimate purchase.

Applause.

Right, Lyft mused, *family business. Which family and what business, huh, Ali Senior?*

Lyft rocked on the name, but immediately realized the whole scenario was going to fall into place. He decided he'd learn more by listening rather than preempting the speech and thereby missing something by letting his mind race.

"You all have been invited here as trusted comrades in our mutual enterprise. That enterprise is about to unfold. All of us are allied in our effort to rid this wonderful country of foreign interference at every level. Indonesia is our country and should be beholden to no foreign influence. Several years ago, when we founded this movement, each of you agreed as a matter of faith to pledge a certain monetary sum to be rendered at a future date. That date has arrived. I now ask you to honor that commitment, without which the activities of this body would cease to exist. Our endeavors are honest, our methods just. We will succeed, and soon, Indonesia's future and financial security will reside in our hands, not those of Britain or the United States. We must be successful, we must be victorious, or else we risk being serfs in our own companies. So have a wonderful time this afternoon. The library is open through the second arch." He pointed across the patio. "One of my most trusted lieutenants will be there to receive your offering on your way out. Enjoy yourselves."

The guests all applauded. Lyft thought of the consequences to any welshers who failed to render unto Caesar. He figured they'd all pay up. After all, they knew what they were here for. Something was gnawing at him as he watched the beautiful people quaffing drinks and stuffing food. He decided that Ali Senior's speech was a cover, clothed in patriotism, but laced with evil. He needed to know more. He didn't believe this was merely the action of a rich financier, greedily striving to wipe out foreign competition. Something else was a motivating factor. He kept close over Ali and his wife.

Ali and Licia ensured they made the rounds, speaking to each guest like good hosts, with never a relevant word as to Lyft's purpose. Not having much propensity for patience, Lyft was getting frustrated hovering over the rotund behemoth who was now sweating freely into his freshly starched shirt. Spots of perspiration were appearing on the back of his tux jacket, with larger stains evident under his arms. Lyft thought that when the entire suit became liquefied, as Ali's water reserve became depleted, he would combust with the ensuing pyrotechnics ending the party. The finale would be a grand explosion rivaling that of Mt. Toba millennia past, and the rest of the guests would fry with him on the patio.

If only, thought Lyft.

Licia leaned toward Ali, relating that perhaps it would be best if they went indoors where it was cooler, as Ali was beginning to show the strains of the day. Ever mindful of her position, she intelligently couched her counsel in terms of what was best for his health rather than telling him he was sweating like a fat hog. Lyft would have taken a different tack, but he could afford to. He wasn't married to the richest man in northern Sumatra, ever mindful of the politics of an arranged union.

Ali thanked his wife for her concern and related that, yes, perhaps it would be best to seek shelter for a bit from the blazing heat. They walked arm in arm through the recently directed archway, into the library, where it was well air-conditioned, paneled in mahogany and teak, where, behind a mammoth hand-carved teak desk, sat the trusted lieutenant, Ahman, who looked to Lyft like a caricature from an old silent movie. His hair was slicked, his mustache oily, his skin sallow, his face hawklike, beady eyes and all.

Lyft noted that four elephants in relief comprised the legs upon which the desk stood. He wondered if that was out of deference to Ali who needed their support as he leaned on the desk, absorbed in daily ministrations. Ali told Licia to leave them, that he was fine and would be along for a change of clothes shortly. She exited through the doorway into the short hall leading to the main living room. Ali spoke first.

"Very warm out there, Ahman. Perhaps we should have waited for a more temperate day."

Finally, Lyft thought. *Maybe now we'll get somewhere.* He quickly looked around, spotting what he thought to be surveillance cameras in the upper corners of the room. *Uh oh,* he thought. *Better be careful.*

Ahman spat disdainfully, "Yes, well, we can control some things, one of them not being the weather. It's now or never, relative to the ensuing action, so we had to do it today. What do our guests know?"

"Nothing. They think a corporate takeover is imminent."

"Ah, just so. How much will we take in today?"

"Just under fifty million."

Lyft gasped inwardly when he heard that.

"Perfect, more than enough. We will have an excess to be used toward future operations."

Ali said, "Ahman, this operation's not even close to that figure. Why do we need so much at this point?"

"We have multiple operations going on around the globe. Surely you knew we were not engaging in a one-shot jihad? Please, have more faith than that."

Ah, Lyft thought. *Ali's really not the head and horns. He's just a paunchy pawn.*

"The council has dictated that we expand our operations. Fundraising such as yours is integral to the process. You are an extremely valuable component of this most holy movement. In fact, you have been looked upon with great favor, some believing you should be in line for succession."

Ali visibly flushed.

That's right, Ahman, thought Lyft. *Massage his ego into holy fervor. This insecure bastard needs all the praise he can get.*

"Money is the key. All the devoutness in the world is useless without the prime mover of finance. We are most appreciative of your efforts. You will be awarded accordingly. How is the situation in the Wakhan?"

"We have sent the signal. We are waiting on confirmation of action."

"From where was the signal sent?"

"From a moving boat on the river."

"Excellent, more difficult to trace that way."

But not impossible, chuckled Lyft.

"We should have had confirmation by now that the plant no longer exists. It worries me that your son could have been found out before he was able to take action. Elimination of that plant will send several countries into orbit. We need to know soon if he was successful."

"I will let you know as soon as we hear something."

With that, Lyft had a thought. He would need access to a phone soon.

Ali inquired, "So what are these other operations you have spoken about?"

"Not yours to know, old friend. The less you know, the more shielded you are from inquiry. You are indispensable. We can't have you risking suspicion and perhaps subsequent torture under government scrutiny. You are not trained for such duress. Better leave that to those who are willing to make the ultimate sacrifice by sowing disinformation while enduring extreme physical discomfort."

"Yes, I see your point. I do not believe I would do well under such circumstances."

Lyft thought, *No, you wouldn't, you dreg of humanity.*

"How would your son do, do you think?"

"I don't know. He's never been in such a situation. As a father, I do believe he would hold up."

"Let us hope we do not have to find out."

"Yes," said Ali, "let us hope."

The lieutenant informed Ali, "You understand there is another council meeting next month. You are not required to be there.

However, the funds are. Our council intermediary, whom you know, Brihamm, has asked how to deal with the checks not clearing in time to be liquid. You know it takes more than ten business days for checks of this magnitude to clear."

"You need not worry. I have set up a dummy corporation in anticipation of just such an eventuality. All that needs to be done is for you and I to go to the bank where we make you a signatory on the account. Once that occurs, you can write checks to your heart's content, as I will ensure there is the equivalent amount of money in the dummy account relative to what has been raised here."

"Ah, my good friend, you never cease to amaze me."

Nor me, thought Lyft.

"One minor contrivance I will need from you," spoke Ali softly. "This has nothing to do with trust, but everything to do with the tax authorities. I will need a dummy receipt for each expenditure you undertake. You know how it gets around here at audit time. I can't even escape the microscope. Goddamned Americans with their Sarbanes–Oxley Act. They infected the world with their new accounting rules. So, my good friend, we would be keeping each other out of hot water if we adhered to the dictates of our green-shaded, backroom number crunchers."

"I must compliment you on your thoroughness. I would not have thought about this situation."

"Well, most networks are investigated beginning with the money trail. If there is no trail, or the trail exhibits at best twisting convulsions leading nowhere, at least it gives us time to move finances, go offshore, wash the money, et cetera. So the better we're covered, the worse it is for the investigators. In this manner, we have the edge, and they don't."

"Bravo, my friend, bravo. You truly are a genius."

"Not so, only experienced in these matters. Just as you are in other matters. But thank you for the compliment. It means a great deal to me."

"You are most welcome."

Lyft could have slapped both of them, propelling them across the room into the bookcase. He needed more information. He did not want this conversation to end just yet. He sensed it was coming to a conclusion, which would not do at all. And he was going to need a phone soon, to get to Bashirin. He had an idea. He wasn't sure it would work, but it was worth a try. He looked down at the phone on the library desk. At its base, it had the house number etched into a white plate.

Thank the Lord they haven't gone digital yet, he mused. He then flew out of the library at near supersonic speed, seeking an errant cell phone. He looked madly around the patio, all the animated guests now in full-blown party mode, centering on one rather inebriated soul, teetering into his companion, and attempting to have a discussion on some matter of importance known only to him.

Must be non-Muslim, thought Lyft.

Lyft, always the expert pickpocket, riffled his pockets gingerly until he found the gentleman's cell phone in his outside pocket. He grabbed some decorative rice paper from one of the buffet areas unobserved and then zoomed to one hundred feet, punching in the house number as he went. Getting the paper ready to be crinkled for static interference to help disguise his voice, he tucked the phone under his neck, preparing himself for the ensuing conversation. The phone rang twice, and then a third time. *The men were sitting right next to the phone,* Lyft thought, cursing to himself, *why don't they pick it up?* He was relieved to hear Ali's voice just as the fifth ring began.

"Hello?"

"Let me speak to Ahman, if you please."

Crinkle, crinkle, static sounding somewhat like a washing machine.

"Certainly, he's right here."

Ali handed the phone to Ahman.

"Yes, may I help you?"

"This is Brihamm. We will need Ali at the council meeting. Tell him the location. And ensure that he is there, Ahman," Lyft said curtly, attempting to make the command hold just a touch of a threat in case Ahman found himself tempted to argue with his new directive.

"As the council wishes."

The phone was hung up. Lyft ended the call, shut off the Nextel so that it would not operate on walkie mode, pocketed the phone, and then zipped at light speed back into the library as Ahman began speaking. He arrived just in time to hear Ahman saying, "It will be in Jakarta."

Lyft listened intently, memorizing the details, giving himself a mental high five for his ingenuity. The scam had worked, at least temporarily, until Ahman tried to independently contact Brihamm. He would have to work on that detail. Lyft wondered how coordinated the action at Georgetown was in conjunction with the council meeting. Coincidence or were the two events planned around each other? He figured evil serendipitous coalescence was at work, as the liquefied natural gas tankers had schedules and so did the council. The action planned against the tankers was the variable frosting.

The guests began entering the library. Payments ensued, large checks written from larded bank accounts. Lyft thought he'd better use the cell phone quickly, so he went back out over the patio and called Bashirin, telling him in detail what had transpired. They both agreed that Lyft should attend the council meeting in Jakarta. Salvo had determined that the tankers were under American control, so the alert of the impending plot passed through the U.S. Navy had been painless. The decision was made to keep to the schedule heavily protected and on full alert at all times. Bashirin was adamant that they dig out the roots of this cell to determine if the connection was worldwide or confined to Indonesia. Lyft couldn't have agreed more. Lyft also asked what had occurred with Ali Junior while he'd been investigating Ali Senior. Bashirin related that when Ali went to investigate why the various charges had not released, he was nabbed, being placed into confinement at two o'clock on the morning Lyft had departed.

Lyft said, "I need his signal sent to his father that the plant was blown to pieces. Do you know what that signal was?"

"As a matter of fact, yes we do. It was to be three calls to the library phone, which is on a separate line from those of the rest of the house. The first call was to be two rings, the second three rings, and the third two more rings, with no conversation on any of the calls. This would tell his father that all went as planned."

"So you have Ali's phone?"

"Yes, we do. All we need is the library number."

Lyft gave him the number and assured him that an immediate conveyance of the signal would complete the evening for "two incarnations of evil whose souls were about to be tortured for eternity."

Bashirin replied, "Think no more about it. I will place it immediately after we conclude."

"So far, so good. I will call you when I can."

"Good luck, my little friend. Stay out of harm's way. Jeff sends you his very best, as do we all."

"Likewise."

This time, Lyft kept the phone on. He propelled himself back into the library, where the pilfered gentleman was in the process of taking his checkbook out of his inside pocket. Lyft deleted the calls and then, unobserved, gently placed the cell phone back into the same pocket where it previously resided, just as the phone on the desk rang twice. Both Ali and Ahman looked expectantly at the phone, and Ali pressed his hands together, looking skyward. Ahman looked with narrowed eyes toward his fat companion, swallowing heavily. When the phone went silent after two rings, Ali smiled. A few seconds later, three rings pealed, and then a short time later, two more. Ali bowed, as if saying a quick silent prayer. Then he nodded at Ahman. Ahman stood and addressed the audience still in the room.

"My friends, Allah has bestowed great beneficence upon us. We have just had great success in buying out an international company up north, over which we have just now taken total control. May Allah be blessed, and may we continue with our successes."

Lyft's drunken friend, spewing his inebriated breath over Ahman and Ali, who were mightily offended by being this close to alcohol, chortled, "Well, let's celebrate."

Lyft thought he had celebrated quite enough, until he changed the one to a seven with six zeros after it on the check.

Go ahead, you jackass, thought Lyft. *Add another three zeros onto it, and really break the bank.*

In spite of being highly offended by his behavior, both Ali and

Ahman fawned over the gentleman as if he were their long-lost brother. Lyft thought he was going to be ill in the wastebasket next to the desk.

Finally, the last of the guests left. Ahman and Ali totaled up the amount, in excess of sixty million U.S. dollars.

What a fund raiser, thought Lyft. *Too bad they don't give it to their own tsunami survivors over in Aceh.*

Lyft felt there was little else he could do here, except plague the wait staff with another run at the buffet. Never one for leftovers, he decided he'd had enough of the entrées but that perhaps it was time for a little dessert and champagne. As the bartenders were consolidating their inventory, their attention was distracted from the ice buckets, the center of Lyft's attention. Not one in these circumstances for niceties, Lyft upended one bottle of Dom that had only been slightly depleted by one glass, finishing it off with a large belch that everyone in the patio heard. All looked at each other, thinking the other had done it, not realizing that more was on the way.

Lyft spied the two-tiered cake on a table in the corner of the patio, surrounded by candles. He went over, taking several slices and cramming them into this mouth. By this time, his belly was distended from all the varieties of food he had consumed. He was decidedly uncomfortable, so he let out a booming fart that blew some of the candles out around the cake. One of the girls servicing the buffet area nearby screamed. All turned their attention to her, thinking perhaps she was the culprit. Sensing their accusations, she shook her head no, it wasn't her. Lyft decided he'd had enough fun for one night, so he zoomed over to the headwaiter, wrapped his arms around him, and gave him a big kiss on the cheek. The waiter screamed that an agent of Satan had him in his grip, and dear Allah, what offense had he committed to be subject to this?

As the tortured waiter was running around the patio wild-eyed and gesticulating and shouting to anyone who would listen, Lyft exited the scene, thinking of how he should deal with Brihamm. As he was slightly tired from his exertions, he decided to go back to the boat in Lama, where he would sleep on top of the wheelhouse to give it some thought. He'd come up with a plan. He always did.

CHAPTER NINE

Mid-Atlantic Ridge at the Intersection of the South American and Antarctic Plates

Even though Lyft thought he could not find enough skilled labor to undertake another plant, somehow, probably through sheer bribery via any number of corporate storefronts he utilized, the second plant was taking shape. It was a recycler, although a large one. Its platform was in place, while the plant was rapidly being constructed on top of it. The same principle was employed here as in the oil industry—time on, time off. Here it was thirty days straight with one week off. Lyft was a tough taskmaster, but he knew what was at stake.

Again, there was a military presence on board. Colonel Spencer Jackman of the U.S. Air Force was in command of the project's security. In addition, Jackman held a PhD in meteorology, weather being his primary concern more than the threat of terrorism, as there was no landmass for thousands of miles. Weather there was borne along the currents from Cape Horn, converging with storms brewed in the Antarctic, mixing with the currents flowing off the coast of Africa. It was a volatile mix, sometimes generating rogue waves one hundred feet high that had swallowed tankers and container ships, leaving no trace.

Sometimes Jackman wondered why this location had been

chosen for the project. He knew the answer, but he had little faith in the longevity of the plant, knowing full well what weather conditions could be in the area. He remembered the extensive damage done to the oil rigs by hurricanes in the Gulf of Mexico in the summer and fall of 2005. It took six months to get those back into production. He speculated on their chances of survival if a megastorm blew up from Antarctica.

Lyft had anticipated such an eventuality, however. As monstrous a project as it was, the whole thing could be moved in the event of a disastrous storm. It was the only rig in the world that was self-propelled. It could do five knots, seven with the current, which would transport the rig out of harm's way toward Africa. And there was the backup of the largest platform ship in the world, which could either tow the entire rig or lift only the plant onto its deck for transport. The key was for Jackman to predict the weather patterns accurately and succinctly in time for the system to be activated and then the move implemented. The survival of the project depended on it.

As with many new advanced technologies, the current ability of the platform to move was hampered by technical difficulties. So for the time being, they were stationary, at the mercy of Mother Nature. One could only hope she was in a benevolent mood. As the seasons were reversed from the northern hemisphere, perhaps they could get through the next few temperate months without incident. Regardless, Jackman was on perpetual watch, with the help of satellite radar and continual communications with shipping plus ship-to-shore hourly updates with various weather services. If anything were brewing, he'd be one of the first to know about it.

The construction of the plant had gone smoothly over the past few months. In spite of the apparent success of the construction and the amiability of the crew and construction workers, something was niggling at the back of Jackman's mind. He could not place it, couldn't identify it, had no reason to have it, yet it was there, day and night. He could not shake the feeling of the thunderhead beginning to block out the sun. It was what kept him constantly alert. He'd had this feeling before, often. His intuition had served him well. Without it, he would have ceased to exist five times over.

So he waited for the inevitable. He just wished he knew what form it would take.

The weather was perfect, perhaps too perfect for this time of year. Maybe that was it: it was too warm for this latitude. In his mind, all the talk about global warming was wasted. He had seen it begin years ago when he was stationed in Alaska as the permafrost deteriorated. No one listened then, and no one was listening now. All it took to make him a believer in permafrost deterioration was a home plunging into a sinkhole one summer as a robin took flight nearby. Native Alaskans had no word for the bird, as it had never appeared there before. Now it was commonplace to see them arrive in June. The home, well, it was a total loss, along with all its contents. The State of Alaska fully reimbursed the homeowner, probably because of the guilt it felt in contributing to the home's demise by all the oil it was pumping south.

Talk about the circle completed, he thought. *Oh well, what the hell. Even if we decide to get off our fat asses, China and India will bring us down along with the other developing countries right behind them. I can smell the sour crude from here.*

As these happy thoughts pinballed in Jackman's head while he sat at his well-equipped console, facing south, overlooking the sea several hundred feet above its surface, the ship to shore crackled. It was from the icebreaker *Atlantis* operating in the Antarctic on a geological survey.

"To the platform Abzu 2, we have extensive calving, excessive iceberg activity to our south. Be advised. Over."

"Roger, *Atlantis*, read you loud and clear. Thanks for the heads-up. Over and out."

"Over and out."

Jackman placed a call to a secure NASA number in Washington DC, relating the transmission. NASA said they'd get their satellites on it ASAP. They'd call him back with any unusual activity. He said he had nowhere to go, so he'd wait for the return call. There was a chuckle on the other end of the line as the phone disconnected.

The ship was over fifteen hundred miles to the southeast, so Jackman was not particularly worried about any ice moving his way. Most of it got caught up in currents within its confines, swirling about, banging into other ice, until reduced in size and either reattached or floated aimlessly into warmer currents, where it melted. Admittedly, large pieces on the edge of the ice shelves could be of concern, but the chances of those breaking off with the intent of a direct hit on the platform were negligible.

As Jackman mused on his status as a bull's-eye, the phone jangled. It was his close friend, Ross Shellfing, NASA's head meteorologist.

"Spence?"

"Yeah, Ross, how you doing? Good to hear from you."

"Likewise. Although I wish I had better news."

The hair on Jackman's neck rose.

"We've got something of concern on the most recent satellite image of the shelf near your position."

"By my position, you mean due south?"

"Ten degrees east, but close enough for concern."

"Huh—let me have what you've got."

"We'll send you the image on your screen via satellite so that you can see for yourself. A substantial portion of the shelf has broken off, probably due to the inordinately warm weather we've had over the past two years."

"How large is substantial?"

"Over three thousand square miles."

"Mother of God, that's double the size of Rhode Island."

He leaned forward, peering out the window, as if willing it to loom in the distance.

"True, or larger than the square mileage of Jamaica, if you wanted to save Rhode Island from continual bashing."

"Why didn't *Atlantis* report this?"

"Because it's so large, they missed it. The only way to tell if something like this has occurred is by satellite. To get the magnitude of the event, this is the largest floating object on Earth right now. It will have its own weather system, it's so large. It's over one hundred miles long, about ten miles wide, and about three hundred feet off the ocean's surface."

"And of course, you called because you feel it could be headed toward me."

"Don't really know yet. The split just occurred, so there's little movement as of now. We need to do some research relative to currents, wind speeds, ice movements—you name it, we'll do it. But that will take a while. Then we need to redo our calculations to ensure accuracy. We'll get back to you in a week or so with more info. Meanwhile, we'll beam the image to you so you can see what you're potentially up against."

"Thanks. Your good work is greatly appreciated, my friend."

At that moment, the image appeared on the Sony screen to the right, hung overhead. At Jackman's disposal was an array of electronic equipment in the console, with multiple screens hung around the room, his pride and joy. Made for NASA, they were of the highest resolution. He leaned back in his brown leather swivel seat, not believing the size of the berg. It wasn't a berg, it was a floating country. Jackman wondered if there was any wildlife stranded on it. Hopefully, they felt the jolt when it separated and abandoned ship. He studied the image, shaped in the form of a longneck wine bottle, which was good news, because the neck would have the potential of breaking off, rendering the berg less potent. As he mused over the image, he realized there was little he could do but wait for NASA to call back. And that would take a while.

He exited the console room, ensuring he went down the galvanized narrow stairs backward to the next level, holding the two railings with both hands. Too many individuals had pitched forward through the years in similar circumstances, thinking their balance to be in order at the first step, so safety regulations now dictated backward movement on one-man stairs.

As he leaned against a rail on the lower level, he noted with satisfaction that construction was on schedule. He saw the foremen directing giant PVC tubing via a huge crane, which would shield the piping for the liquid nitrogen eventually to be pumped through it. As he overlooked an anthill of activity, he placed the worry about the iceberg in the back of his mind. He had other things to concentrate on. The berg would just have to melt in place for a while, or so he hoped.

CHAPTER TEN

Barge off Pulau Simeulue

Colonel Ivan Minsky hated the heat. He'd rather be in Chechnya, fighting terrorists. As commander in chief of the final link in Lyft's scheme, he knew his responsibilities and was not about to shirk them. But this heat was ridiculous. Even this far out at sea, there were few breezes to ease a tortured soul who desperately missed the low humidity of the northern Russian climes. Boredom was not really a problem, although he missed carousing with his best friend, Bashirin. There was enough to do to ensure the project's completion. They had thwarted one pirate attempt, were constantly on the alert for more attacks, and had a daunting schedule to keep.

The recycler composed of four surplus U.S. Army barges, which Minsky and crew now called home, was arguably the most innovative island ever constructed. Each barge was one hundred fifty feet long and fifty feet wide. The barges were pinioned together with giant bolts so that the entire structure acted as one large vessel in the swells. Off to the right, independent of the island, was the newest the Army had to offer, a U.S. Army barge derrick, outfitted with a crane capable of lifting an Abrams battle tank off a Navy cargo ship. Two hundred feet long, eighty feet at the beam, it had accommodations for a crew of thirteen enlisted and two warrant officers. Equipped with a full galley, mess hall, staterooms, a hospital, a laundry, and a state-of-the-art communications system, it was as if the vessel had been placed there for R & R, but Minsky knew better. When the time came, it would do the heavy lifting, securing the synthetic tunnel from the seabed to the nitrogen recycler on the barge system.

Of particular note, spaced around the barge perimeters were sixteen innocuous compartments flush with the deck. On command, elevator systems popped up through the deck circumference, raising sixteen platforms. On each was situated a fifty-caliber Gatling gun, capable of ripping anything less than a fully armored ship out of the water within a nautical mile.

From his elevated office on the rear of barge number two, Minsky could see the galvanized steel structure of the recycling plant begin to take shape. He noted the Dewars standing upright, patiently awaiting impregnation. He looked over at the tugboat next to the giant barge, seeing little activity, probably, he thought, due to the excessive heat. *Just as well*, he mused. *They'll all be busy soon enough.*

In his forties, stocky, exhibiting a closely cropped crew cut, a muscular build, and a square face that showed a ready sense of humor, Minsky was a true professional. He was like Bashirin, only slightly lighter on his feet, as his good friend had emptied too many distilleries of his favorite clear refreshment. He was one of the select few who had been recruited by Uncle Sam, able to retain their status, yet keep a full-time commission along with their paychecks from their native countries. A true double-dipper, Minsky understood his allegiance to two paymasters. Like Bashirin, he had no problem with that, as long as the larger dogs refrained from showing their true dispositions by exercising what they thought to be their territorial imperatives. There were too few fire hydrants to go around these days, so the fewer raised legs, the better.

Minsky was getting bored. It was too quiet for him. Having met Jackman several times, he decided to call him on the ship to shore to see what was up at fifteen degrees south, sixty-five degrees west.

He radioed, "Yo, Jack, this is Minsk, what's up?"

The reply, "The usual, man. What's up wit' yous?"

"Hey, I like the Brooklynese. Pretty quiet here. Maybe too quiet, you get my drift?"

"Yeah, same here. Somethin' ain't right, ya know? I got this hairy feelin' on the back of my neck, like a premonition or somethin' that won't go away. Like a bad dream, ya know?"

"Yeah, I got the same thing buggin' me. Somethin's gonna blow, but I'll be damned what. Just a bad feelin' I got," Minsky said, chuckling at his rough version of Russia meets New York, happy to hear Jackman's voice. "Plus, it's hotter than hell here."

Dropping the accent, his friend replied, "Well, we're not as warm as you guys, but it's warmer than average here as well. How hot is it there?"

Minsky peeked out his window at the thermometer secured to his office window frame. "One hundred two in the shade. And we're fifty miles out."

"Jeez, that is hot. It's fifty degrees here, but it should be thirty."

"You make me envious, my friend."

Jackman replied as the phone crackled in Minsky's ear, forcing him to hold it away from his head for a moment, "True, it's more comfortable here, but you know, we're really screwing up this planet. Do you have grandchildren?"

"Not yet, but we're hoping."

"Well, when they come along and grow up, they will see a very changed world, my friend, from what we know today."

"You're right. And it may not be pretty."

"The North and South Poles maybe, but not anywhere else."

"Can you imagine? The equator being one hundred fifty degrees or worse on a good day, and the poles being temperate? The poles would then get crowded and look like Moscow or New York."

Jackman chuckled into his receiver. "Now, is that a good or a bad thing?"

"We'll just have to wait and find out."

"Heard you had a little incident several weeks ago."

"Yes, but sorted out quickly. You know, our mutual friend is a dynamo, and it takes little to piss him off if he feels his friends are threatened. I would hate to be on his bad side."

"Me too. He's a whirlwind. I've heard stories from Bashirin about him, and I do believe they are all too true."

"After what I saw, I'd believe anything."

"Well, my friend, I need to sign off. Got to check on an iceberg that broke off the continent some time ago."

Minsky laughed. "Why don't you send it here? We could use a little air-conditioning."

"I'll do that and send you the bill for delivery while I'm at it. You know, iceberg delivery these days isn't cheap."

Minsky guffawed. "How big's this thing you're tracking?"

"About double the square mileage of Jamaica."

"Whoa. That's huge."

"Exactly why we're tracking it. We hope it breaks up before it becomes a problem."

"Man, all that ice and no vodka."

"Who are you kidding? We have plenty of vodka here. If it gets too close, I'll know how to put it to good use. I'll call you to ensure I'm making only the most correct of Russian martinis."

"Yeah, you do that. But I'll give you a hint on that score. Drill a hole in berg, insert vodka bottle. When appropriately chilled, pull out bottle, and drink. Forget glass. It is superfluous."

Minsky howled, noting the sweating, shirtless workers on the barge below, struggling with some pipe being lifted by a small crane threatening to disengage from its chain. How he wished he could offer them his favorite refreshment.

Jackman laughed audibly. "My kind of martini."

"Take care, my friend. Let's hear from you often."

"Will do. Keep the pirates at bay."

"Roger that, over and out."

"Over and out."

Minsky signed off feeling that, even though it was good to have human company for a short while over the radio, the sense of imminent peril hadn't dissipated. He was too professional to ignore his intuition, so he'd stay alert to stay alive. He'd keep a sharp lookout, and sleep be damned.

He decided to take a break, and as he made his way over to the crew-quarters barge, he noted numerous sea skaters on the surface of the ocean.

Huh, he thought.

It was the first time he'd seen skaters out this far. Normally they stayed closer to shore. He wondered why. He looked closer, and as far as he could see, the glassy surface water was covered in black by the insects riding gently on the swells. Not overly alarmed, as they did not bite, it was more curiosity than anything else that prompted him to go down to the barge to get a closer look at their activity. Having seen them previously nearer to shore, he noted no change in their apparently random routine, other than the fact that there were millions upon millions of them swarming around the barges.

I wonder what they know that I don't, he thought.

He would soon find out.

CHAPTER ELEVEN

Original Selkirk's Island, Four Hundred Miles off the Coast of Chile, Near the Juncture of the Nazca and South American Plates

When Lyft said that the other major plant was to be built in South America, we all thought that meant the mainland. We should have known better. One of his tenets was to not only pick the appropriate latitude but to place the location away from prying eyes. Even though the island, once known as Selkirk's Island, had around seven hundred inhabitants, they were mostly hardworking fisherman who kept to themselves and wanted to stay that way.

This is the island the Chilean government renamed Robinson Crusoe's Island in 1966 to help promote tourism. Although many believe Robinson Crusoe to have been an authentic historical character, he was made famous in the fictional novel written by Daniel Defoe in 1719.

In 1574, Juan Fernandez, an explorer out of Peru, stumbled on three islands as he was sailing west to avoid the south winds. He named them Santa Clara and Santa Cecilia; no one knows why he did not name the third island in the chain. Later, the islands were renamed, Mas a Tierra, "closer to land," Mas Afuera, "farther from land," and the original Isla Santa Clara.

In 1704, a Scotsman, Alexander Selkirk, aboard the ship *Cinque Ports*, which was cruising in the area, believed the vessel to be unseaworthy and demanded to be let off on Mas a Tierra. As the captain had had enough of what he deemed to be an unbalanced individual, he obliged, leaving Selkirk on the island with little except a gun, a knife, a hatchet, navigation books, a Bible, and three days' rations. He remained there until almost five years later, when he was discovered by the *Duke*, captained by Woodes Rogers. He was found half starved, clothed in skins, and unable to converse in his native language. It was fortunate he was found still able to be identified, as William Dampler was on the ship that had originally let him off and also on the voyage that found him, probably wanting to check to see if he was still alive. From then on, the island was referred to as Selkirk's in honor of the fact that Alexander survived his ordeal.

One of the attributes of the island was that it was inhabited by wild goats and chickens. It also had an abundance of fresh water available, so it became a convenient stop for pirates needing to replenish their vessels on raids to and from the coasts of Chile and Peru. For the past three hundred years to the present, rumors have abounded of buried treasure on the island, the most notorious of which was known as the Treasure of Vera Cruz, supposedly consisting of eight hundred bags of gold, assortments of Incan and Aztec gold statues, ten papal rings, and an assortment of jewelry. The unsubstantiated rumor centered around General Don Juan Ubilla y Echeverria, the general of the Spanish fleet stationed in Vera Cruz, Mexico, who decided to plunder the Bourbon dynasty in Mexico after the Spanish War of Succession. Thinking this to be his retirement plan, the story went that he stole eighty barrels of gold and jewels, burying them on Mas a Tierra.

One of the hurdles Lyft had in convincing the Chilean authorities to locate the plant on the island was that the entire archipelago had been a national park since 1935. But through Lyft's subliminal messaging while negotiating through high-level intermediaries, the Chilean authorities became convinced of the merits of the Abzu Project, finally giving permission to build, but only if they had oversight of the project with the eventual construction contracts pertaining to the plant proper being signed with Chilean companies. Lyft and company agreed, while stressing the timetables that had to be met.

Initial construction had begun, with the small dirt runway of an airport being upgraded along with a dirt road to the plant site being built, as the stirrings of the foundation of the workers' structures began to manifest themselves above ground level a mile away from the runway. Lyft's thoughts of treasure were of another type, mainly finishing the plant to regale in the greatest treasure of all, the return of Mother Earth to good health.

Colonel Rodrigo Alvarez, U.S. Army Corps of Engineers, of Spanish descent but decidedly American in every way, chafed at the Chilean oversight imposed upon him by the construction agreement. His piercing gray eyes squinted as his wiry five-foot-eleven frame tensed with the thought of that fat bastard, General Ricardo Emillio Estavez of the Chilean Army, coming weekly to check in, note the progress, and then leave. According to the agreement, Alvarez had to submit an after-action report daily to update Estavez on each day's activities. He religiously did so. He doubted Estavez ever read them. Estavez, having bought into the rumor mill long ago, came to the island to see if Alvarez had hit upon any buried treasure. Never seeing any hint of that, he feigned interest in the project, asking cursory questions, and then left on his private plane. One wondered how a general in the Chilean army was able to afford a private plane. Alvarez decided he did not want to know.

Alvarez had also heard rumors about buried treasure on the island. Being a practical individual, he doubted any of them had merit. However, if he stumbled on any, he sure as hell wasn't going to tell Estavez about it. He had already decided that if anything occurred of an unusual nature, treasure or anything else, he'd radio Bashirin to keep it within channels. Bashirin, as Abzu Project manager, could then do with the information what he wished. But Alvarez was damned if he was directly going to aggrandize Estavez to the tune of a penny. He figured the Chilean general had amassed enough illicit funds.

Work was beginning on the section designed for the living

quarters of those who would be servicing the plant. The construction crew was temporarily living in sparse but comfortable Quonset huts. Smaller than the Wakhan operation, there would not need to be as many units. Although a Chilean company had the rights to eventually build the plant, the United States retained the right to build the living quarters with a U.S. crew. Lyft and all did not want bugs built into the walls of the housing units.

Master Sergeant Mack Henley was a twenty-year Army veteran, having seen it all, or so he thought. He was overseeing the digging of the foundation of the living quarters approximately five hundred yards from the plant site on a thirty-foot rise overlooking a beautiful pebbled cove. His crew was on a much-deserved break. It being a warm day, they were on the beach sampling the water, which was in the fifty-five degree range, fine for seals, but chilly against human flesh. Some of the men went in anyway, emitting howls of agony. He smiled as he looked down upon the self-torturous activity, happy that he was not part of the goose-fleshed group.

As he turned back to the site, something caught his eye, a glint in the dirt reflected from the sun. He walked over to it, scraped the dirt off it, and exclaimed, "Well, I'll be damned. What have we here?"

It looked like an iron bar, caked with dirt and grime. He could not make anything out on it, so he decided to take it back to his hut and clean it up. One edge showed a yellowish hue, but he had already discounted the theory that it could be gold. Coins, yes, but gold bars, he didn't think so.

He went into his hut, ran some hot water over the piece, and scrubbed it with a soft abrasive sponge. The more he cleaned, the more excited he became. He knew he could never get it to museum standards here on the island, but perhaps he could clean it up enough to identify it. Sure enough, it was beginning to reveal itself. Holy Mother of God. It *was* a gold ingot, about seven inches long, a half-inch wide, and about a fourth of an inch thick. He was able to clean it enough to discern the letter "M" on the left side of the bar, which meant minted in Mexico City. Could they have stumbled on the Vera Cruz treasure? In spite of wanting to go excavate the site by himself, he knew he needed to get to Colonel Alvarez, as this was going to be bigger than just him. He was smart enough to understand the ramifications of letting out the word that treasure had been found on the island. Every man's dream, stumbling on the mother lode, and they were in a position to do nothing about it. He left the hut to find Alvarez, placing the now-dry ingot under his blanket at the foot of the bed.

He walked to the other hut, knocked, and was told to enter. He saw Colonel Alvarez wrapping up a conversation with Bashirin on the mobile satellite telephone.

"Yeah, Mack, what's up?"

"Sir, I think you'd better come to my hut. I found something at the foundation excavation that you're not gonna believe."

"What is it?"

"Sir, I was hoping you could tell me. I believe it to be a gold ingot, but I'm no expert, so I think you'd better take a good hard look to make sure I'm right."

"You know something? As exciting as it would be, I hope you're wrong, I really hope you're wrong, because if it's the real thing, all hell's going to break loose. Let's go take a look."

They walked over to Henley's hut. He uncovered the blanket at the foot of his bed, revealing the ingot, which appeared shinier now for some reason. The colonel sucked in his breath.

"It's an ingot all right."

Alvarez picked it up. "You obviously cleaned it up some. Did you see anything else over there?"

"No, sir. But then again, I didn't look very hard. I wanted to get this piece under cover before the crew came up from the beach, which won't be long, because they're freezing their asses off."

The colonel smiled. "Good thinking. Let's clean it a little more and take a closer look."

They used a mild soap with some warm water, letting the gold sit in the sink for a few minutes to loosen some of the embedded grit. This time, after scrubbing it gently with Henley's toothbrush, it began to show nicely.

Alvarez was looking for something on the far right of the ingot when he exclaimed, "Ah, there it is. Each ingot was stamped with the weight in Roman numerals and also with its worth in escudos. See, here we find the obverse side of an eight-escudo piece stamped on the ingot, along with the letter 'V,' which means five old Spanish ounces. This, my friend, is a hell of a find."

"Yes, sir, thank you, sir, but what do we do about it? I can't have the men continue to dig in the site knowing that there might be buried treasure there. They'll be coming up from the beach any minute."

"That's why I picked you, because you are a thinking sergeant. Tell the men I got a call today from that lard bucket, Estavez, telling me to hold off the foundation work due to some bureaucratic snafu. Leave everything as is at the site until you hear from me. Meanwhile, give me the ingot. I need to research it. Having been an avid coin collector when I was younger, I still have a passing interest in these things. If this is what I think it is, then there might very well be some loot buried around here. If so, we'll find it, but not on company time. I need to get to Bashirin on this."

"Yes, sir."

Henley handed the ingot to his colonel, whom he trusted implicitly.

The colonel felt the same about his sergeant. The two had been together for the past fifteen years, each having developed a profound respect for the other, in spite of the differences in rank.

Alvarez tucked the ingot inside his shirt under his belt loop. In spite of its size, it was slightly heavy. He wanted to ensure it did not protrude underneath his shirt as he walked back to his hut, so he bloused his shirt slightly so that it billowed out more than normal from the usual dress code.

He encountered no one on his walk back. He cleaned up the bar some more, finding royal seals and other initials, probably those of the assayer who produced the bar. This had to be from a treasure trove. He looked on the Internet, finding a duplicate of what he held in his hand, from a wreck in 1733 that had been salvaged by Treasure Salvors in 1973. So there was more than one bar around. He dated it by the information as being from the mid 1600s, minted under Philip IV's reign. It must be worth a small fortune. However, as exciting as this was and as hard as his heart was pumping, Alvarez had the intellectual acumen to realize that this could turn into a major publicity disaster if word got out. Construction would have to stop, and construction could not stop. There was something bigger than buried treasure at issue. If they were unsuccessful in their quest, there'd be no one around to discuss it, much less dig for it. He sat at his beaten-up oak field desk and picked up the telephone, placing a call to Bashirin.

Bashirin answered almost immediately on the ring tone.

"What, you miss me already? We just hung up fifteen minutes ago."

"Must be your winning personality. I just can't keep away."

Bashirin guffawed on the other end of the receiver.

"Colonel, we've got a situation here that just developed, and you need to hear about it."

Alvarez's tone was such that Bashirin became highly attentive.

"Yes, go ahead."

Alvarez took a breath, noting the dim light shadowing a cross on his pillow from one of the recessed window frames.

"As you know, we've begun the foundation living quarters for the maintenance folks who will eventually run the plant. While excavating today, Sergeant Mack Henley, you know Henley, found a gold ingot at the site. He and I cleaned it up, and it turns out it's from the reign of Philip IV. I've dated its production to somewhere in the mid 1600s."

"Rigo, paisan, are you telling me you've stumbled on buried treasure?"

"Yes, sir, I am. Have you ever heard of the Vera Cruz treasure?"

"No, can't say that I have."

"Well, it's long been believed that a Spanish general hid it here centuries ago after raiding the treasury in Mexico City, which was then under French domination. No one ever placed much credence in the story except dreamers and a lot of folks who don't like working for a living. I'm not saying we've come upon that particular treasure, but finding a gold ingot in the dirt is suspect. I would venture to say there is more, kind of like roaches. If you see one, you can bet there are more hiding behind the walls."

Alvarez stood and slapped at a moth, its flickering shadow irritating him, fluttering around one of the two naked lightbulbs hanging from the ceiling. The moth pitched onto the plywood floor as Alvarez grabbed a Kleenex, wiping the moth's cottony detritus from his fingers.

Bashirin laughed. "This is serious. If word of this gets out, there'll be hell to pay. First, construction will be stopped by the Chilean government, and then the infighting will begin as to whose jurisdiction it is. Then the islanders will get in on the act, figuring that the island and subsequently the treasure are theirs, and since the government never helped them out when they needed financing of their fishing fleet, then why should they return the favor by letting the government have the treasure? On top of that, there'll be the salvage company negotiating its share, and of course, the U.S. Army, which found the treasure in the first place. I can see it all now, with the press having a field day. The best thing would be to have never found it in the first place, but it's a little late for that."

"Yes, sir, it is."

"Well, one thing's for sure. You can't let anyone else know about this."

"Yes, sir, we understand that, although we were hoping we could dig it up on our own time."

"How do you control your crew?"

"Sir, they've been with me for years. I've trusted each one with my life on several occasions. We'll all be in this together."

Alvarez glanced at the ingot on his tightly blanketed olive green army cot centered by its black U.S. Army letters, almost in relief in the glancing light. The thought of royalty supported by service flitted into his mind and then out again as Bashirin queried, "What are you going to do with the treasure if you find it?"

Alvarez intoned, still glancing at the ingot, "I think it best if our mutual acquaintance solves that issue."

"You mean the acquaintance with the initials L. F.?"

"Yes, that mutual acquaintance."

"Good idea. Let me see if I can contact him somehow to get a resolution on this. Until then, I suggest a subterfuge so that you can stop excavation."

"Yes, sir, already implemented."

"Good man. I'll get back to you. Take a short vacation until you hear from me."

"Yes, sir, gladly. Over and out."

"Over and out."

Alvarez hung up and then stood, tucking the ingot back into his shirtwaist under his clothes. He left his hut, walking directly to Henley's. When he reached Henley's place, he was let in after a few knocks. Alvarez related the conversation he had with Bashirin, that they were to wait in place until further notice. The good news was that Bashirin had not emphatically said no to eventual further hunting. The bad news was that they had to wait for directions from higher up on the food chain before work of any type could continue. So they would wait, communing with nature, knowing that there, in all probability, was an empire's fortune beneath their feet.

CHAPTER TWELVE

Back in Belawan, Lyft slept on the wheelhouse roof until the blasting horn of a passing freighter propelled him a hundred feet into the air.

Damn, thought Lyft. *I ought to stuff some of that freight down their horn spout for that. And I was having such sweet dreams of Mrs. Faetels.*

Lyft's two companions had abandoned ship earlier, opting for more comfortable quarters in which to spend their evening. Lyft had noted no security present, but he felt, just the same, the vessel was probably being kept under some type of surveillance. Not that it mattered much to him in invisible mode, but he found it interesting that no active security was nearby. Lyft figured word had gotten around pertaining to severe penalties for anyone tampering with the boat.

It was a little early to call Bashirin, but Lyft felt he would need access to a phone sooner rather than later. Since it was four thirty in the morning, he decided to go back to the warehouse to do some snooping. Perhaps he would find an operable phone there. If not, he was sure he could find other ways to entertain himself.

Lyft flew leisurely back to the warehouse on the edge of the city. Located in its own block, it was a large structure made of wood and heavy sheet metal with several small doors for administrative entrances along with oversized padlocked doors allowing truck entry. Across the front of the building was printed "Sastroamidjojo Corporation" in large red letters, spanning nearly fifty feet. Lyft noted that nothing looked amiss, in spite of the previous evening's activity. There were no windows on the first level, but many opened on the second, which had screens.

So much for air-conditioning, thought Lyft.

He flew up to one of the screens, punching a hole in it large enough for him to pass through. No alarm sounded. He zoomed down to the office, seeing no blood or bodies on the floor. He figured Licia had informed Ali Senior about the commotion and that he had expeditiously cleansed the scene. He wondered how she had explained her rescue. In spite of an office cleanup, the glass was still broken, which meant the office was open. Lyft only hoped he could gain access to files that might tell him something.

He began looking around the office, which occupied a substantial space. It was air-conditioned, with the hot air spewing out onto the warehouse floor from the unit.

So much for the benefit of the workers, Lyft thought.

He clicked on the overhead light and turned off the air-conditioning so he could hear if someone outside the office approached. He found a wall of file drawers, which were, of course, locked. He went to the desk, which had been fortuitously left open in the haste of departure the evening prior. There in the top drawer was what he presumed to be a set of file keys. He took them, trying the master key, which subsequently opened all the drawers simultaneously.

"Aha," he said aloud. "Now we get down to it."

Not knowing where to begin, he decided to alphabetize his search, so he started with the As. Luckily for him, Licia, and whoever else ran this aspect of the operation, was detailed and organized. After ninety minutes of panning, he began to find gold. The Os, Ms, and Ss yielded the most information. "Operations" gave up the scope of activities in which Sastroamidjojo Corporation was involved. The file labeled "Munitions" told Lyft that there were one hundred cases of Stinger missiles in his current location. The "Shipping" file detailed to whom all the most recent shipments had been made, outlining the dates delivered along with those for future delivery. As Lyft had a selective photographic memory, he immediately discarded useless information, keeping in his head only that which was relevant toward any future operation pertaining to the Sastroamidjojo organization.

As he closed the last file drawer, ruminating on the best way to deal with the missile issue, he heard cars pull up outside the warehouse. He turned the air-conditioning back on while simultaneously clicking off the light. It was now six forty-five. He thought he'd literally hang around to see what was to transpire.

He was surprised to see fat Ali with the two slicks from the boat, Ali dressed in a sweat suit, which Lyft thought only too appropriate, and the other two in typical Armani casual. They had come in through the front administrative entrance, turned on the warehouse lights, and were now standing in front of the office.

Lyft mused, *I wonder if they dress in anything else or if that is as casual as they ever get. They've got plenty of blood on their hands, but I'll bet grease is too messy.*

Ali began to converse. "You understand, your crew threatened my wife. No one threatens my wife, or any member of my family."

"Yes, sir, we understand," said beige shirt. "They did not know that was your wife in the office last night."

"Regardless, what type of people take ax handles and go after a woman? I ask you that.

"My wife knew nothing of these proceedings. She thought your crew were hired thugs—it appears she was correct. Your henchman apparently never showed."

So it wasn't Licia who was supposed to have paid the crew. Lyft wondered who the culprit was.

"So your contact took the money and ran?" Ali pressed.

"Evidently," said maroon shirt, who had changed to navy, but would always remain maroon in Lyft's mind.

"Well, find him and deal with him."

"Yes, sir," they replied in unison.

Ali queried, "What did you do with the crew?"

"Shark food in the bay," said beige shirt.

"Appropriate punishment," Ali replied. "So no more screwups. Vet your new crew from top to bottom. Radical fundamentalists would be appropriate rather than the wharf rats you usually hire."

"We understand," said maroon shirt. "Unfortunately, it is difficult to hire fundamentalists from the interior with seafaring experience. Most true believers are not coastal dwellers."

"Well, find some crew you can trust, and find them fast. We've a schedule to keep. My superiors will not tolerate any mishaps, is that understood? It all flows downhill to the most expendable, so make sure your house is in order when we are ready to move. There will be no second chance in this operation. We keep to the appointed schedule."

"We understand," said beige shirt.

"You are dismissed."

"Yes, sir," they replied in unison.

They left the warehouse to attend to their ministrations. Ali unlocked the office, turned on the overhead, and sat at the desk, noting that it was unlocked. He took a key from his pocket and locked the center drawer, checking the other drawers to ensure the key had done its task. Satisfied, he looked around the office, seeing nothing out of order or in disarray. He then stood and exited the office with a notepad and pen in hand, waddling over to a mound of what appeared to be crates along the rear wall, covered with tarps. He peeked under the corner of one tarp, satisfied that all was in order.

Lyft mused, *I'll bet I know what those are.*

Ali then walked back to the office, looking down on the mess on the floor.

"We'll need to get this glass cleaned up and the window replaced today, first thing," he said aloud.

He scribbled on a notepad to remind himself to call an affiliated service company when he went back to his house. He got up, rattled a few file drawers to ensure they were locked, turned off the light and the air-conditioner, locked the office door, and then exited the building. Lyft heard the car drive off.

Now, how best to deal with these Stingers? thought Lyft. *Take the easy route and blow up the warehouse? Disassemble them in the crates, ensuring failure upon operation, and then wait for havoc to rain down on Ali's head? Tell Bashirin to mount an operation to liberate them?*

Lyft ruminated for several minutes before he hit upon the answer. It would take some time, but he felt the best way to accomplish the goal of interruption, discredit, and subsequent humiliation was to open each crate and remove the battery coolant units, or BCUs, which had to be inserted into the hand guards. Insertion of the units shot a stream of argon gas into the systems as well as a chemical energy charge that activated the acquisition indicators, the identification of friend or foe, and the antenna and which also gave the missiles power. Without the BCUs, the missiles were inoperable. Lyft got to work.

In one corner of the warehouse, there were drawers of hand tools. Lyft knew he had only a certain amount of time to accomplish this mission, as the warehouse probably opened at nine. He found a portable battery-operated heavy-duty screwdriver with a Philips head and began, as quickly as the screw head would turn, to remove the covers on the missile crates. He removed the BCUs from the crates, and then screwed the crate covers back on. As the inventory had already been opened and checked, he could only hope that no one would again decide to physically double check the interior components. He piled the BCUs behind the crates, having the thought to move them to one of the garbage dumpsters outside the building. He had made his way a quarter through the inventory, when he heard a car outside. He quickly took the BCUs out of the crate he was working on, placed the lid back on, and screwed it shut, just as Licia walked in through the administrative door. She had a minder with her who looked to Lyft like a one-man army. Lyft hid the screwdriver behind one of the crates.

I'd hate to meet that dude in a back alley somewhere, thought Lyft.

The minder was around six feet, six inches, heavily muscled, with a hard, shaven face. He had a turban on, making him look more like a Sikh than a Muslim, sporting a blue cotton sleeveless vest and lightweight drawstring canvas-colored trousers, along with open-toe sandals on his feet. He stood with folded arms outside Licia's office as she settled into her work routine.

Looks like Ali's not taking any more chances with his wife being alone, mused Lyft. *At least he's got that going for him, he cares for his spouse. I wonder how many men he's killed?*

Lyft changed the subject in his head, thinking that he needed a diversion to get them out of the warehouse so that he could finish his sabotage. He floated over to the tool area, where he spied a ten-pound hand sledge, just the thing for his rapidly developing plan. He picked it up and flew to the ceiling of the warehouse, almost directly over the minder, at a slight angle. He launched the sledge, hoping the minder didn't move as the missile sought its target. Bull's-eye. The sledge struck the man's toes with a sickening thud, breaking the big toe immediately and crushing several others. The minder screamed in agony, looking all around, unable to determine through the pain what had transpired. Licia jumped up from her desk, opened the door of the office, and rushed to the now prostrate bodyguard to determine the cause of the commotion. He was holding one leg around the knee in the air to relieve any pressure on his foot, rolling back and forth on the cement floor, ahhing in agony, unable to speak. Blood was dripping from his foot, staining the floor. Licia asked him what had happened, but he was mute in his pain, so she helped him to the Mercedes outside, locked the outside door and drove off.

"Well, finally some peace and quiet to complete the job," said Lyft aloud.

He sought out the screwdriver, continuing his work on the rest of the crates, figuring he had maybe another hour at most before reinforcements arrived. He was ten minutes short. He had completed 50 percent of the crates when he heard a rush of vehicles skidding to a halt amid squeals of brakes. Paramilitary shouts, boots on the ground, rushing through the doorways, setting up an inside perimeter throughout the warehouse. What they found was nothing. Lyft had hidden the BCUs in the rear of the warehouse under tarps that housed a plethora of paraphernalia. Even if Ali's guard unit had looked there, they would never discern what was hidden.

The police commander, evidently a colonel in the makeshift unit, was perplexed, as he and several squads of men looked high and low to find the source of the attack on the Sikh. They found nothing other than the sledge, still in position on the cement floor, where it had landed resoundingly on the foot of the guard. This time, Lyft hid the screwdriver on a beam overhead, sensing that a more than perfunctory search would reveal it. He was glad he did. The squads were going between the crates in the hope of flushing out any perpetrator hiding in the alleys. They found nothing amiss, reporting such to their commander.

"This sledge," he commented to no one in particular. "This sledge must have fallen from a beam. That is the only explanation. We do not believe in ghosts, and tools do not launch themselves into space. We will check overhead."

Lyft had to act fast. He scooted to the beam, removed the screwdriver, tucked it under his tunic, also making it invisible, and flew at near sonic speed to the open tool drawer. He placed it back in its original position, gently shutting the drawer. He then took a larger sledgehammer leaning against the wall, again tucked it under his tunic in the back so that the part sticking out of his uniform would be shielded by his body, and flew to the beam, where he gently placed it unseen as the activity began to unfold on the floor of the warehouse. Then he watched in amusement as the commander attempted to operate the cherry picker. He told two of his men to climb onto the platform while he fiddled with the controls. They did as ordered, but not without trepidation, holding on for dear life as the commander jerked the platform up and down while they gripped the side rails, white knuckled and wild-eyed. Finally, he got the hang of it, as he positioned the platform so that the men could inspect the top of the beam. One shouted as he spied the sledgehammer, motioning for the commander to stop the vehicle. He reached over, grabbed onto the hammer, and set it on the platform while he motioned for the commander to continue the vehicle's forward motion. The beam yielded no more evidence, so the platform was lowered as all gathered around the vehicle to view the booty.

The commander felt vindicated when shown the tool, as his premise was proven true. Now he could report something concrete to his boss, Ali. He wouldn't have to deal with the supposition that spirits inhabited the warehouse, a premise supported by the Sikh who was now in the hospital, sedated, still mumbling about flying tools thrown by nefarious apparitions. The commander took the sledge as exhibit number one, gave the order for his troops to disperse, and left five men to guard Licia when she returned to the warehouse. She would come back in the early afternoon, as she had other errands to attend to, the commander informed his men, so they best be on the alert for her.

What a break, thought Lyft. As soon as the commander left, he'd deal with the guards, giving him enough time to finish the crates before noon. *C'mon, move it, get your men out of here, let's go. I've got work to do*, he shouted in his head.

Eventually, warehouse doors were shut, trucks were mounted, engines roared, and the convoy sped off, leaving the five troops inside the warehouse near the office.

It was now slightly past ten. Lyft was torn between trying to find a cell phone for a call to Bashirin or continuing his present task. He decided Bashirin could wait until noon. He was determined to finish by then. Knowing full well he had no time for his usual antics, although several fun-filled thoughts crossed his mind relative to how he could deal with the troops, he decided to dispatch them quickly. He picked up an ax handle that had been left behind by the crewmen threatening Licia, intending to quickly give each man a resounding whack behind either their left of right ear, whichever presented itself most readily. By the time he got to number three, it became more difficult, as the man attempted to shield himself from the onslaught, seeing his two fallen comrades at his feet. It was to no avail. He got it across the bridge of the nose and then on the back of the head. The other two began running for the door, but Lyft banged one of them on the shin, doubling him over. As his helmet fell to the floor, Lyft whacked him on the back of the head, rendering him immediately unconscious as his cheekbone crunched onto the cement. The final trooper was just reaching for the door when Lyft whacked his wrist. He let out a yelp of pain. Lyft poked the stub of the handle into the man's abdomen, doubling him over, and then the final resounding whack sent him into oblivion with his cohorts. Lyft dragged the men behind the crates where he could keep an eye on them in case they came to, but that would not be for an hour or so at least. He went to the tool drawer, retrieved the screwdriver, and went back to work.

He was on crate eighty when one of the trooper's walkies crackled. It was the commander, wanting to know the status quo. Lyft took the unit off the trooper's belt and disguised his voice as best as he could going from memory of the timbre of the combined voices of the troopers.

Lyft's walkie crackled, "Red dog, this is the commander, come in, over."

Lyft replied, "This is red dog, over."

"What is your status, over?"

"All quiet here, over."

"Good news. Be sharp on number one's return, over."

"Understood, over."

"This is blue dog, out."

"Red dog, over and out."

Lyft placed the walkie back into the trooper's belt, continuing on his mission. Finally, he completed all the crates. He took the BCUs, one hundred total, to two tarps, dumping them into small plastic garbage bins in the rear of the warehouse. He replaced the screwdriver in the tool drawer and then hid the ax handle under the extraneous equipment tarp in the rear of the building. He exited just as the troops were coming around with much groaning and exclamation. He went to the garbage bins, taking one at a time in his firmly taloned hands, shooting skyward, leveling off at ten thousand feet. He flew out over the ocean, where he dumped the contents of each bin, wincing at the potential for environmental damage, which panged him; however, he had little choice in the matter. He replaced the bins in their original positions in the rear of the warehouse and thought, *Now to find a phone.*

While Lyft was thinking of how to pilfer a phone, the Pulau Simeulue barge was under siege. Minsky had noted the skaters swarming around the barge in the relative calm, but now something more sinister began to manifest itself. Yellow-bellied sea snakes, millions of them, blanketed the ocean as far as Minsky could discern, separating the skaters as they surfaced, and then in a frenzy, heaved themselves onto the barge, writhing in agony as the sun scorched their skins. They were somehow cursed to always swim in reverse, too slow to nab an honest meal, thusly ambushing their prey with backward snaps of their elongated jaws. Normally borne on ocean currents, they are generally not strong swimmers, but not these. These were jet propelled by their own torture. As they catapulted onto the barge, flying backward through the air, coiling immediately upon impact, the sloshing sound of their twisting bodies made the crew think that their morphologic actions were of a creature with one mind and one body. The crew panicked and ran to higher structure.

Minsky came down a few notches on the second tier ladder to take a closer view and to perhaps determine what had caused the phenomenon. He made sure he did not get near any of the snapping jaws, as the snakes were highly poisonous. From his vantage point on the ladder, he could discern nothing, except more snakes piling onto the barge. One thing was for sure, he mused. Work at sea level was shut down until nature decided to right herself. He decided the situation warranted a call to Bashirin. He then pulled his walkie-talkie out of his belt and spoke to his crew chief.

"Walker, have the men fire up the grills. Looks like we're having an exotic entree tonight."

He made his way up the ladder to call Bashirin.

Lyft decided to go back to Ali's villa to scrounge up a cell phone, since he already knew the lay of the land there. It only took seconds to fly up the hill from the warehouse location, where he hovered over the house for a few moments, determining the best location for a phone. Then he saw Licia's unoccupied Mercedes in the courtyard. He zoomed down into the passenger seat through the window, which had been left open, no doubt due to the excessive heat, where he found Licia's cell phone propped up in the cup receptacle. He wondered at the lack of security exhibited, which he mused seemed always to be to his benefit, as he grabbed the phone and whisked to twenty-five hundred feet. Floating effortlessly, he placed his call to Bashirin.

"Well, my friend, seems like all hell's broken loose since our last communication," related Bashirin after their initial cordial exchanges.

"Oh? Do tell."

"Where to begin," Bashirin said with a sigh. Then he plunged in, telling Lyft first about Alvarez and Henley's discovery on Selkirk's, confirming that he believed the pair might have uncovered the treasure of Vera Cruz.

"You did the right thing, telling them to cease operations. What do you suggest?"

"Well, you know I am a true Communist when it comes to the interest of the people. Not all that bull malarkey with the central party whose rule we were under for nearly a century, but real, honest to goodness communism."

"Yes, we are not so far apart in that regard."

"Ahhh, a fellow traveler. So knowing my propensity to allow the people to retain what is rightly theirs, I suggest that we excavate the booty, transport the bounty to a location only known to you, have your people dispose of it, convert it to cash, make a pact with the island council, and then distribute such to the island populace in the form of a trust fund administered by the council to ensure their future. In this manner, no one would become excessively wealthy, no eyebrows would be raised, yet all would be secure for generations to come. You remember when the central government failed to grant loans to those sorely in need relative to poor fishing seasons due to five successive years of foul weather? People could not even launch their boats. The government thought no one would notice a small island in desperate need getting stiffed three hundred miles off the coast, but the islanders remember, brother, do they remember. One told Alvarez that if they had the means, they'd shoot down Estavez's helicopter. That's what they think of the central government."

"My friend, you're a man after my own heart. This was the tack I was hoping you'd take, and I'm in complete agreement. Due to the weight, we'll have to improvise a method to take the stuff from Selkirk's and get it to New York, where my good friend Isaac on Forty-Seventh Street has buyers waiting at private auction. Don't worry, these buyers exhibit the ultimate in discretion. They would do anything to remain anonymous, and we have helped them ensure that status, so we have built a tight bond of trust. We then place the proceeds in one of our separate accounts and subsequently make regular disbursements to the islanders for whom we will have established an account for their use only. This will be their money, but we will administer it. We will do so under the subterfuge of the agencies operating the plant, paying them a royalty for the use of their land. We will not give them so much as to undercut their livelihoods, but it will be enough so that they can live comfortably, buy new boats when needed, build a decent medical clinic, staff it, you know, provide for the basic necessities and then some. This way, no one will be the wiser, including the two central governments on the mainland.

"Suffice it to say, you have to admit it's pretty exciting to come upon such a find. My people will be overjoyed to view the excavation. We will seek out appropriate buyers, those who wish to remain anonymous from the public eye, who will readily pay top dollar for such a find of historical significance. I believe this will work out nicely. I anticipate your and Salvo's help in the transport."

"Not to worry."

"OK, what's next?"

Bashirin told Lyft about Jackman's iceberg, noting that it was a hundred feet off the surface of the ocean and concluding, "God knows what's underneath the surface."

"Whoa, that's huge."

"That's what I said."

"How far is it from his location?"

"About fifteen hundred miles."

"So no imminent danger?"

"Not yet."

"Hmmm," he mused, looking down, noting that Licia was still not in sight. "That warrants us keeping an eye on it."

"Jackman's having a friend at NASA track it every six hours, to determine sheer and current drift. So far, it appears to be hung up on obstacles on the bottom, but that won't last long. A berg, or should I say, a country, that large will eventually grind its way loose to gain independence in the open sea. The question is, will it remain intact? If not, we could have more to worry about, with the chances of a hit being multiplied by the number of calves it produces."

"Right, provided it or they head in another direction, and then not to worry. However, we may have to take some drastic action if we feel the Mid-Atlantic Ridge project is in jeopardy. You get my drift, so to speak?"

"Yes, sir, I do."

"So what other disasters have befallen us?"

Bashirin related Minsky's recent call.

"You're kidding."

"Not really. I wish I were. He says they are going to have a barbeque tonight, as he's heard that snake tastes a lot like chicken."

Lyft chuckled, "True, it does. It's not bad with a little salt, pepper, and seasoned salad dressing."

"He's worried that some unnatural occurrence is causing the upheaval. He also related to me that there are millions of skaters skimming along the ocean's surface near the barge, which he has never seen before. The snakes are interspersed among them but not trying to eat them. The reptiles are throwing themselves on the barge for no apparent reason."

"Radio him back, and tell him I believe there is a major earthquake or volcanic eruption in the making. He should be in no immediate danger located where he is, but I have seen similar behavior in varied species prior to such an event. He is in no danger of tsunami or lethal gas unless there is an eruption directly beneath him, which is unlikely. What I would like him to do is get into a helicopter to warn the local populace on Simeulue and on the western coast of Sumatra to get to higher ground immediately, as this cataclysm is upon us."

"Hang on while I get him on the radio."

Lyft waited until Bashirin came back on the line.

"He readily agreed. He's on his way. He's already contacted the civil authorities in both areas, who are taking him seriously, as they view him as a scientist engaged in similar research."

"I expect that within forty-eight hours, something's about to either heave or blow in that vicinity."

"Sounds like a bad meal."

Lyft laughed, "Let's hope if it's a volcano, it doesn't have a bad case of indigestion."

Bashirin guffawed into the phone, forcing Lyft to hold it out from his ear.

"So how's my good friend Jeff holding up? Has he found any more connections or other nefarious dealings?"

"None. He's almost through the alphabet. Should be done within the week. It's a very tedious job, but I must say, he's stuck with it in spite of the inherent boredom of file sifting. He's like a dog on a bone."

"Yes, trustworthy to the core. That's why I assigned him the task. He will let no stone go unturned. Tell him I'll see him soon. I may need him over here for a particular exercise I'm in the process of devising. How's Ali Junior doing?"

"Singing like a canary. Unfortunately, nothing useful to date, but we are forever hopeful. It may very well be that his father kept him in the dark as protection, in case an eventuality such as this caught up to him. We shall see. When you return, provided we have not produced anything more, perhaps you would consider a surreptitious interview, if you know what I mean."

"Yes, perhaps sooner than you think."

"So we dig for treasure, we keep an eye in the sky, and we have a Texas rattlesnake barbeque."

Lyft intoned, "I love an optimist, I really do. Is there nothing that depresses you?"

"Yes, when I run out of vodka, which has only occurred once. After that, I make sure there is, how you say, no strike two."

Lyft laughed at the mixed metaphor. He said, "All's well here." And he proceeded to relate the exploits of the past few days to

Bashirin. Lyft told him about the Stingers, which Bashirin thought was great theater. Lyft closed the call by saying, "Hopefully I'll be back relatively soon. However, this connection needs to be exposed and put away. So we'll see how it goes. Tell Jeff to stick with it."

Lyft flipped the phone shut, deciding that perhaps now was a good time to deal with Brihamm. He floated over to the library entrance from the patio, seeing the library vacant. Ali had evidently been at his desk recently, as the desk lamp was turned on. Lyft zipped over to desk, looking around for an address book, something with Brihamm's number on it. He was in the final drawer when he heard footfalls on the tiled corridor outside the library. He gently closed the desk drawer, hovering overhead, just as Ali walked into the room. The behemoth sat at his desk, noticing nothing amiss. Ali reached into his side pocket, pulling out a small black book. He placed it in the center drawer just as the headwaiter, who evidently doubled as the house butler, appeared in the doorway, relating to him that Licia was calling for him upstairs. He shut the drawer without locking it, no doubt intending to come back to do some paperwork after administering to his wife.

Bingo, thought Lyft. *No wonder I couldn't find it.*

Ali left the library, leaving Lyft to pilfer the drawer once more. He took out the book and thumbed through it as quickly as he was able, all the while cursing his talons for such a finite task. He found phone numbers for Brihamm and Ahman, memorized them, and then placed the book back as it was in the drawer. He then flew out of the library hovering at twenty-five hundred feet. Having previously memorized Ahman's voice pattern, he placed a call to Brihamm, saying he felt that, because of the excellent work Ali had done, he should be invited to the council meeting in Jakarta. Brihamm agreed. Then he called Ahman, pretending to be Brihamm, asking if everything was in order for Ali to attend the meeting. Ahman said yes, he would make sure Ali knew the location of the meeting, not to worry, all would be as planned. Lyft then erased the two phone numbers from the phone, clicked it off, and then shuttled to the car, placing the phone back in the cup holder. He chortled to himself that all was now in order. He only hoped the two would not discuss the phone calls before the meeting, but nothing was perfect in life.

As he exited over the property, he wondered if Ali and Licia ever checked their cell phone bills to pick out unauthorized numbers. He doubted it.

CHAPTER THIRTEEN

Barge Recycler Midway Between Bougainville and Tonga
Trenches, 250 Miles off the Northeast Coast of Australia

Colonel Justin Smythe, in spite of all his travels with the Australian Navy, from battling rebels in East Timor to catching pirates in the Malacca Straits, had never seen a vision such as that laid out before him. As far as he could discern, the sea was alive with every living creature imaginable, and some unimaginable. Shark fins sluiced through the tepid seas, sea snakes roiled the surface, every species of fish known to man was jumping through the brew, snapping back down to the surface, only to reappear, twisting in midair arabesques, encore after encore, needing no prodding from an audience. In several areas within five miles of the barge, columns of smoke had appeared, the sea bubbling forth a sulfuric haze that was beginning to smart Smythe's eyes, as he was downwind from two of the vents that had suddenly sprouted through the ocean's floor.

Hell on Earth, he thought. *We've finally done it, pushing Mother to the brink. No going back now. Only one way to go, get the project completed, and hope it's not too late.*

Located near the Solomon Islands, southeast of Papua, New Guinea, the barge was the final connector to the Selkirk's Island project off Chile. The water temperature should have been in the mid eighties Fahrenheit, but when Smythe dipped his hand in, he knew it was over one hundred degrees.

No wonder these creatures are in agony, flopping around as they are. They're being burned alive, he mused to himself. *It truly will be the end if all the oceans react this way. I can only hope this is localized.*

As he gazed out on the milieu, his question was answered. The entire nightmarish pageant was rapidly moving away from the barge, an amorphous slick upon the ocean's surface, until finally Smythe and his crew were left wondering if what they had just witnessed had actually occurred at all.

Like a forest fire, Smythe thought. *Nature's way of protecting her beasts is the heat shield approaching so that they can sense to flee. Only man is the fool to try to control it. All the other animals with any sense get the hell out. Unlike us. So we stay to try to fix our mess. Good luck.*

An eerie silence enveloped the barges. The sea was dead calm. Smythe almost wished for the return of the sea creatures to dispel the notion of an impending cataclysm. He felt relatively safe in his location. If there were a major undersea disruption, the barge could not be swamped by a tsunami. That could occur only if they were near land. If a major volcanic eruption occurred near them, they had filter masks and plenty of oxygen if needed. What did worry him was an eruption occurring directly beneath the project. He had heard about giant methane bubbles boiling up out of the sea as rents in the ocean floor opened up to release their burden into the atmosphere above, but he knew little about them.

Not unlike a giant fart after a glutinous banquet, Smythe thought with little amusement.

Suddenly, in the distance on the Australian side of the barge, there was thunderous explosion. An ash cloud began to form, with a pyroclastic flow spreading over the sea. To the right of the newly formed volcano, the sea seemed to be displaced for a few seconds, and then an upwelling followed by a popping roar ensued. When the shock wave hit the barge, it was so loud that several of the crews' eardrums were perforated. Smythe saw them bent kneed, holding their hands to their heads, blood streaming down the sides of their faces. He signaled other crew to help them to the infirmary.

As his attention was drawn back to the distance, hell had broken loose. The popping sound evidently was a gigantic methane bubble released from the ocean floor due to excessive seismic activity thousands of feet in the Earth's mantle. The methane had ignited at the volcano's cone, causing a massive fireball in the atmosphere, as if a midair nuclear explosion had been discharged. The air roiled in gargantuan greenish flame, extinguishing itself in seconds. Fortunately, the methane dissipated quickly with the flames lasting only as long as the fuel source was active. One of the more proactive crew had filmed it with his camera, so when Smythe reported it, he'd at least have an unofficial record to which he could refer, so no one could accuse him of being completely insane, although he realized he had to be slightly ajar to have accepted this assignment in the first place.

Now I know why the sea animals left in such a hurry. Good luck to them, Smythe thought.

Fortunately for the barges, the pyroclastic flow was heading directly south, parallel to the barge system. Behind it, the sea was superheated. Those sea creatures in a ten-foot water column under the surface not lucky enough to be able to flee its two-hundred-mile-an-hour onslaught would inevitably perish. Smythe felt sorry for them. He wondered how many more volcanic births he'd witness and if they on the barges were destined to be in the path. With what they had just witnessed, they realized they were lucky, as the volcano did not well up from the sea, but had erupted on a small island already formed. The action of the methane bubble was not enough to cause a tsunami, and there had been no major earthquakes that they could feel, so the coasts of Australia, North and South America, and Asia were safe for the moment. Even so, he needed to report this to NOAA for a potential tsunami alert, and then to Bashirin. He made his way to the office to do just that, hoping that he had time to place the calls before the sea exploded beneath him.

CHAPTER FOURTEEN

Selkirk's Island

Colonel Rodrigo Alvarez and Master Sergeant Mack Henley had wasted no time planning the unearthing of the riches of Vera Cruz. When the call for a "go" came in from Bashirin, they immediately assembled the men, relating to them what they would be about. Some of the men were incredulous, until Alvarez produced the ingot for all to see. Then there was genuine excitement.

"OK, men, OK, calm down. You all realize what we are up against here. No one can know, not even those at home you care so much about. This will be one of your toughest assignments yet. You must, and I repeat the word, *must*, treat this like a secret op. We've been on plenty of those before, so zipping your lips on this is no different."

Alvarez proceeded to outline in detail what could happen, indeed, what *would* happen, if anyone let slip that they had found the treasure of Vera Cruz. He also related to them exactly what the plan was to spirit it off the island to New York, where the appropriate parties would dispose of it and turn it into cash, subsequently setting up an account for the islanders. Most importantly, they did not want Estavez snooping around and spoiling the fun. Alvarez indicated that Estavez did not have the welfare of the islanders in mind. Neither did the Chilean government. As it was every man for himself, Estavez would use every means at his disposal to insure his own future. Alvarez outlined what had occurred between the central government and the islanders when they had almost starved during a sour fishing season. He figured he knew his men well enough to know that the Robin Hood scenario would be motivation enough for them to operate on a higher plane.

So with that in mind, Alvarez outlined a plan to excavate the treasure, while at the same time repositioning it into another underground site, just under the Earth's surface, in a cement tomb. Each piece excavated would be cleaned to the best of their ability, cataloged, segregated by category, and then packed in ammo crates, ready for further disinterment, and then transport. He appointed an excavation team, a washing detail, a cataloging team, and a packing crew. Henley would be in charge of all excavation, with the teams rotating once a week, so that everyone got a shot at discovery; Alvarez knew that would be half the fun. He told them they would have to work quickly, as Estavez eventually would be snooping around the site, wanting to know when work would again be progressing. But for now, Alvarez knew Estavez was content to dispense with the weekly visits to what he thought a miserable destination, reeking of fish alongside what he deemed to be an ignorant, surly populace.

Work at the site was progressing well. Within a week, they indeed had stumbled on the mother lode. They found kegs of coins in rotten barrels that disintegrated at the touch. They figured there were over one hundred fifty barrels of coins so far, each barrel containing about twenty-five hundred pieces. Some of the barrels had been packed with stone on top, probably passed off as ballast to ward off any suspicious interlopers years ago. Either that or to lighten each barrel, as the gold was so heavy it became cumbersome to move them about with each filled to the brim.

Most of the coins were the two-escudo piece, although here and there were a few half-escudos. They were shaped like blunt arrowheads, stamped with shields, or escutcheons. Each weighed between six and seven grams. Each coin was worth about five thousand U.S. dollars on the open market, so they had unearthed to date six hundred twenty-five million dollars worth of coins, not including the premium of the Vera Cruz trademark. They figured each barrel weighed between forty and seventy pounds, so it must have taken a while for the pirates to have transported it and then to have buried it.

They were excavating gingerly now with picks and shovels, having traded in heavier machinery for more exact implements. They were down about twenty feet when Henley yelled to Alvarez that he had struck something wooden. Alvarez came down into the pit, hoping they had finally found the coffins containing the gold ingots, as no more had turned up since their initial find. Excited, some of the men gathered 'round the top of what appeared to be a wooden crate. Then one of the other men digging to the right of Henley yelled that he had also struck something, and then another yelled the same. It seemed the pirates had a sense of order, as a pattern began to develop. Heavy wooden crates laid side by side on the bottom, barrels on top. All excitedly brushed off the top of the crates and then carefully dug around them, finally exposing them to the air. They were not overly large, but they were exceedingly heavy. Each was about two feet long and about a foot wide, perhaps eighteen inches deep. They had to pry shovels under the crates to get a handhold and then it took two men on each end to move them. They finally got one up to level ground above the pit, where they could get a better look in the sun at what hopefully would put an end to the excavation. There were ten crates in all, but for now, they would concentrate on this one. The crates were sealed in pine tar. Alvarez really did not want to destroy the crates in the process of opening them, as they were in extraordinarily good condition. He figured that whoever buried them knew what they were about with their preservation methods. He told Henley to go to his quarters and retrieve his bayonet. Henley came back in a few minutes with a freshly sharpened blade and handed it to Alvarez. Alvarez was impressed.

"You normally keep this so sharp?" he asked Henley.

"Yes, sir, I do. Might never know when you need it to stick a pig like Estavez."

The men roared at that one, as did Alvarez.

Alvarez said, tongue in cheek, "You know that you just disparaged a superior officer in front of the men."

"Yes, sir, I do. Perceptually, guilty as charged. In reality, there's only a uniform. The man in it doesn't qualify."

The men gave another roar along with a "hoo-hah" or two.

Alvarez just smiled. "Well," he said, "let's see what we've got here."

Alvarez began to saw the knife under the crate's lid. He was happy the blade was so honed, as the pitch had solidified, necessitating actually cutting through it rather than attempting to pry the lid open. Progress was slow, but finally, a sweating Alvarez completed the mission around the four corners, dulling Henley's knife substantially in the process. They gently lifted the lid off, where oilskins covering the top of the contents were revealed. They peeled them off, all collectively gasping at what was displayed underneath.

The crates were compartmentalized, separated by a wooden divider, each containing a pile of gold ingots. Alvarez yelled for a tarpaulin so that they could lay out the bars to get a count. A private pulled one out of the back of a deuce and a half parked nearby, spreading it out on the ground next to the crate. They carefully took the ingots from their resting place, setting them in rows on the tarp. Now they knew why each crate was so heavy. Although each ingot weighed approximately a third of a pound, they counted exactly five hundred laying out on the tarp. That meant the contents of each crate weighed about one hundred sixty pounds, with the crate alone adding another ten. Alvarez figured that each ingot was worth one hundred twenty thousand dollars, give or take, if his math was correct. Multiplied times five hundred, each crate was worth in excess of sixty million dollars. So far, they had counted ten of them. His mind reeled as he sat to catch his breath, the realization of what they had found suddenly careening around in his head. The coin plus the ingots having a value of over one billion dollars was staggering. The men gathered around him, asking him if he was all right.

"Yes, I'm fine, although somewhat overwhelmed. Gentlemen, most of you have been with me a long time, and those of you who haven't were picked for this mission because of your exemplary records. I cannot begin to relate to you the significance of this find. Number one, if word gets out about this, the entire Abzu Project will be finished. As exciting as this all is, believe it or not, we are working on something more precious, saving this planet we all live on. So I ask you to put this in perspective. Yes, ten of these ingots each could set all of you up for life, but what type of life will it be if the Earth splits apart? These ingots will not do anybody much good in that instance. So mum's the word. Do I make myself clear?"

A combined "yes, sir," loud and clear, echoed across the site.

One trooper piped up, "Sir, what do you think this is all worth?"

"Well, since you all worked on it, you have a right to know. Although I'm not an expert in these matters, I give what we have found so far an estimate of over one billion dollars."

"Holy shit!—Sir. Sorry, sir."

"At ease, reaction understandable. Now you have an idea of what we're dealing with. So as I said, each of you is a combat veteran, each of you knows what security is. This will be the toughest yet to contain, but, gentlemen, it is a must that you understand what we are about here. We are excavating this horde to get it out of the way to continue the mission. Plain and simple. Keep that in mind. I need you all to work collectively to that goal."

Another "yes, sir" resounded across the excavation zone.

"Now what I need you to do, as we are running out of time, is the same as we have done here with the other nine crates. Not to put a damper on things, but I hope this is the end of the excavation. We'll have to see. At any rate, we need to lay all the contents out, catalog them, repack them in the original crates, secure them with rope, as the tar will no longer hold, and then rebury them in concrete tombs. Then we wait for transport. Then we continue the mission. Everyone with me?"

A giant hoo-hah reverberated in Alvarez's eardrums.

"OK, then. Let's get with it."

Henley organized details on each crate, while Alvarez took inventory once the ingots were laid out. Each one had exactly five hundred ingots, with one exception, which counted out at 499 due to some rotten wood underneath the crate. Alvarez took his ingot and placed it on the tarp, evening the count to avoid any appearance of impropriety relative to his crew. Once all the crates were taken out of the excavation pit, Alvarez instructed the operator of a small backhoe to go back into the pit to ensure there was nothing stacked in the earth beneath the level where they had found the crates. Alvarez knew they were taking a chance on destroying any containers they might find with the hoe's blade, risking losing more treasure by spreading it into the dirt, but he was too far behind on the construction schedule to have any other choice.

It took them half the day to complete the inventory. They repacked the ingots as they had found them, placed the hardened oilskins over the gold, and then loaded them onto trucks. On the opposite side of the hill, two cement tombs had been sunk into the ground, construction having commenced when the gold coin had been found earlier that week. Each tomb was appropriately eight feet deep and four feet wide. Each was lined with cement to the six-foot level. Each had a cement lid that would be placed with a crane. Earth would be dumped in over the lids so that the appearance of newly scraped earth, legitimate in a construction zone, would never be questioned. As they were loading the last crate onto a truck, the backhoe operator shut down the machine and yelled for Colonel Alvarez to come quickly to the pit.

Oh, no, thought Alvarez. *Not something else to slow us up.*

The operator had evidently hit something else of a metallic nature. He was out of the backhoe, shovel and broom in hand, beginning to dig around the object. As he unearthed it, he laid down the shovel and swept off the top of it with the broom. As Alvarez approached, both discerned that it was an iron chest. As the outline became more defined, Alvarez figured the chest to be about three feet deep, four feet long, and about thirty inches wide, made of solid iron. He told the operator to get back into the hoe to see if he could get the blade underneath the chest to lift it to ground level. The operator succeeded, placing the chest on the lip of the pit, on a tarp. Some of the crew then dragged the tarp with the chest on it out of harm's way so it couldn't fall back into the pit. The item was secured with an ancient padlock, and as there was obviously no key, Alvarez called for a set of bolt cutters, which he detested using on a valuable item, but he had no choice. The cutter arrived. He instructed the hoe operator, who had initiated the find, to cut both arms to the lock, which he did. The operator then opened the lid to another set of oilskins, which were removed to reveal every type of jewel imaginable, set in rings, necklaces, bracelets, tiaras, and pendants. In addition to the precious stones, there was every assortment of pearl jewelry as well.

They began the arduous process of inventory onto two tarps this time, as each piece had to be cataloged like the others. All the pieces were in relatively good shape. They were fortunate they did not have to reinstate the washing detail. As they made their way down through the chest, they noted that it had been packed with some care, with the smaller items on top, the heavier on the bottom. Excitement grew as they pulled out bejeweled replicas of the Spanish fleet, solid gold miniatures of ships adorned with diamonds and rubies on the bowsprits topped with emeralds on the masts. Solid gold and silver daggers encased in sheaths, inlaid with every imaginable precious stone on the planet were next, and beneath that were two matched sets, still in leather, of wheel-lock pistols, inlaid in gold and precious jewels, no doubt the king's showpieces. Real excitement was generated upon exposure of these pieces. Alvarez had no idea as to the market value of each pistol, but wagered in his head that each was worth well over a million dollars. And there were four of them.

The sun was beginning to go down as the last of the precious cargo was gently placed back into its original container. In order to preserve the chest, Alvarez ordered that it be placed on a pallet so a forklift could get under it to gently lift it onto the back of a truck. They would have to secure a separate location for the trunk, as a forklift could not get into either tomb to extricate it later for transport. He placed a guard detail on the truck overnight until they decided how to handle securing it until its final move. He hoped that was the end of the excavation.

How ironic, he thought. *Here I am wishing for a quick end to this, where if things were normal, I'd only wish for more. Isn't life a kick in the ass sometimes?*

With those thoughts, he made his way to the mess tent, where the buzzing about the day's activities was at a hundred decibels. Hungry and tired, he waited in line with his men, preferring not to be served at the officer's table as he ruminated over the previous sixteen hours. He sat at the table, bowing his head. The others saw the gesture as grace. He was really praying that no more treasure be unearthed and that they complete their mission before the Earth split apart. Only time would tell.

CHAPTER FIFTEEN

Jaffna Harbor, Sri Lanka

Lyft sat on a bowsprit of one of two trawlers snaking its way through the small islands and treacherous shoals on the way to the warehouse district in Jaffna's inner harbor. South of Jaffna at Mannar, Hindu mythology determined that the limestone shoals leading to the Indian subcontinent were the remains of Rama's Bridge, sometimes referred to as Adam's Bridge, destroyed by a cyclone in 1480, never to be rebuilt. One could almost walk from Sri Lanka to the Indian town of Rameswaram on the limestone shoals in the Palk Strait, but not quite. Sharks formed a barrier in the deeper shoals, so floating transport was desired, although that too was fraught with danger. There were any number of uncharted hidden reefs and underwater upheavals in the area. One had to know what they were about when plying the waters around the southern tip of India in the Bay of Bengal and in Palk Bay. A testament to human ignorance were the hulks of vessels just underneath the surface in various areas, noted by markers to warn mariners of potential collisions. No such problem here, however. The two captains seemed intimately familiar with their surroundings, ignoring the peril surrounding them. Lyft sensed they were well versed in smuggling routes throughout the Indian Ocean.

Lyft was getting bored. He wasn't used to so much inactivity. Between the heat and humidity and the uninteresting terrain of northern Sri Lanka and the stupidity exhibited in the inane conversations of the small crew on board, he was agitated, beginning to exhibit an ill humor. He knew it was the price of seeing the exercise through, but every guttural expletive issued from the crew after another foul joke smoked the air was grating on him like a rasp on metal. He was looking forward to the conclusion of the day.

The one hundred Stingers, loaded in Belawan, fifty crates to each trawler, were awaiting inspection by two of the Liberation Tigers of Tamil Eelam, non-affectionately known in Northern Sri Lanka as the LTTE. Partially eliminated after an eradication attempt in the 1990s by Sri Lankan military forces, followed by a truce, they lately had resurfaced due to the inability of the government to reduce previous sources of discrimination among Tamil youth, which led to high unemployment and lack of opportunity, subsequently leading them to become general outcasts from society. The Tamils demanded a separate state in Northern Sri Lanka. Each wore a cyanide capsule in a small vial around his/her neck, ensuring they not be taken alive at the prospect of capture. The suicide bombers of today are the educated children of the Tamil terror movement, having picked up on the Tamil's tactics, which began in the early 1970s. They were the original progenitors of self-elimination to achieve their higher purpose. Martyrdom was essential to their philosophy, and they practiced it with élan. To Lyft, it was somewhat of an oxymoron that the Tamils were headquartered in the ancient city of Yaalpaanam, which means "city of the lyre." There had not been much music there lately.

As Lyft was thinking of ways to alleviate his boredom, he spied two men standing at a distance on a pier, outlined against the tin sheet metal of a warehouse. He figured they were part of the operation. Time to find out what they're up to, he thought.

He flew to their location, hovering over them as they conversed, learning that they were two brothers, appropriately named Yaalchelvan, pride of Yaalpaanam, and Yaalmani, gem of Yaalpaanam, waiting on the shipment. He noted the capsules around their necks and knew what they meant. Understanding the Tamils was to understand that, in the backs of their minds, their lives would be shorter than most, giving them comfort to disparities in daily operations, somehow soothing their souls, knowing that beyond it all was a higher purpose, that paradise awaited them with open arms. It made daily operations all the sweeter. It also ensured a greater attention to detail, as anything else would offend the mightiest power of all. Being familiar with the radical fundamentalist mindset, Lyft thought great theater was in the offing upon the crates' delivery. He flew back, hovering over the bowsprit of the lead boat.

The trawlers now had the warehouse in sight, a decrepit structure, a sheet metal affair, exhibiting rotting pilings supporting a gap-toothed pier.

What a dump, thought Lyft. *But smart. No one would go near the place. It looks condemned, even in this society.* He continued to hover overhead.

Back in Belwan, Ali had instructed maroon shirt to subcontract the shipment to Akbar, the pilot of Lyft's boat, and to Ifsham, the commander of the other. Maroon shirt and beige shirt had other duties preparing for the liquefied natural gas conflagration in the Straits, and even if they could have delivered the Stingers themselves, Ali knew they were unqualified to pilot the boat into Jaffna Harbor. He decided to rely on past experience, as the two experienced pilots had never failed him. That was about to change.

The two Tamils waited on the quay, and as the trawlers drew near, they signaled to the boats to stay where they were. Akbar reversed engines and idled in place. Ifsham followed suit. Lyft noted that there were two other trawlers moored nearby, now figuring that this transfer was never going to touch land. Pride and Gem each climbed into a rowboat tied to the pier and made their way to Akbar's boat. They were helped on board with a rope ladder, greeting Akbar with familiar salutations, friendship all around.

So, thought Lyft. *This isn't a first. This ought to be interesting.*

Akbar offered tea as they sat on the rear deck, sipping and exchanging stories of families and recent exploits. Trust was implicit, as no one seemed in any particular hurry to enact the transaction. Lyft saw no baggage for cash, so he wondered how the exchange was to be concluded. His notion of coziness between the Tamils and the council was about to be confirmed.

Pride said, "Please relate to Mr. Ali that, as usual, upon satisfactory inspection and initial usage of the cargo, he will find in his account the agreed upon sum. It won't be long. We have several actions planned for next week."

"I will be sure to do so," Akbar replied.

"So let's get to work, shall we?" said Gem.

"Indeed," said Akbar.

He took the tarps off the crates, subsequently unscrewing several of the lids with a portable battery-powered screwdriver, exhibiting the contents. It was clear to Lyft that Akbar didn't know the workings of a Stinger missile and had no inkling of missing components as he looked down with satisfaction on the contents of the crates. Pride and Gem looked closely, studying the contents, straightened up, looked at each other and then at Akbar. Lyft watched Akbar's face reveal that he sensed something was amiss. He queried, "Is there something wrong? They look OK to me."

Lyft could see the redness working up Gem's neckline to his face, his eyes flashing. He spat to Akbar. "Allow me to teach you about these missiles," he said, staring for a moment into the other man's eyes and then gesturing for Akbar to look closely at the useless Stingers. "Here is where the battery coolant unit should be. The missiles are inoperable without them." His eyes were cold and hard as he hissed, "You might as well take them out into the middle of the Bay of Bengal and dump them overboard."

Akbar's eyes went from utter amazement to rage. "You mean to tell me we took this trip for nothing?" he spat. Then he looked quickly at Gem. "We will find out who did this."

Lyft felt like piping up that he knew, but he felt it the better part of discretion to remain silent for now.

Akbar called over to Ifsham to unscrew the lids on the other missiles and to look to see if the BCUs were in the crates. Ifsham called back over that he didn't know what to look for, so the two trawlers were brought alongside each other, bumping tires, as Gem hopped aboard the other boat to confirm the loss. Sure enough, they eventually determined that the BCUs were missing from all the crates.

Standing on the deck, Pride gesticulated, hands in the air, exclaiming, "Well, this presents a problem. It is obvious that Ali's organization has somehow been compromised. I suggest you tell him so, although, if you do not want to return, I will understand, and you can take temporary refuge here. We will be most happy to inform him of his ineptitude. When things settle down, then you can return with the cargo for his review. If there are any repercussions, you know you always have a home here." Pride outstretched his arms. "You have been loyal transporters for us all these years, so we hold no enmity toward you." Pride's eyes narrowed. "Toward Ali, well, that's another matter. We shall relate to him that we will find another supplier. There are plenty of Russians willing to do business who have an excess of arms on their hands. This will change the strategy of the operations impending for the next few months, but we have no shortage of true believers, so we have other tactics we can employ to ensure the viability of our operations."

Lyft saw Akbar look at the vial around Pride's neck, clearly understanding the implication of his words. He opted to remain in Jaffna until Ali was contacted by the Tamils. Lyft didn't blame him for fearing the ultimate retribution. Pride agreed to his plea, as did Gem. Both captains would be housed in Tamil households until it was deemed safe to return.

Akbar queried, "But what of the cargo? What are we to do with it now?"

Shrugging his shoulders, Pride replied, "Well, it's essentially useless, but we will determine that with Mr. Ali. It is still his, so he can take responsibility for disposing of it. We will see. Come with us; we will get you settled and then place a phone call."

Both boats anchored in the harbor, and then all were eventually transported to land, where they made their way to several households willing to take in the two captains and their miniscule crews.

Well, thought Lyft. *This is certainly progressing with minimal fireworks. Not quite what I expected from a group of rebels. Highly educated and articulate, I'll say that much. Perhaps they'll have a chance at overthrowing the government if they are as smart as I think they are. I don't approve much of the tactics, but I understand the concept. Too bad governments worldwide don't get it. If they did, they'd look out more for their citizenry rather than their own self-promulgation. Sad, but so be it relative to the insanity continually exhibited in humanity.*

He wondered how Ali was going to take the news of the sabotage. He decided to find out. He hoped for brilliant theater.

He followed Pride and Gem to their offices on the second floor in the rear of the warehouse, where, hidden from prying eyes, there was a state-of-the art display of computers and electronic devices, including marine ship-to-shore and satellite communications, along with multiple servers housing database information over which the government authorities would salivate. The two Tamils dialed a secure speakerphone directly into Ali's library, where Lyft imagined the porcine figure to be pouring over his books, looking with satisfaction on his multiple dealings, the greed oozing like sweat from his pores. He answered the phone.

What transpired in the library, Lyft could only imagine. When the two related what had occurred, Ali became dangerously apoplectic. Lyft imagined his blood pressure rising into his neck and then his whole face becoming fire-engine red, the sweat soaking his collar as it ran down into his shirt. He yelled into the phone that it was that bitch Licia's fault, as she ran the warehouse operation. He never should have entrusted that aspect of the business to her. Gem and Pride both agreed, saying certain things should not be entrusted to women. That only incensed him more, as he didn't tolerate others criticizing his wife. Lyft, to his delight, heard books and implements being thrown in the background, confirming the wrath of the leviathan on the other end of the line. When he was told the two felt his organization to be compromised, indicating it would be best to find another supplier, Ali completely lost what temper he had remaining, telling them they were the dregs of humanity, that he could find other avenues for his business, that there were plenty of other buyers. Gem and Pride then informed him he would have no clients left if he kept shipping faulty matériel. He slammed down the phone, ignoring the discussion relative to the disposition of the two crews and the cargo. Gem and Pride looked at each other.

Gem intoned, "That went well." Pride shrugged, already beginning to lose interest in Ali. Gem continued, "I'd hate to be in Licia's position at the moment. Somehow though, perhaps she can fend for herself."

Lyft chortled to himself. As expected, he surmised that this was the beginning of the downfall of the Sastroamidjojo family empire. He was happy he was intimately involved in its destruction.

CHAPTER SIXTEEN

The Wakhan

Having had enough fun and games with the Sastroamidjojo family, Lyft decided to fly back to the Wakhan, for him a relatively short direct flight of just under three hours. Feeling no rush to return, he detoured, paying surreptitious visits to the Pulau Simeulue barge and the Bougainville project, noting with some alarm the recent volcanic activity at the latter and the number of new smokers bubbling on the ocean's surface.

Six more months, he thought desperately. *Mother, just give us six more months to cool you off. I just hope to God the project works.*

Seeing how the situation had deteriorated gave him a new sense of urgency. As most of the journey was over the ocean, he had no worries about breaking the sound barrier, affecting only a few fish. He flew back to the Wakhan from Bougainville in just under an hour, half his normal time. He found Bashirin first, briefed him on the situation at the barges, and then made his way to find me. I was just wrapping up the computer project when I heard the rap on the door.

"C'min," I yelled.

"Don't mind if I do," I heard Lyft say.

The door opened and shut. I felt the familiar clump onto my

shoulder, with a little squeeze added, perhaps his way of saying he was happy to be "home."

"We have a meeting with Salvo and Bashirin at two this afternoon. How are you coming with your project?"

"Nice to see you too. No, 'Gee, Jeff, good to see you. How ya doin?' Or better yet, 'Gee, it's good to be back. I've missed it around here.' None of that. We couldn't have any of that, now could we?"

"Sorry, I'm just a little preoccupied right now. There's a lot going on at Bougainville, and I don't like the looks of it. New volcanoes spawning, right up through the ocean. Mother's angry, getting ready to blow, and we're behind schedule. I'm worried we won't make it."

"Ah, well, that is serious. How far behind are we?"

He began flitting around the room in agitation, hands extended. "Well, we keep getting delayed by horse manure like what happened on Selkirk's. That put us behind by at least a week. Then we have this stupid Sastroamidjojo business, with them wanting to blow up the planet. I ought to just wait, because soon they'll get their wish. All they have to do is continue to keep me busy, unable to attend to the serious side of things, while they plot and scheme to determine the next target they want to blow into oblivion. I hate humans sometimes; I really do."

"We are an obstreperous lot, I'll give you that. But look at it this way. You've got some really good people who have your back, even though some of them don't even know you exist."

I reassured him as best I could, reminding him that all the rest of the plants and barges were on schedule. The only question was whether our schedule would have us done before there was a major cataclysm.

He lit on the mantel over the fireplace, next to the small bronze bust of Napoleon. I stifled a humored grunt.

He replied earnestly, "Yes, that's the question with no answer. Only time will tell." He raised his arms in supplication. "I can't speed anything up, because we're already using the world's entire workforce that has experience with the construction of these plants."

I sat on the sofa opposite the mantel to engage him, but then he floated over to the marble counter separating the dining area from the kitchen.

I got up, crossing the room, attempting a face-to-face. Standing, I said softly, "Would you like something to eat? You seem to be edging in that direction."

"No, thank you, too much to think about at the moment—my stomach's upset from all the upset." He flew to the back of the sofa.

"Look," I reasoned, turning toward him, arms outspread, palms up, "this plant here's almost online. When that happens, we transfer the workforce to Selkirk's and let them at it hammer and tong."

Exasperated, he said, "I know the plan. I just wish we could speed it up somehow."

This time, I went to the chair in the corner near the fireplace that faced the sofa. I queried, "How are the tunnels coming? The whole thing's no good if the tunnels aren't ready when we are."

"The minikins are progressing nicely. There are fifteen thousand of them working nonstop. They are halfway around the globe, with no major setbacks. Provided all goes according to plan up here, we'll be ready down there when the switches are thrown." He flew back to the marble counter. This time, I remained in place, the Pied Piper rat in me beginning to rebel.

I said soothingly, forgetting my consternation, "Well, we keep at it and say some prayers."

He began flying around the room, his agitation evident, not so much talking to me as just expounding at length to any inanimate object he felt would listen. He piped to the air, "I have a nasty feeling we are not going to get out of this unscathed."

"What do you mean?" I said, getting dizzy watching him swirl around the room.

"In the next half year or so, Mother's going to have to blow off some steam somewhere. The Pacific near Bougainville is my best guess, but if not there, then somewhere else. I don't like what I see happening."

I croaked, not able to watch him anymore, "We can only do what we can do. If something blows, then it blows. Some things can't be controlled, as much as you would like to have mastery over it all."

He stopped in midair, hovering in front of me, finally something centering his attention. The sarcasm could have rent the air as he looked me dead on. "Very philosophical of you."

I threw my hands up. "Hey, what do you want? Me running around here wringing my hands like Chicken Little? I'm not one for that."

He placed a hand on his chin, still hovering in front of me. "Perhaps you have a point."

I leaned back in the chair. "Listen, we'll make it. This is the largest project ever attempted on Earth, so kudos to us that we've made it this far. I have great faith in you. Now I have something that is really going to piss you off."

"Great, I can't wait to hear it." He began buzzing around the room again.

"Well, *60 Minutes* called. They got wind of the project from some Afghans who complained to their village elders about the continual helicopter noise over their village, which then went to the local UNESCO official who took it to State. The State Department said they knew nothing about it but would look into it. State was being interviewed by *60 Minutes* that day on Iraq, and one of the interviewers happened to overhear that there was an abundance of helicopter traffic in the Wakhan, which he thought unusual, knowing the history of the area. Then *60 Minutes* somehow got access to air transport and did a flyby yesterday, snapping pictures and all. Now they want a full-blown interview."

Lyft stopped, hovering in the center of the room. He raised his hands on high. "Ah, God, it never ends."

"Nope. Now why don't you stop flitting around and making me dizzy. Relax, and I'll get us a couple of Cokes and some peanuts. Stay stationary for a minute so that I can get my equilibrium back."

A harrumph from Lyft. I noticed he settled onto the back of the sofa. I went into the kitchen, took two cans of Coke Classic out of the refrigerator, snapped the ice maker into action, half-filling the glasses, and then poured the coke, listening to the ice crackle as the glass filled. I walked over to the cupboard and reached up to get the peanut jar, which I noted had a loose lid as I placed it on the counter. My sense of order offended, I yelled out to Lyft, "Who's the last guy to put the peanuts away, huh? The lid's loose, and they're probably all stale. Don't blame me if they're lousy at the first bite."

He boomed, "My God, you are a pain in the ass. Have you nothing better to think about than peanut lids?"

"Well," I yelled back, "you'd be the first to complain if they were stale."

I took out a blue ceramic bowl patterned with an idyllic Chinese farm scene, filling it to the brim and sampling a peanut or two. They weren't stale after all. I thought about bringing in some egg and smearing it on my face, as it was going to end up there anyway. I put everything on a faux mahogany server and walked it into the room, setting it on the glass coffee table in front of the couch.

I intoned, "The peanuts are OK, not stale, just so you know."

"Well," he huffed, "I think I could have figured that out for myself. You're losing it, you know."

I sat on the couch, he angled on the arm, looking at me to my left. I said, "You're not the only one under stress, so let's just leave it at that. Like I said, *60 Minutes* wants an interview."

He flew over to the table, picked up his coke, and grabbed a handful of peanuts. He settled himself back on the arm, nibbling and munching between sips, the ice rattling against the glass.

He nonchalantly said, "Actually, I'm surprised it took them this long to get on to us."

Taking a sip of Coke, I asked, "So what do you suggest? I certainly can't be interviewed," I said.

"No, that's true. I think this is one for Bashirin and Salvo."

"What? And reveal the project?"

"Why not? What harm will it really do?"

"We have to think about this one."

"Why?" he said between nibbles. "How long, really, did you think this project could stay under wraps? Look at the amount of people involved with it already. It's not going to stay secret forever. And why should it, really? Humans worldwide do have a vested interest in it, as well as you, you know. Perhaps it's time to let the world know what a state Mother is really in. Then maybe mankind will begin to cease its nefarious *schwachsinn* and get serious about getting along not only with each other but with the Earth as well."

"I can just see all the environmental groups instituting lawsuits to stop the project. And how the hell do we explain the tunnels? How's that going to work?" I piped, setting my Coke down on the tray.

"We don't." Lyft began pacing slowly on the couch arm.

I looked at him, wondering if he ever sat still. "What do you mean, we don't?"

"Just what I said. We don't tell them about the tunnels."

"How do you propose that will that work?"

He stopped and looked directly at me, arms raised, peanuts in one hand, Coke in the other. He began to gesticulate, not receiving my full attention, as I was sure something was going to spill. I thought to myself that I really needed to work on my focus, trying to put his antics out of my mind.

"Like this. We just tell them that we have, with the help of a group of esteemed scientists, picked hot spots that need to be cooled off by pumping liquid nitrogen into cavities near plate junctures to reduce the stress level created by what has been deemed to be an excess of volcanic activity. It is believed that due to some sort of absorption of global heat, the inner core of the Earth has increased its spin slightly, expanding the tectonic plates, which, in turn, has the potential to create general havoc. The Earth's overheating has resulted in an increase in volcanism worldwide, increasing the potential for major earthquakes, tsunamis, et cetera, with the final scenario being a nuclear winter if Mother really decides to blow her top. We don't know if what we're doing will work, but it's better than nothing."

I raised my glass with a question. "How do we explain the recyclers? They are not nitrogen producers, they just move the stuff along."

"Tell the truth." He finished the final slug of peanuts in his grasp and then floated over to the table where he grabbed another handful. He then settled himself back on his perch.

I exclaimed, almost spilling my Coke, "Are you nuts?"

"No," followed by a quaff and a nibble.

"You just said don't tell them about the tunnels," I yelled.

"The major tunnels. No one would believe it anyway. But there are not enough resources to build all the plants needed, so we built recyclers to move the nitrogen along to specified locations yet to be built, transported in tunnels under the surface to the expected locations. In other words, we are getting our ducks lined up. Let *60 Minutes* figure out another scenario for themselves if they don't believe ours. What are they gonna' do? Go down with the minikins and find the tunnels themselves? They wouldn't get ten feet, so how are they going to disprove what we tell them? I say we should come across as honest, earnest people, directed by a consortium of governments worldwide, who are making an attempt at giving mankind a chance to survive what could potentially be the unkindest cut of all."

I placed the Coke on the tray and sat back, arm stretched out along the back of the couch. "This just may work. I'm so happy I'm in your employ. What would I do without you?"

"Probably figure it out yourself, but I'm happy I could be of assistance at any rate. When do they want to do the interview?"

"In two weeks."

"Hmm, that may give me time to wrap up this terrorist connection so that I can be here for it. I would like that."

I looked up at him with a lopsided grin. "I'll bet you would."

He wrinkled his forehead as he raised his eyebrows. "What does that mean, exactly?"

I laughed. "You know you want to be in show business. You already are to a degree. You just can't crow about it visibly to the public."

He said agreeably, "It's true, you know me too well. I do like to be at the center of things. I seem to have more control that way."

"Yes, I've noticed. On another note, what's this meeting about at two o'clock today?"

"I need some help with this terrorist thing over in Sumatra. I have a plan that I would like to run by you all."

"Uh-oh. Does this mean impending travel?"

"Perhaps."

"By perhaps you mean yes?"

"Well, we'll see. But I may need all three of you, as I can't be in more than one location at a time, even though I am pretty quick to relocate sometimes. How are you coming with this project of ferreting out any more suspects?"

"I am officially through, as of today. I have found no other potentials that have the capacity to cause trouble."

"Well, that's a modicum of good news." He took a large gulp of Coke and a large mouthful of peanuts.

"Yes, I thought you'd be pleased. It looks like Sastroamidjojo's the only sleeper."

"Well," he muffled through a mouthful of peanut butter, "that means you're free to engage in other escapades."

"It would seem so."

"I'm hungry," Lyft exclaimed. "Why don't you cook us breakfast?"

"Good God, we've just finished two Cokes and half a jar of peanuts. Plus, you said you weren't hungry. Now breakfast?"

"I changed my mind, and why not? It's eight in the morning somewhere."

"Good point. Sausage, eggs, English muffins, orange juice, and hot coffee sound good to you?"

"Excellent. I'll have a dozen eggs scrambled, please."

"Whoa, you are hungry. Good thing I've got two cartons in the fridge. A dozen for you and three for me. You really are a chow hound."

"Something you already knew. Yes, I decimated several buffet tables in Belawan, I'll have you know, but that was some time ago. I really haven't eaten much since."

"I would have liked to have been a fly on the wall watching those escapades. I'll bet you did us all proud."

"Yes, you could say that. The headwaiter didn't seem too pleased when I gave him a rather large goodbye kiss on the cheek as I wrapped my arms around him on the patio. That was quite a scene."

I lapsed into hysterics over my mind sight of it, almost falling off the couch. Lyft just casually looked on, clearly wondering if the laughing jag was going to continue all day or if he eventually was going to get something to eat.

"Anytime you're ready to start cooking, I'd be most appreciative. I'm really quite hungry, you know."

"Well then, don't paint anymore scenes like that in my head so that I can concentrate on the task at hand. You are rather humorous, you know, even though oftentimes it eludes you."

"I'll admit, I do have my moments, some being more playful than others. Most often, it's to see how someone reacts that prompts me to do silly things. Sometimes, it's out of sheer boredom. The headwaiter thing, well, that was out of spite, because he was such a total jerk to his staff. Petty dictator, that sort of thing. I thought he needed to be put in his place, so I ensured a little humility into his day."

I began to laugh again, but decided it was time to get busy. Still laughing on the way into the kitchen, I felt it best to have the humorous scenes in my head interspersed with attention to the stove. The eggs were mixed with a little green pepper, onion, and cheddar cheese. I poured them into a large buttered pan, and as they began to bubble, I mixed them thoroughly. The sausage was simmering on another burner, so I asked Lyft if he would mind putting the English muffins into the toaster.

"Not at all. Glad to help."

He did so with a click. We'd soon be ready. I set the table quickly, pouring out large glasses of orange juice. The coffee had already been brewed. I always made extra, never knowing who was going to drop by.

I dished out the pan, literally filling Lyft's plate with a low-rise hill of scrambled eggs. I had to get another plate for the sausage and muffins for him. We sat down on the living room side at the table abutting the marble counter to converse about past and future activities.

He began, "Have you ever thought much about cause and effect?"

"Sometimes, but not lately."

"For instance, there is a reason the Sastroamidjojos feel the way they do about things Western."

"What, I'm supposed to have empathy for jerks like that?" I dug into my eggs, topped off by a snap of bacon between my lips.

He waved his fork in front of me. "No, that's not the point. The point is, if you know from what something emanates, you can understand it better. Let me give you a slightly archaic example. Say you wanted to undertake a study of the rise of trade in Europe. Where do you think you would begin?"

"With Europe's economic development."

"Exactly. And how do you think Europe's economy developed?"

"Through trade," I said as I jellied an English muffin.

"Bravo. And so how did this trade develop?"

"Don't think I have an answer to that one."

"Aha. Ever hear of the lateen?"

"Nope."

Lyft scooped a mouthful of eggs onto his fork, shoveling them home. "Well, it's the triangular sail on a mast attached to a moveable boom that allows a ship to catch the wind from any direction, thus having revolutionized trade in Europe. Before it was discovered by the West, one could only sail before the wind in square-sailed vessels. In other words, you had only one direction in which you could go."

Waving his fork again, he asked, "Say, could we have some juice? And some coffee? What kind of chef are you anyway? I'm drying out over here."

"Sorry—you were so intent on substance, I forgot the liquid. Coming up."

I went into the kitchen and brought the unplugged percolator, steaming hot, along with mugs to the table. It took me a second trip for the juice, sugar, cream, and spoons. I settled in again.

"Thank you, that's much better." Lyft poured himself a mug of coffee, took a quick sip and continued. "As I was saying, no one wanted to risk changing ship design as there was so much invested in building ships. This design was fine for traders who crossed the Indian Ocean, as the wind only blew in one direction for six months of the year and then changed direction for the other six, but not for Europe, where the winds were extremely capricious. As Europe prospered in the twelfth and thirteenth centuries, traders took notice of the various contrivances in other parts of the world. Eventually, the lateen took hold, enabling more and more ships to be put to sea."

He wrapped talons around his juice glass, picking it up without a hitch. I was waiting for it to slip and crash onto the table, but he brought it to his lips, taking a sip and then set it down without incident. I still couldn't figure out how achieved his dexterity.

He looked directly into my eyes, somewhat exasperated, holding his fork aloft. "Are you paying attention?"

"Well, yes. Yes, I am. How the hell do you pick up your juice glass without it slipping out of your grasp? That kind of fascinates me."

He rolled his eyes as he stood against the edge of the table at rib height. I thought he was going to throw his fork at me, tines forward. "You know, I think you have attention deficit disorder. What's wrong with you? The way I'm able to pick up the glass is in the same manner in which you pick up yours. I don't give it a second thought. Do you?"

I looked up sheepishly, the student getting a stern lecture from the master. "No."

"So there, now no more about it. These lessons I'm giving you at a considerable expense of my time are the fundamentals of history, important for your overall education, so listen up."

I could have reached over and slapped him, knocking him off his pedantic perch, but I thought the better of it.

He prattled on. "Now where was I? Oh, yes, the rudder. Without a rudder, the ships were difficult to control, and as necessity seems often to be the mother of invention, the earliest display of a ruddered ship appeared on the city seals of Ebling and Wismar, two Baltic seaports, enabling ships to be maneuvered more easily while putting to dock. And thusly, the evolution progressed to the container vessels we have today, or should I say moving islands?"

I finished off an English muffin. "So you're telling me that the use of a sail on a movable boom propelled Europe to new heights of prosperity?"

"That and the rudder. The ships eventually got too large for the old fashioned steering oars, but again, through exposure due to better sailing techniques, the rudder, probably invented in China, spread to the Arab world and then on to the Mediterranean, and finally Europe."

"Huh, who would have thunk it?"

Lyft took a sip of coffee, a talon wrapped through the thumb hold. "Thunk it, huh?"

"My own idiomatic expression, thank you."

He looked down at his plate, contemplating his next assault. "More like an idiotic expression, if you ask me."

I ignored his bait, finishing my eggs.

He continued, fork pointing in the air, "You know, you really should read *Connections* by James Burke. It's about change throughout the history of mankind and the causes of things. It's fascinating. My example is taken from that book."

"I'll make a point of it. You know how I like history."

"This is better than dry history. This deals with technology in a historical context."

"Point taken. Interesting historical tidbit, but what's this got to do with us?"

He placed his fork down, all business now. "Well, the book talks about cause and effect—a need arising and then being addressed. It seems like the universal prod of cause and effect is the need, brought about by any confluence of circumstances. Sometimes things happen plainly by accident, but more often than not they happen through the search to satisfy a need. We have the same problem with our project. We have an effect, but we do not know the cause. If we knew the cause, we could address the need. The need in this instance is to find the cause. Exactly why *has* the Earth's core increased its rate of spin? All I hear are theories." He waved his arms quickly in the air. "I've been dealing with this problem ever since we felt there was an issue with the Earth's magnetism over three years ago. Then, I had no conception the core was spinning out of control. Global warming? Forget it, has nothing to do with it. What's happening on the surface would not affect the core. It's something more fundamental. But what it is is beyond all of us at the moment."

I leaned forward, intent. "So what do you think it is?"

He looked me directly in the eyes. "I think the Earth's axis has increased its tilt."

Incredulous, I croaked, "What?"

"Just what I said. There has been a shift in the Earth's axis."

"From what?"

He waved his arm across the table. "From a giant plate subduction along the Marianas Trench running down to Bougainville, not far from the barge. There are new volcanoes forming there."

"Why would this happen all of a sudden?"

He shrugged. "Mother Nature taking her course. You know that the Earth's not static; it's continually moving and evolving. As a matter of fact, the ironic thing of it is, the Earth's actually cooling. Has been for millions of years. It seems to be going through a rather bad patch at the moment, though. The tilt isn't much, less than half a degree, but it's enough to raise havoc. There's so much subduction material going into the outer core and basically melting at the moment that the inner core is trying to maintain a balance against its neighbor by compensating its spin due to the pressure increasing against it. You would think it would be the opposite, that an excess of material would slow it down, but nature doesn't work that way. Nature always tries to compensate. If what I believe is true, then we are all in for a real ride, as everything on Earth will be affected, including your pocket compass you have at home. I just hope that what we are about will have some positive effect. Mother does not really care about mankind. Mother is Mother, that's all there is to it, and she'll take her own sweet time to right herself—say, several hundred thousand years or so. We don't have that amount of time to let her take her own course."

I raised my eyebrows, still leaning forward, trying to absorb the gravity of what he was telling me. "Why hasn't someone else come up with this theory?"

He said offhandedly, "They may have, but no one can prove it. They can prove the tilt is off, but that's all they can prove. They can't scientifically prove that subduction is causing it. Even if they do prove it, what are they going to do about it? Nothing. No one has a better plan than we do, so we're doing it. I'm not normally wrong about things like this, so place your bets on me."

He scraped up the rest of the eggs on his plate, ensuring nothing left, and then took a sip of coffee. I toasted my juice glass to him. "I will. So let me get this straight. We now have a cause, do we not, and we know the effect. We also have what we hope is a temporary solution to be implemented. The need is to hopefully cool the Earth's interior, eventually slowing down the spin, which will reduce friction, lowering the thermostat, thusly tempering the excessive plate expansion. This will, if we are successful, prevent the Earth from blowing sky high, no? Am I pretty much on the mark?"

"Bull's-eye," he yelled as he smacked his hands together.

"So what's the problem?"

"It's pretty much all speculation."

I leaned way back from the table. "Whoa, we're going to all this trouble on spec?"

"Yes, something akin to building a magnificent house to throw on the market in the hopes that someone will snap it up."

"So you're saying we may not be addressing the real problem?"

"I'm saying I believe in what we're doing. If I didn't, I wouldn't have undertaken it in the first place. But there's nothing proven here, so we'll have to wait and see."

"Once we're set, how long before it shows any results?"

"Who knows? Could be immediate or could be five years or a hundred years. Nothing's ever been done on this scale before."

"I might be dead before I know whether we've done any good or not." I took a final sip of coffee, hoping it wasn't my last.

"I've got news for you. If you're dead, you're not going to know." He finished the last of his juice.

"Very funny," I mewled.

We chatted on further, weighing the pros and cons of the project, until before we realized it, an icon beeped on my computer, telling us it was time for the two o'clock meeting. We made our way to Bashirin's dacha, where a smorgasbord of Russian pastries and hot teas awaited us. Just what we needed after recently devouring a monstrous breakfast. We exchanged pleasantries, and then Lyft, unfazed by the array, filled his plate with sweets while I did him the favor of making him some black Russian tea.

Salvo came in immediately after our arrival and mimicked Lyft at the buffet, and then we all sat down as Bashirin called the meeting to order. Most of the dachas were similar in design, except that Bashirin's had some rather nice black and white etchings by Russian artists on the wall, one especially expressive over the fireplace of Cossacks toasting around a blazing fire with their horses in the background outlined against a sparse forest. Bashirin queried, "And now, my friend, since you called this meeting together, what is on that devious mind of yours?"

Lyft, chairman of the board and all business, now situated himself on the back of the couch facing the fireplace, with the two colonels, one in each chair, facing him. I was on the couch to his left as he began pacing on the right. "First of all, it's good to be among you all again. As you know through my intermittent communication with you, we have a solid lead into the terrorist network. I know the basic location of the meeting coming up soon, but I need more specifics. Once we find that out, I'll need some help. Jeff, you're finished with your project, are you not?"

"Yes, I finished today, as a matter of fact. I've found no other connections within the workforce here."

"Good. I need you to be the only survivor of the recently blown-up plant. Can you pull that off?"

"Sure, with a little help. What do you want me to do?"

"Ingratiate yourself with the Sastroamidjojos by having been their dying son's confidant."

"I'm missing something here. Was not the signal supposed to be sent that indicated that young Ali blew up the plant?"

"Absolutely, but that doesn't mean he sent it. Get my drift?"

"Ah, got it."

"You know, you can be obtuse sometimes."

"*You* try looking at a computer screen for a month straight for sixteen hours a day and see how *you* fare."

Salvo piped, "Bitch, bitch, bitch," with Bashirin and Lyft joining the chorus on the third "bitch."

I jokingly said, "OK, guys, paybacks are hell. You'll never know when it's coming, so watch your backs."

From Lyft, raising his arms, "OK, enough, we've got work to do and not much time to accomplish it. Jeff, I need you to gain the family's trust so we have enough evidence to arrest Ali Senior and that snake Ahman along with Licia. I also want to break the family financially so they can never recover. We do that by discrediting them, putting dents in their armor, as with the Stinger transfer. Can you handle that?"

"Yes, with help, but I don't speak the language."

"Can you fake a bit of a brogue?"

"Close enough."

"Good. We'll play off the Irish terrorist connection, with which Ali will identify. As to your dearth of language skills, no worries there. I'll help you with that angle. We'll get down to the specifics later, but that's the general game plan for now with that aspect of the plan."

He gazed at the etching over the fireplace. I wondered if he saw himself in the scene, toasting to success upon completion of the mission.

Momentarily distracted, he continued, "Then I need someone to watch the boat while we are at the summit council. The call for launch could come from the council, and as I can't be at two places at once, I need someone on the boat." He pointed at Bashirin. "For my good Russian friend, we'll make up some bull about you being a disaffected Russian officer who decided to get religion during an operation in Chechnya. You shot your commanding officer, taking out half your unit before switching sides, and you've been on the run ever since. You need a home, you need cover, you need sanctuary. You also need some money. You speak passable Arabic?"

"No, Chechen. But it's related. I may very well be able to get by. What nationality do you think the two bastards are who are running the boat?"

"Hard to tell. Could be Jordanian. They definitely aren't Indonesian."

Bashirin took a large bite of pastry, looking into space, concentrating. He paused and then said, "If they're Jordanian, that's perfect. Chechen is well understood in Jordan. There is a large minority in the country who understand it for whatever reason, I don't know why. Don't worry about me, I'll get along."

"Good. And now, my good friend Colonel Salvo," Lyft said, turning his attention away from Bashirin, "I believe it best that you stay with Bashirin on the boat. You could be from North Africa, Moroccan, no? Immigrated to Italy, disillusioned with the West, feeling its decadence in your soul, chomping at the bit to practice jihad because of all the corruption that surrounds you. Any language connection?"

"Fluent French."

"That should cover you, as over half the people speak French in Morocco. Even though the official language is standard Arabic, you could say you were brought up by a French family after having been orphaned as a young child, you know, make it into a real tearjerker. As for Arabic, they shielded you from the true religion, which you found coincidentally enough after you made your way into Italy. Western ways did not agree with you, so you sought out contemporaries at local mosques, where an imam took you under his wing and made you see the light, that sort of thing. If our friends are Jordanian, chances are they are fluent in French. If not, they may speak French anyway. I know Bashirin speaks French, so if need be, he can translate for you. Sometimes, keeping your mouth shut is not such a bad tack, as I'm sure you know. You two will have to work out a connection as to how you teamed up. I know you're both up to the task."

"No problem, we'll practice our fervor religiously," said Salvo.

We all laughed.

For the rest of the afternoon, we strategized, agreeing that we would play our roles on each other for the next several days. Lyft had decided that I would be best presented to the Sastroamidjojo family in a somewhat disheveled state, introduced through the same bartender in Belawan who we thought by now had attained religion through his previous encounter with Lyft. Bashirin and Salvo would present themselves similarly but on another day, so as not to arouse too much suspicion. Lyft also said he had to interview young Ali for the "hook." I asked what that meant. He replied, "Wait and see."

Chapter Seventeen

The Straits

The jumping-off point was arriving all too quickly. I called Barb back home, relating to her what I was up to in general terms, not wanting to alarm her about any specifics. She told me to take care, that all was well on the home front, but that I was missed, which only made the ache all the worse.

Bashirin, Salvo, and I decided to go overland to Islamabad, fly from there to Yangoon in Myanmar (previously Burma), proceed to Kuala Lumpur in Malaysia, and then by boat, cross the Straits to Medan. All air transport would be standby with the exception of the last leg of the journey, a ferry out of Port Kelang, Kuala Lumpur's port city, directly to Belawan, an all-day journey. I was actually looking forward to crossing the Malacca Straits; I had heard so much about it.

As the day for departure rapidly approached, it seemed our frenetic activity would outstrip our schedule. There were plant briefings to be held to ensure adherence to the building and opening schedule; *60 Minutes* had to be called, postponing their insertion into our business; travel papers had to be arranged; inexpensive accommodations booked for me, many into youth hostels where we could get away with it; itineraries planned and double checked, in case Ali's family snooped into our immediate backgrounds;

connections made for the small caravan that would escort us to the outskirts of Islamabad; and the route carefully planned for breaking out of the Wakhan corridor and making our way to Islamabad, the toughest exercise of all. Even though I was not actually engaging in the physical exercise of hitchhiking along the Karakoram Highway, the story had to be plausible as to how I made my way to Islamabad. So we poured over maps, studying the landscape in detail, all the villages and towns I would have visited, until we had the following scheme mapped out:

After having befriended Ali and gaining his trust, he planted his cell phone on me with instructions as to what to do with it should something happen to him. Sure enough, he appropriately went up with the plant. I decided to leave the area soon thereafter, as there was no help forthcoming, with the plant a total loss. Supplies were running short, and I had no means of communication with the outside world, other than Ali's cell phone, which was essentially useless, as there was now no way to charge it. I would be shutting it off, hoping to preserve the charge.

So I decided to hike to the Hunza River, which runs out of the Wakhan into Pakistan through the towns of Mor Khun and Baltit, with the three remaining mules in camp. At Gilgit, it is joined by the Indus, which becomes the main river system of Pakistan, running all the way through the country. Fortuitously, the Karakoram Highway runs along most of the length of the Indus River down to Islamabad. Once I made it to the highway, it was pretty much road travel from Baltit to the capital city. However, that does not mean it was safe.

The Karakoram was built in a twenty-year period beginning in the 1960s. It covers over 760 miles between Kashgar, China, and Islamabad. Over one thousand lives were lost in its construction. The word "karakoram" means "crumbly rock" in Turkish, and the highway lived up to its name. The highway runs through several mountain ranges, including the Pamirs and the Karakorams, which are geologically active, raining down on the highway everything from large boulders to the sides of mountains when so inclined. Earthquakes are frequent, as is inclement weather, frequent fogs, along with the omnipresent highway banditry, drug smuggling, and smatterings of terrorist activity, a highway to be approached with trepidation. Elevation of the highway runs from over sixteen thousand feet just over the Chinese border to about seventeen hundred feet in Islamabad.

Some of its most spectacular scenery is displayed in the descent into the Hunza River Valley, seventy-eight hundred feet above sea level. The road was blasted into the mountainsides, following the twist and turns of the river, with hairpin turns and precipitous drops of over five hundred feet in some locations directly into the turbulent waters below, a recipe for rapt attention to driving. Glaciers come right down to the road, the Batura in Northern Hunza and the Ultar glacier in Karimabad, their melt adding to the waters of the Hunza. They are the lifeblood of many of the local village economies. The river splits the Karakoram Range, many of the peaks soaring to over twenty-five thousand feet above. In Karimabad, the Rakaposhi peaks, the Golden, the Ultars, and the Princess Boboli, a missile in disguise, seeking thinner atmosphere, give cricks in the neck, as it is impossible to not continually gaze skyward.

And so for about half the length of the Karakoram Highway, I had to research each stop, memorize the topography, the foods offered, including the ubiquitous wild thyme tea, known to cure everything from gout to diarrhea. I had to know of the various languages and local customs, where the most spectacular scenery was, where I stayed, and some of the names of the proprietors who took care of me en route. It was a monumental exercise. By the time I was through, I looked liked I had made the trip on foot, disheveled as I was due to the lack of sleep entailed in all the labors.

Finally, the day arrived. We were actually to be helicoptered to Peshawar and then taken by truck to Islamabad, where we would catch a night flight to Yangoon. I thought what an adventure it would really be to take the Karakoram all the way down through the river valley of the Indus, but that was not to be. I had no time to be a tourist.

Lyft said he'd meet us from time to time en route. I told him his arrival would surely coincide with meal times each day. He saw no humor at all in my quip.

For travel purposes, I was to be passed off as a rouster on an oil rig, heading for work in the Straits. Contacts within Petróleos Mexicanos had assured my paper work would be authentic. My other two companions had work as crew on a boat in Belawan, as evidenced by their Indonesian passports and other work documents.

International flights in that part of the world, no matter the length, always took off at night, so we timed our arrival in Islamabad several hours before flight time to avoid searching for accommodations in the capital city overnight. We could not afford to waste precious time waiting for the next flight twenty-four hours hence.

The flights to Malaysia normally were relatively uneventful, with the exception of the animated jabbering at ticket agents of would-be passengers who had either been bumped from their flights or who had finally showed up due to other late flights to find there was no room on the plane. The constant scenes of chaos made American flight check-in leisurely in comparison. Salvo told me there had been a shooting two nights previously at the Kuala Lumpur airport by a man who had become so incensed that his family had been bumped by an airline that he ran to his car, retrieved a machine pistol from the trunk, and then began shooting up the Malay Airlines passenger terminal. The police shot him dead outside the security area in the main lobby of the building. I asked why would the man have a machine pistol in his car. Salvo turned to me, saying, "Think about it. Normal citizens don't do that, so who was the guy really?" Not having much sympathy for terrorists or others related, I do believe my good friend Salvo thought the world a better place without the individual. He was probably right.

The main city of Kelang was a bustling traffic nightmare. The port was two hours from the airport by bus, so we decided to stay overnight in a center city hotel and then go to the port area in the morning. I was impressed with how modern the main city was, with its skyscrapers of steel and glass and its clean streets. The port areas were a different matter, however. The actual port is about five miles from the city of Kelang, actually separated into three ports: north, south, and west. It is rated as one of the busiest ports in the world, obviously growing as its freight traffic increased. It was accented with warehouses, storage facilities, including those for oil, and low-rise offices. It was anything but pedestrian friendly, as the bus and taxi terminals were well away from the passenger ferry docking area. An unpleasant, unsafe walk awaited those attempting to walk from their public transport drop-off points to the terminal loading area.

We took the Transnasional 126 bus to the port area the next morning from a stop outside the hotel, walking a little over a mile to the ferry building, where we bought tickets and waited. We had wisely partaken of breakfast at the hotel, as there was only an unsanitary greasy spoon in the ferry building that looked as if it was exempt from the local food inspector. Our boat was scheduled for departure at ten thirty aboard the Sabang Marindo II, operated by NKH Ferry Services, direct service to Belawan. We had about an hour to wait, which was no problem, as we fit in with the rest of the accumulating passenger list. We were purposefully unshaven and somewhat disheveled, most passengers exhibiting the same wan look, especially mothers carrying multiple infants, all of whom had not had enough sleep. A stray dog or two ran through the terminal chased by small boys, beggars abounded, infants yowled, and mothers jabbered until the cacophony was finally put in its place by the thundering bourdon of the arriving ferry.

It took thirty minutes for the ferry to off-load and then another few minutes for it to be readied for departing passengers. At ten fifteen, we began boarding, children, dogs, and all. In spite of the heat, the three of us decided to sit on deck, as there would at least be a breeze once we were underway. I was afraid I'd get seasick, a propensity I have never tamed, even though I've been on the water a good deal. The crowded, sweating bodies packed into the large un-air-conditioned accommodations below, along with the noise and the anticipation of eight-to ten-foot sea swells, did not make a good mix relative to the finely tuned equilibrium of my inner ear.

It was a seven-hour voyage directly northwest to Belawan. Most passengers stayed below, having more sense to remain out of the heat. The blast from the ship's horn sounded, reverberating around the deck and giving apoplexy to those not expecting it who were near its funnel. We made our way through the harbor and out into the Straits, where every type of imaginable shipping was to be seen. The water was dotted with Chinese junks, fishing and shrimp boats, container ships, cruise ships, freighters, barges, Indonesian and Australian naval vessels, the occasional high-end sailing vessel, and the ever-illicit cigarette boats always seeming to be in the distance, like the shy cousin at the sweet-sixteen party.

We'd been out about four and a half hours, located on a latitude with Sibolga, on the opposite coast of Sumatra, some forty miles south of Belawan. Lyft had clumped down onto my shoulder about ten miles ago, now snoozing lightly, rocking to the gentle swell. I was beginning to drift off as well to the rhythmic hum of the ferry engines intermingled with gentle humid sea breezes. Suddenly, the boat jerked violently to a stop, throwing the three of us along the deck until we rolled up against the cafeteria bulkhead. Lyft was propelled directly into the steel wall head first with a mighty muffled clang that would have broken a mere mortal's neck. Instead, bitter complaints emanated from thin air, screeching about the incompetence of the captain. Salvo had a nasty cut above his left eyebrow with blood streaming down his face, Bashirin thought he had broken his ankle, and I was OK except for a ringing in my ears caused by slamming my head into Bashirin's knee.

There was pandemonium on board. Women were screaming, children were crying, dogs were barking, people were entangled with one another, some piled four deep. Many exhibited physical injuries of broken bones, lacerations, and bruises, but the most dangerous result of all was panic. There was such bedlam that it was useless to attempt any calming influence. With over twelve hundred passengers aboard, it was everyone for themselves.

We gathered around each other to examine our injuries. I grabbed one of the knapsacks that had a first aid kit in it, pulled out some butterfly bandages, squeezed Salvo's wound together, and stuck on the bandages, hoping they would hold in the heat. Bashirin was deftly beginning to put pressure on the ankle he thought he had broken, exhibiting that he could support his weight on it after all. That was a relief, as the last thing we all needed was for one of us to end up in a Medan hospital. I asked Lyft if he was OK. He replied yes, that he was, in spite of the clumping he had received. Lyft said he had something to do, that he would return shortly, and that we should make ourselves as comfortable as possible until he came back.

He was back in less than five minutes.

"Where'd you go?" I queried.

"To the wheelhouse. The captain's not doing so well. He's out cold."

"You mean he's drunk?"

"Far from it. He hit his head on the impact. He's flat out on the floor of the wheelhouse. Evidently he was as surprised as we were."

"Is he going to live?"

"Yes, albeit with a nasty headache for while."

"What the hell happened?"

"Just a supposition, mind you, but I think we hit an unchartered reef of sorts."

"How could that happen? I saw charts galore when I walked by the wheelhouse earlier in the voyage."

"Yes, well, they may need updating. You remember the tsunami in 2004 that swept the Straits?"

"Who wouldn't?"

"Right, who wouldn't? Well, closer to shore, the upheaval from the displaced fault line changed the bottom topography of the Straits, even though the incident occurred on the western coast of Sumatra. The fault line was 735 miles long, and the displacement of water where the rift occurred changed the seabed forever. It looks like we've become a party to that tumult."

"Great. I wonder how we get out of here."

"Hopefully it's low tide. Even if it isn't, I don't recommend swimming in shark-infested waters. Perhaps the incoming tide will lift the boat."

"Provided it's low tide."

"Yes, provided it's low tide."

As Lyft was giving us an oceanic geography lesson, I noted black smoke creeping up the side of the vessel, disseminating into the air. A smell of sulfur was growing stronger, until the deck was enveloped in it. My eyes began to burn. Bashirin and Salvo took handkerchiefs from their pockets, placing them over their faces to help stem the stench.

"Great," I said. "Now the boat is on fire."

"Bah, the boat's not on fire, but something else sure is," pronounced Lyft. "Let me take a look. Stay here. I'll be right back."

"'Stay here,' he says. Where the hell else would we go?" I shouted.

In spite of their aches, Bashirin and Salvo gave a hearty laugh.

Bashirin said, "It never ends with you two, does it?"

"Nope."

True to form, Lyft returned after several minutes, dripping wet, sitting heavily on my shoulder.

"Ouch, that hurts. Take it easy."

"That's for your wisecrack a minute or so ago."

"Have a nice swim?"

Lyft poked me in the shoulder with a talon.

"You know, you keep that up, and I'll make sure I go pub crawling alone from now on."

The pressure eased.

Lyft said, "Here's what we've got. The boat hit a reef all right, but not just any reef. The keel has opened up a smoker. We're sitting on top of a newly minted volcano."

Bashirin asked, "Do you have any good news?"

"Not really. The water temperature around the boat is anywhere from one hundred thirty to one hundred sixty degrees, so swimming for it is useless, unless one can swim fast enough to get away from the hot spots before being overcome with fatigue. Not an option."

I piped up, "Can the bottom of the boat burn through?"

"Exactly what I was checking. I don't believe so, as we are not directly over the vent. Close enough to raise havoc, but not to do any real damage to the boat. I suggest we wait for the tide, as my best estimate says we are at slack tide."

I said, "What if the damn thing erupts?"

Lyft replied, "Then we all go up with it. If I had to, I could latch onto you all by the belt loops and fly you out of here, but I'd prefer not to do that. Might raise too many eyebrows."

Sweeping an arm to the sky, I said, "I'd prefer that option rather than becoming a human guided missile, thank you."

"Let's hope it doesn't come to that."

The bedlam had not subsided on the boat; it had increased with the smoke and foul stench of the sulfur. Some thought the gateway to hell had been opened, some thought the boat was on fire, and others thought it was the end of the world, with some screaming for the captain's head, as they were sure he had to be drunk to lay this curse on them. Evidently, the crew was incapacitated as well, as there was no one in charge of the passengers. People were screaming that it was time to abandon ship. They began ripping at the lifeboats, screaming about jumping overboard.

I yelled at Lyft over the noise, "You are the only one who knows a universal language that will be understood by all these people. You need to get on the PA system and stop the panic. If you don't, hundreds of people may be killed."

"How much do I really care about that? If these idiots want to jump, let them."

"Lyft, you don't really mean that."

"Oh, I suppose not. But it would serve them right, except for the children. I've never seen such idiocy."

"C'mon, be a sport. Do your thing in your best Godlike voice. Go wow 'em over the mic."

"I'm only doing this for you, just so you know."

"I understand, but it needs to be done and done quickly. So go."

I felt the pressure lift from my shoulder. In a few minutes, we heard the booming voice of Iblis once more.

"Now hear this. Now hear this. This is the first mate speaking. I want everyone to calm down and listen. There is no need for panic. There is no need to abandon ship. Now *listen*!"

Even I jumped on that one.

He explained the situation, noting that the captain was hurt and had not been drinking, assuring the passengers that they were in no immediate danger and that the crew would be around with first aid kits followed by helicopters to remove the most severely injured among them. He explained why they shouldn't attempt to swim and concluded with the admonition, "If you need water, go to the cafeteria on the upper deck, and take what you need. There is enough for everyone. Women and children first, please. No running, and no panic. Remember, panic kills."

Lyft then called an SOS, which was received by numerous ships in the Straits who said they would relay the message to the proper authorities. He returned to the three of us, who were sitting down, relieved to have heard his masterful act.

Lyft queried, "Does anyone know how to shut off the boat's engines? It might be a good idea to take the strain off the engines, as we're not going anywhere for a while."

"I think I can figure it out," said Salvo. "I've been around boats all my life. Jeff, give me the first aid kit, and let's see how our captain is doing."

Salvo and I made our way forward to the wheelhouse, where the captain was still stretched out unconscious on the floor. There was a small pool of blood by his head, so we assumed the worst until we heard him moan. I tended to him, where I found a nasty gash just beyond his front hairline. As he was coming to, he began making motions that his chest hurt. He coughed and spit up blood. I opened his shirt but couldn't see anything wrong.

"Probably jammed himself against the wheel when we hit the reef. He may have broken ribs and punctured a lung. If so, we've got to get him immediate attention," noted Salvo.

Salvo was studying the controls as he spoke, trying to figure out the language.

"I can't read the damn language on the console. Can't figure out which switch is which," exclaimed Salvo.

Luckily for us, Lyft arrived with Bashirin in tow, offering to help.

"How may I be of service?" Lyft inquired.

"Well, you can tell me what's what on this console here so I can shut down the engines," said Salvo.

Modesty an anathema in his vocabulary, Lyft proceeded to go through the console and lecture Salvo on the purpose of each function displayed. I could see that Salvo was getting agitated.

Finally, he blew. "Shit, Lyft, just tell me how to shut down the engines. I don't need a lesson in marine navigation."

Imperiously, Lyft intoned, "I disagree. But to alleviate your temporary insanity, here's the shut-off switch."

Salvo flipped it, and immediately, they began to wind down.

"Now as to your consternation, you may very well have to know these functions. Where's the first mate, huh? Where's the petty officer? Where's the engineer? Where's the rest of the crew or anybody who can sail this tub off this rock when the tide comes in? For all we know, they're incapacitated or worse. So you may be the guy. You'd best listen up."

"If it comes to that, I will certainly sail this thing to port," Salvo said, raising his chest and conceding begrudgingly. "But surely they'll have a harbormaster in Medan someplace they can bring out here to get this thing home."

"Well, what if they don't? We'll have to handle it like we do everything else. So, my suggestion is to learn these functions, get a slip of paper, make a map of the console, and then spell it out in English so you know what you're doing, just in case. Would anyone disagree?"

Silence.

"Good. Then I'm not such a didactic ogre after all. I think the captain needs medical attention."

"Brilliant observation," I quacked. "Our diagnosis is concussion and cracked ribs, with maybe a punctured lung. What's yours?" I queried sarcastically.

"My, we are out of sorts. What's gotten into you?"

"You and your attitude. Instead of being such a know-it-all, perhaps you could explain up front why something should be done so you don't make people, especially those close to you, end up disliking you. Remember that you need us as much as we need you. It would seem that we are in a mutually cooperative effort, so why don't you act in accordance with that precept?"

"Excuse me, I think I need some air."

Lyft departed the room.

"Kind of rough on the little guy. You think he'll be OK?" Bashirin said softly.

"He'll get over it," I said. "Sometimes he needs a boot in the arse. He'll come around. Let him nurse his wounds a little. Do him good."

We issued another mayday for medical emergency. There was no dearth of ships around, so we received several answers that help was on the way. Luckily, there was an Australian Hospital ship in the Straits heading north to Aceh, which dispatched a medevac helicopter to our location. We heard it in the distance. Realizing that it had no place to land on the ship, this would be a cable and winch operation. Two medical personnel were lowered onto the rear deck, and then a folding stretcher was lowered, along with oxygen and other supplies. They quickly made their way to the wheelhouse, where they assessed the situation. They loaded the captain onto the stretcher, initially concurring with our amateur diagnosis, and took him to the rear deck, where they gave him over to the crew on the winch. They returned as soon as he was loaded into the chopper.

"How are the other casualties?" they inquired.

I said, "We're not sure. There must be others, but we've been busy here. We figured out how to shut off the engines and have been tending to the captain, but as to the rest of the boat, that's a question mark."

"We'll make the rounds and see what we find."

"Thanks for your help."

"Hey, it's what we do. Let's get to it," one said to the other.

Another helicopter joined the first, with the first making way so that more medical personnel could be lowered. This time, six more people were dropped off, who would be needed, as there were over twelve hundred passengers on board. They made their way through the jumble, separating the badly injured from the rest, bringing those hurt the worst to the upper rear deck, where they soon would be transported to the ship. Meanwhile, the hospital ship had made its way toward us and was now anchored about a mile distant, waiting on its errand of mercy.

Miraculously, there were only sixty-five serious injuries. It appeared that the same thing that had happened to us had happened to a lot of people, mainly that most folks caromed into each other, with the most seriously injured those who were catapulted into unforgiving objects, such as bulkheads, rails, and fixed seats. No one had been killed, which would not satisfy the media, but it suited us just fine.

It took the majority of the day to get everyone off-loaded into the choppers. Lyft still hadn't materialized. We did what we could to help the medical personnel administer to the injured, giving the wounded water and comfort where we could, although the language barrier was an issue from time to time. Finally, the last of the casualties were whisked off to the hospital cruiser, where they would eventually be deposited in the hospital in Medan. Salvo's eye had been stitched up, with compliments to me closing it so rapidly, which made sewing it easier. Bashirin's ankle was swollen but not broken, a sprain that would heal if he kept his weight off it. He said as long as it wasn't broken, he could deal with it. That and a little vodka for pain and relief.

The Australian Navy had sent the equivalent of a U.S. Navy Seal team over to inspect the bottom of the ferry. They found no significant damage and pronounced the vessel seaworthy. They also believed the incoming tide would raise it off the bottom. By this time, high tide was near, so the issue arose as to who would take command of the ferry once it was afloat. We had petitioned the authorities in Belawan to send a pilot to guide the ship to port, but no one was available. The Australians had no one available either, nor any of the surrounding countries bordering the Straits. No one on board was in any shape to operate the vessel, as the first mate and engineer had been medevaced off the boat, and anyone else left in the crew had less experience than we did in the wheelhouse. Salvo was becoming exasperated, beginning to envision himself piloting the ship past Medan to Belawan. We were all beginning to be infected with stage fright.

"Shit," he yelled. "Is there no one to sail this tub up the coast? I really don't feel competent to do this. What are we supposed to do? Float around the Straits, bounce off other ships like a pinball, praying for no tilt? They just can't leave us here. This is insane."

"I agree. What do they expect us to do? This is nuts," I yelled.

Just then, a familiar presence clumped down on my shoulder.

"Told you so," he said softly.

"Oh, you're back. Nurse your wounds, eh?"

"Actually, yes, and you were right. I apologize to all assembled here. I was out of order, which is unlike me. I feel it was due to the pressure of the moment."

"I disagree with the part about it being unlike you, but we'll let that one go. We need some help here. There's no one to take this tub to Belawan."

"*Sukiny deti*," yelled Bashirin. "None of them will help us."

Lyft intoned, "I can take this tub to Belawan, with a little help. Would that suit you?"

"Very much so," we all replied in unison.

"I'd say we've another hour to high tide. You feel that? The boat just moved a little. We're as good as there. Here's the game plan. When the boat floats free, we crank up the engines in reverse to get us away from the reef, for about a half mile, I'd say, so we can eventually skirt around it, giving it a wide berth. Then we swing to starboard and go down the middle of the Straits, instead of hugging the coast as our previous pilot did. Then we pitch to port and go straight down the river to Belawan. Hopefully, by the time we get there, there will be a harbor pilot to take us in, as that could get messy."

"It's *up* the river to Belawan."

"You know," Lyft yelled at me, "I'm not the only one who's impossible around here sometimes. I ought to let you take the controls and see how you fare with this monstrosity you call a ferryboat. You'd reverse us back to Kelang, where we could take this enjoyable journey all over again."

"You might have a point there."

"Touché for me. Now, let's take a crash course, pun intended."

Bashirin and Salvo guffawed at that one, and I even let out a chuckle, having been properly put in my place. So far for the day, the score between Lyft and me was one–one.

Salvo actually had made a readable map of the console, which outlined pretty much all the needed functions of commanding the boat. Some were not intuitive, but together, we figured out most of them. The ones we didn't, we would try on faith. We surmised that we could do no worse than what had already been done. So a little experimentation might serve us well if we had to navigate the behemoth up the river.

High tide was upon us. We felt the boat beginning to have some movement to it, but it had not yet floated free. We agreed that perhaps the ship needed a little nudge, like a newly minted teenager at her first prom, confronted with her first girls' choice. Lyft had Salvo fire up the engines.

Lyft got onto the loudspeaker and, in his best command voice, said, "Now hear this. Now hear this. We have found a pilot to take us to Belawan. We are going to reverse the boat sharply to get it off the reef. Everyone must take a seat immediately, as we are about to perform this maneuver. Everyone please take a seat and hold on tight. We are about to reverse the boat. We are about to reverse the boat. We will give you five minutes to get settled."

He spoke in three different languages, including English, to ensure all understood what was about to take place. He gave the passengers the allotted amount of time, and then told Salvo to place the boat in reverse. We gave the boat time to adjust, and then Salvo gunned the engines. The propellers whined, and the boat jolted, but it did not come free. He wound down the engines and then tried again, with the same result. We felt we were close, but our teenager needed another type of nudge. Lyft got on the loudspeaker again.

"We need all passengers to come to the rear of the boat. We need to take the weight off the front and midsections. All passengers to the rear of the boat. We will try to reverse again in five minutes."

Again in the allotted time, Lyft told Salvo to try once more. This time, the boat slid off the reef gently, the reluctant teenager tentatively engaging in her first dance. A great cheering roar went up from the passengers, as they realized that this was not their day to perish after all. Salvo kept the boat in reverse for the designated half mile, and then Lyft instructed him to place the ship in neutral, and then forward, directing the vessel into the center of the Straits, making way for Belawan. Lyft over the loudspeaker directed the passengers back to their seats and told them the immediate danger was past. I noted that he used the term "immediate danger," because he was as unsure as the rest of us about the remainder of the voyage. Salvo kept hitting the ferry's horn to warn other shipping to stay clear, his only defense against his inexperience. We all agreed that six knots, although decidedly slow, was an appropriate speed. Lyft, ever watchful, hovered in full sight, as there was no one else in the wheelhouse but us.

As we made slow progress, Lyft began another educational monolog. As he plowed into more diatribe, I noted the dimming light through the windscreen, allowing the console lights their due. They reminded me of Christmas decorations, placed with thoughtful care, some having their functionality color-coded in greens and reds intermixed with the obligatory golden hues of dials and needles encased in glass.

"Did you know," he pontificated from his perch on a revolving stool, "that the total energy released by the 2004 earthquake was just shy of a gigaton of TNT? Or, to put it another way, the equivalent of eleven days of energy consumption in the United States? The Earth's surface oscillated anywhere from eight to twelve inches, and the entire surface of the Earth heaved vertically to one centimeter. The shift of mass altered the Earth's rotation slightly. It caused the Earth to wobble on its axis as well, by about an inch in the direction of 145 degrees east longitude." I noticed a wobble in Bashirin as well, as he repositioned his leg on a stool opposite the one he was sitting on to avoid placing pressure on it. Although he could walk on it, he preferred to rest it to minimize any swelling. Lyft continued, "It has since recovered due to the tidal effects of the Moon. I won't bore you with some of the other statistics, but Mother put on quite a show, I'd say. And I fear it's not over yet."

I asked the sage, "What do you think is the worst that could happen if Mother decides not to wait on our scheme?"

He spun to me, taking his attention away from the windscreen. "That all the plates expand at the same time, resulting in concurrent upheavals a thousand times worse than the 2004 incident. The Earth as we know it would be totally destroyed."

"That pretty much sums it up," I quipped.

"Yup."

I looked out onto the Straits, able now to see the lights of ships all around us, hoping they all understood maritime etiquette. I didn't want to contemplate the thought of an unlit vessel anywhere in front of us. I said, "But you don't think that's going to happen, do you?"

He turned his attention to the front again, peering out through the thick glass. "Hard to say. If we can get the plan together in time, I really do think we have a shot at averting catastrophe. What I think will happen, even before we implement, is that Mother will blow off some steam, kind of like the sewer covers in New York City that blow up from time to time for one reason or another."

"Apt analogy," I intoned. I looked at Salvo, understanding his reticence, as his aquiline features were tensely concentrating on the task at hand, blowing the ship's horn at thirty-second intervals.

"Yes, I rather thought so," replied His Eminence.

As we slowly made our way north, we kept radioing the port authorities in Belawan, who finally answered, yes, they would send a pilot out at the five mile mark. It was a good thing, otherwise we would have to operate the ferry in the dark, as the day was rapidly waning. Lyft asked how we would know when we arrived at the marker, and the reply was, when we passed the five-mile marker in the shipping lane. Lyft replied that we were not in the shipping lane and that he didn't even know where it was, so how could we know to radio back when we would obviously miss the marker? This went on back and forth until the radio man in exasperation told them to radio back when we saw the MV Alpine, the storage and floating production system for the Langsa Oil Pool north of Medan, situated in the Straits. Once that came into view, we would be approximately five miles out from the entrance to the port. But we had to edge our way west on the course heading he gave to us in order to eventually see the facility, as we were now plodding down the center of the Straits, which would take us past the oil pool most probably without even seeing MV Alpine.

We maneuvered as instructed, and sure enough, after a few hours, we saw a large facility in the distance as promised. We radioed the port, and soon a helicopter arrived. The pilot was let down on the rear deck by cable. He made his way to the wheelhouse. Luckily, he spoke passable English. He was not the same individual

Lyft had spoken to earlier, which made things easier, as suspicions would have been aroused if anyone asked for the person who had spoken his native tongue previously on the radio.

The pilot expertly took over the controls, cranked up the engines, and placed us at the ferry terminal without further incident. It was past dark by the time we arrived, so we decided to get something to eat and find a place to rest for the night. It was a wise move on our part, because we would need every ounce of our reserve to cope with what awaited.

Chapter Eighteen

Santiago, Chile

General Ricardo Emillio Estavez, a Spanish look-alike to Ali Sastroamidjojo Sr., was at the moment pressed by many concerns. His two mistresses were braying for more money, saying they would leave him if he didn't treat them in accordance with their stature. This was getting out of hand, intermittently punching hold buttons, yelling at one and then the other. He wished he had them in front of him in his office so that he could strangle them both and be done with it. He rolled his eyes, swore to the air, and then told each they were already treated in accordance with their station in life, whores on a street corner. If they didn't like it, they could go public, adding that they would do so at the risk of their lives. That seemed to shut them up for the moment, but he knew they'd be back for more. He figured he needed to dump them, perhaps take them both for a plane ride on a purported sightseeing journey to an island, where he knew there to be buried treasure. They'd be just greedy enough to want to go along. Then he could push both of them out the rear door of the plane.

While fantasizing about the elimination of the two thorns in his side, the phone rang again.

"Mother of God," he yelled to no one in particular. "This better not be one of those two bitches calling me back. I'll kill whichever one it is."

Ready to explode and give better than he took, he grabbed the phone, ready for battle. It was his wife, Maria, the diminutive, sweet lady of his life on whom he continually cheated; she knew it but had no recourse but acceptance. She had long ago reconciled herself to a less than perfect marriage with her fat, lout husband. As long as the baubles and money were in the pipeline, she was content to let him do as he pleased. She would make his life a living hell if he failed to keep her as she wished, however, and he knew it. He treated her with great deference, making up for his lack of performance in the bedroom by ceding the power of the marriage to her. She liked it that way. Sex could be obtained anywhere. Power to her was a stronger elixir, harder to come by and much more fun to wield.

She cooed into the phone, "Darling, when are you going back to that nasty little island to make sure those gringos don't stumble on that treasure you know is buried there? I want to make sure no one steals our birthright."

Estavez chuckled. "I was just thinking about going back there, as a matter of fact. The last time I was there, there was no evidence of anything amiss, so I wouldn't worry if I were you. Why, would you like to come along?"

"No, darling, just checking to make sure that you aren't holding out on your dear Maria. I know you so well Emillio. It would be just like you to discover something and not tell me."

Making a sweeping gesture to the air, ending with one palm up as if she were in front of him, he cooed into the phone, "Sweetheart, I would never do that. If anything is found, you will be the first to know."

"No, if anything is found, the press will be the first to know. I'll be the last to know. That's how I know nothing's been found. You know, the islanders hate you with a passion, so if there is any hint of a find anywhere on that island, they'll make sure it goes public immediately to ensure they share in it. So you had better be the first to find it, if you can find it, which I doubt you can, and keep it quiet when and if you do. But my fantasies run away with me. I think this is your fantasy, not mine. Mine are already being fulfilled and in that regard. How about filling my checking account this week? I'm a little low on cash. I've only got a hundred thousand left in it."

Estavez looked around his office, focusing on the painting on the opposite wall of a stunning view of Santiago, evidently rendered from the top of one of the ski resorts that looked down upon the valley. How he wished he could be up there, away from the minxes who continually brought stomach acid to his throat. He said absently, "Only a hundred thousand, you say? Well, we can't have that. I'll tend to it right away. Anything else, my sweet?"

"Yes, the Rolls needs servicing, and I need a new mink."

"You just bought a new mink last week."

"That wasn't a mink; that was a sable. I need a new *mink* for my new outfit I bought last week. The sable won't do. It's too dark. I need a lighter mink for the party next month."

Estavez crumpled a piece of paper on his desk, balling it in his fist as he replied, "Why don't you just go out and buy it? You've enough to handle that in your account."

"Oh, I'll buy it all right, but I'll charge it to your account. My account isn't for my clothes, you remember, we discussed that. My account is for me, and your account is also for me, remember? My account doesn't buy mink coats, yours does. Remember, it's the man's job to take care of his wife, no?"

"Yes, my sweet, anything you want. Make yourself happy, and do as you wish." He threw the paper ball with a snap of his wrist against the painting, watching it fall on the carpet.

"Now, that's a lot better. Good luck on your little visit to the island. I hope you come back awash in gold."

"Yes, thank you, little one, that would be very nice. Goodbye."

"Goodbye."

He hung up the phone, thinking of a way to get all three of the vipers on the plane to rid himself of the albatrosses hung from his neck. He'd have to work on that.

He called his pilot, who was always on standby, to ready the plane for Selkirk's. Not really expecting to find anything there, he figured this to be just another short pain-in-the-neck excursion to eat up more of his day. He left his office and went downstairs to the waiting driver who transferred him to the airport. He greeted his pilot who closed the door of the plane after him, taxied to the end of the runway, and then took off after receiving clearance. Although the flight would be about an hour, at least he was away from those hyenas who continually nipped at him over the phone. He sat back to rest, falling fast asleep, his snoring a resounding bellow inside the cabin.

The plane landed with a jolt fifty-five minutes later. Estavez came awake with a snort, noticing with disgust that drool from his open-mouthed medley had dripped down onto his uniform. He grabbed his handkerchief, attempting to dab his uniform dry, when he stuck himself in his middle finger with a pin that had come loose from one of his medals, welling up a small mound of blood on the tip of his appendage.

"Shit," he screamed in frustration.

He squeezed the finger to drain the pinprick quickly and then sopped it up on his handkerchief. He stuck the hanky back in his pocket and made ready to exit the plane. The pilot came through the cockpit door to ask if things were OK with the general, having heard a yell.

"Yes, I'm OK. I received a wound from one of the pins on my shirt, which, frankly, hurts like hell, but I'll live."

"Oh, well, is there anything I can do? We have some alcohol on board in the med kit. Perhaps it would be best to put some on the wound to avoid infection."

"No, thank you. Alcohol stings badly. I will be fine."

The pilot turned, rolling his eyes in his head, wondering what the fat baby would do if he had suffered a serious injury. He'd have to undertake a psychological study of this sociopath in order to understand how one so squeamish could dispense such cruelty to others. He figured it was something in the general's childhood and left it at that.

Estavez always liked to arrive on the island unannounced, hoping to find Alvarez's crew in the midst of scurrying to hide newly discovered treasure. Although he had been involved with several treasure hunts subsidized by private financiers, nothing was ever found on the island, in spite of one company promising that if there were metal buried anywhere on the island, a new machine recently invented could find it. What it found was zero, as it failed to operate as advertised. Having been let down often, Estavez had few expectations of ever finding anything. However, since there was an excavation going on, why not snoop around just in case?

The pilot went to the shed that housed the Jeep next to the tarmac, unlocked it, and brought the Jeep to the plane. The general climbed in, the drool between the rows of ribbons and medals having dried in the sun as he waited on the driver. They proceeded to the construction site, where he saw Alvarez overseeing the excavation of the pit, noting that not much progress had been made since last week. He climbed out of the Jeep, all smiles as he approached Alvarez, the medals and ribbons swaying with each step, resembling a syrupy fruit cocktail splattered on his chest.

"How are you, my friend? It's good to see you once again."

"Why hello, General. On your weekly checkup I see."

"Yes, and not much progress since last week I note. Tell me, why is that?"

"We had a change of plan, and instead of locating the housing here, we decided that the main plant would go here, so the excavation had to halt until new plans for the foundation were approved for the specific site. We are now back in business, so you will see much more activity and progress from now on."

"Why did you decide to relocate the plant site?"

"The soil in the other location was too unstable to support the weight of the facility. This site has proven to be a better fit for the substructure underpinnings of the plant. As you know, this plant is relatively large, so it requires stability to support it."

"Ah, yes, I see. So no sign of any buried treasure, eh?"

"Unfortunately for us all, no. However, you'll be the first to know, you being the official representative of the Chilean government. Alas, so far, nothing but dirt and more dirt. Some sand once in a while, but mostly just dirt. It would be exciting to find something though, don't you think?"

"Yes. Yes, it would. I would like that very much."

"Yes, I'll bet you would. Well, we'll let you know if we come across anything."

"Thank you. However, people have been digging out here for years finding nothing. I expect the same from you, no insult intended."

"None taken."

"Well, I'll be off. I'll see you next week."

The fat general climbed back into the Jeep, moving away, when it suddenly stopped near the area where the tombs were buried. Alvarez knew there was no way suspicions could be aroused, as the truck traffic passing over the site all week had rendered it looking like the rest of the area. He went over to ensure the cover story.

"Something else I can do for you, General?"

"No," Estavez said with squinted eyes, looking over the site. "I was just looking over the expansion, which is larger than it was last week." Estevez reminded Alvarez of a greedy hog, eyes narrowed on a barnyard find.

He said evenly, "Due to soil samples; we were testing various areas to relocate the plant. The one being excavated proved most effective."

"Ah, I see. Well, best of luck. I look forward to steel in the ground soon."

"We too."

"See you next week."

"Yes, I look forward to it."

The Jeep moved on. Alvarez hoped he had averted any suspicion, indeed, if any suspicions had been raised. What he really wanted was for Lyft and company to re-excavate the treasure and get it the hell off the island. The sooner, the better.

CHAPTER NINETEEN

Belawan

After a restless night in an un-air-conditioned flophouse, we found a small café, where the coffee was passable and the sweet pastries delicious. We decided to take our time, as the bar did not open until eleven in the morning, although chances were that one could obtain a drink in that establishment at any time with the right connection. After our feeble attempts at rousing ourselves with coffee, we made our way back to the "hotel" to change into clothes more suitable to our purported stations. Bashirin had packed some old Russian Army fatigues, filthy boots, and a dirty motor pool cap. He looked like a different person in them. His ankle injury, luckily for us all, turned out to be a slight twist, so the swelling was minimal. Salvo had more traditional dress: standard Italian street clothes, the disheveled Armani look, needing an upgrade but not being able to afford it. If anyone asked about the bandage above his eye, he'd simply tell the truth about the ferry accident. I had on torn kakis, a dirty olive green T-shirt, black construction boots, a gray sweatshirt stained with grease, and a jaunty black cap with a snapped visor. When I looked in the mirror, I really did look like a lost soul in a foreign land, pinched face from no sleep the night before and all. It was going to be a long day.

Lyft felt it best for Salvo and Bashirin to scout around the boat. He gave them directions, and they said they could get there on their own, even though it was some eighteen miles up the river. Lyft thought it would perhaps be a better plan if I went into the bar alone to inquire after the Sastroamidjojo clan. He, of course, would be with me, but he preferred to remain invisible after his last encounter there. The last item of concern was young Ali's cell phone. I almost forgot it. Lyft made sure it went into one of my front pockets. It would be proof of my contact with young Ali, provided the battery was not completely dead.

As we prepared to leave, Lyft said, "Sit down a minute. I need to talk to you."

I sat on the edge of the bed.

Lyft floated in front of me, all business. "You remember I said I was going to interview young Ali for the 'hook?'"

"Yes, I remember it. I really didn't know what you meant, but I thought it had something to do with convincing the family of my sincere intentions."

"You are a quick study, I'll say that. And that's exactly what it is. Ali has left a message on the cell phone. You can't listen to it, because you are not supposed to know what it is, plus the battery is probably dead. You just know it's there. Ali confided in you that if anything were to occur to him, since you two became confidants at the plant site, you were to contact the family, handing over the cell phone to them so that they could listen to his message. Sure enough, Ali went up with the plant, you struggled out of the Wakhan on the route previously stipulated on the Karakoram, making your way here through kind benefactors. They must listen to the message in short order for this to work. We do not want them waiting for a week, making funeral arrangements before they hear it. I am counting that the father will be chomping at the bit to do so, once he's learned his only son has been killed. The problem will be to get the phone charged."

I looked directly into those intelligent eyes centered on me. "I understand. The phone's been off ever since we left the Wahkan. There should be some charge still left in it. Cell phones generally run down with usage. So we should be OK there." I took the phone out of my pocket and clicked it on to see the charge three quarters down, enough for our purposes. I clicked it off, not wanting to use the charge more than necessary. "Looks OK—good enough, anyway. By the way, how did you ever get Ali to leave this message on the phone?"

Lyft raised his arms to hip height. "I didn't. Bashirin did. He simply threatened to kill Ali's mother and father. It's amazing what incarceration against one's will can do to the mind. All sorts of things well up in isolation. We had little trouble with the boy cooperating. I actually felt kind of sorry for him. He was as unprepared for being captured as he was for his overall role in this escapade. It gives you an insight into what kind of man the father is for promoting the scheme in the first place, using his only son for such bidding. We'll deal with the old man, though. We'll break him, if all goes as planned."

I looked out the small window and then back again to Lyft. "Yes, I believe we will. Are we ready to be off?"

"I believe we are. Remember, I will be close by, hearing everything, so not to worry."

I stood up, happy to be relieved of the depressing atmosphere in the small room, which contained nothing more than a cheap iron bed, a nightstand and lamp, rough wooden floors that, at one time, had seen maybe a coat of varnish, and a small, useless overhead fan. The dismal light green walls desperately in need of paint reminded me of an old hospital room in a war zone. I stated, "I'm not worried. A little nervous, maybe, but not worried. I would be if you weren't here, though."

"Thank you for that. Now let's go."

We went out into the street, making our way into the seedier area of Belawan, where we found the alley leading to The Blue Lady.

Lyft said into my ear, "I used Bahasa on the bartender, which is the official language around here, but you won't need to do that. I believe he speaks passable English. I exercised that caution because of subterfuge. You need not employ such a tactic, as English is native to you, and you will be expected to know no other form of communication, being an Irish expat. Ready?"

"Ready."

"You make your way up the alley. I'll go in and check out what's going on inside the bar."

"Right."

I did as instructed, waiting a few seconds outside the bar until Lyft settled upon my shoulder.

"Bar's pretty empty. Not much going on at the moment. A couple of seedy characters sitting there, looking like they've been there a while. Same bartender, though. He probably opened up early for his regular customers, if you can call them that. Now would be a good time for you to make your entrance. I'll be right near you."

"OK, here we go then," I said in my finest Irish brogue.

The door opened outward with a long, loud creak, ensuring all in the bar were now aware of my presence. I would have to ask Lyft how he got into the bar unnoticed, invisible or not. I thought the lack of door maintenance to be purposeful, an early warning sign due to the continual illicit activity within. I wondered if my paranoia was getting the best of me.

I wandered up to the bar and ordered a draft, throwing a five-dollar bill on the bar. Although it was five o'clock somewhere, the beer tasted rancid on top of the recently consumed coffee and pastries. *Anything for Mother*, I thought. I noted that the mirror behind the bar had been replaced. I wondered if the hole behind it had been repaired as well. After a few sips, I began what I hoped would not be a one-sided conversation with the bartender.

"So, do ya speck English, lad?"

"I speak a little, yes. I have not seen you here before. What's an Irishman doing in Sumatra?"

"Ah, a good question, that. I'm about the Sastroamidjojo family, trying to find the old man, ya see. Don't happen to know the address, now wouldja?"

"Many people lately seem to be interested in this family. The last one with such an interest tore up my bar and nearly killed a man in the process. Except that we could not see who was doing it. A very strange occurrence. But Allah works in mysterious ways, no? What would be your business with this family?"

"Ah, lad, I'm unfortunately here as a messenger with bad news, yeh, bad news, mind ya. But I can only tell the family that, you see, not wanting the news to get ahead of me, if you get me drift, so I need the address to relate what I've got in me head."

Lyft whispered in my ear, "Brilliant performance. You deserve an Oscar for this. I shall see that you get one."

I ignored him.

"I see. Let me make a phone call. You seem like an honest chap. Please remain here while I place the call."

"Many thanks for that, me friend."

The bartender went down the corridor leading to the unisex bathroom, where a pay phone was located. I figured that the bathroom was really a men's room, as I couldn't conceive of any women ever frequenting the establishment, much less ever wanting to utilize the facilities. Lyft, ever watchful, told me he thought the bartender in all probability was calling one of the two slicks who oversaw the boat up in Lama Village. I just nodded slightly, exhibiting that I had heard his comment.

The bartender returned.

"There will be someone here within the hour. If they believe whatever story you have to tell them, then they will have the responsibility of deciding if you get through the Sastroamidjojo gates. Until then, enjoy your beer. It's on the house."

"I appreciate your hospitality, me man. Very kind of you, very kind indeed."

In spite of the fact that I was confronted with free beer, neither my taste nor my mood matched the bartender's benevolence. It was imperative to think clearly pertaining to whatever lay ahead, so I ensured I took no advantage of his offer. I nursed the beer to the half-hour mark and then ordered another to be polite. Luckily, they tasted like a few hops in sink water.

Five minutes before the designated hour, the two slicks walked into the bar. True to form, they were dressed in maroon and gabardine. The bartender nodded his head toward me. As they approached, they said nothing, but they motioned for me to come off the bar and be seated at a table in the corner. I did so, scraping a chair out from under the round table on the rough-planked floor.

They took seats, were offered drinks by the bartender, and waved him off, and then maroon slacks began. We were situated opposite each other, maroon leaning forward, hands folded on the table, gabardine seated back, arms folded. I leaned forward, clasping my hands together, relaxed, but all business.

Looking me directly in the eyes, he queried, "You speak English?"

Looking directly back at him, "Yes, lad, I do."

"Irish?"

"It's the truth."

"Where from?"

"Kilkeel in County Down."

"I don't know that place. What is it like?"

Figuring they may very well know what it was like, I had done my homework. These two weren't stupid.

"It's a fishin' village with one the largest fleets in all Ireland, a beautiful place, where the Mountains of Mourne come down to meet the sea," I said, waving one arm in an expansive gesture, as if to picture it in the air.

"Northern Ireland?"

Placing my hands back together, I replied, "Aye, lad, it's a fact."

"And how did Kilkeel come by its name?"

"In Irish, it's Cill Chaoil, meanin' 'church o' the narrow place.' There's an old fourteenth century church overlookin' the town on a narra hill, and from it, the town was named."

"What type of fish are caught in this vicinity?"

"Mainly herring and shrimp. Some cod."

"For what is Kilkeel famous?"

"Well, not really much, ta tell the truth. At one time, perhaps as far beck as the eleventh century, Kilkeel, a proper Christian community mind ya, was the capital of the ancient Kingdom of Mourne. Today, it's better known as commemeratin' the brave soul of Robert Hill Hanna, who won the Victoria Cross in 1917 in France. The tale has it that he took out a machine gun nest on top of a hill while under fire. Although Canadian with a Canadian company of men during the war, he was born near Kilkeel with lots of relatives still around, so we take him as one of ours, mind ya. His sword hangs on a wall in the Kilkeel British Legion in the village."

"Anything else?"

I flapped both arms in the air in a frustrated gesture. "This is a proper inquisition, isn't it so? I mean, boyos, I'm here to do the Sastroamidjojo clan a bit of a favor, but here we are, wastin' time with the queries. This to me is a right load of bullshit, if ya don't mind me sayin' so. I mean, I can take or leave tha task as it stands; it's nothin' ta me. Just say the word, an' I'll be on me way." I leaned back in my chair, arms folded.

Maroon pointed at me, a flash in his eyes. "And we are here to make sure people like you approaching the family are on legitimate business. Surely with your background you can understand a bit of caution."

I remained in my posture. "Surely I do. So have at it. Mind you, I get bored rather easily, so much more of an inquiry an' I might be forced to forget why I came here. Like I said, in me eyes, I'm doin' a dyin' lad a favor."

That got them going. They looked at one another and paled when I mentioned the "dyin' lad" part.

Slightly contrite, maroon pressed on. "We will continue, but we will be brief. So, what else is your part of the country famous for?"

I put my hands up to shoulder level, palms up. "Well, there's always Percy French."

"Who is that?"

"One of Northern Ireland's most beloved poets. He was a painter and musician as well. He painted the Mountains of Mourne, from which he drew inspiration for the song o' same."

Maroon finally leaned back, beginning to relax, hands on his knees. "How does it go?"

With this, Lyft whispered in my ear that he would carry the tune, but did I know the words? I jerked my head yes, pretending that I had a slight crick in my neck. How he knew the tune, I would have to ask him, as I could not fathom a Klinque knowing anything about Irish music. I would also have to query about the telepathic part of the equation.

"Well, it goes like this, with apologies to dear ol' Percy."

Lyft began the tune in my head, something akin to "Sweet Betsy of Pike" but more melodious, slower, and with a little more soul.

> Oh, Mary, this London's a wonderful sight,
> With people here workin' by day and by night.
> Sure they don't sow potatoes, nor barley, nor wheat,
> But there's gangs of them digging for gold in the street.
> At least when I asked them that's what I was told,
> So I just took a hand at this digging for gold,
> But for all that I found there I might as well be
> Where the Mountains of Mourne sweep down to the sea.

> I believe that when writing a wish you expressed
> As to how the fine ladies in London were dressed,
> Well if you'll believe me, when axed to a ball,
> They don't wear a top to their dresses at all,
> Oh I've seen them meself and you could not in truth,
> Say that if they were bound for a ball or a bath.
> Don't be starting them fashions, now Mary mo chroi,
> Where the Mountains of Mourne sweep down to the sea.

> You remember young Peter O'Loughlin, of course,
> Well, now he is here at the head of the force.
> I met him today, I was crossing the Strand,
> And he stopped the whole street with a wave of his hand.
> And there we stood talkin' of days that are gone,
> While the whole population of London looked on.
> But for all these great powers he's wishful like me,
> To be back where the dark Mourne sweeps down to the sea.

> There's beautiful girls here, oh never you mind,
> With beautiful shapes nature never designed,
> And lovely complexions all roses and cream,
> But let me remark with regard to the same:
> That if at those roses you venture to sip,
> The colours might all come away on your lip,
> So I'll wait for the wild rose that's waiting for me
> In the place where the dark Mourne sweeps down to the sea.

Lyft had expertly carried the tune just ahead of me so that I could follow it easily, signing softly to keep my ear to his music.

"Well done," the two slicks intoned together.

Evidently, my musical debut had convinced them I was authentic.

"What is your nature of business with the Sastroamidjojo family?"

"Well, it's for Ali Senior's ears only, lads. I wouldn't be goin' tellin' 'im this, but let's just say there's one less on the family tree."

"This will kill Ali Senior," gabardine said softly.

"That's why ya lads need to lave it ta me to do the dirty work. Nothin' I'm not used to, mind ya. Ya just pave the way, so ta spake."

Lyft whispered, "Now we're getting some place. Brilliant performance. I shall recommend you to the Royal Shakespeare Company in London. Bravo."

I could see that what was needed here, immediately if not sooner, was a giant swift kick in Lyft's posterior region.

"Wait here while we make a phone call," said gabardine.

Both got up, exiting out into the alley, where the ubiquitous cell phone was displayed for a call, hopefully to Ali. I saw them both passing the phone back and forth, probably Ali being careful, corroborating the story, not wanting any foreign entanglements at this delicate stage of operations. I saw a head shake yes, hopefully a positive sign.

The two came back into the bar and sat down, with maroon leading.

"We have a car in the street beyond the alley. The master of the house agrees that you should be admitted to the grounds. He will give you an audience in his study. The time to go is now, as he has impending important business and has little time for such discussions. I did not tell him the exact nature of your business. I believe you are correct in that regard. Some things need to be done in person. So he does not know exactly why you have come. I told him you had word about his son. That's all I said. I leave the rest to you. Good luck, my friend. I would not want to have this unpleasant task. Shall we go?"

We all stood up, exited the bar, and walked through the alley to the street, where a black Mercedes S65 AMG awaited us. It looked like the family business was prospering. I figured this could outrun anything around Belawan, Medan, or the entire country, for that matter, with its 604 horsepower V-12 twin turbocharged engine growling under the hood. Maroon opened the rear door, I climbed in behind the passenger seat as he shut the door, and then he went around the car and entered from the other side to fill the backseat. Gabardine sat in the front, commanding the chauffer to take us to the Sastroamidjojo compound. Lyft had zipped into the back with me, deciding to sit on my lap to avoid any physical contact with maroon. The roads in Belawan are not known for practiced maintenance. Many are of cobblestone, especially in the warehouse district. If lucky, grooved cement replaces the cobbles on the hillsides, as the frequent rains demand traction for vehicles going up and down the steep terrain.

Although the Mercedes is advertised as offering an unparalleled ride, the locale was proving to overcome the promise. Sitting in the backseat, having had little to eat and less sleep, a slight beer buzz in my ears, the car swaying and bouncing over stones and into potholes, Lyft bouncing up and down on my lap essentially threatening to crush my testicles, I began to turn a little green.

Maroon looked over at me and said, "You OK? You don't look well."

"How far is it to the house?"

"Not far, five minutes without traffic, ten with. You going to be sick?"

"Not if we get there soon. Not used to ridin' in the backseat, ya see. Never could, even as a child."

"And you from a seafaring nation."

"Ah, lad, some o' us are just cursed, don't ya know."

Maroon laughed, as did gabardine. The chauffer was mute, as befitting his station.

Lyft cooed, "Oh, good one. You get better and better, even if you are going to soon engage in reverse peristalsis. Did I ever tell you about the time I—"

I gave him a sharp pinch with my right hand, shielded from

maroon. A large "ouch" echoed in my head, but at least it shut him up temporarily.

The sweeps and curves up the hill did little to abate the ever-darkening shade of green I was exhibiting. I really needed to get out of the car, or the upholstery was going to have new definition in the backseat. Suddenly, we arrived at the gates of the compound. The chauffer rolled down the window, as did maroon in the back. The guards, upon recognition, signaled the tower to the right to hit the button, tripping an electronic switch that opened the gates inward. We proceeded up the hill, past magnificent gardens, mini waterfalls, pools with expensive koi roaming for food, until finally we arrived in the courtyard where we parked next to Licia's Mercedes. I noted the cell phone Lyft had made such good use of still in plain sight, figuring she must have a duplicate since she always seemed to be leaving this one in the car.

It was a relief to get out of the car and into the air of the day. I leaned against the car for a moment to clear my head, the feeling of carsickness rapidly dissipating. Lyft decided not to sit on my shoulder, probably fearing distraction.

Maroon and gabardine allowed me a few moments of respite as my stomach settled down.

Lyft intoned in my ear, "I will be with you all the way. Don't worry. I'll be your close ally through all this."

"That's what I'm afraid of," I hissed, irritated that he had not warned me about his proclivity to sit on my lap, exacerbating the backseat phobia I often exhibit.

Gabardine asked, "Did you say something, my friend?"

"No, no, just sayin' to meself I was afraid I was goin' ta be ill, but I fully believe the moment's passed on now, don't ya know. Sorry for any inconvenience, mind ya."

"Not to worry. Let us proceed this way. Perhaps the view on the patio will settle your constitution."

I hate to admit when slime is right, but he had a point, as we walked through the archway connecting the cobbled sand-colored parking area with the large patio of terracotta tile, surrounded by a stuccoed cement railing all around. The patio contained giant planters, some of palms, others of plants and trees foreign to me but native to Sumatra. It looked out over the entire harbor, and for those who became bored with their surroundings on top of the hill, there was a telescope mounted toward the front of the patio that swept two hundred seventy degrees. The house shadowed the patio toward evening, rendering the space into perfection for the cocktail hour. Maroon told me to look through the telescope, becoming more friendly, as he found no duplicity in my demeanor. I took a stance at the railing, looking out over the scene, admittedly impressed with the view, as well as with the magnification of the telescope, my stomach pretty much coming back to normal.

Gabardine took a call on his cell phone and then signaled that we should go inside. In my head, I decided to refer to him as "gabby" from then on. It seemed to fit somehow. The library was across the patio in the facing left corner. The door was open.

Here we go, I thought.

The three of us entered what looked to be a black patch in a wall. The library was just as Lyft had described it. Ali Sastroamidjojo sat behind his monstrous desk, looking over what I presumed to be journal entries relative to his business, a green-shaded, expensive-looking desk lamp illuminating the desktop, which was organized and neat. The gold scrolling in the leather inlay, the subdued recessed ceiling lighting, and the books lining the walls reaching all the way to a twelve-foot ceiling gave the room an aura of the antique book room at the Library of Congress rather than a library belonging in a home. When I saw the size of Ali, I wondered how he could get that close to his desk to read the journal. Then I realized that the desk had a cutout behind it in order to accommodate his excessive girth. No detail too infinite for the master of the house.

He looked up from his desk, motioning for me to sit down in one of the two leather chairs, with no offer of a handshake or introduction.

He said to the two others, "Gentlemen, please wait on the patio. We shan't be long."

I hadn't heard the word "shan't" in a very long time, contrivance at its best. But he was not the only one engaged in that pursuit.

He looked me straight in the eye. "So you have word of my son. How do you two happen to know each other?"

He was still using present tense. This was going to be good theater. I could just imagine Lyft, sitting in the other leather chair, taking it all in.

"Actually, I'm not in the chair at all, but looking over this marvelous collection of books he's amassed. There are some fabulous first editions here. I shall have to steal a few for my library. But I'm listening, so continue on. Don't let me interrupt you. You are doing wonderfully well."

A mind reader to boot, I railed inside my head. I nearly jumped out of my skin. Had Lyft been reading my mind this whole time? And why had he left this tidbit out until now? I'd guessed I'd have to be careful. I swallowed and got back to Ali's question, hoping he hadn't noticed my distraction.

Trying to be composed, I replied, "Well, it's a long story, ya see."

And so I told him about me signing on with the work crew out of Mexico, as I'd been trained as a pipe fitter on oil rigs in the North Sea, and that the skill was sought after with this project, the disciplines being similar. I'd jobbed out several employments with Petróleos Mexicanos but was getting tired of Mexican heat and dirt, so I wanted to do something farther north. The Wakhan fit the bill, so I jobbed on with the crew headed there. Some of the chaps I knew and some I didn't. Ali, overseeing some of the electronic installations in certain areas of the plant, seemed like a bright lad, and as our professional paths frequently crossed, we developed a kinship, so to speak. As the plant was nearing completion, he brought me into his confidence, stating that if anything were to happen to him, he asked that I give a call and let the phone ring here the allotted number of times, and then he wanted me to make my way here and give his cell phone to his father, as it had a message on it.

Ali paled when I mentioned the part about "if anything were to happen to him."

"What do you mean, if anything happened to him? What has happened to my son?"

"Well, sir, as ya know, the plant blew up. We can only figure that Ali had somthin' ta do with it, but we'll never really know, as unfortunately, me friend, he di'na' survive the blast, oh don't ya know."

"But, but, I received the call. The call meant that he was alive. He sent the signal."

"Sir, that was me sendin' the signal. I sincerely, regret to bring ya this information, but a promise is a promise. I couldn'a go back on it."

Ali was pale and sweating profusely. "You are a good soul to travel all this way to tell me of my son. Please, let me have the phone so I can listen to his last message."

"Surely. Here's how you get in to listen ta it. Mind ya I have na done so. I would na feel proper ta breech a confidence I promised ta keep, so I have na heard it, I want ya ta know. Would ya like me ta leave so ya can have some privacy?"

"Please, that would be most kind of you. You may wait on the patio with the others. I shall call you when I'm through. You are most considerate."

"No problem at all, me friend. I'll be right outside."

I joined the other two on the patio. "He's lis'nin' to his son's message now," I said. "Poor man, hearin' his son's last words from the grave. 'Tis a hard thing, truly 'tis."

To top off my sentiment, I brushed my eyes with my hand, turning away to ensure my body language befitted the moment.

None said anything further on the patio. After a few minutes, Ali came to the doorway, with tears in his eyes as he walked out onto the patio. He addressed maroon and gabby.

"This man," he choked, placing his left hand around my shoulders. "This man will now be considered as part of my family. He may stay with us as long as he likes, forever if need be, and will be extended every consideration as if he were my own blood. Is that understood?"

"Yes, sir," they both replied.

"This message tells me of your friendship and loyalty to my son. It is more than any father could have asked as a last message from one so loved. In it, he tells me of the love for his father and mother, his country, and you, my lad. He has told me to treat you as one of my own, and I will do so. This tape will be a great comfort in the future as we mourn our loss. This will kill his mother, but with Allah's help, we shall overcome this wretchedness. Now, if you all will excuse me, we have a funeral to prepare. Tell me, my friend, what are we to call you?"

"Me name is Keegan Killroy, sir."

From Lyft on high, I heard, "Keegan Killroy? Oh, brother, where did you come up with that?"

Ignoring the message from the ether, I tuned into what Ali was saying.

"I don't suppose there are any remains we could obtain for a proper burial," Ali fairly sobbed.

Gabby and maroon turned away, embarrassed by the display.

I looked at Ali and said, "Sir, the plant went up in a fireball. Once the liquefied natural gas was let loose into the atmosphere, the charges incinerated everything in a five-hundred-yard radius. Even the wee gophers around the plant were obliterated. I'm so sorry, sir, but there's nothin' left o' anythin' in the vicinity o' the plant site. Just a tangle o' charred metal. I stayed around for a week or so, pickin' thro' what I could, livin' on some supplies left over stored away from the plant until there was nothin' left to live on. Then I made my way here, which I'll relate perhaps at a more appropriate time. To answer your question in the short term, however, sir, there are no remains. I checked and double checked, but I'm afraid, sir, that the intense heat o' the explosion turned much around the plant ta ash."

"I understand. In that case, we will have services immediately. I must now go and inform his mother. Please make yourself at home. Arthurio, our headwaiter, will see to your needs."

From on high, "So *that's* his name. I'll be having some more fun with him. I wonder how he's recovered from our last encounter?"

Again, I was forced to ignore the comment, barely suppressing a guffaw at the memory of Lyft recounting his exploit with the waiter.

"Thank you, sir. I'm sure to be comfortable in such luvely settin's."

"My assistants will see to your transportation and anything

else you need off the premises. Now I have unfortunate business to attend to. Good day, gentlemen."

"And ta you, sir," I replied, the others nodding in unison, as Ali went into the house.

In seconds, Arthurio appeared on the patio, asking me if I had any luggage. I told him no, it was all in my hotel room, but that it was of little consequence, as I had recently arrived in the country with basically the clothes on my back. He told me to follow him to my room, where I'd be staying from now on. Maroon and gabby said they were at my beck and call if needed.

I followed the waiter into the main entranceway, where two giant curved staircases arched around to the second floor, centered by a huge chandelier lantern hung from the ceiling. From the upper levels of the house emanated a primal female screech that could have rendered the interior plaster to dust. Ali had done his worst and was now paying the price. They both were.

Arthurio showed me to my room, which was magnificent by any standard. He told me there were clothes in the large walk-in closet, and if they did not fit, he would see that I received new ones. I hoped they were not young Ali's, and he, evidently reading my mind, said they were not the young man's but were placed there for other guests if needed for various occasions. They were all clean, some brand new and never worn, so I told him I would try them out and let him know the outcome. He said he would leave me alone to freshen up and perhaps take a bath, a subtle hint, and to call him if I needed anything. He seemed to frown as I sat on the white-lace-covered duvet on the king bed, capped by an exotic Indonesian wood headboard carved with a wild boar on the charge. I thanked him as he left the room, closing the door behind him.

I looked around the room, thinking this was not a bad place to have lodgings versus the dump I had just vacated. I walked over to each of the two end tables framing the bed, turning on what looked to be hand-painted lamps in pastels of native flowers, their height perfect for reading in bed. Across from the footboard of the bed was a large six-drawer bureau, chest height, complete with brass antique swirled drawer pulls, and over that was a gilt-edged mirror, large enough to reflect the bed setting. I noted that all the wood in the room matched, thinking Ali had a very good supplier or he had the furniture custom made. To the left were two oversized windows looking onto the courtyard and then out onto the bay, framed by sheer curtains, giving the room an airy feeling. To the right of the bureau was the entrance to the bathroom, to the left of the door, the closet.

Lyft made himself visible. "I've checked for bugs and video. I didn't find anything, so we're safe to talk."

He floated in front of me. I said, exasperated, "You know, sometimes you drive me nuts. Your comments can set me over the edge, you know. What if I reply, forgetting that I shouldn't? The whole thing would be blown. You really need to keep quiet when I'm engaged, you know."

"You'd think you'd be used to it by now. Rather touchy, aren't we?"

"Cautious is more like it. I can't risk a screwup."

"True. I'll take your counsel on this one."

"So, tell me how you entered The Blue Lady without the door squeaking."

"Easy. I went in through one of the upper open windows."

I said to the floor as I leaned over to untie my boots and pull off my socks, "You know, you might have warned me you were going to sit on my lap. Damn, I really almost got sick in the car."

"Sorry about that. I had nowhere else to sit, however, and I needed to be there in case of trouble, so what else would you have me do? You're lucky I was with you."

"Right. I could have handled myself nicely, thank you." I sat back up, my feet blessedly airing, wiggling my toes.

Lyft put a hand to his face, as if saying, phew. "Hey, don't forget, I'm your insurance in case things go awry. Show a little appreciation. You know, you really do need a bath."

"No kidding. OK, so you're appreciated. Now what?"

Lyft began floating back and forth as he thought a second. "Now we break him."

"We've done a pretty good job of that already."

He stopped, motionless in front of me. He put his hand up, as if to stop me from leaving. "Whoa, wait a minute. We're far from through. We've just started. And besides, don't forget, his son's alive. He'll soon be joining his father in prison. The whole family can have a suite together."

"Probably deserve it. I have something else to ask you."

All nonchalance, floating again before me, he quipped, "Ask away."

"Since when can you read people's minds? You spooked me in the library earlier today."

"Well, I can't read everyone's. It seems only certain individuals have the magic mix of brain waves in simpatico with mine. It doesn't happen very often, and sometimes it can't be repeated with the same individual, although sometimes it can. Maybe it depends on what people have eaten the previous day. I've never been able to figure it out."

I wiggled my feet some more. "Scientific, to say the least."

"Yes, very. Say, have you ever heard of the term *sodai gomi*?"

Uh-oh. Another pontification on the way, I thought. "Can't say that I have. What's it mean?"

"It's the Japanese term meaning 'large garbage.'"

"What the devil has that to do with anything?"

Lyft threw up his hands, still floating in midair before me. "Just listen for a minute. In Japanese, phrases often bespeak mindsets. This term, *sodai gomi*, you would think would apply to certain trash collectibles put out on the curb for collection, but there's more to it than that. It really pertains to the psychological implications of how Japanese men feel inside their marriages, especially when they take the time to look inward on those marriages from the perspective of their work environment."

I stood, beginning to peel some clothes, wanting a bath more than a lecture. The pontiff continued, "For the Japanese male, work is everything. Their entire life and psychological well-being revolve entirely around their employment and their status within the organized structure of the workforce. That leaves the women running families, with many women feeling no better than hired house servants in loveless marriages. Each evening when the man comes home, he enters a foreign land in his own household."

I thought to myself as I stripped down to my shorts, *Yes, and*

I'm in a foreign household in a foreign land, and I can't wait to get home. He prattled on, "Most Japanese men would prefer to remain in the office, sleeping in their chairs, rather than come home to the indifference and feeling of uselessness they encounter upon walking through their own thresholds. Their wives technically have no use for them, nor do the children, as the men put no time into fostering familial relationships. It is an uneasy truce, the men wishing they were always at work, the women wishing for something better, but in the absence of that, thankful that the men only stay home for eight or ten hours and then leave, so they can organize the family and their lives the way they choose without any outside interference."

Lyft, who'd been hovering near the closet, evidently surveying my selection of attire options as he delivered his lecture, flew over and settled once again in front of me as I sat on the bed, almost naked now. "So where does this take us, you ask?" he inserted, not waiting for confirmation that this was what I was about to ask. "Many Japanese men have disparagingly labeled themselves in the context of their marriages as *sodai gomi*, large, useless trash, akin to broken television sets or inoperable refrigerators, ready to be collected on the curb to either be recycled or placed in the landfill. Either way, useless to the family in its current state. Believe it or not, Japanese societal stability depends on the tenuous family structure as it now stands."

Lyft began floating back and forth. "What we want to do is instill in Sastroamidjojo the feeling of *sodai gomi* relative to his stature in his organization. We want to break his arrogance, make him see what peril he has fostered upon the head of his only son, make him see with clear vision the error of his ways." He stopped in midair, raising his arms, sweeping them out from his body, almost in supplication. "In short, we are talking about the full conversion of a human being, if you want to call him that, in his current state. It's already begun with the Tamils. We now need to ensure it across the board."

I looked up at him. "Wow, and I thought we were just going to ruin him financially. You're talking about the whole package."

He raised a foretalon. "Yes, total war. It's embedded in my

psyche. If he's not broken, he'll just return to do this all over again, like wasps returning to the same nest each year unless the nest is eradicated."

I raised my forefinger in return. "We will render *ichiban sodai gomi* on his head."

Lyft chuckled heartily. "Very good, oh, go to the head of the class. Yes, number one large garbage. I like that."

I raised a leg, propping the ankle on the opposite thigh, realizing that the conversation preempted the bath. "So now that we're in, how do we go about this?" I queried.

"The difficult part is accomplished. You have gained his confidence. Now we do the easier part. You know, it's always easier to destroy than build, don't you think?"

I grabbed my crossed leg with both hands. "I really never thought much about it."

Lyft raised his foretalon again. "There is a use for philosophy in this world, you know. Just thought I'd let you in on that secret."

"Sorry, I'm practically oriented and am probably too old to change now."

"Bah, never too old, but we don't have time for your conversion at the moment, so for the short term, I'd agree with your philosophic regard for the practical. What we need to do is get to the press. Who's the nemesis from *60 Minutes* we're supposedly dealing with?"

"Ed Hazelit. He's on *Your World Today.*"

"Do we have a way to contact him?"

I asked quickly, "Who'd Bashirin place in charge back at the plant?"

"Major Dumont."

I began picking at my toes, realizing that my toenails needed a cutting. "Well, if Dumont can find the info in my computer, we can make contact. Otherwise, it'll be tough going through directory assistance from a Sumatran cell phone."

Lyft had one hand under his chin now. "Right. Well, you work on that angle. As you have few people to call, I would not advise you asking for a communications device from the family here. It might raise a suspicious eyebrow or two."

"Agreed." I picked on one troublesome toe, the skin peeling under my onslaught. I hoped I had not contracted some foul Far Eastern foot disease.

"We'll work three angles. One, the financial, trace the money trail, expose the network. We'll need to get to the books and get a copy of them. Two, we work the angle of discreditation. You remember the missiles I disengaged? Well, the Tamils are not too happy about their delivery. We should get Hazelit involved there, provided there's time. That should be fine theater. When word begins to get around that Sastroamidjojo runs an unreliable operation, his reputation will sink like a stone."

"What's the third angle?"

"The liquefied natural gas tanker off Georgetown. We'll need a presence there when the operation goes sour. *60 Minutes* is going to be busy."

"Are they ever."

"So first a bath and new clothes for you. There are a few things in there," he said, gesturing toward the walk-in, "that will likely fit you, hopefully anyway. We really don't have time for dalliance in men's shops outfitting you in Armani. Then we need to get something to eat. I'm starved. Maybe I could get Arthurio to whip something up for us."

"After what you did to him, he'd probably like to whip you."

"I'm sure he would if he knew about me. But since he doesn't, I might just have a little fun with him while you get your wardrobe together."

"How 'bout a little smoked carp from one of the koi ponds?"

"Cute, very cute. Have you no regard for God's creatures?"

"What? I heard smoked carp was a European delicacy."

"That's because they ran out of other fish due to mismanagement of resources. I'll be off now to plague Arthurio. Get cleaned up, and maybe you can join me somewhere in this morgue for a bite to eat."

Lyft exited out the window, not wanting to alert any staff passing by as to how a door could open by itself. I decided I would heed everyone's advice and take a bath, and then explore for clean clothes. I looked in the substantially stocked closets, where there was an ample wardrobe, divided up by sizes. Evidently Ali's houseguests wanted for nothing. Shoes were always a concern of mine, as I had a triple E width to consider. I found no shoes I could wear, but there were several sets of sandals that fit. Now that my mind was eased, hopefully I could relax in the tub.

The bathroom was a grand affair, all done in white. The small checked tiled floor, the marble counter over the substantial porcelain sink, the oversized tub under the large window, again looking out on the bay, the fluffy towels hung through silver rings on the wall near the tub, along with the large mirror over the double sinks all lent the room an air of beneficent elegance. I ran the water in the tub, thinking a person could drown in it. It filled surprisingly quickly. I climbed in, relishing a few minutes to myself.

While I was taking care of business upstairs, Lyft decided to do the same on the kitchen level. Not one to purposefully miss a meal, Lyft, as I would soon learn, reentered the house through the library, making his way down the hall through the massive dining room to the kitchen beyond, where the swinging door into the dining room was open into the kitchen foyer. There he found Arthurio and the chef, talking over the evening's dinner menu at the large wooden table centered in the kitchen on the terracotta floor. Lyft noted from the conversation that the chef's name was Peter as he took in the kitchen, which was the ultimate in modern convenience, featuring a giant Viking industrial cooktop consisting of ten burners; six wall ovens; four wall broilers; two oversized stainless-steel refrigerators with freezers; two sets of stainless-steel sinks, one for pots and pans and the other for general utilitarian purposes; two large butcher-block carving tables with gravy drains; four built-in dishwashers; overhead a large cast-iron pot rack with hanger hooks from which hung every conceivable copper pot and pan; not to mention recessed ceiling lighting and glass-enclosed shelves with four different complete sets of china. In the rear, near the marble-topped eat-in alcove for six, was the access corridor leading to the back entrance of the house, where two recessed walls of wine, one refrigerated and one not, were stocked from the cellar daily so that the chef did not have to interrupt his duties for libationary requests. Lyft noted that the air-conditioning was keeping the room at a cool seventy degrees, the ultimate luxury in this part of the world.

It looked to Lyft that although dinner was underway, it would be some time before the main event would come to fruition. He cruised over to the wine rack, discovered an expensive bottle of Châteauneuf-du-Pape, pulled it out, and then hid it on the floor behind the door. He went into the kitchen, where he surreptitiously slid open a drawer unobserved, but alas, no corkscrew. He did the same to four more drawers, until finally he found the implement of his desire. The chef and the headwaiter were too engaged to notice any peripheral movement, so he was able to spirit the tool to the rear nook, where he had located the bottle. He then went back to the rack, where he found a bottle of 1996 Taittinger Comtes de Champagne Blanc de Blancs that he grabbed as well. He exited through the rear this time, as he had implements in his possession that he could not render into invisibility. He flew up to my window, then proceeded to seat himself on the closed toilet lid with his spoils of war.

"What are you doing? Can't a man have a little privacy?"

"Sure, but then you can't partake of the ultimate luxury, drinking outstanding wine or champagne, whichever you prefer, while bathing in the tub. And as to your privacy, it is of little concern to me whether you are clothed or not. We Klinques do not ruminate on nor do we care about such things."

"How did you come by these fabulous offerings?"

"I stole them."

"So I thought. Won't they be missed when they decide to do an inventory for dinner?"

"Who cares?"

"Well, I might, as I'd be the likely suspect if they find something's gone missing. Ever think of that?"

"Hmm, you might have a point." Lyft ruminated for a few seconds, placing his hand under his chin after setting this booty on the tile floor. "You do have an alibi, although a weak one. You are so new here that, if questioned, you would not have known where anything is, so how could you have the acumen in such a short time to have scoped out the house to such a degree? I believe that would work, should the subject come up."

"You're right, it's weak, but I suppose I could use it if necessary. Now, pour away. Did you find anything to eat?"

"There's plenty to eat, I just couldn't get at it. But as usual, time is on my side. I just need someone to leave the premises for five minutes. Then they'll see the damage I can do. We'll have to use the bathroom glasses for these. I couldn't bring any proper stemware here. It would have been noticed." He zipped to the marble counter over the sink, taking the two glasses conveniently placed there, as he looked at himself in the mirror while he floated in midair. "What a handsome devil I am," he exclaimed.

I rolled my eyes as I sat in the tub, wondering if I should let the provocative declaration pass or if I should let vanity rule the moment. I decided on the sarcastic course.

"Yeah, you're a real Humphrey Bogart, and I'm James Mason. Can I have some *vino* now?"

All I received as a return salvo was a harrumph. He collected the bottle from the floor and then floated in front of me as he poured, handing me the glass. I took a sip.

He then floated back to the toilet seat and poured his own libation, sitting on the front edge with his feet dangling off. I began to chuckle, wondering if his breed had minitoilets in which they did their business. I decided not to pursue that line of thought, obscuring it instead by gushing, "Outstanding. What a wine. We need something to eat with it."

"I know. Just give me a few minutes. I'll scout out the kitchen again shortly."

Having uncorked the red wine, Lyft began working on the Taittinger. The cork opened with a resounding pop.

"Now, for this, no food is required, so let's have a few quaffs."

Lyft retrieved a few more glasses from the top of the bureau in the other room, that were more appropriate to the occasion, being at least regular cocktail glasses. He poured a little of the champagne in each.

"Now," he said, "that's what I call a champagne."

"Agreed," I chimed. "But I can't have too much of this stuff, or

I'll get loopy and slip up with the accent. Then there'd be hell to pay."

"OK, I get the hint. Let me see what I can do about obtaining something of a little more substance to go with these outstanding vintages. I'm surprised, though, that no order had been put through the kitchen for lunch."

"Probably due to the upset in the house. Remember, there's a funeral in the making."

"Oh, that, right. I keep forgetting, because the kid's still alive. Actually, he's lucky I didn't kill him myself. I thought about it, believe me, I did."

"I'll bet you did. Now on to happier thoughts and getting us something to eat."

"Right."

Lyft zipped out of the bathroom. Provided he was to be successful, I decided to get on with the bath, getting serious about actually bathing rather than just sitting. I set the glass down so I wouldn't step on it exiting the tub, scrubbed up, rinsed, and then stood and retrieved a towel from one of the rings. I placed the towel on the edge of the tub, noting the rapidity of the water swirling down the drain. A dark ring replaced the water line; something for Arthurio to enjoy cleaning up, I mused. I walked over to the back of the door, where a freshly laundered white terrycloth bathrobe was hanging on a hook. I put it on and walked back into the bedroom, where I sat at the substantial lawyer's desk, noting that it was a reproduction centered with faux leather.

Suddenly, Lyft zipped in through the bedroom window, a large plate of seafood in each hand. I was about to ask him what he was up to, but could see he was intent on a mission. He quickly left and then reappeared shortly with two enormous plates of the all-berry pie, two forks, and some paper napkins. He set everything down on the table and sat opposite me in the other facing chair.

I asked him how on earth he had accomplished this feat. Lyft stated that when he went back into the kitchen, Arthurio and the chef were pondering what to do about the fact that no food order for luncheon had been placed with the headwaiter. They thought it a highly unusual circumstance, but they knew better than to speak unless spoken to, knowing they could be dismissed with the snap of a finger. So without any standing orders to contend with, they decided to whip up a little feast for themselves, which Lyft thought a splendid idea. They had collaborated on a menu of seafood salad; some leftover baked quiche filled with ham, onions, and spinach; some freshly baked homemade squash rolls, that were, as evidenced from the conversation, Licia's favorite from her short time spent in Boston; and for dessert, some leftover all-berry pie from the previous evening. They decided on a Pouilly-Fuisse, Chateau Fuisse, M Vincent et Fils, 2003, for lunch. And they said to each other, if no food order arrived by one o'clock for the afternoon, they would crack another bottle and have one each. It sounded like a pretty good plan to Lyft as well.

He went on to say that they each began their preparations, with the chef having made a mound of seafood salad on a platter, complete with parsley, sliced lemon, every type of seafood imaginable, and whole lobster claws and tails garnishing the heap. Arthurio said he had to go to the cellar, and the chef said he needed the men's room, so they agreed to begin the repast as soon as they returned. On the way to the men's room, the chef noticed the hole in the wall where Lyft had pilfered the Châteauneuf du Pape. However, luckily for us, he dismissed it as carelessness in a previous inventory, evidently thinking little of it.

Lyft explained that he had to work fast. He found two plates, scraped half the platter on to one each, grabbed some utensils, and then sped out of the kitchen by his usual exit, coming back into the bedroom. He then left and flew back to the kitchen, which, luckily for us, was still vacant, seized the pie and utensils, and arrived back with the bounty.

"A feast for the senses," he declared.

From down in the kitchen, there was a commotion and much yelling, as the chef and Arthurio were no doubt blaming each other for more than half of their missing meal. Lyft and I clinked glasses.

"To the victor go the spoils," Lyft announced.

"To the victor go the spoils," I repeated.

We sat in relative silence for a while at the writing desk,

munching and quaffing. I had to give Lyft credit. It was really an excellent meal.

"So," I said as I was finishing up the pie. "What's our next move?"

"As you know, the council meeting is coming up shortly in Jakarta. I will need to communicate to you three what's coming out of it relative to the liquefied natural gas fiasco and anything else on their plates. They got too close to us once, and we can't let it happen again. When Bashirin quizzed young Ali about how they knew of the Wakhan plant, Ali said through a network of informers. Now someone tell me there's no worldwide terrorist network. All it takes is some seed money among the various disaffected local populaces in targeted areas of the world to breed a network—or the building of a local school or bailing some farmers out in a bad year or telling certain growers in an area that you'll provide protection and a market for their ever-expanding poppy fields. These people are smarter than most governments and state departments. Their foot soldiers are literally at the grass roots level, whereas governments distribute aid through channels to other governments, which only serves to line the pockets of those tasked to serve those less fortunate. No wonder there's rampant terrorism in the world."

"So, how do we know the other projects aren't compromised? After all, there's one on the opposite coast here."

"In actuality, we don't. That's what we need to find out. But I'm the one who needs to go to this meeting. You need to stay here and find the books, provided they are not taken to the meeting, which I don't think will be the case. This is a strategy meeting, not a CPA convention, and besides, Ali doesn't even know why he's been told to go to the meeting. First, we need him to get through the funeral or whatever they're going to do for his brat son, and then we get down to business."

"Any idea how this funeral thing will progress?"

"Well, I figure an imam will show up soon, gather family and friends together in the large patio outside, and say *Salat-i-Janazah*, traditional Muslim funeral prayers. Then there will be a reception from which I will mightily pilfer, followed by three days of mourning. During this time, the family will accept condolences from all over the world. After that, Ali will go back to work. No, knowing him, he'll work through the mourning period. Licia will not recover until she finally sees her son, which she will, by the way, but on the opposite side of a jail cell. Soon thereafter, she will be joining him, so the family will get their wish, that they all be together again.

"Although I know the location and could be there early, I figure I'll just tag along with Ali in invisible mode on the way to the council meeting until we arrive at the destination. Never know what one might learn inadvertently by just hanging around, so to speak. Always have an alternative plan, I say."

"So we just chill until after the mourning period?"

"Unfortunately, that would seem to be a side effect of our plan. However, not all is lost. You can wander around, become familiar with your surroundings, ingratiate yourself further with the clan, and let me know what you find. While you're at it, you can make friends with the headwaiter who also, it appears, doubles as the butler around here, and also with the chef. My cardinal rule in these situations is always make fast friends with the chef. You never go hungry that way."

"Good advice. So I think I'll get dressed and wander around a little bit, centering myself perhaps in the kitchen, although I'm not at all hungry now. How are we going to get rid of these dishes?"

"Leave it to me. When they are out of the kitchen, I'll spirit them into one of the dishwashers after I give them a little rinse. No problem."

———

I took Lyft's advice, wandering at leisure around the grounds of the house, paying particular attention to the library, confirming that it was under video surveillance from cameras peering through small bubbles from the four corners of the ceiling. Getting to Ali's books in his desk was going to be an interesting exercise. I did not discern any of the other portions of the house being under watch, with the exception of the outside grounds, especially around the main gates. The estate was surrounded by a magnificent handmade wrought-iron fence, needing continual maintenance due to the humidity. It depicted scenes of many of the native animal species of Sumatra: elephants, clouded leopards, tapirs, tigers, Malaysian bears, and the ubiquitous varied species of snakes. Every twenty feet or so were cameras mounted on top of the fence at its intersections, where sturdy wrought iron poles were stuck deep in the ground. The cameras at those points were ten feet off the surface, so no one could get at them, even though they were cleverly shielded from view by natural vegetation that had been strategically planted to diminish the impact of an eyesore but maximize the advantage of a security shield.

The service had taken place on the patio as Lyft thought it would, with the guests staying on for a reception in the house. Lyft had great fun at the buffet, becoming mildly inebriated while severely plaguing Arthurio, driving him nearly mad with pranks until the headwaiter really did think the house was haunted by evil spirits. Lyft thought it best that he ease off, not wanting to raise unwanted suspicions at this delicate balance of the game. I noticed that Arthurio was his only victim, however. True to his word, he left the chef and the other servants alone, playing out his game plan to have the staff believe Arthurio really was crazy so that his authority would be undermined. Lyft hated petty dictators even more than major ones who caused so much trouble in the world. It went against every fiber of his true communist upbringing.

While Lyft was having fun and games with Arthurio, I was engaged in the thought process of how to obtain the books for ten minutes and, better yet, how to make a copy of them. They were locked in the side desk drawer. There was no way I could obtain them without being seen by the cameras. I related as much to Lyft that evening when we were ensconced back in my quarters. I was lying on the bed, my hands propped behind my head, elevated by three pillows. Lyft had settled himself onto the footboard at great peril to its exterior carving.

Lyft said, "Ah, the cameras would seem to be a problem. However, let us really think about this. The security room is behind the parking area, correct?"

"Correct."

"And it is always manned?"

"Yes, but briefly unmanned during shift changes. Sometimes the guards are lax when they greet each other outside the hut."

He raised his arms. "That's our chance then. We disable the system to the library for a very short period so we can jimmy the drawer to get the books."

"And by *we*, you mean that *I'll* disable the system and jimmy the drawer, I suppose."

"The problem," Lyft continued, ignoring the comment, quickly adjusting, centering on me as the agent provocateur, "is how do you get a copy of the books once they are out of the nest? You'll have to work fast. You can't just take them to the local Kinko's. You'll need to photograph them and replace them quickly." He paused, thinking for a moment, and finally acknowledging my comment, added, "It would be too difficult for me to operate a camera with these talons I have anyway, which sometimes really irritate the hell out of me for purposes such as this, but it can't be helped. We all have our handicaps," he said, waving his talons at full extension, like curved lethal shanks awaiting impalement.

"My, we're humble today. What would you say my handicap is?"

"Being sarcastic."

"I shouldn't have asked."

"At any rate, I'll have to steal a camera somewhere, and you'll have to take the pictures—extraordinarily fast, mind you. We don't need the whole journal, maybe just five or ten pages. Perhaps we could review them in our room before we send them off, although there might not be enough time for that."

"Our room?"

"Where do you expect me to stay? On the wheelhouse of the boat in Lama Village? I've had enough of that routine, thank you."

"OK, so *our* room."

"Your generosity overwhelms me."

"I can be rather magnanimous to those who deserve it."

"Oh, brother. You're beginning to sound like Ali."

"Heaven forbid. Shoot me now."

"Now there's a thought."

"Listen, this isn't getting us anywhere."

Lyft pointed a talon at me. "You started it."

"Yeah, so now let's end it. What do we do once we photograph the books?"

"Well, the first thing is to put them back and then get them to Hazelit at *60 Minutes*. However, we don't have Hazelit's contact information here, do we?"

"Nope, another interesting exercise in the offing."

"Ah, yes, but doable. We can contact Major Dumont to access your computer files back in the Wakhan for you. And here, don't forget, you will need a computer, as I intend to steal a digital camera that will enable us to send the pictures via e-mail."

"I won't have much time," I mused aloud, trying to think of what would best facilitate a speedy file transfer.

Lyft said, "Right. Perhaps you could use one of the computers in the house while Ali's at the council meeting. Now wouldn't that be sweet."

I thought it out. "That would be perfect, if I could get away with it. I won't need much time. You could even scout out the make first, being sure the camera download operation is compatible. That would be the best course."

"Consider it done."

Lyft floated back and forth over the footboard, clearly in thinking mode. Then he stopped, looking directly at me. "Let's use Licia's. She has less use for it than anyone else in the house. You can get to hers, as she probably will go with Ali to get away from the house during this period. He will tell her it will do her good."

"What if she doesn't go?"

"Trust me, she will."

"More brainwashing?"

Lyft nodded.

"Does Major Dumont know who you are?" I asked him.

"No, you'll have to make the call," Lyft said.

I wondered aloud whether Licia's cell phone was still in the car, and Lyft left to check. He was back in less than ten seconds, urging me to hurry. I quickly dialed the phone, getting to Dumont. I told him what I needed, gave him my access codes, and told him to immediately call me back when he found it on my computer. In less than ten minutes, he was back on the phone. I scribbled

Hazelit's information on the pad on the writing table as he related the information, said thanks to him, and then told him I would be in touch. He wished me the best of luck, inquiring into the whereabouts of Bashirin. I told him he was fine, respecting his concern for his fellow soldier, but that I had to go. I told Dumont not to use the number again and then erased evidence of both calls. I clicked off, giving the phone back to Lyft who then zipped out the window and replaced it back into Licia's car.

"So," I said, "now the next thing is to obtain a camera. You may have to go to Medan. I don't think there are many camera shops in Belawan."

"Right. That will be my task today."

"And don't forget to get the USB cable. I can't hook up to the computer without it."

"And what, pray tell, is that?"

"It's a thin cable that connects the camera to the computer, allowing me to download the photos. I can't do anything without it, so make sure it either comes with the camera or you pilfer it separately. Either way, I need it. Most will fit into any computer. I'm sure Licia has the finest in state-of-the-art equipment at any rate."

"No doubt."

"So off you go. No time like today."

While Lyft was engaged in petty theft, I thought I'd wander around the grounds near the security shack located to the left of the parking area, not far from where Licia always parked the Mercedes. It being a rather temperate day, I saw that the door to the hut was open, with the guard reading a newspaper, looking up from time to time at the monitors surrounding him, less attentive than if he thought there were a real threat imminent.

Boredom, the ultimate enemy of the vigilant, I thought to myself. *What these guys need is a major security breech to wake them up. Maybe we can help in that regard.*

The guard noticed me wandering around, but only nodded to me in recognition. It seemed he had been briefed that I was no security threat. In fact, I was pretty sure he'd been told to treat me with the utmost deference. Although not confirmed, I assumed that gabby and maroon were tasked with security of the overall operation, which included the grounds of the mansion. I figured the more visibility I gave to the security personnel, the less future risk I would have of suspicion if seen in an inappropriate setting. The ploy was beginning to work. I was given as much thought as the occasional stray cat on a hunt for vermin.

Later that day, Lyft returned with the camera and cord. Sitting on the bed in "our" room, I briefly looked over the directions, quickly realizing that they were pretty much the same as mine at home, so felt relieved that I could download the pictures quickly. He fluttered over my shoulder.

"Lyft, I will need Licia's password to get into the computer. Since she's in a state of shock, how do you propose to obtain it? She probably won't be using the computer much."

"Not true, she used it this morning. She's e-mailing her lady friends all over the world, getting condolences in return. She seems to be comforted by it. As a matter of fact, Ali can't get her out of her study, she's so glued to the back and forth with her girlfriends. People do mourn in strange ways. And I figured you would need access to her machine, so here's her password, ALIJR1. Probably every time she types that, it consoles her." He chuckled. "I notice it's not ALISR1."

"No, it wouldn't be that. I think she really hates the man."

"If she didn't before, she does now, he being responsible for the loss of her only son. However, she's not blameless. She's a part of the operation, a willing participant. No one coerced her into her warehouse duties. She knows very well what's going on. As a matter of fact, we might be able to use what she knows as an admission to the operations underway during a little *60 Minutes* interview. We should think about that. We could use the exposure of Ali Junior's existence against her for a confession to Hazelit in a private setting somewhere. The more I think about it, the more I like it. That plus proof of the money trail in Ali's books ought to put a lid on his activities for the duration."

I said, "I like your thinking. Brilliant, as usual."

He deadpanned, "Yes, I must admit the scheme has a luster to it."

"Modest too, I see."

"Yes, to a fault."

"So," I asked, "what about disabling the guard shack?"

"The question is, do we disable the electronics or the guard? It might be easier to disable the guard, to tell you the truth. A little something in his coffee and then closing the door for, oh, say, fifteen minutes. I picked up something in town this morning that should do the trick."

Lyft extricated a nondescript small brown bottle labeled "Chloral Hydrate" from his side pocket. I took the bottle from him, examining it, small cork stopper and all. "Ah, chloral hydrate, the ol' Mickey Finn. FYI, this doesn't go in coffee, but it sure would work nicely in something with alcohol in it."

Lyft queried, "A nice frozen margarita or something similar perhaps?"

I said, "Yes, a nice fruity punch, so to speak, that doesn't exhibit much alcohol but still has a good wallop to it. Let the chef and me work that one out."

Lyft exclaimed, "Done."

"OK, so the rudiments of the plan are in place. What's next?"

"Well," Lyft replied, "today is Monday. Wednesday is the council meeting. I'll stay really close to Ali on the way. During the meeting, well, that's another matter. I'll have to see how it goes. I might tear the place up, or I might be complacent to just tune in to gain access to the rest of the network. All depends how things go during the meeting."

I said thoughtfully, "Either way, we need to be in contact with each other. It won't do much good for you to tear up the place without us gaining any further knowledge about exposure of the network. We can't very well have *60 Minutes* interview *you*. Don't forget, it's proof we need more than anything else. I think you should take another tack and record the entire meeting."

He floated in front of me, puffing himself up. If I'd had a pin, I would have poked him to see if we would have exploded with a thunderous pop or just whizzed around the room helter-skelter as the air rushed out. Instead, he let out his own hot air. "I take umbrage at the notion that I would be less than a suitable interviewee on national television. They would be privileged to have the opportunity for an exchange with His Kingliness regaling past exploits. They'd be mystified not only by my presence, but by my many deeds that have been the salvation of humanity."

I gave him an eye roll from my sitting position on the bed. "Yes, and after you've told them about your empire, they would start digging all over the Earth in the hope of discovering your kingdom. I can see the quiz shows now." I waved my arm, brushing his regal vestments. "Instead of 'dialing for dollars,' it would be 'digging for Klinques.'"

He scoffed, "Very amusing, I'm sure."

Back to business now, I said, "I think it best you stick to the recording plan, no interviews and no exposure. You know, I wonder if anyone there records the meeting. Probably not, as it might be leaked. There probably aren't enough individuals there to warrant a microphone. But if there were a central sound system in the room to which a tape recorder could be patched, then we'd be golden. You would have no use for a recorder other than to hook it up immediately in advance of the meeting. If you're lucky, the hotel will have that type of capability."

He began floating back and forth, the thought process kindled once more. "Good thinking. Perhaps we can get more information about impending events from our host."

"Perhaps I can help in that regard. As I'm staying here, I am perceived as no threat to Ali. Let me have coffee in the morning with him. I'll see what I can glean out of a conversation then. I'll be wandering around the patio, pretending I couldn't sleep late. As he has coffee out there each morning, looking over his beloved harbor, I'll stumble into him, wangling an invitation for a little java. Leave it to me."

He stopped in front of me, a talon in the air. "The student has now become the master. Brilliant."

"I've been taught well."

"I appreciate the compliment."

"So stick around the coffee klatch tomorrow morning. You might pick up on something I miss."

"Good idea. While I'm at the council meeting, you will do the e-mail to *60 Minutes* with the pictures of the books? You might want to compose a quick summary to Hazelit, telling him what you're doing."

I said quickly, "Right, but I'll have to do it fast, because someone like that nosy Arthurio might come into the room." I stood up and began to pace parallel to the side of the bed, speaking rapidly. "However, there's one thing I can't reiterate enough: he can't go public with any information until we give him all of it. The media has gotten so competitive that any odor of a story is leaked to the public before the final outcome is brought to fruition. That can't happen here. If it does, then the council members will melt into the fabrics of their own societies, and we'll never be able to pull them out of the weave again."

Lyft was floating with me at shoulder height. He turned and looked at me as I sat back down on the bed. "I like the metaphor. However, don't preach to the choir over here. You need to tell Hazelit of your concerns, not me."

"Yeah, I do get a little animated at times discussing the media."

"And rightly so."

I raised my hands. "So we've got a plan."

"Yes, and a good one."

Slapping my hands back down on my thighs, I said, "Let's see if we can implement it."

"Oh, we can, and we will."

I wish I continually had Lyft's confidence. However, my continual questioning of my abilities probably sharpened my performance. I could only hope so in this case.

CHAPTER TWENTY

Bashirin and Salvo had hitchhiked to the boat location in Lama Village, finding the *Lotus Blossom* tied up to the quay. They did not trespass onto the boat; they just needed to know its location. Now they had to make contact with the two slicks running the operation.

Four days after I chatted with the bartender in The Blue Lady, the duo decided that Salvo was better outfitted than Bashirin to deal with the bartender. They decided to concoct a story linking them to the Irish connection, having met me in Kelang, the friendship cemented on the ferryboat over. They thought this easier than reiterating the previously scripted journey down the Karakoram. Bashirin would stay in the background, pretending that he only knew Russian. Salvo would use French along with heavily accented English, fronting his Moroccan connection, but beginning in French to give the introduction an air of authenticity.

Into the bar they went. It being midafternoon, a round of beer was in order. They sat quietly at the bar, finishing their first and then ordering a second. Midway through the second round, Salvo began the inquiry.

"*Parlez-vous Français?*"

"No."

"Do you speak English?"

"Yes, I do."

"We're looking for work, and thought perhaps you might know of someone needing some help, preferably as deck hands on a boat, that sort of thing."

"I might. Where you from?"

Salvo proceeded to relate the story and then threw in the clincher.

"Say, you wouldn't have seen an Irishman in the past few days, would you? We made friends with him over in Kelang and traveled with him on the boat. Seemed like a fine fellow."

The bartender, apparently not wanting to relate more than he should, played it tight.

"Can't say that I have. Let me make a phone call. Perhaps there are others who are able to give you more information than I can."

He went to the same phone, placing a call to gabby and maroon. They said they'd be there in thirty minutes.

He came back to the bar and said, "Wait here for half an hour. Some folks will be along who perhaps can help you find the work you seek. In the meantime, have another beer. It's on the house. What about your friend? He doesn't say much."

"He's Russian, knows some east European languages, but that's about it, so he normally keeps quiet as he doesn't understand many conversations in this part of the world."

"Ah, that explains it."

Salvo related in Russian to Bashirin what was taking place. Bashirin just nodded.

They had another beer, sipping slowly for the same reasons I did. Finally, gabby and maroon entered the bar. The bartender nodded toward Salvo and Bashirin. The two slicks made a motion that they should join them at a table, the very same one I sat at four days ago. They were quizzed in similar fashion, soon convincing the two henchmen that they were authentic. Luckily, since they were not requesting an audience with the chief potentate, their grilling was not as extensive as mine. Bashirin in the interview asked if either of them spoke Chechen. Maroon replied yes, and so he and Bashirin conversed at length, finally with Bashirin asking after the Irishman named Killroy. Maroon wanted to know how the two came to know this Irishman, so they told him about their travels over from Kelang on the boat. This seemed to impress the two slicks. They inquired as to where the two travelers were staying. They were given the name of the fleabag where I had lodgings. This would arouse no suspicion, as it was the only hotel in the waterfront vicinity, where people traveling by ferry with little money would be expected to stay.

Gabby and maroon told them to wait outside the hotel in the morning, where they would be picked up at eight o'clock. They would be shown the boat and interviewed on board to see if they knew what they were about. They thanked the two interviewers, ambling back to the bar for another round, as they were now officially on the house for as many rounds as they could consume. Gabby and maroon left the bar, stating on the way out that Killroy was staying with a prominent family on the island and that, if all went well, perhaps they could remake his acquaintance. Salvo and Bashirin said they would like that, thanking the two once more. They had one more round and then exited the bar, making their way back to their hotel.

So now the plan was fully in place. Pending their final interview on the boat, all the pieces of the puzzle were beginning to fit nicely. Now the waiting game began, the toughest, most difficult piece of all.

Chapter Twenty-One

Lyft and I were conversing in our room the day prior to the departure for the council meeting. Bashirin and Salvo had passed their onboard inquisition in splendid fashion, having become accepted as bona fide crew. I'd had no chance to interact with them, but Lyft had been in constant contact, shuttling back and forth between the *Lotus Blossom* and the house. That morning, the two deck hands had been told to move from their hotel to the boat, stow their gear, and wait for further orders. Bashirin seemed to have acquired maroon's trust via his incessant moronic Chechen jokes, with gabby rendered to spectator status, as Chechen was alien to him.

"So," Lyft fairly chortled, "it looks like we're pretty much set."

We were sitting at the desk, he standing in his chair, facing me in mine.

"Yes, provided all goes as planned. One thing's missing in my mind, however."

"And what would that be?"

"I thought you were going to help me work out the details of getting into the library."

He rolled his eyes. "Must I plan out everything?"

Slightly frustrated, the level of my voice rose as I raised my arms. "Listen, I don't have a problem knocking out the guard with a little cocktail. The issue is, how do I disable the cameras? That seems to be a problem to me. I can't just waltz into the library in plain sight making my Broadway debut on tape, you know."

"No, you can't very well do that, I'll admit. The solution is relatively simple if you really focus on it."

I fairly shouted, "What? Throw blankets into the air up in the four corners of the room hoping to cover the targets?"

Lyft, all rationality, said quietly, "Well, that would be the ultimate in stupidity, wouldn't it? Think about it. You're already halfway there by eliminating the guard. So now, what's the other half?"

"Eliminating the video."

"Right. And what's the easiest way to do that?"

"Shut off the cameras?"

He raised his foretalon. "Bingo. Equation complete."

"Won't there be a gap on the tapes?"

He raised his arms. "Sure, but who cares? You don't really think those tapes are reviewed every night, do you? I'll bet they're only rerun infrequently and only if there's sufficient cause. If the guard wakes up to all being normal, all monitors on, nothing amiss, then he'd have little cause to be suspicious. As added security, he won't want his superiors to know he nodded off on duty. After all, who does he ultimately report to? Gabby and maroon. Would you want to report to them that you had a security lapse, that is, went to sleep on duty? I think not. So chances are 99.99 percent he won't want to know what he missed. Therefore, the gap, in all probability, won't be discovered. If it is, it'll be after the books have been made public. By then, it'll be too late. I take it you do know how to shut off the cameras, yes?"

"Sure. The guards and I have become great friends. I bring them coffee from the kitchen in the morning and frozen fruit drinks in the afternoon. They've come to trust me, even as I watch their operations."

He raised his arm, fluttering the finger forward. "Perfect. Couldn't be better. You've become a master at subterfuge."

"I'd be flattered if you weren't such a pain in the arse."

He leaned forward on the desk, palms on the faux leather. "You know, I often am, but consider this as part of your training. With minimal help, you have figured this out yourself. You'll not always have the luxury of my invisibility to help you muddle through."

"Point taken. However, there's still one thing missing."

"Oh? And what would that be?"

I leaned back in the chair, arms folded across my chest. "I have never jimmied a drawer, so I'll need to get into the desk somehow."

"Ah, I almost forgot. I obtained a little tool downtown, in anticipation of just such a need. You know, the handyman's special for around the house. It's a small knife with a picklock on it. Works every time."

"Thanks for telling me about it. Do you have it with you so I can practice in my room on the desk there?"

"Sure, here it is. Like I said, you just insert and give a little twist, no problem. Works on 99 percent of all locks."

I leaned forward, took it from him, and while examining it, said, "Wonder what I'd do if I'd forgotten to mention not being able to get into the desk? That would have been cute, me running around the house trying to find a tool while wondering when the guard would wake up. I think you're losing it a little, you know?"

"Perhaps sometimes I might have a lapse or two, but I've a lot on my mind. Speaking of that, I've been meaning to ask you, why Killroy? Why not O'Farrell or Jameson or Casey?"

"Do you know the origin of the story surrounding Kilroy?"

"No, but through the years I've heard many references to 'Kilroy was here.' Never thought much about it though."

"Well, for once, maybe I can educate you."

I got up from the chair, as it was beginning to bother my back, and then lay down on the bed, arms folded under my head on propped-up pillows. Lyft centered himself on the footboard. I told him that the phrase emanated out of World War II and that, although there were variations on the theme, the most plausible story was that a ship inspector, James J. Kilroy, wrote the phrase in yellow crayon on the hulls inside ships in the Quincy, Massachusetts, shipyard after he had inspected them to keep the riveters honest. Some riveters evidently had the propensity to double count their rivets. Kilroy wanted to let his superiors know that he was on top of the job, number one, and, number two, that his signatures told other shift inspectors the count was complete so that the rivets were not counted again on the following shift. Once the ships were put to sea, the troops on board saw the markings, and it all escalated from there. Graffiti spread all over Europe, stating that "Kilroy was here," driving the Axis crazy. In fact, Hitler was so incensed with the notion that Kilroy was a super agent of the Allies that the German high command had orders to find Kilroy and shoot him on sight. Even Stalin later wanted to know who Kilroy was. During the Potsdam Conference in 1945, someone had scribbled in outhouses built for the dignitaries "Kilroy was here." After Stalin had used one of the facilities, he came out with a perplexed look on his face, asking through an interpreter, "Who the hell was Kilroy?"

I concluded, "I thought perhaps when this gig completes itself, I'd leave the same message, you know, something akin to a Parthian Shot, even though I've chosen a different spelling, using double L instead of the usual one. Didn't want to risk alerting anyone in case they knew a little of the story, you know."

Lyft exclaimed, "Yes, I totally approve. Bit of history laced into the operation. Always a hearty 'bravo' for good theater."

"Yes, I knew you'd agree. And I have just the mechanism for it."

"And what would that be?"

"It's a secret. But you'll eventually find out. It'll be perfection itself, oh, don't ya know."

"I must say, the accent is pure Thespian."

"Oh, thank ya, lad."

Lyft inquired, "By the way, were you able to obtain any more info during your coffee klatch with Ali? And might I add, I'm highly offended at being an afterthought in the mix. I got caught up over at the boat."

Ignoring his offense, with me having no defense, I ignored his quip. "Nope, no info there. I was hoping for the meeting room name in the hotel, but he made no mention of upcoming events. Just small talk. Why don't you just call the hotel and ask for the room name?"

Lyft, with his arms out, said, "Might arouse suspicion."

"Makes it a little complicated to set up the recording equipment ahead of time, no?"

Lyft began floating back and forth over the footboard. "It surely does, but I was expecting that curve ball, so no matter. I'll manage. Bribery works every time, and that's what I'll do, albeit at the last minute. I sincerely hope the location remains in the hotel, however. One never knows if the location is real or just subterfuge. If not, then that could be a real complication. However, I'm counting on the location to be legitimate. What other choice do I have? Ali and the council are paranoid, and I know already for a fact that the meeting is booked as a company function, so as not to alert any law enforcement authority. Ali has these types of company meetings all the time throughout this part of the world, so no one will be the wiser."

"Since you need to maintain your invisibility, how do you propose to let the audiovisual people know what you are about?"

Lyft floated, centered over the footboard, raising a talon, "Why simple, through the written word. Some graft now, much more to come later when the job is complete and the tapes delivered and subsequently reviewed. Works every time."

"I've no doubt of it. Say, have you ever thought about the concept of things not being as they appear?"

Lyft said, "Often, as a matter of fact. What brings that question to mind? Kind of a segue isn't it?"

"Perhaps. I was just thinking of it because of Ali and his organization and you and your invisibility. On the surface, a seemingly innocent conglomerate, operating in accordance with the rules, generating no suspicion, just doing what conglomerates do. Nothing unusual. But scratch the surface, and lo and behold, there appears a nest of vipers. And you, well, when you're invisible, things certainly aren't as they appear."

"I agree with you; things aren't always what they seem. Sometimes it takes a little digging, some research, if you will, to determine why something is as it seems. Often, we have to follow a red herring to discover the actual substance underneath."

"Huh, red herring. I wonder where that term originated?"

Floating gently back and forth, in full lecture mode now, Lyft said, "I believe the English invented the term. As perhaps you are aware, a salted herring, when smoked, turns brownish red. During fox hunts, red herrings were dragged across the trail to throw off the dogs so that the fox would not be cornered too soon. The term has come to mean a distraction of an issue due to the insertion of an irrelevancy. This is called in Latin, *ignoratio elenchi*, which means 'ignorance of refutation.' It can be brilliantly used in debates. I've used it myself on occasion. It can totally confuse the promoter of an original premise, making him forget what it originally was by igniting a refuting argument totally irrelevant to the expectation of his conclusion. Most individuals get into the quagmire of irrelevance accidentally by tangentially asking unrelated questions to the point or giving similar answers of no consequence, because they either do not understand the original premise or do not know the correct answer, yet feel they have to say something other than 'I don't know.' This can be a dangerous exercise in certain situations, such as in a serious interrogation. It takes a skilled verbal artisan to utilize such a tactic and be completely effective."

Lyft settled back onto the footboard and centered on me. He explained that Aristotle was one of many who were historically famous for using such tactics. He pointed to his 350 BC treatise, *On Sophistical Refutations*, noting that Aristotle was probably the first to address the tactic so thoroughly.

When I inquired into the tactic's modern use, Lyft was full, as usual, with an answer. "Take a look at labor negotiations," he said, floating up from his perch, coming closer, hovering over my stomach. I hoped his air wouldn't run out due to his pontification, causing him to plunge bedward and pierce me with a talon. "Look at how long it really takes to get to the central issue during a protracted labor dispute. What about a Senate filibuster? C'mon, you can't tell me a filibuster is central to any issue. It's a stalling tactic to wear down the opposition, totally unrelated to the main issue of concern, used to throw off the opposition to hopefully augment their original premise. How would you classify Eisenhower's tactics at D-Day, convincing the Germans that a beach other than Normandy was going to be used as the landing point? What about the husband who comes in late to an angry wife, maybe having had a little too much of a good time, who suddenly complains of chest pains, diverting one attack to another? All one and the same, me boy, oh, don't ya know."

"It's not like I didn't know those tactics were used, just not in any philosophical context as you've explained it."

"And that's the difference: knowing to utilize it as a tactic, not as a knee-jerk emotional reaction, rather, to understand when to use it and, better yet, how to use it. Really invaluable sometimes. People use it subconsciously all the time as a defense mechanism, but ask them to explain why, and they crimson with embarrassment or make a feeble attempt to relate their action to the main issue, which only leads to more embarrassment. I look for the one who is not embarrassed, who uses it as a conscious tactic, and then I find a thinking individual. He is the one to be watched, like friend Ali, using the ultimate in subterfuge to shield his true organization."

"Got it. Thanks for the philosophical illumination. I'm sure now that I'm cognizant of it, I might very well begin to use it."

"One can only hope a lesson turns into a practice."

"So where to from here?"

"We wait for departure."

"Then may I suggest dinner in the kitchen with the chef?"

"A capital idea."

Chapter Twenty-Two

The following day, early in the morning, the limousine came to collect Ali and Licia for the short journey to the Medan airport.

Lyft and I were bantering in our room, me getting dressed with one arm in the closet, he floating around the room in a perpetual state of activity. I quipped, "I'll make sure to tell your friend, Arthurio, how much you miss him while you're away—that you'll be happy to regale him with your exploits upon your return."

"Oh, you really can be something, you know?"

I thought briefly, *Nothing like a lover's spat before the onslaught*, and then put it out of my mind. I retorted, "And you can't? One of the things I live for is getting even with your incessant barbs. Never had this much fun in the other job, planning conventions. Trust me, working there was the nadir of intellectual stimulation. Working for you, my intellectual curiosity is continually aroused, at least to the point of verbal retribution. I even lose sleep at night wondering how I can reverse the cannonade constantly fired my way." I put on a rather nice pair of sand-colored linen trousers with a drawstring in the waist, quite comfortable for the climate.

Lyft imperiously replied, "I'm only too happy to be your moving target. However, I have approximately a thousand years of philosophical and practical experience on my side, give or take a few hundred. So strategically, you're pretty much at a disadvantage," he said with a grin. "I'm off for now. I'll be in touch somehow. Take care of yourself. I would hate to rescue you from the local jail."

We wished each other good luck as he disappeared through the billowing sheers framing the window, that I had opened earlier to vent the mourning from the house.

Knowing him, he took up the position somewhere in the rear of the limo, closest to the refreshments in the side pocket. As I stood near the side of the window, I saw the car leave, the guards at attention as the car cobbled through the courtyard, snaking its way down the winding drive. I closed the window gently, intent on avoiding a Sumatran insect feast.

Although Ali and I had conversed only briefly during a few occasions in the past few weeks, there was no doubt as to his intentions that I should have the run of the house in his absence. He even offered me his library, in the event I would like to read some of the splendid titles he proudly exhibited on his well-stocked shelves. Evidently no wastrel in the intellectual department himself, it looked to me as if Ali's passion centered on first editions, duly signed by the authors themselves. It was the perfect ruse, me being allowed in the library, my presence having been previously sanctioned to the guards by the master of the house, absolving them of any responsibility in the event of any unfortunate circumstance.

And so I spent as much time in the library as I could, careful not to sit in Ali's chair at the desk, but rather in the comfortable leather ensemble in one of the room's corners, where I had the luxury of placing my feet on a beautifully sculpted deep brown leather hassock, just the right height off the floor to avoid any excessive leg strain. I dug into Churchill's memoirs, often letting my attention flag, falling asleep, and then awaking with a start, probably to the amusement of the guard on duty in the shack. I often went for a snack in the kitchen and then took something out to the guard, practicing *ignoratio elenchi* in its rawest form.

As the library was the only area of the house to be videoed, I felt relatively secure in using Licia's computer to contact Hazelit at *60 Minutes*. After a few days of nodding off in the corner of the library, lulling the guards into false security with the insignificance of my presence there, I felt secure enough with the plan to act and get it over with. I'd been around the house too long, frankly getting bored with the guards' inane jokes about their continual nightlife exploits, which to me sounded like pure fiction, typical bovine rhetoric from those with no aspiration in life other than how to spend their next paycheck.

And so, as planned, I had the chef make two very large piña coladas, one for me and the other for the guard in the shack. I took the vial of chloral hydrate out of my pocket on the way out to the parking area, dumped it into the first drink, being careful to note which was which, and stirred it in with the straw, trying not to disturb the little plastic umbrellas with their tiny clips the chef had attached to the sides of the glass, as I made my way through the back corridor to the outside cobbled archway. I hoped Lyft had the right dosage so I didn't kill the guard. What I didn't know was how long the concoction would take to act, so I decided the best course was to hang around the shack until I saw the effects. As I came out of the house, I noted the guard shack door open, so I headed toward it, enunciating a greeting so as not to startle Sammy, as he had become known to me.

"Hey, Sammy, what's up? Look what the chef made. Thought I'd join you for a little refreshment to pass the time."

"Wow, look at those. The chef's really somethin' no?"

"Yes, he is, very accomplished at what he does. I think he put a little somethin' extra in there for us, oh, don't ya know, so don't drink too fast. Might put you ta sleep."

I entered the shack, a tarred shed roof affair, handed him his drink, and took the other chair in front of the console on the bench. There was a large rectangular window looking down the drive, the side door normally always being open to the house. There were numerous monitors overhead, depicting the library, the courtyard, the drive, and entrances to the house. There were also four for the perimeter grounds. If one were diligent on duty, he would be relatively busy keeping track of any activity about the property, but good help was tough to find these days. I scraped the padded chair along the plywood floor, turning it to face him as he scoffed, "Bah, these girly drinks are nothin', man, you should have seen me last night. Pounding 'em down, man, pounding 'em down." His accent was a cross between Jamaican and Indian. I could not place his country of origin, not that it mattered much. He'd soon be history. "No one can hold their own wit' me when I get goin'."

I raised my glass in toast. "Ah, sounds like a drinkin' contest. I remember those in college, although I was never a participant, only an observer, mind ya. I remember once gettin' a kid to the local hospital 'cause he thought he could outdrink anybody else under the table, ya know. Pretty much cured him of his drinkin' games after that, lad."

This barb went right over this head.

"No, man, no drinking games last night. Chasing pretty women last night on arrack."

"Is arrack an island?"

He guffawed at that one.

"No, man, arrack is liquor from Bali, made from tuak, a sweet wine from the coconut palm flower. So good, man, you think you died an' wen' ta heaven."

"Really, well I'll have ta try some."

"Better try it here, man, 'cause you can't get it off island. Only made here to drink here."

Trying to stay interested, I asked with good cheer, "If it's so good, why hasn't someone exported it to other places?"

"Beats me. All I know is the more that stays here, the more there is for me. That's the way I like it. Haw, haw, haw," he bellowed.

Knowing that he was totally inebriated last night, I hoped, would work in my favor when the chloral hydrate was introduced to his hangover.

"Well," I intoned, "here's to arrack."

"Here's to arrack," he repeated.

He downed half his drink, trying to impress me with his assimilative alcoholic skills.

Go ahead, you stupid bastard, I thought. *Suck it all down. Then it's sweet dreams. You're soon to be unemployed.*

As we engaged in small talk about the merits of downtime in the pursuit of carnal pleasure, I noticed his bloodshot eyes becoming droopy. He slurred once more, "Here's to arrack," finishing his drink and then laying his head down near his computer keyboard.

Almost immediately, he lapsed into the breathing of a regular sleep. I shut off the video to the library, which was on a separate circuit from that for the surrounding grounds, and then rapidly walked across the courtyard to the patio that juxtaposed the library.

I entered the room, walking quickly to the desk, where, sure enough, Lyft's tool worked as advertised. I rifled through the drawers carefully, finding what looked to be an accounting ledger in the top center drawer. Sure enough, it was an entry journal, and it looked genuine, as it made no mention of any illegitimate activity that I could discern. Although not an accountant, I had seen plenty of balance sheets at work, and I decided that this was not what I was seeking. But where the hell were the false entries? In the warehouse? I didn't have all day to look around the house. Where would be the most logical place to keep them? They had to be here, as Ali spent more time here than in the office. My pulse started to pound in my temples as I began to more thoroughly search the drawers, attempting to not dislodge anything that might lead to suspicion that the desk had been pilfered. I found nothing. I stood up, walked over to the library shelves, and looked intently at each, wondering if perhaps a volume could have a false cover. After six shelves, the sweat began to course down the back of my neck into my shirt. We would not have another shot at this, and the exercise was getting dicey. *Look at chest height*, I thought frantically. *You don't have all day. The fat bastard would not want to bend over all the time to get the journal.* I took my own advice, an electric vibe coursing through me as I stumbled upon *The Biography of Admiral Lord Nelson*, seemingly out of place with the other first editions near the left doorway entrance to the library. I quickly pulled it out from the shelf, placing it flat on the desk. I opened it, and sure enough, it was a fake volume, with hand entries outlining accounting activities. Luckily for me, it was in English, as Ali had interests overseas, subject to other countries' scrutiny. I took the digital camera out of my pocket, turned to the appropriate pages, and began snapping as fast as the flash reconstituted itself for the next shot, attempting to prevent the sweat coursing off my chin from dripping onto the book. What I was looking at was a goldmine of information, with numerous pages noting all the shells set up to receive illicit funds.

60 Minutes was going to have a field day with this. Many entries were organizations I'd never heard of, which were going to have to be researched, but no entity could do it better than the press, not even government agencies, it seemed.

I'll bet the State Department's going to have a new watch list out of this, I mused as I snapped away.

After about ten minutes, I felt I had enough material, plus the camera's battery was beginning to run low. I had photographed more than half the book, but I had a few more to take. I noted the rear half of the book had blank pages, awaiting more odious entries. I closed the book, which exhibited on the front, etched in gold into the exquisite leather, "The Journal of Admiral Lord Nelson."

In spite of the stress I felt, I laughed to myself, thinking of Ali equating himself to the nineteenth century British naval hero. I clicked off two pictures to ensure I had the cover to substantiate the content. I then opened the book to the first insert, which gave the inception date of the journal along with some ruminating thoughts pertaining to Ali's operations, briefly stating the purpose of the journal and what he hoped to accomplish through its use. I photographed that as well.

"This isn't an accounting ledger, it's a manifesto," I breathed out loud. Ali was obviously secure in his belief that no one could get to the book. Wouldn't he have a hell of a surprise upon his return?

Time to go. I took my handkerchief out, wiping down the book, placing it back exactly as I found it on the shelf. I relocked the desk drawer, wiped down the desk, just in case, and then quickly went upstairs to my room and deposited the camera in the top desk drawer, taking the key with me. I then went down to the guard shack, breathing a sigh of relief to find the guard still asleep, turned on the video monitors to the library again, and then quickly exited the scene, thinking the best course of action was to let the guard wake up naturally on his own. As Lyft had stated, what he didn't know wouldn't hurt him.

I went back to my room, unlocked the desk drawer, and looked through the photos, which were of excellent quality, clear and precise, when a knock on the door echoed through the room.

"Sir?" Arthurio's voice resonated through the door. "The master of the house is on the telephone for you. He said to take the call in the library."

A jolt of electricity went through me. My pulse began pounding again. How could Ali call me now, right after I'd photographed the books? Was there a security system I'd missed? Had he watched me the entire time I was in the library? I swallowed hard, attempting to keep my stomach out of my throat, valiantly retaining self-control as I said, "Thank you, Arthurio. I'll be right there."

"Very good, sir."

I heard him walk away. I placed the camera under the bed with a line to a hidden outlet to ensure its charge, telling myself to walk calmly back to the library, that the timing of Ali's call had to be coincidental. I prayed that Arthurio failed to recognize the angst I felt I was exuding. I realized that my shirt was soaked, the sweat running down my cheeks from my sideburns.

I made my way to the library and sat at Ali's desk, where the phone was located.

Noting the red hold light flashing, I took a deep breath and then picked up the phone, slippery in my hand, and said hello.

"How's it going?" came a familiar but entirely unexpected playful tone.

"What?" I stammered. "Lyft?"

"You didn't think ... oh, you *did* think I was Ali. How else did you think I was going to keep in touch?"

I'd momentarily forgotten about Lyft's skills as an impressionist. I said apprehensively, "Aren't you afraid someone's listening in?"

"No, not on the library phone. I pretended to be Ali on the other line for Arthurio's benefit. Once the call's transferred, the line's secure. You picked it up while it was flashing, didn't you?"

"Yes."

"Then there's no way with the security system they have in place that anyone can listen in."

I breathed a sigh of relief. "What about the security cameras?"

"They have no voice capacity. Just keep your head downward so that there's no lip reading going on."

I said, lips against the receiver, "I think the guard's still asleep anyway, but he should be waking up soon."

"Ah, so the mission is accomplished?"

"So it seems. I haven't had time to send them yet, but I'm working on it. Just as I was reviewing the pictures in the camera, Arthurio knocked on my door to tell me the 'master of the house' was on the phone. How do you like being viewed as master of the house?" I had to try my damndest not to laugh out loud.

"Has a nice ring to it, if you ask me."

"Yes, I thought you'd say as much. By the way, excellent choice of camera. Everything came out better than expected."

"Outstanding."

"So where are you, and how did you come by a telephone?"

"Licia's again. She's still so distraught, she's forgetting everything. And I'm at the Dharmawangsa Jakarta, a magnificent hotel. I'll say one thing for our friend, he has impeccable taste, if nothing else."

"So," I sarcastically rasped, waving one arm in the air, "you're living in the veritable lap of luxury while I'm engaged in the ultimate of nefarious activities, risking incarceration, torture, and lack of habeas corpus, to say the least?"

"Correct," Lyft deadpanned. I could have goalposted him, provided I could have caught him.

"Well, I hope you enjoy yourself," I fairly shouted.

"Oh, I am. Let me tell you a little about the facility. It's in Kebayoran Baru, probably the nicest area of the city. Mostly residential, it's literally an oasis in the midst of chaos. It even has butler service."

I rolled my eyes, my head down, angled toward the desk. "And have we availed ourselves of that?"

"But of course. I even had my wonderful silver suit cleaned in anticipation of a night out."

"And how did we manage that? Wasn't anyone suspicious as to its size?"

"I put it on Ali's bill as a woman's suit top."

"Brilliant. Don't tell me you have your own room."

"Absolutely I do. I finagled that at the front desk while no one was looking. I registered myself in the computer and then signed myself in as part of Ali's entourage: room, tax, and incidentals, all to the master account. I'd wager on a room service smorgasbord tonight, if I were you."

"I'd lose the bet."

"Yes, you would."

I queried, genuinely interested, "So what does Dharmawangsa mean? It must have some significance."

"Oh, yes, it does. The name refers to an eleventh century Hindu king who ushered in the Golden Age of Java under the empire of Majapahit. Much of the design of the hotel reflects the artistry of the Majapahit culture. For instance, there are recurring yellow marble disks in the floors representing the sun's progress across the sky, a central element in Sanskrit, the main written language of the empire. This motif is evident in much of the design of the hotel and in its accessories."

"Sorry I'm missing it." I looked around the library, wondering if the conversation was going on too long, thinking that perhaps the guard had by now woken up. I kept on, "But at least I have the chef to talk to."

"It could be worse. He could be a lousy cook."

"True. So what do you have to report? I can't gab all night with you on the phone. The guard might wake up wondering why I'm on so long, or at all for that matter, with the 'master of the house.'"

"I really like that ring. I think I'll have you address me as such when I return."

Exasperated, thinking I'd be caught out on the phone, I hissed, "Oh, for God's sake, what do you have to tell me?"

"Well," Lyft sheepishly said, feigning hurt, "not much. They seem to be keeping the exact location of the room under wraps. I may have to do some fancy footwork with the audiovisual company shortly, but luckily for me, they're out of house and, by default, have no loyalty, so that should all work out. Oh, methinks room service is knocking. Let me run."

In spite of camera security considerations, I began to laugh, unable to help myself. I chuckled into the phone. "How do you plan to open the door?"

"I won't. He has a key. I'll pretend to be in the tub. Now let me go before I fade away from hunger."

"Oh brother, and I thought you were going into harm's way. Was I deceived."

"Yes, but only due to your own misconception. Now, I have a sumptuous repast to attend to, so I must disconnect."

"Yes, so must I, as I have a date with the chef. As a matter of fact, I'm late, so I must sign off as well. Toodle-loo."

"Oh, toodle-loo to you, pain in the arse."

"Call me when you have some substance to report."

"Bah."

He clicked off, which was just as well. *I wonder what I would have done if Lyft had called me while I was at it in the library, assuming it really was Lyft on the phone. Wouldn't that have been a kick?* I mused. Then the thought occurred to me that, similar to a marriage, one should never end a phone call or terminate a conversation with a close friend or loved one in an ill manner, since one could never fathom fate. I would have to remember to relate that thought to him, although in thinking about it, I was probably just as guilty.

I didn't have a date with the chef, but in actuality, it was not a bad idea. It was still a little early for dinner, at least for me. For Lyft, anytime was too late for dinner. I called the chef from the library, asking what was up for that evening. As usual, he said he was sharing it with Arthurio. By the tone of his voice, I noted some dissatisfaction with his date. He immediately asked me to join him, whereupon I accepted. He sounded truly delighted, saying he'd make something special for dessert in honor of the occasion. Dinner was at seven.

That left me free for several hours to pursue Hazelit on Licia's computer. I could only hope I didn't run into Arthurio near her room. Irrespective of the chance of discovery, I had to undertake the quest. Some decisions are easiest when there is no choice of action. I went to my room, placed the camera in my pocket, and traversed the upstairs through the main second story corridor, where I found her room open. I noted Arthurio in the kitchen plaguing the chef as I made my way earlier to my room. I just hoped the chef didn't become aggravated with his antics, forcing him to leave the kitchen. Arthurio was in the habit of slithering around the house, popping up at inopportune moments.

I felt the best course of action was to leave the room accessible. I knew there was little that got by him, and he would remember that the door was supposed to be open. Luckily, the computer was to the right of the entrance, so if he did walk by, he couldn't see me at the desk. Unluckily for me, I probably could not hear his footsteps on the carpet outside the door.

I sat down at the desk, fired up the computer, and keyed in the password. I accessed my own AOL e-mail account. I quickly explained to Hazelit what I was about, inclusive of a major impending terrorist action, relating there would be many pictures downloaded to him, that he should immediately bring a crew to Sumatra with access to a helicopter ASAP, and for him to remain mum about what was transpiring until he had a phone call from me. I never typed so fast, not even bothering with the spell-check function. I thought I heard a noise in the corridor just as I downloaded all the pictures. *C'mon, c'mon, damn it, why does it take so long,* I railed in my head. My pulse started hammering again. I wondered briefly how much stress my heart could take, envisioning myself in a Medan hospital with monitors beside the bed. The thought was eclipsed by the upload finally terminating. I deleted all I had composed, shut down the computer, got up, and literally almost jumped into the closet, the computer screen dimming as Arthurio's weaselly form peered into the room. Satisfied that all was in order, he exited, turning down the corridor, heading toward my wing of the house.

I needed to get downstairs fast. I waited a few seconds, peeked out into the corridor, seeing it vacant, and crossed quickly to the stairs, going down two at a time. I then proceeded to the kitchen, where I had a chat with the chef, trying to pry the night's secret out of him, but he would not relent, so I told him I was going up to my room to rest and freshen up. I took a detour out to the shack, where Sammy was wide awake, studying the video monitors, his drink empty near his computer keyboard.

Beautiful, I thought. *Just as Lyft promised.*

My heart rate almost back to normal, I then went back to the pantry, going up the other secondary staircase to my room, so I didn't have to go back through the kitchen. There I saw Arthurio, skulking outside my room, evidently awaiting my return.

"Why, g'day, Arthurio. How are ya?"

"Fine, just fine," he sighed in a tone that indicated he was anything but fine. "Chef Peter can be so demeaning," he added, tagging along, attempting to follow me into my room.

"Oh?" I said, blocking the door and hoping it would seem I'd stopped to give him my full attention rather than to keep him out. "I don't find that atall, at least not wit' meself, mind ya. We seem ta get along quite well, oh, don't ya know."

"Well, I think he's an utter beast," Arthurio spat, the insult seeming to straighten his posture. "And I'll not eat with him tonight. I'll take my dinner in my room. Would you like to join me?"

I sensed a very lonely man underneath the petty tyrant's suit. My first propensity was to make an attempt to tell him to look inward, but I figured it would be a total waste of time, as his personality dictated it was him against the world, with the world always being wrong.

"Ah, lad, 'twould be delightful, I'm sure, but I've made the chef a promise, ya see, and a man can't go back on his promise, oh, don't ya know. So I'll be eatin' with the chef tonight, I'm afraid. I'm truly sorry to disappoint ya."

"I understand," he sniffed. "I shall entertain myself grandly tonight, in any case. I may even go out on the town a bit. I have many friends in the area, many who have requested my presence at numerous functions. As a matter of fact, there's quite a bash down the road I've been invited to. I think I'll go and leave this wretched place for a while."

"A splendid idea if I ever heard o' one. I'd join ya, if I hadn't made the promise, ya see. Sounds like a smashin' good time."

"Oh, 'twill be, yes. 'twill be. I'm sorry you can't join me."

"Another time, me friend."

"Yes, you'll have to make good on that. Well, good night."

He turned, walking toward his room, no doubt cursing the chef and me under his breath. I could see why Lyft liked to torture him, although I couldn't see the use of it, as I was fearful it would drive him over the edge. Undoubtedly, knowing Lyft, that was the whole point. I was certain Arthurio had no such plans as previously advertised, that he'd be in his room at the stroke of midnight, complaining for most of the next day about illusory symptoms relating to stomach pains from sabotaged food.

Thinking of the pathetic creature's psyche, I made my way to my room, where I lay down for an hour, subsequently showered, and then duly joined the chef in the kitchen at seven.

The surprise was blueberry cobbler, made with fresh Maine blueberries, a la mode with homemade vanilla ice cream. We had a delightful discussion about food and wines, he stating that it took one week to obtain the blueberries from request to delivery. I told him how amazing I thought it was that I could have a dessert of such quality in a tropical climate obtained from the opposite corner of the globe. As we finished an excellent French Sauterne, I realized what an interesting evening this had been. I thought of Arthurio stewing in his room, me happy in the thought that he hadn't participated in the festivities, which, for a certainty, would have been ruined by his boorish, petulant behavior. I bid the chef good night with a hearty thanks for his culinary artistry, stating that I hoped we could partake of each other's company in similar vein again soon. He said to be sure of it.

The next day saw my anxiety operating at an elevated level. At three that morning, I had sneaked into Licia's room to check my e-mail. There was a bounce-back message from Hazelit, stating that he was out of the office on business, only being able to check e-mail occasionally. I was worried about Lyft, wondering about Hazelit, and, in general, was distracted by my own dark thoughts. Essential communication was key to any successful operation, and there was damn little of it being practiced in my estimation.

My communication with *60 Minutes* was a one-way street so far. I didn't even know if Hazelit had seen the information. So much for field work.

Then, to calm myself, I began looking at the scenario from Lyft's point of view. It little mattered, in his estimation, whether *60 Minutes* was in on the act or not. His central tenet was to destroy a network that was attempting to stop his project, thusly endangering his beloved Mother Earth. The press's role was frosting on the dessert—a warning to other groups that they could be ousted and a warning to the public to be diligent, that no one was safe these days. So to a degree, the press was irrelevant.

As to the part about whether or not *60 Minutes* got the scoop, it would eventually get its due. It occurred to me that part of the reason Lyft wanted *60 Minutes* in on it was for our benefit. Probably Lyft figured that if Hazelit landed this one, he'd owe us, perhaps backing off from the interview in the Wakhan. I personally doubted that would happen, as I knew the press to be akin to bloodhounds intent on a scent. Anyway, the interview was the least of my concerns.

I tried the library, feigning reading in my usual corner, when Arthurio finally interrupted me to announce that the "master of the house" was once again on the phone. I asked Arthurio how his night was, and sure enough, he said he had acquired stomach pains around nine thirty, probably from that monster's food preparation, and that he had little opportunity to avail himself of the extended invitation down the road. I sympathetically told him that perhaps it was best that he had remained at home after all. I excused myself to take the call, wondering about domestic interaction in other terrorist households.

I walked over to the desk, sat down, and picked up the receiver cautiously. Relieved to find Lyft on the other end, he informed me that the council had set the operation for the day after tomorrow, and that they'd all be home well before the zero hour. In fact, they'd be home tomorrow.

"Good," I said. "I'm getting bored and tired of the subterfuge."

"Just a little longer, and then we'll be out of there. Although, I can't say this has been a bad gig. Pretty nice hotel here."

"Well, just so you know, I had a terrific dinner last night with Chef Peter. I really don't think he's part of all this, a real innocent caught up in a nasty situation, if you ask me. Arthurio's not so innocent, but Peter, he's another story. I don't think we should bring him down in all this."

"I agree. We'll take care of it. Have you communicated with Hazelit?"

I told him the issue and that I wished I could call him. Lyft said he used Licia's cell to call Hazelit, pretending to be me. I couldn't help but almost hear the smile in his voice.

I queried, "What about Bashirin and Salvo?"

"They'll get the message through gabby and maroon. They know what to do."

"I've no doubt of it. So what happened at the council meeting?"

"Most interesting, I assure you. There are some really heavy hitters here, all pretending to be something they're not. I have names, company affiliations, enough to bring down the whole network. Hazelit is going to have a field day with what I've obtained. What's unique about the council is that it's not made up of any governmental authority, just a loose affiliation of people with a common interest, irrespective of the perverse nature of their exercise. I have every tidbit on tape, stowed away in my pockets. I really need to get rid of them, as they are weighing me down."

"Why? How many tapes do you have?"

Lyft quipped, "Sixteen—thirty minutes each."

"Ah, that *is* a lot to carry."

"For your information, I'm burdened with the video version as well."

"Is that not on a CD-ROM?"

"Yes, it is, but I'm not used to carrying much in my pockets, and remember, I'm a lot smaller than you, so to me, these things take up a lot of room. Plus I have multiple copies of everything, so we don't have to hassle with reproductions in Sumatra. I feel like a plastic Christmas tree, for God's sake."

"Apt analogy for one so secular."

"Oh, you're getting better, I'll give you that."

"So I can't just believe you sat there the entire time behaving yourself listening to these demons hatching terrorist plots."

"No, there was ample opportunity for mischief. I had to be careful, mind you, so as not to disrupt the meeting. This one had to be seen through. Much of what occurred centered around the buffet at meal times, some under the conference table, with the main event taking place in Brihamm's room."

"The buffet I understand, but under the conference table? What perversions took place there?"

"Really, you have such a filthy mind. It needs purging, you know, when you begin to think that way."

"Human nature, I guess."

"Right. Exactly. At any rate, harmless fun abounded under the table. But we'll get to that later. Brihamm became the prime target. I started off on him with something easy. While no one was looking, as he inspected the buffet during a break, I gave him a resounding whack on the back of the head with a rather large, freshly caught side of wahoo, which I immediately placed back on the tray. The blow knocked him into the dessert station, where he fell face first on the minitarts and other assorted pastries. Needless to say, he was mortified."

I chuckled under my breath. "OK, so then what did he do?"

"What *could* he do? He looked wildly around the room, didn't see anyone, was convinced he had been accosted, yet could prove nothing. He had no alternative but to go to his room to change. Unfortunately for him, I'd been there first."

Lyft explained how he'd looked up Brihamm's room number earlier in the day and pilfered a key from the front desk. He'd taken all his clothes to a Laundromat, where he'd washed his finery in the hottest water available, subsequently placing them in the dryer. By the time the clothes where ready to be brought back, they had shrunk several sizes, being of the very finest fabrics never to be touched by a compound as simple as water. Lyft chortled as he explained that Brihamm went absolutely nuts when he found that none of his clothes fit. He called down to the concierge, blaming the hotel for its incompetence, how could they make an attempt to clean his clothes without his authorization, how dare they, he'd sue, on and on it went, until he finally realized that he was missing a substantial portion of the council meeting. He slammed down the phone after the concierge assured him for the twentieth time or so that the hotel had nothing to do with his unfortunate circumstance, that someone must be playing a practical joke. This only incensed him more, as there was no room in his life for fun of any type, a serious man with serious concerns on his mind, namely murder. For Lyft, this was fuel to the fire. While Brihamm sat on the edge of the bed, mulling over his predicament, Lyft tied all his shoes together in tight square knots. He had also redyed them the previous day to a fire-engine red.

I laughed, "Why fire-engine red? Why not some gross concoction of puke purple and green or other obnoxious combination of colors?"

"I'll have you know the color red has incendiary qualities relative to certain personalities. I sensed I had one of those here. Now, let me continue."

Lyft then related that Brihamm got up and went to the bathroom, needing to relieve himself, only to find an ice sculpture of a giant sea snake of mammoth proportions situated in the toilet, melting around the toilet ring. He jumped about three feet into the air when he first noticed it, and then he began swearing in Arabic in running commentary. When he finally settled down, Lyft noted that he peed in the tub in a most undignified manner and then washed it down with the running faucets.

By this time, Lyft had me in hysterics, tears spilling out of my eyes as I took in the picture painted of his further chipping away of this particular tyrant. It seems that while Brihamm was making a futile attempt at freshening up, Lyft planted a blowup doll—one of the really sleazy ones easily obtained in the sex shops—in the man's bed, tucked in under the overlying bedcover, propped up a little bit, leaving her breasts exposed so that Brihamm could get an eyeful as he came back into the room from the bathroom. Sure enough, having been unsuccessful in his ministrations in the bathroom, he entered the room in a foul mood, only to be greeted by the bombshell in bed.

Lyft continued that he'd done a double take, thinking at first that it was a real person. Then, as there was no movement or sound, he realized he'd been scammed, screaming "Blasphemy!" and "Who on God's earth would do such a thing?" et cetera, et cetera. He had grabbed a ballpoint pen from the desk, one of those with the long points opposite the tip, whereupon he then repeatedly stabbed the doll with the reverse point, puncturing her on the first jab but continuing to take out his frustration with successive thrusts. Lyft related that Brihamm had penetrated the mattress on several occasions, until finally, the pen broke in two. Upon that occurring, unfortunately for him, the refill went the way of the plastic, spattering ink all over the bed, the deflated doll, and him. He broke into a real tirade then. He picked up the bedside lamp, a lovely, heavy, white ceramic, bowl-shaped piece etched with elephants, and smashed it on the floor, whereupon he duly obliterated two lovely handmade floor tiles.

Those tiles, Lyft informed me, must have cost the hotel about one hundred dollars each. In certain sections of the room, they were hand-etched in Sanskrit, wishing the traveler a safe journey filled with peace and tranquility. Whichever artist conceived them should have designed one relating to retention of the traveler's sanity, as what Lyft saw next assured him that Brihamm was losing his.

When he got up to go to the bathroom, he noticed his shoes dutifully tied together on the open closet floor, like soldiers at attention, their brilliant, shiny red luster beckoning what little mental prowess remained to leap over the precipice. He ran to the closet, gathered them all up (he had no choice, as they were tied end to end as well as together), and then, with a mighty heave, hurled them into the large, gorgeous mirror hanging over the desk, framed in gold relief of the native animal species of Java. The mirror, of course, shattered, cascading glass fragments about that section of the room, consequently making the area impassible for the idiot to now walk from the bedroom to the bath without grievous injury. Then, to complete the mosaic, the phone rang. Ali was on the other end, asking obsequiously why Brihamm wasn't in the council meeting? Brihamm, in a supremely agitated state bordering on incoherence, babbled that he was being sabotaged.

He then haltingly managed to relate what had happened. Ali gently suggested that he would take care of everything immediately.

Brihamm was shouting that he needed relief from the insanity taking place in his room, a man bordering on the brink. Ali tried his best to placate him, realizing that he was becoming unhinged. He just needed Brihamm's sizes, and he'd have the concierge deliver a new set of garments.

Lyft then continued, "Brihamm then related his sizes to Ali, but I was quicker than the concierge. After Ali had called, I zipped into the adjoining room, placed a call, and immediately cancelled the order. So the clothes never arrived, implicating Ali in the scheme of disbelief and, worse yet, disloyalty. After thirty minutes, Brihamm was fuming. He called the concierge, shouting what in hell's name had happened to the clothes order Ali had placed, only to be told that someone had immediately cancelled it. He swore at the concierge, calling him incompetent, ripped the phone out of the wall, and flung it across the room, where it smashed into an original glass-framed watercolor of Lake Toba. By this time, Brihamm was literally on the verge of insanity. The council meeting had been adjourned for several hours.

"Finally, duty overtook humiliation. He eventually reappeared in a too-tight white shirt with rolled-up sleeves, red shoes, pants that were a good six inches above his ankles, and no suit top. The entire council tittered upon his arrival. As head of the council, you can only imagine his consternation with having to present himself in such a state. He took the seat at the head of the table juxtaposed to Ali, attempting to mask his consternation with a business-as-usual attitude.

"As the proceedings moved forward, I zipped under the table and massaged his thigh, whereupon Brihamm jumped from his chair, glaring at Ali, closest to him, ranting that a perversion was taking place under the table."

Lyft then went on describing a scene I would have given up a good portion of my operating budget to witness firsthand.

Ali subsequently placed his hands above the table, and of course, Lyft continued the exercise. Brihamm, then on the point of losing what little sanity remained, hurled his notepad at Ali, who fortunately ducked as the notepad sailed over his head and into the wall. Ali protested that he had done nothing, that whatever was going on, he was not a part of it. Brihamm became enraged, thinking Ali a liar, suggesting that perhaps it was time to take their differences to a tête-à-tête in the private room off the lobby.

The council, by this time, was agog and shocked at the insane behavior of their leader, so Ahman at the other end of the table suggested that perhaps a short break was in order to let the two work out their issues in private. A collective sigh of relief could be heard. Ali acquiesced, not fully understanding the agenda. But of course, Lyft followed them to their destination in hopes of plaguing them further, thusly creating more disharmony. As usual, his instincts were correct. They proceeded into the small conference room, Brihamm leading, whereupon he gave him a little love pinch on his right buttock. After all his outrage and humiliation, whatever self-control was left deserted him. He turned rapidly, swiftly cocking his arm and smashing Ali directly in the nose with the flat of his fist. Ali's nose exploded, blood all over him, down the front of his shirt, streaming down his suit, spattering his shoes, speckling the magnificent tiled floor. Brihamm became a mad man, screaming he'd been accosted by a pervert in the employ of Iblis. Ali sprayed back, how dare Brihamm hit him in the nose, for what reason, he never touched him, how could he do such a thing? He told him he was becoming unhinged, dotting Brihamm's shirt with speech-propelled droplets of blood.

Brihamm bellowed, "Unhinged? I'll show you who's unhinged."

He then grabbed a conference chair and hurled it at Ali, who fortuitously ducked. The chair sailed above the stooped-over Senior Sastroamidjojo into the magnificent, hand-etched glass wall defining the conference room partition from the lobby. The etchings had depicted lyrical events in the ancient Majapahit Empire. The chair, along with innumerable shards of glass, splayed out into the lobby, severely frightening the guests and staff who thought, at first, there'd been a terrorist attack in the hotel. The concierge came running over to investigate, and when he discovered the source of the commotion, he screamed at Brihamm, Lyft quoting for effect, "You? You again? You've been nothing but trouble. I'm calling the police."

Brihamm thundered back, "Who do you think you're talking to? I'll have your head on a pike, you miserable little bag of shit."

Then the concierge yelled to him that he was a disgrace in his own country, that he'd done irreparable damage to the hotel, and that he must get out. Brihamm thundered back that he could buy the dump if he wanted and that the concierge should shut up, that he'd have his job for his insubordination.

By that time, hotel security had arrived, along with the hotel nurse. The nurse tended to Ali, leading him across the lobby to the nurse's station, giving him a towel to hold over his nose as she escorted him by the elbow, avoiding the broken glass as best they could.

Security detained Brihamm, one officer on each side of him while they ensured he remained at the conference table. He was ranting about sabotage, about how his hateful enemies had hatched a sinister plot to overthrow his sanity. The guards attempted to appease him in an attempt to have him relax, which only agitated him further. Each now had a hand on his shoulder, ensuring he remained seated. Finally, the official police arrived, duly noting the raving delusions of a lunatic.

Brihamm, by this time, was so out of control that they could illicit no sense from him whatsoever, so they took him away to the police station, telling the concierge that he would have to eventually pay them a visit, along with Ali who perhaps should file a complaint pertaining to his recent physical assault. The concierge told them he was off duty at three that afternoon and that he would relate the message to Ali after his nose returned to some semblance of normalcy.

Unfortunately for Ali, Lyft informed me, normalcy would no doubt mean surgery, as his nose looked like it had been broken in several places. As he was being tended to by the nurse, he muttered that not only was he going to sue Brihamm for millions, but that he was also going to get rid of that millstone Licia who'd been hanging around his neck too long; dead son or no dead son, it was time to make some changes. He was now going to be in succession for chair of the council. Everyone could see that Brihamm, for whatever reason, had fallen into the clutches of evil spirits who now dominated his mental processes. He was finished, as he could never be trusted to hold a position of responsibility again, even if he did ever regain his mental composure. Now it was time to assert what should have been rightfully his all along. Yes, there'd be some changes made. Lyft said that if Ali had only known their scope, he would have been engaged in a liquidation sale.

I asked Lyft if he had preplanned Brihamm's decent into insanity or if he had ad-libbed it, which I'd seen him do masterfully on occasions before.

Lyft replied, slightly imperiously, "Actually, I had the general plan in mind some time ago, but the details manifested themselves at opportune moments, so I'd say, yes, much of it was ad-libbed for sure. Shows a certain mental dexterity, don't you think?"

"Absolutely, I'd be the first to give you accolades for this masterful orchestration. A true maestro fine tuning his orchestra."

"Yes, an apt description. The composition played to perfection. So to conclude the narrative, Ali's nose was finally placed on hold, and Licia, evidently tired of the lobby antics, called that slithering creature Arthurio to book an early flight back to Medan, inclusive of a limo pickup. So she'll be returning this evening."

"Glad you told me. And this all occurred when? My frame of reference is a little off."

"I figured that information might be useful. This all occurred yesterday, for your information."

"So what are you doing today? Taking a vacation day?"

"Very funny. I'm ensuring there are no loose ends, like Ahman, the new de facto council head. Anyway, let me continue, or we'll never get through this."

Lyft recounted how Ahman finally reconvened the council, now sitting in Brihamm's place. Lyft noted that Ahman had waved for Ali to take the number-two seat. I could just picture Ali's two monstrous black eyes flickering through a haze of pain. Lyft pointed out that he resembled a Sumatran raccoon who'd tipped over the garbage, having found too much arrack. It seemed that his swollen, crooked nose acted like a beacon to the assemblage, who could not avert their gaze. Here was the new successor who had engaged in combat on their behalf, or so they thought. Not only was their attention riveted forward due to Ali's immediate change in physiognomy, but also due to their respect of the victorious warrior. Then Lyft shouted, a little too loudly, "To the victor go the spoils."

"Amen. You know there are no raccoons, in the traditional sense, in Sumatra or anywhere else in the Far East, for that matter?"

"Ah, trying to one-up me, eh? Of course I know that. They only have their cousins, the red panda, otherwise known as the lesser panda, which have been hunted to protected status. But they look similar to a raccoon, so my analogy stands."

"Granted."

"Oh, you're too kind. So anyway, it was agreed that the action in the Straits would be scheduled for the day after tomorrow and that the council would operate pretty much the same as it had. Ali will have to obtain certain information from Brihamm, for which we cannot wait. I'll take care of that while he's incarcerated. Actually, he may be incarcerated for a good, long time. We need to know the extraneous tentacles of the network so that Hazelit can conclude what we've begun. That's imperative, as we need to get back to work. This has been nothing but a distracting aberration from our main purpose, albeit in pleasant surroundings."

"Agreed. So when will I see you?"

"Probably in the morning or soon thereafter, after I'm finished with Brihamm. Hopefully I won't have to totally destroy him to obtain what we need. There *is* that possibility, however."

"Well, if you do, you do. He'll get whatever he deserves."

"Yes, well, there's that. So I think I'll sign off now. I've a lot on tape, probably enough to do the job, but it'll take too long to separate the wheat from the chaff, if you know what I mean. By the time that occurs, some of the wheat may be blown to the wind. The network has to be taken down quickly and fully, otherwise it'll sprout up somewhere else. Not that others won't, but getting rid of this one would be a particular coup. So I'll see you tomorrow, and then we'll liaise with Bashirin and Salvo to make sure they're in the loop."

"OK, tomorrow it is. Although it probably doesn't mean much, my commendation on a job well done."

"Actually, it means quite a bit. See you soon."

He clicked off the cell phone connection. I figured if Sammy questioned the length of the call, I'd tell him Ali and I were discussing possible employment, as I was rapidly attaining primogeniture status within the family.

As it was now past noon, Arthurio came into the library, inquiring if I would like to join him and the chef in the kitchen for luncheon. His timing made me wonder if he had overheard any of the conversation. Then I thought, who cares, Lyft had done all the talking. In reviewing my abbreviated responses on the phone, there were few items that could have been misinterpreted to have betrayed me. Dumb luck or haute intelligence? I thought of it as a compromise, terming it blind instinct.

"So, Arthurio, made up with the chef, 'ave we?"

"In actuality, sir, it was *he* who made up with *me*."

"Ah, I see. Well, da na matter either way, as long as it's done. I'm glad we're one large, happy family again, as I detest strife in tha family, ya see. Never could tolerate me sisters an' brothers fightin', drove me bonkers, oh, don't ya know. So I'd be delighted ta join yas in the kitchen. Now, what time would we be congregatin?'"

"Chef says he'll be prepared in thirty minutes."

"Perfect. That'll just give me time to freshen up a bit. See ya then."

I made as if heading toward my room and then veered off toward the kitchen. I needed to quiz the chef on his future aspirations so as to gauge his interest in going with us, ensuring that the reptile Arthurio wasn't lurking nearby. There I found the chef diligently preparing a fresh seafood salad, the likes of nothing I'd seen. Grilled calamari in light pesto, garlic, and oil; blackened mahimahi; fresh wahoo; cold grilled marlin steaks vinaigrette with hot grilled vegetables; oysters and clams on the half-shell; mussels marinara; and fresh ahi tuna cooked to perfection.

"Chef, what's this, for cryin' out loud? There's only the three of us, don't ya know."

"True, true, but the mistress is arriving home this evening, so I thought I'd prepare a little extra. A fresh feast for us, and leftovers for her. Ha ha."

I smiled at that one. Having previously determined his Swiss culinary heritage, I knew that his loyalty was to food, not necessarily to people. His statement reinforced my opinion.

"Chef, we need to have a conversation in private, lad, about what's happenin' to this family. I've some information of some importance relatin' to yer future I think you'll find of interest. Namely, that ya haven't got one."

That got his attention. His head snapped up, and his jet blue eyes narrowed. He towered over me, his six-foot-six height exaggerated by his tubular chef's hat.

"What do you mean, 'haven't got one?'"

"Just what I said, lad. You've no future here. In less than two weeks, I'll wager, you'll all be unemployed. But I can't discuss it here now. The walls 'ave ears, oh, don't ya know."

He stared at me a few moments, trying to fathom my meaning, when Arthurio came skipping into the kitchen.

"Oh, you're here early, kibitzing with the chef regarding me, no doubt. So what were you two discussing? I know it was about me, so out with it. I want to know what schemes you've been hatching."

The chef glanced at me, now understanding my reference to acute hearing. He rolled his eyes as he edged toward the counter, evidently preparing for some intervention with Arthurio.

"Why, Arthurio, lad," I mellifluously intoned. "Our conversation had nothin' to do with you. Rather it had everything to do with the future and what the chef's goin' to do with his. I'll ask the same question. What are you goin' to do with yours?"

Arthurio snarled, "I heard what you said. I don't believe anything you say. You're nothing but a smooth-talking Irishman, taking advantage of a grieving family, making every attempt to insert yourself into their good graces. You're untrustworthy, and I think you're a cad. And my future's none of your business. I work for the most reputable of families. I plan to remain in their employ as long as they'll have me. The master and the mistress have my undivided loyalty, and I would gladly give my life for either of them. That's more than you can say, you slick-talking ingrate."

"Well, Arthurio, it'll take a much larger man than yourself to put a steamer under me arse. But I can think of one ta put under yours. As a matter of fact, we were discussin' what a slimeball y'are, nasty to the staff with yer feckin' imperious attitude on exhibition every minute. We were both sayin' what a waste of a human being y'are, ya feckin' little Napoleon. So why don't ya take yer scaly reptilian presence outta here ta yer bedroom where ya can go feck yeself?"

Arthurio slinked back like I'd threatened to punch him. Then he drew himself up, unconsciously straightening out his uniform, and turned from me, avoiding me like I was trash. "Chef?" he said, clearly forcing his voice into a professional tone. "Do you acquiesce to the sentiments of this upstart?"

"Actually, I'm in complete agreement," the chef replied, almost chortling at his counterpart's obvious discomfort. Then, his temper gaining steam, he yelled, "You're nothing but a pain in the ass to all in this house, especially to me. I've tolerated you long enough. Now get out."

Arthurio cried, losing all composure now, "You can't throw me out of this kitchen. It's as much mine as yours."

With that, Arthurio picked up a rolling pin, preparing for battle, but the chef exhibited surprising agility for a man of his proportion. He quickly crossed the kitchen and, before Arthurio could react, gave him a resounding smack on the side of his face with a solid stainless steel spatula with an extra-long handle. The impact sent Arthurio's black toupee flying across the kitchen, where it landed in a stainless vat of boiling chicken stock simmering on the stove. A large, rectangular red welt was rapidly manifesting itself on Arthurio's face under his left ear.

Apparently, the battle was over as soon as it was begun. Arthurio, clearly in shock, began to cry. This probably was his first time on the receiving end of an assault, and he clearly was incapable of retaliation. The chef screamed at him to leave the kitchen. It was evident that Arthurio was not cognizant of his missing hairpiece, substantial though it was. He slowly exited the kitchen, perhaps finally comprehending that his perceived authority had been severely compromised.

I looked at the chef with newfound respect.

"Nice shot. Couldn't 'ave placed it better meself. Cleared out the room for a nice heart-to-heart, though. Couldn't 'ave orchestrated it to a better perfection, lad, if I don't mind sayin' so."

"I greatly appreciate the compliment. Remind me to wash the spatula to remove the grease."

We both had a hearty laugh at that one.

He said, "So now that the weasel has been chased into his lair, let's have an enjoyable luncheon. I have it all prepared; the Pouilly-Fuissé is icing nicely, and the crème brûlée has been singed. So let us begin without Arthurio's evil spirit hovering over our repast, and also without his toupee." The chef set the pot with the chicken stock in the sink for future disposal.

"I'm ready when you are."

He told me to grab a plate and help myself to the buffet while he poured the wine, a superb nectar from 1991. The food was exquisite, permeated with the freshness of the sea.

We sat across from each other in the alcove. He began, "So what of your reference earlier about my employment?"

I directly looked at him, finishing a mouthful of seafood salad. "Well, my newfound friend, I've come across some information implicatin' Ali in some seriously nefarious activities, oh, don't ya know. Terrorism would be at the top o' the list, with murder a close second, tax evasion a large third, and child abuse a resoundin' fourth. It goes on and on."

Peter raised his eyebrows, slightly incredulous. "And I'm working for such scum? How did you come by this information?"

I concentrated on another forkful. "All in good time, lad. Some things can't be divulged. You remember the one I mentioned, child abuse?"

"Yes," he said slowly.

I swallowed and said, fork poised in the air, "Well, Ali had his only son ga inta harm's way ta plant explosives in a liquid nitrogen facility in Northern Afghanistan. Ya remember the funeral, tha wailin' upstairs, the depression these two reprobates had thinking their son had been killed in the explosion he was supposed ta have orchestrated? Well, the kid's alive and well, incarcerated an' scared half ta death. Only these two arseholes don't know it and won't for a while."

Peter placed his utensils on his plate, looking directly at me, his chef's hat wavering slightly. "Good God, man, who are you?"

I looked directly back at him. "Someone who has your best interest at heart with serious things to do. We figure you're pretty much an innocent in all this. That's why I'm talking to you in such a manner."

Surprised, Peter queried, "What happened to your Irish accent?"

I laughed. "I'm about as Irish as you are, oh, don't ya know."

He picked up his fork again, intent on spearing a piece of lobster. "Well, you carried it off pretty well. Had me fooled."

I pushed my plate forward as I folded my hands on the table behind it. I leaned toward him. "I may have to lapse into it again at some point, so mum's the word. The organization I work for would like to talk to you about employment, but not until we bring Ali down along with his network. You need to do as you've always done and, above all, continue to act clueless until we tell you it's time to make an exit. Capiche?"

He put his fork in the air. "Capiche. I appreciate your faith in me."

I pulled my plate back, intent on more salad. "You should appreciate the faith you have in yourself. Trust me, Arthurio will not be in the mix. He'll sink on his own."

"Understood," he said as the piece of lobster disappeared.

I mused out loud, "I wonder what the little rat bag's doing right now?"

The chef was piling it in now, as he said with his mouth full, "Who cares? What can he do?"

I thought to myself, *He can rifle my drawers and find the camera, that's what he can do.*

"Excuse me a minute, but I think I'll go and ensure he's not turning my room upside down."

I went quickly upstairs, going by Arthurio's room, hearing sniveling within. At least he was in his own quarters. I went quickly to my room and unlocked the desk drawer, where I found the camera, undisturbed. I placed it in my front pocket, leaving the charger in my room. Juicing the battery could wait until the evening. I went back downstairs to continue what turned into an extremely enjoyable afternoon after all.

Everything now hinged on Lyft's return. Licia's was irrelevant, Ali's of more import, and Lyft's most important of all. The next two days needed orchestration to perfection, but for now, there was nothing to do but enjoy the wine and relax, becoming acquainted with a new friend.

Chapter Twenty-Three

General Ricardo Emillio Estavez was having trouble with Maria. Her casual inquisitiveness regarding the supposed buried treasure on Selkirk's had now transformed itself into a fanatical obsession. She harangued him during his meals, and she woke him up from deep sleep by pounding on his bedroom door, screaming that he must be holding out on her. She continually had her nose buried in stories relating to the treasure, until she had what she thought to be the accurate details memorized, which she then spouted at him over the telephone or in person in his office when she popped in, now during frequent intervals of at least every other day.

After one of her particularly nasty telephone tirades, during which she had threatened to go to the press, he placed his head in his hands, realizing that he had to take some action before he killed her outright in his own home. He could have her committed, but could he take the chance that the doctors would prove her sane? He would lose it all if he proved to be unsuccessful. He could take her on the plane to Selkirk's and then dump her out, but what about the pilot? He'd know there'd be no round trip for her. He doubted the pilot's loyalty, so that scheme was out. He could easily hire someone to dispose of her, which might be the simplest way out of their entanglement, but then he was subject to blackmail. Then where did it end? Hire a killer to kill the killer and keep going until the talent ran out? No, that solution was too messy.

Then it hit him. Of course. He had a pilot's license, so he could fly the plane himself to Selkirk's. He could take Maria with him, whether she wanted to go or not, and then dump her out after placing the plane on autopilot. He'd call the pilot, giving him the excuse that he needed some flying time. That was easily arranged, as he'd done it before. What was problematic was how to get her onto the airplane. He didn't want her yakking to her innumerable girlfriends that she was taking a trip on Emillio's private plane, so he'd have to drug her. A little something in the morning coffee. Yes, he'd get up early one day this week, make the coffee with the pretense of having to get to the office early, pressing matters, that sort of thing, not an unusual circumstance. When the lights went out, he'd bring her down the back staircase to the car in the garage, dump her into the trunk, and drive to his plane, where it was parked in a remote corner of the Santiago airport. All he had to do was show the guard at the security entrance his military ID, and he'd have the run of the airport grounds.

Now that he had the general rudiments of a plan formulated, he wondered how he would explain her absence. All her girlfriends knew that she had, on more than one occasion, threatened to leave him. He would use that angle. They'd had a huge fight, she'd told him she was leaving, and he'd said good riddance, but just the same, being a dutiful husband, that he'd make sure she was comfortable in whatever new surroundings she selected for herself, that he felt it best they part, even though she was the love of his life. No, perhaps that was a little thick, might arouse suspicion. Take the hard line, he told himself. It was more in keeping with who he really was. Here's the money, now get the hell out, and don't come back. So be it. They'd buy that for sure.

So, he figured, why wait? Tomorrow would work as well as any other day. He called the pilot, who was grateful for the day off. The pilot told him the plane was fully serviced, ready to go, all he needed was the key, and did he have it? Estavez replied yes, that he kept one in the house. Estavez said he'd return by evening, and the pilot said there was a front moving through in the next few days, that Estavez had selected a good time to go, and that he hoped all went well. They clicked off the conversation.

Stage one out of the way, thought Estavez. *Now for stage two.*

Morning couldn't come fast enough. He tossed and turned most of the night, desperately needing the coffee he was so intent on making. Maria came down around six in the morning. Sure enough, she started in on him as soon as she entered the kitchen. When was he going to Selkirk's, how was he going to know if treasure was discovered while he was shuffling papers in his office, how could he trust men he didn't know doing excavation on the island, and how could he be sure nothing had not been found? He'd better not be holding out on her.

"I think you and those men out there have found something and are hiding it. I am convinced of it. How do you have all this money if you haven't found something? I don't trust you."

"My sweet, how can you say that? Here. I've made the coffee just the way you like it. Have some. It will calm you."

"You know why I don't trust you? Because you've two mistresses. Everyone knows it too. You've humiliated me. I'm the laughing stock in this city. My girlfriends are the only ones who understand. You know something, Emillio? I hate you with a passion. A passion, I tell you. You're a miserable, selfish son of a bitch."

This was pretty strong, even from her. He wondered what had set her off on this tangent so early in the morning.

"My dear, you know very well where the money that supports us comes from, from my numerous enterprises. Do you really think we could live as we do on my army salary? Please, give us both some credit. You very well know the arrangement." He sipped his coffee and eyed her coldly over the rim of his mug. "If you like, we can easily part company. I give you an allowance for life, you remain in the lifestyle you want, doing what you want, without my encumbrance. It would certainly suit me, so I wouldn't have to hear you screeching like a cat about these perpetual fantasies regarding buried treasure. You know people have searched every inch of that island for years, turning over every stone, only to come up empty-handed time and again. So there *is* no buried treasure. We have to protect the fiscal arrangements we currently have with our clients and put aside this talk of buried treasure, otherwise we will take our eye off the ball and lose our lifestyle. Now we would not want that, would we?"

"Of course not, Emillio, and perhaps I was hasty in judging you. I don't want to part company."

"And why is that? I surmise it is because you do not trust me to keep you in the style to which you are accustomed."

"Exactly."

"One thing, Maria, I cannot accuse you of being stupid. A real bitch on occasion, but never stupid. You very well know I cannot give you a lump-sum payment, I do not have that type of capital. So you've really no recourse but to keep the status quo."

"I know, and it kills me. It kills me, I tell you. What woman wants to be constantly cuckolded in public? For that matter, what *person*? I would not do that to you, so why do you do it to me?"

"That's what this is really all about, isn't it? The unfaithful husband the object of the wife's wrath."

"How could it be anything else?"

"Well, I really thought it was about the treasure, but that's not the case at all. I'll tell you why I do it, because I like sex, plain and simple. You don't, at least you never exhibited that you did, so this is what you get. I like the curve of a woman's back and the feel of her naked breasts against my chest. You could care less about the physical act of love. You can't have it both ways, Maria. You can't have everything you want in life and shut your husband off in the bedroom. Life doesn't work that way. Perhaps if you'd shown me a little more deference, a little more love, a little more passion, things would have been different. But no, your greed took you over, to the point that you've become mentally ill regarding this stupid treasure, all because you think you've been wronged.

"Well, I've a life to live. I'll not sit idly by while it rips on down the road without me. If you feel cuckolded, look inside yourself to find the responsible party. And you know what the worst part is? I don't even want you anymore. There's no appeal left, hasn't been for years. We now participate in a marriage of convenience, nothing more. And frankly, it's barely that, with you carping at me continually, paranoid that I'm multiplying the wrongs. You know what? I'm so busy trying to keep the main event intact so that we have income for us both, the only time I think of you during the day is when you call and caterwaul on the phone."

She said nothing, her head down, both hands on her coffee cup as she occasionally brought it haltingly to her lips, her tears dripping into the brew. Now that all was out in the open, Emillio could see that she realized how badly trapped she was in a loveless marriage, he even imagining how she might ache as well for the human touch again. But he figured she was as aware as he that it was too late for any attempt at reconciliation.

She began murmuring about their courting days, their wedding day, their honeymoon in the Andes, the fun they used to have when they were young, and how she had dreamed of children, and then related how fast it had all changed. She supposed it had to do with wanting a material lifestyle more than a family. Now she croaked into her coffee that she wished she'd had those children so she could be surrounded by loving faces, but even that was too late, at least with Emillio. She began ranting that she'd just turned forty, he fifty-four, and that they'd been married twenty years, with the last ten at each other's throats. She said that needed to change, that she could no longer go through life like this.

She was getting drowsy, beginning to say something, slurring her words. Emillio looked on with satisfaction, waiting for her to place her head on her crossed forearms on the kitchen table.

Her words stumbled out, "Emillio, maybe it's not too late. Maybe we still have a chance. Maybe we should try again. I'm soooo tired. I just need to rest my head a minute."

She was asleep within seconds, her breathing at regular intervals. Now to get her to the car, nightgown, bathrobe, and all. He cleaned up the kitchen, rinsed the coffee cups, and then placed them in the dishwasher. He picked her up, slinging her over his shoulder like a sack of potatoes, making his way unsteadily down the stairs to the attached garage. He used his electronic key button to open the trunk of the Mercedes, gently placing her in its confines. No sense in damaging her yet, there was plenty of time for that. Plus, he didn't want any blood dripping around in the trunk.

He exited the garage, closing the door behind him, noting that all was quiet in his neighborhood at that hour, only an occasional jogger or cyclist out for their early morning training. He leisurely drove to the airport, flashed his ID at entry, and was saluted on his way through the gate as he headed to the private tarmac area of the airfield. He was in luck, as the area was deserted. He parked the car in his designated spot, went to the plane, made it ready with the door open, and then went back to the car.

Now the dicey part, he thought. *If anyone sees me, I'm finished. Look around, Emillio. Make sure no one's snooping around where they shouldn't be.* Seeing no one, he whispered to himself, "Let's do this."

He hoisted Maria out of the trunk, carrying her in the crook of his arms. He shut the trunk and hit the lock button to lock the car. Just in case someone should inquire, he could say he was taking his sick wife to a specialist out of the country, that she was very ill and there was no time to waste on transference paperwork and other administrative matters. But no one saw him. He placed her on the floor of the plane near the rear door. He then went to the pilot's seat, requesting clearance and runway instructions from the tower. Upon hearing the answers in his headphones, he noted with satisfaction that his pilot had filed a flight plan for him the previous day. Everything was going perfectly. His freedom would soon be assured.

He took off into the wind that fortuitously was coming directly from Selkirk's. It was only about an hour's flight, so he figured to dump Maria halfway. The currents could then take her all the way to Africa for all he cared.

On the way, however, something unusual began to occur. He began to have a conscience. He ruminated on her still-beautiful face, the good times they had shared in happier circumstances, how empty the house was going to be without her presence. He thought of himself in the role of a widower and was having trouble envisioning the condolences, the tribulations to her that would be forthcoming, after he'd been the one responsible for her disappearance. It was different getting rid of someone unknown, ordering departure from this life by the snap of the finger. That was detached, had no messy consequences, and even if suspicions were aroused on occasion, there were few to question him. But this, this was different. This was looking directly into the enemy's eyes, wondering if the cojones were there to accomplish the deed. This was murder. The other, well, that was business, pure and simple. Even though the law did not necessarily differentiate the two concepts, he did, and that was what counted.

Then he began thinking, if he failed to dump her out, what would he do when she woke up? How would he explain her presence in the plane, and how would it be for the future, she knowing that he'd almost carried out a scheme to kill her? What type of a relationship could they formulate then? She mentioned in the kitchen that perhaps there was still hope, but that was just the drug talking, he was sure. No, once begun on this course, it needed to be seen through. There could be no hesitation.

He looked at his watch and the dials, realizing that he'd been daydreaming way too long. He was getting too close to Selkirk's. In a few more minutes, it would be too late. He placed the plane on autopilot at twenty-five hundred feet, clambered out of the pilot's seat, and then walked back to where Maria lay in a heap in front of the rear door. He gazed down at the slightly pouting lips that had so attracted him in the past, her flush figure, the beauty of her light skin against her dark features, and the pangs began again. He used to love her fire. Now all it did was burn him.

Best he move her now, before losing his nerve. He finally managed the door open, and then he unceremoniously pushed her out of the plane. At slightly over two hundred miles per hour, she was gone in an instant. He shut the door, making his way back to the pilot's seat. The sweat was running down his face, soaking the open collared shirt, sticking him to the back of the leather seat. His breath was coming in gasps, and for a few minutes, he thought he was going to have a heart attack. He began to feel sorry for himself, envisioning he and the plane plummeting together into the shoals of Selkirk's.

But that was not to be his fate, at least not today. The island was getting closer now, so he made preparations to circle and land. He calmed himself as he mentally prepared for the visit with Alvarez. Not that he expected to find anything, but one never knew. The thought of potential treasure warmed him, soothing his soul. Maria's face was already fading from his consciousness as other more pressing matters dimmed her spirit.

Much later, Lyft would do the calculations after he figured what had occurred.

It took Maria approximately fourteen seconds to fall eighteen hundred feet. Subsequently, for the remainder of her fall, she attained terminal velocity, plummeting ten thousand feet per minute for the remaining seven hundred feet in four point two seconds. The chances of her surviving were minimal, at perhaps one in ten million. She must have been the ten millionth person to have done so—perhaps it was divine intervention. Whatever the reason, after hitting the water, she actually skidded, as her forward acceleration was still somewhat active. The skid broke her fall, and also multiple bones: her left arm, her right leg, her right collar bone, her nose, several ribs, her left ankle, and her wrist, along with all the fingers on her right hand. When she hit the water, Lyft pointed out, she likely would have awakened from the drug, but as she was still being tossed around like a rag doll, she probably had no inkling of her surroundings. If she had been conscious during the fall, he surmised, she would have instantly died upon impact. Undoubtedly, her relaxed state saved her.

Although Estavez ensured there was no one around when he pushed her out of the plane, he failed to notice a small fishing craft near Maria's ocean entrance point. The craft was only about one hundred yards away. Being self-propelled, it quickly pulled alongside Maria, using nets to take her on board. The gentleman fisher gently laid her down on the bottom of the craft using the hydraulic net minder, and then, realizing the gravity of her condition, he full-throttled it toward the island. He dared not attempt to make the run to the village. It was too far on the other side of Selkirk's. He would have to take her to the U.S. Army outpost, where they were digging the foundation of a plant. He figured they would have at least minimal equipment to deal with her injuries, and they could get her to a health facility faster than any of the village folk could.

It took him fifteen minutes to get to the island, where he ran his small craft right up onto the pebbled beach. He sounded his fisherman's horn, and the Army crew came running.

Henley was the first on the beach. "What's up?" he yelled.

"I have a woman here who's badly injured, Señor Sergeant. She needs medical attention right away."

Henley looked into the boat and whistled. He took one look at her and yelled at the other crew members to get a stretcher.

"Where on earth did you find her?" he asked.

"In the ocean. A small plane threw her out."

"Holy shit," exclaimed Henley. "You did not see what type it was, did you?"

"Si, señor. It was the plane General Estavez flies. I would recognize it anywhere. I believe he landed on the island as well."

"Oh, boy," Henley muttered. "This is going to be interesting. I hope she lives, but she doesn't look good. Hey, where's the stretcher?" He turned and called over his shoulder, "I need that stretcher."

Four men reappeared over the rise to the beach, two running the stretcher down to the boat, the other two following.

"Take her to Colonel Alvarez's hut. Get the medic ASAP. Let's move it, gentleman. We may not have much time. Gently, gently."

Henley told the fisherman, Ernesto, to tell no one of what happened and to get away from the beach immediately, back to fishing or whatever he was about. Ernesto did not have to be told twice.

They carefully loaded Maria onto the stretcher and took her quickly to Alvarez's quarters. Alvarez was just coming across the clearing when they reached his hut. He ran at a hard clip to meet them just as they were opening the door to deposit her inside. The medic was immediately on his heels.

The medic bent over her, noticing the multiple fractures apparent in her distorted limbs.

"This woman needs proper medical attention. We need to medevac her right away. We'll stabilize her in the chopper and hope to God we make it in time to the mainland. Let's go, gentlemen. Colonel, we need to get this done right away."

"Whatever you need, Doc, it's yours. Anything you can do to save her, you do."

"Yes, sir."

In less than ten minutes, Maria was in the air, headed to Valparaiso, a slightly closer destination than Santiago.

Alvarez turned to Henley and asked, "How the hell did this happen, out in the middle of nowhere?"

"The fisherman, Ernesto, said she fell out of a plane. He said the plane belonged to General Estavez."

"Ah, how interesting."

"Yes, sir, he said he'd recognize the plane anywhere."

"Where is the fisherman now?"

"I told him to get lost for a while, literally."

"That's why I like you, Henley; you're a quick study. Good man."

"Yes, sir. And he said he thought Estavez landed on the island."

As if on cue, all of a sudden, Estavez bounded over the hill in his Jeep, crossing over the location of the two deeply buried sarcophagi, parking in the clearing. Alvarez came out of the hut to the blinding smile and bonhomie of the general.

He thought, *If he only knew what was underneath him on his way in. Hmm, wearing civvies. I've never seen that before. This is getting more interesting by the minute.*

"Good day, General. And how are we today?"

Alvarez shook hands, as if nothing had transpired just minutes ago.

"Fine, fine. I thought I'd take my weekly excursion a little early this week, as I have an official day off. I noticed your helicopter headed toward the mainland. Is everything all right?"

"We had a little accident. One of the men hit in the head by the front-end loader bucket. Knocked the hell out of him, so we're getting him checked out at a hospital in Valparaiso. He's stable, although still unconscious. We're hoping for the best."

"Indeed, I'm sorry to hear of the incident. Well, I see you have steel in the ground, as promised. I'm truly impressed. Are you back on schedule?"

"Not quite, but we will be. Being a man down doesn't help, though."

"Yes, I quite agree. And of course, no sign of any trinkets?"

"No, General, no trinkets. We've hit bedrock, though. Would you like to see?"

"No, that's quite all right. No need to prolong the day. After all, this is my free time. Time for the bar, the buffet, and the boudoir, not necessarily in that order," he guffawed.

Alvarez feigned a good laugh himself, disgusted though he was. He wondered whom Estavez had pitched out of the plane. He'd sure as hell find out. This pig had to be put on a spit, and he was the one who was going to roast him.

"Well, General, we'll be getting back to work then. Good day to you."

"Good day, Colonel."

Then Estavez walked to his Jeep, clambered in, and drove off with a wave. Alvarez coincidentally waved back as he walked to the foundation site, without looking up.

CHAPTER TWENTY-FOUR

Licia returned as scheduled, keeping to herself, asking Arthurio to bring her dinner in her room. Lyft arrived the next day early in the morning, zooming into "our" room through the open bedroom window.

"I could either crow like a rooster or strip the covers from the bed, whichever you prefer. It's time to get up. We've got a lot going on today," he cackled from his perch on the footboard.

"Good morning to you too," I groaned. "So what's the prognosis with Brihamm?"

"Certifiably insane, especially after last night. I interviewed him in his cell. By the time I was through, he was convinced the walls were talking to him. I have it all on tape using a very high-tech portable recorder. The audiovisual people will be able to set up their own company with the graft I've liberally dispensed. So for once, everyone is relatively happy, including Brihamm. I pretty much convinced him that he had been under too much stress, that he should let the proper authority take care of him for a while to nurse him back to balanced mental health. I may visit him from time to time, just to ensure his continued incarceration. Won't take much, just a few phrases from the walls, or the ceiling, for that matter. That's not really all that important, 'cause he's no threat even if he were to get out. What's important is that I've got the whole network ready to be brought down. I need to get this to Hazelit right away, along with all the other paraphernalia with which I am burdened. I spoke to Hazelit (posing as you, I might add). He's here on Sumatra, staying in a fleabag at the airport. I told him I'd drop off the tapes today and that the action was scheduled for tomorrow. Obviously you can't be the delivery man, as you have no way to do it, so I'll do it. I told Hazelit I'd leave them in the lobby for him under his name. I'll need to do so when the clerk is away from the desk or has his back turned. I'll need a bag for this stuff. Can you find one somewhere?"

"I think that can be arranged. The chef basically knows what's up, so he'll help. We need to watch out for Arthurio, though. He's not part of the mix. He chose the dark side."

"Yes, well, I've no time to deal with him. If I did, he'd go the way of Brihamm. But we've more important things to do. So up and at 'em."

"Can I at least have coffee first? And would you like some?"

"What a splendid idea. Nothing better than Sumatran coffee. Yes, I think that's a capital idea."

"Anything else? I'm sure the chef is up. How about breakfast?"

"Even better. Yes, I do believe we've time for such liberties. With sausage, if you please."

"Yes, oh, master of the house."

"Has a nice ring, no?"

"Oh, definitely."

I called down to the kitchen, Peter good-naturedly answering, and told him I'd be down for a giant platter of scrambled eggs, a dozen sausage, a triple rasher of bacon, a basket of toast, a quart of orange juice, a little mixed fruit, and a pot of coffee.

"My, someone has a hell of an appetite this morning. If I didn't know better, I'd say you had company up there."

"I do, but it's not what you think, you dirty old man, so get with it," I said good-naturedly. "I'll be down in a few minutes to bring up the food."

"Give me fifteen minutes, and we're there. See you then."

No shower, but at least I had a chance to brush my teeth and wash my face before I had to retrieve breakfast. Not normally being much of an eater before noon, I fended off Lyft's protestations at my only having coffee and a small bowl of fruit. Without further argument and even less hesitation, he plowed through his breakfast in record time.

"Looks like you haven't eaten in a week, but somehow I seriously doubt that."

"As a matter of fact, I had an outrageous room service banquet last night, but it still left me somewhat unsatisfied. You know those froufrou hotels where they give you miniscule portions at astronomical prices. Those hotels are for models cavorting around the catwalk, not for me. No, sir. Not for me."

"Dare I ask what your room service bill was for the short three or so nights you were there?"

"Well, it's really Ali's bill, but sure you can ask. It was just shy of five thousand dollars."

"Blessed Mary and Joseph. What in earth's name did you eat?"

"It wasn't so much the eating, but the drinking. Several bottles of Screaming Eagle and multiples of Cristal seemed to put the bill over the edge. Ali will never know what hit him."

"I can't believe he's that stupid."

"Well, he's not, but when he sees Brihamm's signature on his bill, what's he gonna do? Go after him in the loony bin? I think not."

"God, you are a master."

"Master of the house, don't forget."

"Yes, that too," I conceded, taking my coffee mug to the open window. Looking out beyond the patio, I ruminated briefly that I was going to miss the view. "So what's the plan, and where do I fit in?"

Lyft was still shoveling it in, but he took a pause between forkfuls to say, "The plan is for me to go to the boat, give Bashirin and Salvo the heads up, then go to Hazelit's hotel, dump off the tapes, and zip back here. By that time, it will be close to lunch. I trust the chef is in superior form."

I raised my mug in toast, still near the window. "You are truly amazing. What am I supposed to do? Sit here and twiddle my thumbs?"

Lyft retorted, with some derision in his tone, "Well, you

could, but that would be a royal waste of time. If I were you, I'd be selecting in my mind the titles of those first editions you covet in the library. Then I'd have some boxes ready to place them in so you can expeditiously pack them and get out of Dodge. Then I'd be scouting out where the car keys are kept, because I can't carry you out of here when all hell explodes. You'll pretty much be on your own when it all comes down. I would get on the Internet and make sure I knew the route to the ferry, because that's how we'll leave. Nothing spectacular like hijacking an airplane. If all goes well, we'll swing back and pick you up in the *Lotus Blossom*. But if something goes awry, you'll have to catch the ferry. We'll meet you there."

I queried, "How are you going to meet me there if the *Lotus Blossom* is out of commission?"

He filled his face with a mountain of eggs on his fork. "If I have to, I'll fly Bashirin and Salvo onboard the ferry, but things shouldn't come to that."

"Best laid plans ..."

"Nothing's gone wrong yet, and I don't plan for it to do so now. But one never knows with you humans what wrinkle will turn into a tear, so best to plan for contingencies."

"I don't disagree." I turned toward him and raised my hands in the air, taking the risk of a coffee spill. Wondering why I couldn't have equal billing, I asked, "But why can't you fly me the hell out of here if you can fly them?"

Lyft fairly scoffed, the eggs somehow staying lodged in his face. "Because I can't be in two places at once, you dolt. Think about it. I need to be there at the same time you leave here, or close to it. I've no leeway in the schedule, so you, being least at risk, are left to your own devices, which I believe you can handle quite well."

Somewhat chagrined, I replied, "Sorry, didn't mean to be obtuse. I see the logic in it."

Lyft waved his fork in the air. "Plus, you need to get the chef out of here. Did you forget him?"

I came across the room and sat down at the writing desk in the chair opposite him. "For the moment, yes, but you're correct, of course. I wonder what he wants to take with him?"

"Ask him. This place will be foreclosed to some corrupt entity anyway, so you might as well take what you can. None of it came here legally in the first place, so I say every man for himself."

I slapped my knee. "My God, I like your style. Too bad we don't have a U-Haul."

Lyft finished his breakfast, scraping the plate clean. "Well, look at it this way. Would you really want Ali's stuff in your home? Think about it, really. Books are one thing. They are knowledge, and frankly, he doesn't deserve them. I'd be willing to bet he's never read any of them anyway. They're just showpieces to him to assuage his own ego. But you have a love for books, especially the classics, so wouldn't those books be happier in your home than in his? I think so." He dabbed at his mouth with one of the linen napkins the chef had sent up and leaned back, clearly satiated. "But would you want his wife's jewelry, for instance? I think not. What a disgrace it would be to even come in contact with it. It was given out of obligation, not love, to show her off in society. It has her sweat on it, so it's defiled as far as I'm concerned. And his money. Let's take a look at that. It's blood money. It's killed people all around the globe, financed corruption, bought him a place in society. Would you really want to be tainted by it? His paintings?" Lyft pointed to the one over the headboard, which was nothing more than an expensive print of a Sumatran jungle scene—attractive, but not an original piece of art. "He really doesn't have any of substance. None of them are worth much, most being expensive prints in highbrow frames. So what's left? The tiles in the floor? The carpet? The scattered Orientals? There's nothing here of value if you really think about it. And trust me, all the wealth in the world cannot equal what my Klinques are sitting on deep within the Earth. If you could see what we have access to, you'd faint straight away upon its revelation. So what you see here is less than a pimple on the arse of humanity or less so, if I can be so crass."

"Yes, I see what you mean, and I agree with you. I need to get to the chef. How much time do we have?"

"Not much. By noon tomorrow, you need to be out of here."

"Gotcha. Will do."

"So now I should be off. I've much to do. I need a bag for these tapes, which are nothing but a pain in my arse."

"Here," I said, handing him the one I'd brought from the kitchen. It was transparent like cellophane, but tougher. "I thought you'd feel less obtrusive this way. Better than a black garbage bag flying through the air."

"Yes, quite. This should do nicely."

Lyft then proceeded to unload his pockets, dumping the contents into the bag. By the time he was through, the bag weighed a good six pounds.

I said, "Quite a load of tapes. Hazelit's just made his career."

"You mean *we've* made his career. At any rate, this will keep *60 Minutes* in high profile for months. Just remember, he owes us a favor for this."

"I won't forget. Now go. You've got work to do, and so have I."

He zipped out the window, bag in tow, like Santa Claus. I could have sworn I heard a ho-ho-ho in the distance.

Merry Christmas, Hazelit. Happy New Year, 60 Minutes, I thought.

Lyft delivered the tapes without incident. It turned out that the clerk slept in the back room until the next shift came in, so Lyft had no trouble dumping off the tapes with a note, leaving almost immediately upon arrival. He then went to the *Lotus Blossom* in Lama Village, where he found Bashirin and Salvo making last minute preparations for their sortie. He settled himself on the roof. Gabby and maroon were not visible at the moment.

"Gentlemen, I am here, on top of the wheelhouse. Where are your compatriots?"

Bashirin answered, "Good to hear from you. They left the premises some fifteen minutes ago, saying they had business to attend to and that they'd be back within the hour."

"Perfect," said Lyft.

"So, what's the plan?" queried Salvo

"Well, gentlemen, methinks it should go something like this. We go along as if all is well. We meet up with the two junks, let the transfer of engines and weapons take place while *60 Minutes* clicks away overhead, and then let the junks proceed to their rendezvous points. While on route, I'll disable one junk, crew and all. At the order to fire, which will apply to both boats simultaneously, only one will fire. Gabby and maroon will then know there's a problem, but no matter, they'll be able to do little about it. I'll make the missile go awry. Then I'll disable the other junk. You two deal with gabby and maroon. Throw them over the side if you have to or tie them up, wait on the authorities, whatever. My issue with the authorities is that one can never know whose side they're on, if you get my drift. Then we turn and head for the ferry landing where we meet Jeff and the chef. If all goes well, we won't need the ferry; we can use this boat. Simple enough?"

"Yes, but what about *60 Minutes* overhead? They'll be filming the action with telephotos. Isn't there a chance of discovering you, even in invisible mode?"

"You know, it'll be so quick and partly under cover, as the junks have deck tarps under which the weapons will be located, that *60 Minutes* will only understand that an action has taken place. They'll never know specifically what occurred, and it's not in my contract to tell them. No one will ever figure out how the missile erred, they'll just put it down to some fault in the propulsion or guidance system. You boys will be on your own until I can ensure our friends in the press are satisfied. I'm sure you two can handle it."

"True enough. I like the idea of tossing them overboard. Lots of sharks in these waters," chuckled Bashirin.

Salvo too gave an evil laugh.

Lyft said, "I'm happy you two are on our side. God help the opposition." Spotting the pair in question, Lyft warned his friends of their impending arrival, promised to keep watch, and disappeared.

They pulled up to the quay, parked the car, and then walked down the planking to the boat.

Gabby yelled, a little too loudly, "We leave in thirty minutes. Make ready."

"Aye, sir," Bashirin and Salvo said in unison.

As the boat was continually in a state of readiness, gabby's order proved ludicrous. The only action left was to start the engines, cast off, and be under way. Lyft had to laugh at gabby's newfound authority. Maroon just snorted, rolling his eyes at gabby's command. He would be the one they would have to watch closely.

Maroon got on the radio, alerting the junks as to the impending action. *60 Minutes*, although not advertised, was overhead, buzzing about, disguised as a port helicopter, supposedly monitoring river and harbor traffic, not an unusual activity in the area. Maroon became agitated in his conversation.

Uh-oh, do I see a hitch developing? mused Lyft. *Oh, I do hope things don't go as planned for them, I really do. It's only right they should suffer some of the same angst as the rest of us.*

Maroon was yelling now into the two-way mic.

"What the hell's wrong with you? You knew you had to breech the security cordon to get off the shot. What good is it firing the missile outside its range? You need to get within a mile to get off a shot. You knew that. The damn thing has a range of only a mile and a half. The whole idea is to hit the target, not fire and run. What the hell's going on over there?"

The voice whined on the other end, "The crew won't go. They think they'll be blown out of the water."

Maroon fairly yelled back, "We discussed that. You knew that could happen. We do this for a higher power."

Trying to blame others, the voice on the other end emphatically said, "The crew says no. They do the work and get fried, and you get clean away. They say to hell with the money. You want it done, then do it yourselves."

Ah, now we're down to it, chuckled Lyft to himself. *Let's see whose balls are made of steel now.*

Maroon was really out of sorts on the two-way. He said through clenched teeth, the fire flashing in his eyes, "You've been paid a lot of money to do this. What are you going to do, be dishonorable, take the money, and not complete the transaction? Those are not our ways, my friend."

Now the wiseguy attitude came out on the other end, the certainty evident that maroon could do nothing to sway the outcome. "As far as we're concerned, the first 50 percent went to refurbishing the junks. We've made little out of the deal to date, so since the money did not go toward personal gain, we've not dishonored the bargain. We figure if we continue, we won't be around to collect the second half, so who's dishonoring who, eh?"

Maroon had to think about that one for a few seconds before he replied.

"The council has directed this action. Does that mean nothing to you?"

"Not really. Half my guys are mercenaries, so they could care less. As for me, I'm thinking of getting into a new line of business. There's plenty of tourist activity over here with the economy's resurgence. Now that the junks are refurbished, they look like something out of the eighteenth century. Since we're armed already, we can protect ourselves from piracy in the Straits, so we believe there to be a lively untapped market for tourist exploration of the many islands in and around the Straits, especially for romantic weekend getaways on authentic junks."

"I can't believe this," screamed maroon. "We're in the midst of an action that could change history, and you're discussing the tourist business?"

Derision in his tone, the speaker laughed. "Who sold you that bunk, the changing history part, I mean? What's an action like this got to do with history? You're an idiot if you think that. The only thing that's going to change is there's going to be two less lunatics in the Straits when it's all over. Me and my crew say amen to that. Now buzz off to your destiny, don't let me delay you. I'll look forward to hearing of your demise on the seven o'clock news tonight. Over and out."

The other end clicked off. Lyft noted maroon staring into the distance, a vacant look of resignation on his face. It was clear that the man was not used to direct action himself, now realizing he was in a box with no way out. He and gabby would have to do this themselves.

He looked over at gabby, a fretful look on his face, forehead wrinkled in concern. He seemed none too pleased at the turn of events.

Gabby said, "So, where do we go from here?"

Maroon spat, "Do we have a choice?"

"Actually, yes. We could just walk away."

Maroon pointed at gabby's chest, looking him directly in the eyes. "That would be dishonorable."

Gabby shot back, "True, but we would have our lives. This plan won't work now."

Maroon raised his hands in the air. "Why not? The Javelins are loaded, and we're ready to go. What's changed, really? Nothing, that's what. We can still do this."

Gabby looked down at the floor. "Yes, we could, but we will not live through it. Either that or we'll be imprisoned for life. It's not a thought I'm comfortable with."

Maroon raised his voice, the fervor building. "Either you are with me or against me. I am not going to sit here and lecture you on the benefits of an afterlife. If you are not a believer, then get off the boat. May you rot in hell."

Gabby turned to step up onto the stern to exit the craft, but before he could do so, maroon was on his back with his left arm around his throat, a knife flashing in his right hand.

"Here's a parting gift. Say hello to my mother and father if you see them."

The knife plunged into gabby's back twice, and then maroon pushed him over the side into the fetid waters lapping the boat. Bashirin and Salvo looked on with feigned shock, more surprised at the ferocity and rapidity of the deed than its actual consequence. Maroon, hot from battle, looked at each of them.

"Any other questions?"

They just shook their heads no.

"Then let's get under way."

He went into the wheelhouse and turned the key in the ignition, rumbling the engines to life. Bashirin and Salvo cast off, leaving gabby's body floating facedown, bobbing in their wake near the quay.

I hope 60 Minutes homed in on that one, thought Lyft.

The boat made its way down the river, through the harbor, and out into the Straits. It was about one hundred eighty-five miles northeast to Georgetown, so Lyft and company had plenty of time to ruminate for the next seven hours. Lyft knew security would be ringed a mile or more around the tanker. It would be interesting to see how maroon's mettle would be tested upon the first shot being fired.

The boat was faster than Lyft anticipated. They arrived close to their destination at two that afternoon, the tanker looming in the distance, dwarfing other vessels, including those of the Australian and U.S. Navies. It made the aircraft carrier stationed close by miniscule in comparison. Maroon stopped and looked about, clearly summing up the situation. With the tanker being about five miles distant, it was evident that he would never get a shot off. Even if he did, he figured the Gatling guns aboard the choppers and on the ships in close proximity would take the missiles out of the air before they had a chance to reach their targets. He might have a chance if he weaseled inside the cordon, but with what he was seeing, he realized there was little chance of that. The whole area was much more heavily armed than he had anticipated, due to the alert Bashirin had issued earlier. He dropped heavily down into the pilot's seat, cursing, realizing the futility of the mission.

He cut the engines, looking over the situation, trying to figure out what to do. Going back with no offering meant disgrace, unemployment for certain, and possibly death. Lyft, perched on top of the wheelhouse, was most amused. He loved to see his antagonists squirm.

Uh-oh, he thought. *Something's brewing in that evil mind of his. I can smell the brimstone burning.*

Lyft noticed by maroon's posture that he was up to something, an alternate plot being hatched in his head. No doubt realizing that he had to go back to Ali with something, he'd suddenly decided on a course of action.

"Make ready," he yelled. "We are going after the carrier. They'll least expect that."

Salvo and Bashirin looked at each other incredulously but played the game.

"Aye, sir," they replied in unison.

Lyft heard him mutter, "At least I've got loyalty aboard. Better than those donkeys' asses aboard the junks."

He swung the wheel around, heading toward the carrier. He told

Salvo to take the wheel, indicating to Bashirin for help uncovering and unloading the Javelins.

"I will shoulder fire the first, you the second," maroon told Bashirin. "We will keep firing until we have no payload left, and then we will exit the playground. They will probably come after us, so be prepared to jump or die. I will show you the operation."

"No need," said Bashirin. "I am trained in such matters. As a matter of fact, I instructed our forces on the use of the Javelin, so you might learn a thing or two from me. Ha ha."

"Well then, we know what we are about. We have to take out the carrier. There will be no stopping us. Allah is great."

"Right," intoned Bashirin.

They unloaded the equipment, checking to ensure all was working properly. They had two launchers with four missiles each. They positioned the missiles on the deck for easy reloading. They now were less than two miles from the carrier, probably four from the liquefied natural gas tanker. Maroon told Salvo to let him know when they were within a mile of the carrier.

Maroon looked up, distracted by the whapping of helicopter rotors. For a moment, the expression on his face showed his puzzlement as to what a helicopter was doing out over the Straits, but apparently he dismissed it, perhaps thinking it must have something to do with the tanker in the distance. Little did he know his every move had been filmed through high-resolution telephoto lenses. He'd soon be a TV star.

Salvo was concentrating on the range finder, zeroing in on the carrier. When the one-mile mark dinged, he yelled at maroon they were there. Maroon told him to proceed another five hundred yards and then shut down the engines. He made ready, hoisting the launcher onto his shoulder. Lyft was already headed toward the carrier to intercept the missile. No sense wasting precious energy in catching up to it.

Salvo called out one hundred yards, then fifty, then twenty-five, and then zero. He idled the engines. Maroon sighted in and pressed the trigger, and the missile was off with a resounding swoosh, heading straight and true toward the carrier. He yelled at Bashirin to fire. No response. Bashirin's eyes were locked on the missile just away, to see if it would malfunction as Lyft had promised. Sure enough, the missile veered off course, plunging into the ocean.

"Whoa," yelled Bashirin. "Did you see that? I've never seen one of these babies do that before. Maybe we've a bad batch."

"Why didn't you fire?" screamed maroon.

It was evident he was having a bad day.

"Because I didn't feel like it, *you* donkey's ass. Now why don't you go and fuck yourself, you piece of terrorist shit. Welcome to my world."

With that, Bashirin quickly placed the launcher down as he traversed the deck in one movement, ramming the flat of his hand under maroon's nose in an upward movement, hoping to send his nose shearing into his brain. Maroon moved at the last millisecond, as Bashirin made contact, only doing damage to one side, basically ripping his nose lengthwise in half. Maroon screamed in pain, but having had some training in terrorist camps, he reached for his knife behind his back in his belt and brought it out, lunging at Bashirin. Salvo, seeing that the fight was on, rammed the engines forward into full speed, turning the boat at the same time, throwing both contestants to the rail. Bashirin gave a violent kick to the side, sending maroon to the deck, with the knife spilling from his hand. Bashirin then pulled maroon to his feet, giving him his best shot to the solar plexus, doubling him over. Then a sharp upward thrust of the knee to maroon's forehead sent him over the rear transom, where he tumbled into the prop wash. When he reemerged some fifty yards later, Bashirin noticed him floating facedown, with one of his legs circling around his head before it sank. Bashirin also saw shark fins heading toward the stew, always ready for an easy meal.

Lyft meanwhile had returned, no longer perched on top of the wheelhouse, but actually in it.

He said to them both, "We're about to be blasted out of the water. You see the patrol torpedo boats over there? They're ten times faster than we are. All they have to do is give us a few bursts with the fifty cal., and we're dog meat, so let's get out of here. You see those two tarps over there? Stretch them out of the deck and lie down on their edges, while I get some duct tape from the wheelhouse. Then I'll roll you up in them and secure you. Do you have goggles with you?"

"Yes."

"Put them on. Button your shirts up around your throats. We're going for a ride."

Lyft retrieved the tape and then rolled them up quickly in the tarps, ensuring that the end of each canvas was taped closed so that the air pressure of the impending ride would not push them out of their shields like champagne corks under pressure. He quickly asked down the canvas tubes if they were ready, each replying yes. He then grabbed the cocoons, one under each arm, tape forward due to wind rip. He propelled himself quickly to supersonic speed, zooming to the landing, flying just over the waves. He made it in exactly 15.6 minutes. He set them down, untaped them, and then gently unrolled them, letting them get acclimated.

"Jeesh, what ride," clucked Salvo. "My face feels like the skin's peeled from the bones."

"Me too," said Bashirin. "How fast were we going anyway?"

"Not sure, faster than the speed of sound," intoned Lyft. "Had to, couldn't wait around to have you two photographed flying around in thin air. Wouldn't that have raised a lot of questions?"

"Right, got it, no need to explain," they both said. "Now what?"

"Now we collect my good friend Mr. Wood, provided he's still at the villa. You didn't happen to appropriate maroon's cell phone during your scuffle, did you?"

"Afraid not."

"Well, no matter. We'll do it the hard way. I'll zip up to the house, won't but take a minute to assess the situation, and then I'll let you know what's up. Just stay here for a few minutes, out of sight if you can, until I return. I won't be long."

"No problem," they both said.

―――――――――――――

Lyft came in through the bedroom window, but I wasn't there. Having thought about what he said, it made sense to pilfer the books, as there was no knowing what could happen to them. The chef had provided me with produce boxes, that were reinforced perfectly to the task.

I was in the library, deciding what books to take, when Lyft made his presence known.

"Ah, decision time on the spoils of war, I see. And have we completed the task before us?"

"Not quite, but I'm getting there. How'd it go?"

"Almost to plan, except that the stupid ass couldn't get close enough for a shot at the tanker. I could have told him that, but he never asked. So he took a shot at the aircraft carrier instead, but of course, the missile erred, so I'm presuming the *Lotus Blossom* was blown to smithereens in the aftermath. I didn't stick around to find out. I had to get Bashirin and Salvo out of there before we were attacked."

"And maroon and gabby?"

"Shark food."

"Ouch. Well, so be it. Bashirin and Salvo OK?"

"Yes, but they had the ride of their lives."

"I'll bet."

"Say, are we on camera?"

"No, the chef fixed that. The plug is pulled, and the guard's sound asleep again."

"My, he's really getting quality rest these days."

"Different guard, same scenario. So how much time do we have?"

"Some, but not much. Are you OK here alone for the moment?"

"Yes, Ali and Licia have gone out, no telling when they'll be back. What's happening in that regard?"

"Well, Hazelit must be back at the portable studio, with a feed back to Atlanta. The boat's gone, so we'll have to take the ferry. As soon as the news breaks, we should plan to steal one of the cars, loading all we can in the trunk, and then get to the ferry. You can pretend you're a book dealer or something. You'll think up some cockamamie scheme to get through customs, knowing you."

"Yes, Irish book dealer, since I've got an Irish passport. Works for me. But don't you want to see Ali taken down? That would be interesting, don't you think?"

"Quite, but I can't risk having you mixed up in this, being incarcerated, and then having bureaucratic snafus delaying your release from the local Belawan jail. Perhaps we can time it so that we steal a car and then make our way to the terminal as the authorities are circling the wagons. That has a nice ring to it."

"I like it," I agreed, pulling out from the shelf a beautiful leather-bound first edition of William Manchester's biography of Winston Churchill, *The Last Lion: Alone*, placing it neatly in the now nearly full box at my feet. Then I turned to my smaller counterpart. "You keep saying we need to leave from the ferry terminal. I disagree. I've found the keys to Ali's private plane. I thought they might come in handy at some point. I think this is it."

"Bravo, ma boy. Kudos all around to you. I shall call the airport to make sure the fuel is topped off and the plane ready to go, using Ali's voice. What a windfall. Do you happen to know how many the plane seats?"

"Ten people, I believe."

"Excellent. And do you know the location?"

"Yes," I said, plopping into my favorite chair, kicking my legs up onto the hassock, savoring the moment. "I happen to have that information as well. Ali was on the phone to them this morning, telling them he had a trip next week and to ensure the plane was moved out of hanger fourteen to the tarmac and made ready by noon on Monday. His parking spot is right outside the hanger. All we need is an Internet connection to study the airport a little before we leave."

"Can you accomplish that while I go back to the landing to check on Bashirin and Salvo?"

"Sure, no problem. I'll use Licia's computer again, but I'd better do it now."

"OK, then I'll see you in a little while. I need to get the guys back up here to take a shower and perhaps get a little something to eat. Do you suppose the chef could whip something up?"

"Absolutely."

"I don't suppose you have access to a cell phone, do you?"

"I thought you'd never ask. I happen to have Licia's in my pocket. You're correct when you say she's absentminded. She can never remember where she puts it down. Here."

"My God, you are priceless. I'll be back shortly."

He zipped out the library doors on his way to the landing. I went into the kitchen to see the chef and then went up the back stairs to Licia's room, where I immediately got on the computer. Just then, Arthurio walked by.

"What are you doing in the mistress's room? This is off limits. You can't be in here."

"Shove it, ya slimy bastard. I'll do what I want in this house. Now get away before I break yer nose, ya rat bag."

"I shall tell the master and mistress straight away when they arrive home that you have violated their privacy in their own home."

"Go ahead, ya feckin' blivat. Tell 'em what you like. I could care less. Now get out of here before I punch yer lights out."

I hadn't had a chance to use the term blivat since college, a made up term, utilizing the short "I," which we used disparagingly to describe someone who was akin to ten pounds of shit stuffed into a five pound bag. In this case, it seemed a highly appropriate locution. I made a move toward Arthurio, who hurriedly scampered down the hallway to his own room. I heard his bedroom door slam.

I downloaded a map of the route to and grounds within the airport. I had to leave the flight plan arrangements to Lyft, but it looked to me there was no reason we could not make it directly to the Wakhan in a matter of hours. It seemed to me like a plan to pursue. Landing at our destination was going to be an interesting experience, as I had no memory of an airport there, but I would leave those details to Lyft and company.

I closed down Licia's computer, changing her screen saver, leaving her a message she would not soon forget. Then I went to the guard shack to do the same. The guard was still asleep. I wondered how many knock-out drops the chef had placed in the drink. The guard had been out a long time. I fiddled with the keyboard, bringing up the screen that showed the library, and put a text message into the system, which was to come up in two days at ten in the morning. Then I went back into the kitchen. The chef and I soon heard a car in the driveway. It was Bashirin at the wheel with Salvo in the passenger seat, driving maroon's Mercedes. I assumed Lyft had come ahead and was already in the house. They came out and walked into the kitchen.

"We're starved," crowed Bashirin. "What's for dinner?"

"Anything you want," cried the chef. "My name is Chef Peter. It is a pleasure to meet you gentlemen. How'd you get by security at the main gate, may I ask? Usually, they're pretty strict."

"They had our pictures. Maroon must have given them to the guards in case we needed access to the main house for some reason. Good thing too. I don't believe his car is armor plated."

We all laughed at that one.

They dug into the chef's offerings, topping off each mouthful with some of the best wine in the house, even though Bashirin would have preferred vodka. There was no hard liquor in the house, however, so wine would have to suffice.

"That snake Arthurio is still running around the house, trying to make trouble. He caught me in Licia's room earlier, threatening me with exposure."

Bashirin asked, "And what did you say?"

"I told him to shove it."

"How apt."

"Yes, I thought it had a kind of poetry about it."

"Well, it's no matter. For them, it's over now. They only have hours to go. How are the books coming along? Someone unnamed told me there were some particularly nice first editions in the house."

"I started to pack them, but honestly, we really don't have time to deal with them. It would probably be easier to leave them here and travel unencumbered. As much as I'd like to take some of them, I feel they will be nothing but a burden."

"Perhaps you're right," Bashirin sighed. "Though I must admit, I wouldn't mind checking out what volumes he has in there myself." He took a long drink of his wine. "Oh well, we have more important things to do."

Lyft whispered in my ear that he needed to make arrangements at the airport. I excused myself, pretending to have need of the men's room so that I could give him the number. I went back into the kitchen. He was gone quite a while, too long for a quick call to the airport, but I paid no further attention to it. After about forty minutes, he returned, settling onto my left shoulder.

"Excuse my tardiness, but I had some other arrangements to make. At any rate, perhaps you could bring some of that bounty up to our room so that I too can participate in this wonderful repast. You were correct. The chef is a master at his trade. I think we can utilize his skills nicely."

Happy to have been vindicated, I piled a platter of food together, grabbed a bottle of Lyft's favorite, Pouilly-Fuisse, Chateau Fuisse, M Vincent et Fils, 2001, this time, excused myself, and headed upstairs. Salvo and Bashirin just grinned at me, knowing full well what I was up to, but the chef seemed perplexed, as I had just finished an enormous meal.

Bashirin looked at him and said, "Don't worry, all will be explained in time. For now, just forget certain things you may see and hear. We are somewhat of a strange crew, but no one gets the job done better than us. What a team."

Salvo shook his head vigorously in agreement.

Lyft was diving into his plate when we heard Ali and Licia arrive in the chauffeured Mercedes. I heard the front door close, wondering if Bashirin and Salvo were still able to remain incognito a while longer. Suddenly, there was a knock on the door. I got up and quickly opened it as they piled into the room. Bashirin said that Peter had given them directions up the back staircase to avoid the couple as he had seen the Mercedes go by the kitchen window as they were finishing their meal. They were lucky, as, evidently, Ali and Licia had gone into the living room. They saw Lyft in full regalia, digging into his feast, not even looking up, he was so intent on the exercise.

"Now there's a man on a mission," chirped Salvo.

Lyft, without missing a beat, shot back, "You mean a *Klinque* on a mission. And yes, it will be a resounding success."

Bashirin and Salvo laughed at that, asking me if they could take a shower. I told them certainly, and they also could have a change of clothes if they looked in the closets. I was sure they could find something that fit, even shoes. Salvo whistled when he saw the largesse. Bashirin told Salvo he could go first, just to wash the tub out when he was finished. That brought a grunt from Salvo who chuckled when he said that Bashirin should be only too happy to roll in his dirt.

The two performed their ministrations while Lyft and I chatted about his previous excursion that day. Lyft related to me the incident with gabby, then maroon, then the boat, and then the flight. Quite a day, and it wasn't over yet. The best was yet to come.

Bashirin and Salvo, in bathrobes, selected appropriate clothes out of the closets, opting for sandals instead of shoes for comfort and general fit. Their previous vestments were left on the floor.

"Now," boomed Bashirin, "I don't suppose there's any vodka here in this good Muslim household, eh?"

"None that I've seen," I replied. "But then again, I didn't go rifling through the liquor cabinets either, if they have any, that is. However, the chef has told me on several occasions there is no hard liquor in the house, and if anyone would know, he would. The wine is kept mainly for guests, although he told me Ali has been known to have a sip or two. A man who knows what he is about."

"I doubt that," Lyft said evenly. "If he knew what he was about, he'd avoid the whirling shit storm headed his way."

Just then, there was a sharp rap on the door. "Mr. Killroy, we need to talk," yelled Ali from the corridor.

"Sure, chief, come on in," Lyft yelled back in my voice.

I opened the door to the red-faced master of the house, who stormed into the room directly confronting me, not noticing Bashirin and Salvo near the window.

"Arthurio tells me you have been most rude, trespassing into restricted areas of the house. He also told me you've been cavorting with the chef in the kitchen, drinking my expensive wine, that you threatened him, and worst of all, that you were in my wife's room on her computer invading her privacy, telling him to get the hell out before you mugged him. What do you have to say to this?"

"Guilty as charged. All true."

"What? How dare you betray the hospitality I have shown you in my own home."

He looked around him, finally realizing that we were not alone.

"What's this? Who are these two, and where did they come from?"

"Ah, these two were the crewmen on the boat that took a shot at a U.S. aircraft carrier earlier today. Your henchman, you know, the one who always wore maroon colors, hired them about a week ago. May I introduce Colonel Bashirin of the Russian Army and Colonel Salvo of the U.S. Army? They now find themselves in your unemploy."

Ali, not being stupid, asked a little shakily, "You used the past tense in speaking of my employee."

"That I did, for he's no longer among us. If you asked the sharks in the Straits, they would say they had a lovely meal."

Ali blanched visibly. "And Jafar's associate?"

"Ah, the one who always wore gabardine. Well, it seems he and Jafar, or maroon, as we called him (never did have a proper introduction), got into a slight altercation. He ended up facedown in the river near the landing due to two knife thrusts in the back, oh, don't ya know."

Ali's head snapped up with my use of the Irish accent again. His eyes narrowed.

"You're not Irish. Arthurio was right. You're a slick who talked his way into my home for God knows what reason. I'm calling the authorities."

"Actually, that would save me the trouble, old sod. They're probably mustering reinforcements to break through your front gate as we speak, on their way to arrest you along with that trollop of a wife you exhibit at cocktail parties. But you're right about one thing. I'm a fast-talking slick who obtained access to your home for a very good reason, to protect humanity and bring your feckin' terrorist network down inta the dust. And that's about to happen, even though you're so feckin' clueless. Television, please."

Lyft, on cue, clicked the power button on the channel changer, tuning to the proper station. I pointed to the television suspended from the ceiling opposite the bed above the bureau where Hazelit was doing a feed from the field. The banner across the top of the screen read "Breaking News," and the reporters were literally breathless with the continual information streaming into the anchor's desk. They showed the murder of gabby on the boat quay, warning parents of the graphic depictions. They showed the body floating facedown. They showed the journey of the *Lotus Blossom* to its destination, the ensuing action, and the disabling of the craft, which was a surprise to us, as we thought it had been blown out of the water. Even better, so they could find the stolen Javelins and trace them. They showed the boat being towed to port in Georgetown, but they did not show Lyft air-expressing Bashirin and Salvo off the boat to the mainland. Either Hazelit had missed it or was savvy enough not to have aired it. I thought the latter, as he would reserve questions surrounding that action until later, if he even saw it at all. Then Hazelit went on to say that much more information needed to be verified before more could be released, but suffice it to say that a major terrorist action was interrupted today in the Malacca Straits.

In Lyft's note to Hazelit the previous day, he had outlined the names and addresses of those involved in the network. He cautioned Hazelit that the proper governmental authorities be notified before he released the information about the individuals to the network. He surmised that the reference to other information related to his restriction on the field man. Lyft didn't want the chaff blowing away in the breeze.

Ali cried, his fatter-than-normal face still exhibiting signs of his altercation with Brihamm, looking akin to a tomato gone rotten, "You can't connect me to this. I had nothing to do with it."

I mockingly queried, "How about the plant in the Wakhan? Did you have anything to do with that?" I took a step forward, throwing in the clincher with a lilt in my voice. "And by the way, we have your son. He's alive and well. As a matter of fact, without his cooperation, we couldn't have come as far as we have. He's really a luvly boy, oh, don't ya know."

Ali paled visibly, the sweat beginning to run down his face. "I need to sit down."

I laughed aloud. "I'm sure you do."

Lyft settled onto my shoulder. He said, "Played to perfection. Your Oscar awaits in the wings. The Academy is all abuzz."

I laughed out loud, as did Bashirin and Salvo who were privy to Lyft's ramblings now.

Ali looked at us in puzzlement, not comprehending the humor.

Just at that moment, there was a scream from Licia down the corridor from her room. She had evidently found my note on her screensaver. She yelled for Ali, who yelled back that he was in my room and for her to come to him, as he was occupied. She breathlessly ran into the room.

"Our son is alive. He's alive in Afghanistan. It's a miracle. We are saved."

"*Au contraire*, my dear," I intoned, "you are fried."

Lyft chuckled at that one.

She looked around the room, seeing Bashirin and Salvo, with Ali in a chair, realizing in an instant that things were different than they seemed upon reading the blessed note. Then she keyed in on CNN, seeing the headline "Breaking News," with telephoto video of the action in the Straits running on an endless loop. Evidently, Hazelit had passed on the rudiments of the action to his cronies at CNN, no doubt owing someone a favor. Her mind being slightly quicker with a woman's intuition than that of Ali, she put two and two together immediately. She ran from the room back down the corridor.

Lyft whispered in my ear, "Hell hath no fury like a woman duped."

"Scorned," I replied.

"Yes, but my bastardization would seem to fit the moment. I shall return posthaste. I would not want Licia to hurt herself or others, jeopardizing what I envision to be an excessively lengthy jail term."

"See you soon," I said out loud.

Ali again looked at me quizzically. I directed my attention toward him and said, "Secret weapon. Comes in handy sometimes."

Bashirin and Salvo guffawed in the background. Ali looked at the ceiling. I could only assume he was praying to Allah that this insanity was but a dream, hopefully to be over soon.

Down the hall, Lyft had confronted Licia in her room. She was insane with anger, yelling to herself. No one was going to take the precious love of her life away from her again, and she was not referring to Ali Senior. It was the duty of the mother to protect her firstborn, her only son, and she would do it with her life if need be. She was rooting around in her dresser, trying to find something, when she suddenly went to the top shelf in the closet, where she pulled out a nine millimeter Glock. Already loaded, she cocked it ready for action when Lyft ripped the gun out of her hand and then knocked her to the floor. Dazed, she quizzically looked around the room, seeing nothing. Then Lyft thundered out of the air, "Whore of Satan. Enemy of humanity. I am the punisher. Be prepared to meet your fate."

The walls shook, the decibel count loud enough to crack the authentic plaster walls. Arthurio came running into Licia's room, and before he had a chance to say a word, Lyft grabbed him by the collar and threw him out through the open window. He landed in the cobbled courtyard with a resounding whack, followed by a scream and then whimpering. The fall had shattered his leg, rendering him useless, although it could be argued that he had already attained that state some years before.

Licia cowered in the corner now, not understanding what was happening to her. Lyft and I assumed that she normally did not engage in devout practices, but she called upon Allah now. She began to weep, supplicating the Almighty.

"Dear Allah, sweet Allah, save me from this abomination. The devil has visited me, and we must drive him out. Allah, be merciful, Allah be praised."

Lyft bellowed, shaking the walls. "The only abomination here is you. Allah's not going to intercede here. Only justice. Now get up and join your husband. You're both nothing but stains on humanity."

Lyft then took the clip out of the gun and bent the barrel so that it wouldn't fire. Licia's eyes went wide when she saw what was happening in the air. She began to tremble, a sweat breaking out on her forehead.

She yelled, "I'm not leaving my room. Go to hell, whatever you are."

"At least you're feisty, I'll give you that. I always appreciate a challenging adversary, unlike that fat blimp of a jellyfish husband you have. But then, you already know that, don't you? Enough with the chitchat."

Lyft grabbed her by the belt and flew her into the other room, she screaming all the way that she was in the clutches of Satan. He dumped her unceremoniously on the bed.

More details were trickling in to the news networks now, about arrests that were being made in various countries around the world, not only in the Middle East and Asia, but in North America as well. Some had been on watch lists and were easily apprehended, some were rooted out of hotels, others were caught in the process of quickly packing minimal belongings, hoping to flee their respective countries to those of safe haven.

As we listened, the Sastroamidjojo name was mentioned. Ali and Licia turned ashen. Hazelit reported that the family purportedly funded the terrorist network and that the Sumatran and general Indonesian authorities had been alerted along with the American military, as the attack took place on an American military vessel. The storm was moving ever closer.

Ali and Licia both tried to jump up, realizing that the game was over. Salvo was quicker, holding Licia down as Lyft quickly settled Ali back into his seat with a thump and groan from the legs supporting the chair.

Licia spat, "What's next? Rape?"

Salvo spat right back, "Don't flatter yourself. We've no intention of harming you. We'll let your own people do that."

Lyft said out loud, "We need some rope to tie these two up. Jeff, see if the chef can find some. Then we need to neutralize the guards. Then we need to get out of here. I don't want any of us mixed up in what's about to ensue."

"Right."

I took off down the back stairs, telling the chef what I needed.

He, being a quick study, ran to the cellar, where he found two coils of clothesline that I thought would suffice. I ran back upstairs. Lyft took the rope, still invisible, tying Ali securely to his chair. He then tied Licia directly to the bed, topping it off by tying her hands and feet to the bedposts, in case Ali toppled the chair over and somehow could get close enough to her so that she could untie him. Lyft, the master, would have excelled at scouting if the Klinques had even offered such a program. I never saw such knots.

He then went out onto the patio to deal with Arthurio, who was pale from shock, groaning that he was going to die. Lyft tied him to one of the cement benches, patted him on the head, and told him that medical help was on the way. He neglected to mention that it most likely would be prison medical attention.

He then went to the guard shack, where the guard was groggily attempting to bring the library video back online. Lyft grabbed the guard's Berretta nine millimeter out of his holster and clouted him on the back of the head. The guard collapsed onto his keyboard, rendering the video screens into an annoying static. Lyft shut them off.

He then zipped down to the main gate. He settled himself into the air between the two opposite shacks booming, "I am Vlad the Impaler, here to serve justice. Open the gates."

The guards, totally confused, drew their weapons but had nothing at which to fire. They looked closely at each other and then centered their attentions to the video screens. Still nothing. Then Lyft, having little patience left, quickly traversed left to right, taking the guns out of their hands and throwing them into the jungle beyond the wrought iron fence. He picked up the left guard, ripping him out of his chair, flew him up into the air, and then jammed him on top of the wrought iron fence at the closest highest point, consisting of two pointed spires. The sharp protrusions impaled his pants under his belt, imprisoning him there, like a giant leg of lamb on a spit. He did the same to the other guard. They were yelling about Satan having accosted them, so he took each of their handkerchiefs and bound their mouths to keep them quiet. Then he gently pushed each one on the chest to ensure they were secure, watching their eyes widen in sheer terror. They no doubt thought the hand of Satan really was upon them.

"Nothing like a little iron to supplement your diet," chortled Lyft.

He then went into the right guard shack, flicking the lever that activated the main gate. The gate swung inward, the road up to the house now exhibiting an open invitation.

Then he came back in through the window.

"Anyone else need neutralizing?" he queried.

"No," I said. "Unless there's a border patrol. I think Ali only has that during social events, however. Although, we could term this one of those, in a manner of speaking."

"I do believe I like your cheekiness," exclaimed Lyft. "Well, we need to think about getting out of here. Since the U.S. military has been notified, I guarantee they'll be here momentarily. One last thing for our friends here."

Lyft suddenly materialized. Ali and Licia almost jumped out of their ropes. Ali shouted, "Dear Allah in heaven." Then Licia said, "We are plagued by the devil." Ali then prayed, eyes to the ceiling in divine supplication, "Dear Allah, deliver us," and on and on.

Bashirin and Salvo were almost on the floor, hysterical with laughter. All I could do was place my hand on my forehead.

"That'll give them something to talk to the authorities about. C'mon, boys, time to go."

We went down the back stairs to collect Chef Peter. He was ready to go, with his bags packed—like I said, a quick study. He also had the Mercedes keys, an extra set he had appropriated from the key rack near the back door. Bashirin and Salvo looked at each other and said, "Wait a minute. We need to take some of this wine with us. No sense in wasting it. Are there any liquor boxes in the cellar?"

The chef said, "Yes, plenty."

They bounded down the cellar steps, coming up with ten boxes.

Lyft interrupted. "Gentlemen, we cannot take one hundred twenty bottles of wine in the car. They won't fit."

Bashirin chortled, "Watch us."

They and the chef went to the racks, where they unloaded and then reloaded the boxes as fast as they could. In seconds, they were ready to go. Seven fit in the trunk, two in the rear on the floor behind each seat, and one in the middle rear in between the passengers.

"See?" said Salvo. "No problem. The chef's suitcases can ride on top. We'll tie them down."

The chef went back into the kitchen to get some twine, which was all there was left to do the job. He diligently tied his belongings through the open doors and up tight around the luggage.

"That should hold at least until we get to the airport," he said.

Lyft had disappeared during the preparations for a hasty departure, but he soon returned.

"We need to go," Lyft said in my ear. He told me he had the contents of Ali's wallet, which was fortuitously stuffed with cash and credit cards, the cash for potential bribes and the credit cards in case the plane needed servicing. "I left his ID in his wallet on purpose," he whispered. He had pilfered extra cash that he'd found in Ali's closet, after threatening the couple with never seeing their son again. He figured less chance of bribery of the authorities shortly due to arrive. He could always burn the blood money later.

He didn't want to meet the U.S. military and the Sumatran Army coming up the drive, so we all piled into the car.

The chef drove, as he was most used to the vehicle, having used it on various food sorties during his employment. We hurtled down the driveway, noticing the two pork cutlets picketed to the fence. Bashirin and Salvo grunted, approving of the methodology.

"You do have a particular *modus operandi*, I'll say that," I whispered to the presence sitting on the liquor box between Salvo and me.

"Don't I?" Lyft said in my head. "Say, do you think now is a good time to reveal me to the chef? He needs to know sooner or later."

I whispered back, "When we get on the plane. He might drive off the road if we were to confront him with that now. One thing at a time."

"Agreed. I'm looking forward to a long acquaintance with him."

I hissed quietly, "Knowing your appetite, I'm sure you are."

We exited the property, taking a left on the road to the airport. Within half a mile, we encountered a military convoy interspersed with police vehicles headed in the opposite direction.

"Looks like we got out just in time," I said quietly.

All agreed.

The trip to the airport was uneventful. The chef kept within the speed limit, as the last thing we needed was to be stopped for a speeding ticket. We easily found our way to the main terminal, passing through the security to the private tarmacs without incident. We pulled up to hanger fourteen, where, sure enough, the plane was in its designated spot, ready to go. We unloaded the car, ensuring we had some wine chilling in the freezer in the onboard refrigerator.

Salvo climbed into the pilot's seat, stating that the plane was standard, piece of cake, no problem to fly it.

We left the Mercedes with the keys in it on the tarmac for anyone who wanted it. We felt it to be our small contribution to the essence of the redistribution of wealth, which these island nations so desperately needed.

Salvo got clearance to taxi out onto the runway to prepare for takeoff. It not being a particularly busy day at the Medan airport, the tower gave him authority almost immediately upon reaching the departure point. We were off, soon able to see the liquefied natural gas tanker in the Straits that, not much earlier, was the critical object of Ali's desire. Strange how we could be looking down on it when literally just hours ago my compatriots were looking at it dead ahead on the water at eye level. I marveled at how quickly things could change. Lyft, sitting next to me, said, "Now?"

"OK, now," I replied.

The chef was sitting opposite us.

"Chef, I've something to relate to you, and I want you to understand the issues surrounding the revelation before you are exposed to it, so that you don't faint and have a heart attack."

"For God's sake, what are you about to tell me?"

"Well, it goes like this …"

I began, where else, from the beginning, back in New York, shoveling the driveway, when I was accosted by a little creature who floated down in thin air in front of me, scaring the hell out of me. On the word "accosted," Lyft gave me a sharp pinch right below my ribs on the right side. I grunted slightly, but ignored the interruption.

I told him about the whole story, from my employment with the dummy corporation in New York, through the present mission along with Bashirin and Salvo's involvement. Chef Peter then said quietly, "If I hadn't seen what I have seen over the last few days, I would not believe such a story. But it all fits. And it all makes sense. What does this little creature look like?"

"You're about to find out."

With that, Lyft appeared floating in the air over the aisle, separating the seats. Peter gasped and snapped backward in his seat.

"Hi, Chef. Jeff tells me you are a hell of a cook. From the small samples he has allowed me, I'd agree."

I laughingly retorted, "What do you mean 'small samples?' You've eaten like a horse in Ali's house."

"Ah, me, all in the eye of the beholder. At any rate, welcome aboard. We are very happy you're with us."

The chef was speechless.

Lyft said, "I love these moments. I have cataloged all the various poses and reactions generated by humans due to my revelation. So far, none are the same; there's something different about every one. This one's no exception. Usually, I get at least a 'Holy Shit' or some such other epithet thrown at me, but only a couple have been entirely speechless. I have noted that those who have been speechless in the beginning have often turned into the most noble of friends. Not always, but often. I'll have to study that further."

The chef then came alive, asking a thousand questions, which were all answered in due time. After an hour or so, Bashirin livened up the party by taking the wine out of the freezer, pouring everyone a round.

I interrupted the festivities by asking, "Has anyone investigated a runway on the other end? I don't remember there being a runway for planes, just pads for helicopters."

Bashirin said, "Don't worry, it's covered. I had Salvo radio ahead so that they could scrape one up for us."

"What do you mean, 'scrape one up?'"

"Just that, scrape one up. They are building one for us as we speak."

"That's what I was afraid of."

"No worries, my men do it all the time. Remember, where we work, there are no runways normally. We just carve them out of the soil. Should be done by the time we arrive."

We had a merry time making our way back to the Wakhan. Salvo, like a good pilot, refused our excessive libations. Bashirin rustled up some sandwiches from the food in the fridge, insisting that the chef on this journey be the guest. Lyft, in typical fashion, devoured his immediately, supplicating Bashirin in Oliver Twist–like fashion for more. Bashirin just shook his head, telling him the directions to the refrigerator.

In a few hours more, we saw the deepening shadows and the sunlit peaks surrounding the Wakhan Valley. Landing could be tricky due to crosswinds and the disadvantage of not always being able to land into the wind, a mantra taught in flight school. However, Salvo was up to the task. He saw the torches placed to the sides of the runway for illumination in the deepening twilight. Luckily, the winds were light. We settled down in a surprisingly gentle manner, the plane coming to a halt near a deuce and a half. Major Dumont and two of Bashirin's men greeted us, helping us unload what little we had, Bashirin telling them to be especially careful with the wine, which I saw he was beginning to enjoy. Perhaps I could convert him from vodka.

It was good to be "home." However, there was still much work to do. But first, a celebration to the victors. We went to Bashirin's dacha, where all hopes of a conversion were dashed, as his vodka consumption proved ten to one of wine.

The next morning saw groans, fuzzy, aching heads, and general malaise, all except for Lyft. He unequivocally stated that what we needed was a hearty breakfast. I reeled, Bashirin threw up, the chef pleaded illness, and Salvo went to the bathroom to retrieve some Advil. However, Lyft was proven correct in his assessment. After some coffee, we all began a slow recovery. The chef, having seen this syndrome before, made a huge breakfast for us all, and by one o'clock that afternoon, we were nearly straightened out. Bashirin and Salvo decided to call a debriefing for their men at four o'clock, so it was back to normalcy all too fast. But I relished it. I also found that I relished field work. I was good at it, proud of my accomplishments. I still had much to learn, but I thought I had handled myself fairly well in my first "op." Relishing the glow of self-satisfaction, I looked forward to more of it. It would come too soon.

CHAPTER TWENTY-FIVE

By the next morning, Bashirin had been in contact with all the sites, with special emphasis on Selkirk's. He'd also been in touch with Hazelit at *60 Minutes*, who related that Ali, Licia, and Arthurio were being held in Medan, currently being interviewed by various military authorities. Ahman was being held in Jakarta, in what we understood to be fairly uncomfortable surroundings—we figured torture was somewhere in the picture. The network had come crashing down, with all but a few minor figures in custody. The story created a sensation. Well over one hundred individuals were arrested, and most were already talking, trying to blame minions, Ali, or Brihamm, with a wealth of information as to how the network was created and how it had functioned.

Relative to our operation, the iceberg south of the Mid-Atlantic Ridge seemed stable, the volcanism off Pulau Simeulue seemed to have equalized, with the other sites holding their own. Perhaps Mother needed a breather, sensing that we did as well. Ali Junior opted to be transported back to Medan, although the Russian and U.S. military authorities were resistant to the move. However, they had no facilities for incarceration in Afghanistan, so they were deciding whether to release him to his native country instead of going through the bureaucratic maze of paperwork, and then the issue of how to try him.

Indonesia had no such issues. Arrest and trial were inordinately speedy in that country, as their judiciary had little case backlog. We were sure that a decision on Ali Junior's status would be rendered within a few days.

The situation at Selkirk's needed to be handled soon, as Estavez was becoming more than an annoying thorn to Alvarez. The incident about the woman was related to Bashirin, who became incensed with the injustice done to her. Alvarez explained that they had been unable to ID her, but he thought it was either the general's wife or mistress who had perhaps complained once too often. Either way, she had been transported to a mainland hospital, and there was no other information available relative to the mystery. One thing was for certain, she fell from Estavez's plane. The fisherman had been emphatic about it. So before we could plan our excursion to Selkirk's, a detour to Valparaiso was in order to interview the woman to see if anything further could be learned.

The main issue before us was how to get the treasure of Vera Cruz off the island safely to New York. It was one thing to find it and rebury it for safe-keeping, but quite another to organize the logistics of spiriting over one billion dollars of gold and jewels off the island through nondiplomatic channels. The only runway on the island serviced small noncommercial jets or props, so the chance of a military transport landing there was not feasible. Otherwise, Bashirin or Salvo would have ordered one, loaded it and taken off before anyone was the wiser. So another plan had to be concocted. If the plan, as envisioned, was to dump Ali Junior off in Medan, as there was the distinct possibility that American and Russian officials would release him to us, and then we would have to go from Sumatra to Perth, Australia, and then to Sydney on the opposite coast, and then to Auckland, New Zealand, followed by the thrilling prospect of an eleven-hour flight across the entire Pacific to Santiago. The Sastroamidjojo company plane could make it to Auckland, but after that, only commercial flights could handle the distance. Commercial flight was no good to Selkirk's, so we needed to augment our thinking to fit the circumstances. The hang up was Ali Junior.

"Guys," I piped up after doing some serious mind twisting. "We're not on the right track. We're letting a junior terrorist dictate our itinerary. We've bigger fish to fry here. Who says he has to go back to Medan? Us, no one else. Are the Indonesians clamoring for him? Not really. It's we who are doing the posturing. We are so concerned with this brat's legal rights that we're bending over backward trying to accommodate the system when it should be accommodating us."

I pulled out a map, pointing to the Wakhan.

"Here we are." I traced the route with my finger, from the Wakhan to Shanghai, from Shanghai to Hokkaido, from Hokkaido to Kamchatka, and from there to Anchorage, and then showed how we could hopscotch across Canada or the U.S. to Cuba. I explained that, the way I saw it, this worked better as far as both issues on Selkirk's were concerned. As to the treasure, we would have control of private transport, enabling us to quickly get the stuff off the island once we landed. We'd have to be careful loading the plane on Selkirk's due to weights and balances and would have to make two trips, but so be it. And hopefully, by the time we arrived, the woman who was injured would be able to speak. As to Ali Junior, well, no one except us really knew where he was, so if we had to, we could transport him to Guantanamo and collect him later. It might do him good to cool his heels a while in such a facility, seeing firsthand what real misery is.

Lyft queried, "How do we deal with the American and Russian military who want Ali Junior?"

"Tell them the truth. I guarantee they'll be happy with the proposal. It solves their problem. You might have trouble with Sumatra, but I'm sure we can figure out something, like he escaped and he's nowhere to be found or he fell off a mountain."

"Fell off a mountain," snorted Lyft. "That's a plausible one."

"Hey, I'm ad-libbin' here. You do better."

"Gentlemen, gentlemen," soothed Salvo, "let's not quarrel. I believe we have here the rudiments of a plan that may just work. It's feasible. What we don't want is a backlash to any action we might take relative to Ali Junior's disposition pertaining to his future legal status. Essentially, if push ever came to shove, he should be tried in the World Court for a crime against humanity. However, in the microcosmic sense, he attacked a joint American–Russian facility.

Technically, we probably could sell the fact that he should remain under those jurisdictions. Since both have agreed to send him to Guantanamo, we should be in the clear, especially since he's an avowed terrorist."

Lyft said, "In essence, he's really not. I understand your argument, but the real culprit is the father. I believe the son was trying to make his bones, and I'm not sure I'm comfortable sending him to be incarcerated in Cuba indefinitely. I would feel more comfortable if he were merely detained in Cuba until we finish our mission on Selkirk's and then handed over to the authorities in Sumatra. To me, that is a better solution. I do believe there is hope for the boy who has seen the fear of God put into him."

I said, "I don't disagree. That begs the question then of why we have to move him at all. Why take him to Cuba and then have him transported back across the world? Why not leave him here until we finish what we're doing and then get him the hell to Sumatra and be rid of him? We're going to do it anyway in the long run, so technically, what's the difference?"

Lyft shouted, "Brilliant."

Salvo shouted, "Bravo."

Bashirin yelled, "Good thinking. Why didn't I come up with this?"

"Because," I said, "sometimes it takes a good deal of circumlocution to arrive at a solution that is not readily apparent, even though it's right in front of you. So, are we all agreed?"

After ascertaining that we all were, I pointed out that we could leave anytime.

"So," I continued, "we horseshoe around the Pacific, maintaining control of the plane, forgetting going across North America. Instead, we go directly down the North American Pacific coast all the way to Valparaiso. I say four days tops, provided Lyft doesn't come along and delay us by trying to find the Shangri-la of banquet buffets."

"Harrumph," quoted Lyft.

Salvo chimed in, "No reason why this won't work. We can file the flight plan from here to Anchorage, where we can lay over, then down to the States, somewhere in Northern California, then on down to Northern South America, and then down to Chile. The plane is eminently serviceable, and we have our contacts at military bases, beginning in Kamchatka, so there should be no technical hurdles at issue."

We decided to head out next week, and Lyft said he'd meet us at the island, as he had business on the other sites. Lyft wrapped up by saying, "I wouldn't want to miss the unearthing of the treasure. That will be a site to behold."

I said, "You mean you're not going to grace us with your company on this world excursion?"

"No, I have some things here and at the other sites that need to be accomplished. Just time it so you're not late. Timing will be everything so we don't meet up with that slob Estavez."

"Why don't you just fly me directly over? Save a lot of money."

"Because I'd land with driftwood instead of Mr. Wood."

"Ah, that would seem to be a good reason. So I go as planned."

"Good choice," piped in Salvo.

So we finalized the itinerary, all comfortable with our marching orders.

Then Lyft had a thought. He felt perhaps it would be a good idea to bring Barb over to help nurse the injured woman back to health. He figured that Maria could not go back to Santiago. She would need to remain in relative obscurity until the mystery surrounding her was solved, and even then, she might have to remain with another identity should she be in danger from another attack. I told him I would contact Barb and see what she thought. His body language told me it mattered little what she thought. As I would need to meet her, I suggested a commercial flight for me to Santiago, getting me there early, as the Sastroamidjojo plane would land in Valparaiso.

I placed the call. She readily accepted. I told her I'd meet her at the airport, which eased her apprehension at being in a foreign country alone. I also related that I would take care of the arrangements from Santiago to Valparaiso for her, which further eased her mind. All she had to do was get on the phone with the travel agent and get a ticket from JFK at the designated time to Santiago. She was fine with that. She informed me that both children would be fine in school and that Lyft had ensured care for the dog.

So husband and wife would be reunited halfway around the world. Lyft was proving to be a true dichotomy, trying on one hand to excise the world of its human detritus while on the other showing the ultimate in sensitivity to individuals in dire straits— more fodder for animated future discussion.

Chapter Twenty-Six

My landing in Santiago was nothing short of spectacular, with the Andes on one side and the Pacific on the other. It was coming into summer on the South American Continent, but there was still plenty of snow on the mountain caps, in spite of what Mother Earth and mankind seemed teamed up to do to the environment. The Chilean coastline is a wonderful place to live, somewhat akin to Vancouver. Always temperate, one could be at the beach and snow ski on the same day.

Barb's flight was not due in for an hour or so, which was accommodating, as I needed to rent a car. I was told not to change money at the airport but to wait until I could find an AFEX money exchange branch in downtown Santiago or Valparaiso, as they were more reliable and had better exchange rates. Lyft had provided me with enough pesos to get out of the airport and to Valparaiso if need be, so money was not an immediate issue. I would need to sharpen my math skills though. It was currently around 516 pesos to the dollar. Better to figure an even five hundred for easy calculation.

Getting the car was an adventure. It was not the reservation that was at issue, but the physical act of the rental itself, and then deciding what to do with the car once rented. The car rental service was off the airport grounds, so after commandeering the vehicle, I had to bring it to the airport, park it at great expense, and then take a bus to the terminal. It took forever. By the time I was finished with the exercise, I thought I'd missed Barb's flight. However, customs was slow, so I was essentially on time. When I met her, we were ready to go, albeit not before another bus ride to obtain the car.

We drove on the toll road to Valparaiso, my having gleaned directions from the clerk during the car rental transaction. Aside from being an important seaport, Valparaiso is supposedly protected as a UNESCO World Heritage Site, due to the beauty of its architecture and the unique setting it occupies. Located only about seventy miles north of Santiago, the city is known for its diverse immigrant communities, steep hillsides accessed by funiculars, and its cultural heritage. It boasts five major universities and is the leading educational architectural center of Chile, with highly trained architects graduating from the Faculty of Architecture and Urbanism of the Pontificia Universidad Católica de Valparaíso, a controversial school due to the avant-garde nature of some of the products emanating from its students. It was interesting to see the funiculars work on the hills, some of which measured 80 percent grades. They were essentially vertical elevators on rails that serviced entire neighborhoods. Not overly large, they were extremely efficient, moving up and down the hillsides at a distance, like insects intent on various missions.

We eventually made our way into central Valparaiso to our very small hotel, the Robinson Crusoe Inn (what else?) consisting of only fourteen rooms. But what a delight it was, at the inexpensive rate of one hundred sixty dollars per night for a two-room suite, shoulder season. Upon arrival, we each were offered a complimentary glass of champagne and then were informed that our rate included a gourmet breakfast. Lyft would have loved that. Situated on a hillside overlooking the port on Hector Calvo, Barb was duly impressed with the three hundred sixty-degree view. There was little to do upon check-in, except to begin a walking tour of the city along with finding a restaurant for dinner. The front desk was extremely helpful in that regard. As they offered only breakfast service, they wanted their guests to be happy, and although I suspected sweetheart deals, they recommended several restaurants nearby, all of which appeared to be excellent. Barb and I found one small café featuring fresh fish, not hard to find in the city. We settled down to an excellent meal, a bottle of white wine, and then bed in that order.

The Valparaiso airport is rather small, with a runway shy of twenty-three hundred feet. Santiago takes all the international air traffic and 90 percent of the domestic flights headed to the general area of the two cities. Salvo, however, could land the plane on less than half that distance, so Valparaiso was well suited for his purpose. In comparing Valparaiso to Santiago, I questioned the wisdom of the decision to have the woman treated in the lesser of the two cities. I thought perhaps the facilities would have been more extensive, offering more surgical services, such as a trauma unit, in Santiago. I could only hope there was the semblance of emergency surgical teams in the Hospital of Valparaiso that I knew were in its sister city.

Salvo was not due until later on in the morning. That gave Barb and me a chance to find the hospital. Located on Ibsen s/n, San Roque, it was pretty much in the city center. Although the street map was easy to follow, it did not say which streets were one-way. We thought the nightmare of continually reversing ourselves would never end. The second challenge was finding the woman who had no name. What I needed was someone who could speak English who knew of her being brought in by helicopter. On my way into the hospital, my cell phone rang. It was Lyft.

"How're things in Valparaiso?"

"A little difficult, at best. The streets are impossible, and it's going to be a challenge finding this woman, with me speaking little Spanish and she having no name."

"That's why I'm calling you. We're hearing reports out of the Santiago press that Estavez's wife is missing. Of course, he's fronting the story that she left him for another man, but the press isn't buying it. They know him too well, it seems. So you may have on your hands one Maria Consuela Estavez, wife of General Ricardo Emillio Estavez. If I were you, I'd keep that one under me lid, if you know what I mean, at least temporarily. She won't be safe if the press gets a hold of this in Valparaiso."

"Got it. We're at the hospital now, making an attempt to assess her condition. We just arrived, so we haven't had a chance to make inquiries."

"Go into the hospital, give me the number, and I'll have her location for you in a few minutes."

"No need, I've got the number right here with me. It's 56-3-220-7700."

"Good. I'll call you right back." It was nice to have a friend who spoke several hundred languages.

A few minutes after we hung up, my cell phone rang. Lyft said, "OK, she's on the sixth floor, room 602, intensive care. I told them you and Barb were coming, that you were friends of those who discovered her near the island, and that you were very concerned about her condition. I'm not sure she's conscious yet. It didn't sound like it from the description the nurses gave to me. I believe they have her in an induced coma to let her heal."

Barb and I went up to intensive care, where we found who we were sure was Maria Estavez on a respirator, appearing more like a mummy than a human being. It looked to us like every bone in her body had been broken. Her face was swollen like a purple gourd. Barb started to cry as a nurse came over to us. Her blond hair in a bun under her nurse's cap, her tan a contrast against her white uniform, she could have just stepped off a movie set, but she was all professionalism.

"Do you speak English?" I asked.

"Yes, some," said the nurse.

"Will she live?"

"We think so, but she has a long way to go. She's very badly hurt, numerous broken bones and serious internal injuries."

"Yes, we understand."

"Are you friends? We do not know who she is."

"We're friends of those who found her near the island."

"I do not understand who could do such a thing," lamented the nurse.

"Nor do we. It is terrible what has been done to this poor

woman. My wife has come all the way from America to help her, as we do not know who her family or friends are. Although we do not know who she is, we believe we have a way to find out."

"That would be very helpful."

I looked around the room, nondescript as far as hospital rooms go. I was impressed that Maria had a private room. That spoke volumes as to the seriousness of her injuries. Some of the prints on the lightly colored beige walls depicted the valley of Valparaiso in pastels with one being an aerial ocean view of Santiago framed by the Andes in the background. I said, looking directly at the nurse, "Yes and no. If we really think about it, someone tried to kill this woman. It is only by the grace of God that she is alive. If someone finds out she is alive and here in this hospital, she might not be safe. So perhaps it is better that she remain nameless until she is able to speak for herself."

Unflustered, but realizing the gravity of the situation, she replied, "I understand. I believe you should speak to the chief surgeon and hospital administrator about this. I will call them on the telephone for you."

"You are very kind."

She went to the nurse's station to place the call. In a few minutes, the leading physician and the head of the hospital came into the room. The nurse left, not wanting to pry into administration business. I related my concerns, telling them that I thought we knew who the woman was, but that, for the moment, it was confidential. They asked what they should do if she expired, and I gave them my cell phone information and the name of the hotel where we were staying.

I asked if there was anything we could do, and they said no, just to stay in touch. She needed to heal, and it was going to be a long process. They anticipated another several days at least before they were able to bring her into consciousness. She was so badly broken up that they did not want her moving in bed in a conscious state, and also, there was the issue of the mind-numbing pain she would have when she awoke. My fears of this being a backwater hospital were unfounded. She was getting the best of care, and these two were true professionals. They said the hospital was affiliated with the Hospital del Trabajador, one of the main trauma hospitals in Santiago, and that this case was of major interest in both facilities. She had the very best trauma physicians looking in on her daily, so all was being done for her that possibly could be done. I reiterated the need for discretion. They implicitly understood.

Barb said shakily on the way out of the building, "That poor, poor soul. I feel so badly for her."

"I know. It's tough to see, but I believe one thing. I believe God saved her for a purpose. I don't think she's going to die. Who gets pushed out of an airplane half a mile above the ocean and lives to tell about it? No one. So I really do believe there's a purpose to all this."

"I hope you're right," Barb said softly. I watched my wife's eyes gaze sadly at the expanse of blue sky surrounding the hospital, and then she become determined. "Well, there's not much for us to do except check on her every day for now," she said. "When she becomes conscious, she'll really need someone. Then during the rehabilitation. That'll be tough." And I knew Barb meant to be that someone.

We decided not to go back to the hotel area, so we found a small café nearby to pass the time. We had a light bite to eat, and then it was time to make our way to the airport to find Bashirin and Salvo. They were due in that morning at around eleven thirty local time, depending on the winds. We decided to wait in the main terminal after parking the car. Irrespective of their private jet status, they still had to pass through customs, so we figured it might be a while. Just as we were headed to the lounge for a Chilean soft drink, my phone rang. It was Bashirin.

"Hello, my friend. Are you at the airport?"

"Yes, where are you?"

"Just completing customs. I must say, they are expeditious here."

"Whoa, you're early. I guess because it's a smaller city, things move faster with that process here. We're in the main lobby. We'll wait for you in the lounge."

"A most sterling location. Colonel Salvo and I look forward to meeting your bride."

"She too. I'll order you both a vodka on the rocks, or is there something else you two would prefer?"

"You Americans, always joking. What other kind of drink is there?" he guffawed. "We'll see you in less than ten minutes."

They cut that estimate in half. They arrived complete with gear, both giving me bear hugs, the introductions were completed, and then we settled in for a drink. They informed me of a little tailwind that provided an accommodating early arrival time and an uneventful flight, the best kind in their estimation. I informed them as to the condition of Maria Estavez. Both whistled, saying she was lucky to be alive. Both men's sense of gallantry had been offended, both wanting to lynch Estavez on the spot. I felt there was a better way.

"You know, I've been thinking. What's the worst we could do to scum like this? We know he is in possession of a monumental ego. We know what type of lifestyle he enjoys. We know how greedy he is. So, each of us utilizing the God-given talent that resides on our shoulders, let's come up with a plan that will completely destroy him, but let him live in a hell on Earth. That, it seems to me, is a just punishment. As a matter of fact, the more I think about it, the more I like it. Here's how I think we should do it—of course with the final approval of His Excellency, Monsieur Faetels."

They had a good laugh at that one.

So I outlined the rudiments of the plan, which they tweaked some, but soon heartily agreed we should implement. I felt it had to be put into practice soon, as we were running out of time relative to issue of the eventual discovery of Maria's identity. I decided to call Lyft.

"How are you?" I asked.

"Fine, why wouldn't I be?"

"Oh, are we in a feisty mood today?"

"Not really, just hungry. Sometimes I get a little cranky when I'm hungry."

"That must mean you're cranky all the time then."

"Very funny. So what's on your alleged mind today, and to what do I owe this fortuitous phone call?"

"When can you be here? I believe we have all come up with a

plan to deal with the promulgator of the most recent heinous act, oh, don't ya know."

"Ah, and you don't particularly want to discuss it on the cell phone."

"Correct."

"Are you all together, malcontents all, planning mayhem and destruction of the upper echelons of the Chilean military authority?"

"Correct."

I suggested a sumptuous, private, gourmet breakfast in my hotel suite at ten o'clock the following morning.

"Perfect. I'm at the Mid-Atlantic Ridge operation, so technically I'm not that far away as the Klinque flies. Only about three hours, I'd say."

I loved the way Lyft turned euphemisms on their proverbial heads. I gave him the details should he get lost, a suggestion that set him off. He cut me short, saying he had things to do, to get out of whatever bar I was in and get back to work. He asked, "By the way, how's our patient?"

"Holding her own, but just barely. You were right; she's in an induced coma. But I believe she's going to make it."

"So do I. She's hanging on for a reason. I hope it's revenge."

"That's what *I* thought."

"Great minds do often think alike. See you tomorrow. Give my best to Barbara."

"Will do. And just so you know, I *am* in a bar, heavily carousing, surrounded by family and friends with several drinks in front of me, lined up like soldiers for battle. Sorry you're missing all the fun."

"Bah," he grunted, although good-naturedly. "See you tomorrow." He hung up.

"So," I said, "looks like we've a plan to present. Tomorrow should be interesting. Let's get the car and get you gentlemen settled, and then you can rest. I'll find out where a great restaurant is located for dinner, and we can meet in the lobby of the hotel later, if that's acceptable to you both."

"Absolutely," they chimed.

I got the car while Barb kept the colonels and their vodkas company, and soon, we were wending our way back to the hotel. The two-bedroom suite I'd arranged for them was even larger than mine, so we changed the breakfast venue and agreed on a dinner time. Then Barb and I left so that the two exhausted travelers could get some much-needed rest.

Barb and I decided that we had just enough time to head off to La Parva, one of Valparaiso's premier ski resorts, located thirty miles northeast in the Central Andes. It had thirty runs with fourteen lifts and was interconnected with Valle Nevado, another resort, which gave it more scope via use of a special ticket. But the main reason we wanted to go was that out of all the ski resorts, this one was set apart, because at its base, one could view the entire valley of Santiago. We would have to hasten our departure from Valparaiso though. From Farellones to La Parva, it was a distance of slightly under four miles. However, traffic was one-way from two in the afternoon until eight at night, coming down the mountain to accommodate those leaving the resort. It now being almost twelve forty-five, we would have to move it.

The good news was an easy drive. The bad news centered on the need for tire chains from Farellones to La Parva. Luckily for us, there were several services for hire that rented chains, each requiring a security deposit. Unluckily for us, the fee was twelve thousand nine hundred pesos, or twenty-five U.S. dollars, per tire, outrageous at half the price, but we had little choice if we wanted to see the resort. So we grudgingly paid the fee, wondering what other surprises awaited the naive gringos.

The resort was as beautiful as advertised. The first thing we did was see the view. It was a crystal clear day, and sure enough, the whole valley lay before us. It was magnificent, looking down on roads just traveled into the pulse of Chile. We could even discern the chain vendors, hard at work, which made us feel better, as we were not the only neophytes taken to the cleaners that day.

We picked up gear at the shops, pleased that it was warm enough that we didn't need parkas, and hit the slopes. The beginner's slope, smooth and gentle and devoid of moguls, was perfect; it allowed us to acclimate to both the sport and the altitude (we'd gone from sea level to approximately eight thousand seven hundred feet in an hour and a half).

After more runs on slopes slightly more advanced, we felt it time to head back.

It was now slightly past five, and dinner was at seven. We stopped as required in Farellones, where the chains came off a lot faster than they went on. The youngsters plying their trade waited expectantly by my window for a tip. I gave them a U.S. dollar each, which they looked down on in their hands with some derision. Evidently, stupid tourists got stupider with the largesse they were distributing to these kids.

Barb said, as we wended our way down the road, "Do you think you should have tipped them more?"

"Nope. The whole scheme is nothing but a big rip off. Enough's enough."

"Well, they're just kids, trying to get some extra pocket cash. Maybe we should have tipped them more."

"Kids, ha. Highway robbers are what they are. Let the operation share some of the loot with them. Fifty dollars for chains for slightly over seven miles? Ha."

The rest of the trip was uneventful. I felt better by the time we arrived at the hotel. I was beginning to feel light headed with some chest congestion in La Parva, so I was just as happy to return. No such symptoms for Barb, except for a little shortness of breath, and she even smoked occasionally. So much for the physical attributes of attempting to stay in shape. I wondered why I wasn't particularly bothered in the Wakhan at pretty much the same altitude, but here, I was. No doubt it had something to do with the rapidity of ascent.

After a quick shower, we met in the lobby, where Salvo announced he'd found a stupendous dinner spot. After a ten-minute taxi ride, we arrived at Bar Inglis, which, as far as its atmosphere, could well have been located in central London. The food, though, was all Valparaiso. The restaurant was known for its fresh seafood, especially for the Calacones a la Pil Pil, a shellfish appetizer stewed in a spicy tomato sauce. I liked mine so much, I asked if the restaurant could make it as an entree. The maître d' said absolutely, no problem. It was one of the best meals I'd had in a long time. Barb had a seafood salad entree, the tanginess of the sea still apparent in its freshness. Salvo ordered grilled dolphin, and Bashirin had a South American bouillabaisse with every creature from the sea imaginable in it in a calamari sauce, different from that of the appetizer.

The restaurant had plenty of vodka on hand, so Bashirin was happy, and we had two bottles of Montes Alpha Sauvignon Blanc, so we were happy as well. A relatively new vineyard established in 1988 in the Leyda Valley west of Santiago, the Montes family was determined to overcome the perception of cheap Chilean wine with tastes to match. This wine was excellent, with hints of citrus and herbs, snapping in the mouth with a crisp, mineral piquant, exhibiting a lush aftertaste well suited to all the meals on the table. If this were a sample of the local wine fare in Chile, we all agreed that they had arrived, at least with the Sauvignon Blancs.

The desserts were homemade that morning in the restaurant. We ordered flan, rum cake, a chocolate torte with ground almonds, and a very thin apple tart. All shared, and all agreed how delicious they were. I feared breakfast at ten the next morning was going to arrive all too soon.

We decided to walk home to alleviate our overstuffing. The streets were not particularly well lit, and we had been warned of the petty criminal element in the city with the potential of being relieved of our valuables on an innocent night out. But there were four of us, two highly trained in the martial arts, one poorly trained, and one not at all, so we felt at relative ease with the decision.

After ten minutes, we heard some hoots and whistles on the street ahead. Sure enough, four youths, who appeared to be in their late teens, blocked our path. The leader demanded what we supposed were our wallets. Bashirin and Salvo came to the front of us, raising their hands on each side face up, pretending they did not understand the command. Suddenly, the leader moved his right arm behind his back and then brandished a hunting knife, like the kind Rambo exhibited in the movie. That was all Bashirin needed to see. He feinted to the right as the youth shuffled in the same direction to Bashirin's movement, and then Bashirin struck, grabbing the youth's wrist with his left hand as the youth made a slashing motion. Bashirin turned his back into the youth and gave him a vicious elbow to the nose, the boy letting out a howl that could be heard to the waterfront. Then, using both hands to secure the boy's arm, he brought his knee up sharply against the underside of the boy's elbow, jerking both his arms downward in a violent snapping motion. We could all hear the arm crack as the boy screamed in agony. The knife clattered to the street. The youth fell down in shock, holding his arm, groaning against a chain link fence cordoning off a vacant lot.

The other boys looked on in shock. Not yet understanding that they were the ones at risk, one made a move toward Salvo. He did a spin kick, connecting with the boy's jaw, flattening him onto the street. At first glance, we thought the youth was going to get up for more, but instead, he was trying to determine why his speech had been altered. We figured it was due to a dislocation.

Then Bashirin said in perfect Spanish, "Go home to your mamas. They'll want to know what happened to you. When they ask, tell them you ran into two U.S. Army colonels with the special forces and that you were too stupid to know the difference. Tell them you're luckily we didn't kill you. Now get out of here."

The other two got the message. They began helping their friends and moved off down the street.

Barb was somewhat shaken by the whole thing, wishing we had appropriated a taxi instead of having taken the risk of getting into a street confrontation. But the moment soon passed, with Bashirin and Salvo cheerily reiterating several incidents of a more serious nature in the streets of Moscow. To them, what had just occurred amounted to the swatting of a mosquito.

Soon we were back at our hotel, Bashirin and Salvo having swapped war stories for the last ten minutes to ease the evening back into its previous harmonic mood. They were masters at psychology. Although intent on the conversation, they remained alert for other intrusions. I have to say, I was happy they were with us; had I been alone with Barb, walking would not have been an option.

We all said good night, Barbara kissing each of her saviors on the cheek, they both blushing as she profusely thanked them. They told her to think nothing of it, that we all should look forward to a wonderful breakfast at ten. She rolled her eyes at the mention of more food. We went upstairs to our suite, where we collapsed in bed. I doubted Bashirin and Salvo did the same. I wagered in my head that they were staying up half the night, drinking vodka, regaling in more war stories now that the initial stimulus had been implanted. Actually, I was wrong. The next morning, I learned they'd stayed up all night.

True to form and to schedule, His Lordship buzzed in through the window at nine forty-five the next morning, materializing on the chair near the writing desk in the living area of the suite. I was already dressed, looking over the morning paper in an opposite chair, although mostly unable to read it.

"Don't you ever knock? I have a lady present here, you know."

"Well, it's nice to see you too. I know very well your wife is here. But I figured you'd both be dressed and nearly ready to go at this the designated hour of the feast, so no foul no harm. Of course, I would have knocked under other circumstances. I may be many things, but rude is not one of them."

"All right, agreed. So how are things? How's the Mid-Atlantic platform?"

"OK, except the iceberg is beginning to move. We think it will take a course toward the project as we look at the currents, but it's too soon to tell. A lot depends on storms, on the wind, and some on the melt rate. We'll have to keep an eye on it, literally, via satellite. We're coming into the stormy season here in this latitude, so your guess is as good as mine."

"Never a dull moment. Well, we could always bomb it and break it up. That's one way out of it."

"Actually, that *is* an alternative. Unfortunately, there are some polar bears on it and several hundred seals, so they would have to be relocated first. But it is an option we've been studying. Instead of nuking it from the air, however, we would seek a gentler method in the form of shaped charges drilled into the ice, utilizing the same principles as with building implosions during urban renewal."

"My way's much more fun."

"Yes, I'll give you that. But not feasible."

Barb came out of the powder room after putting the finishing touches on her makeup.

"Why, Lyft, how lovely to see you. How are you?"

"Fine, my dear, and it's a pleasure to see you as well."

"Did Jeffrey tell you what happened last night?"

"No," I said. "I haven't had a chance to get there yet. Lyft just arrived."

After they exchanged heartfelt greetings, Barb told Lyft all about how her "two knights in shining armor" had saved us the previous night.

"What?" yelled Lyft. He rose up from his chair, zipping back and forth in front of us, exclaiming with consternation, "They know better than to walk around Valparaiso after dark, especially with you two in tow. Oh, I'll have to give them a piece of my mind over this one. Someone could have been hurt."

"Hey," I yelled. "What do you mean with us two in tow? I can take care of Barb and myself, I'll have you know. It's just that Bashirin and Salvo were quicker to the front lines than I was."

"Good thing too," said Lyft. "So what happened?"

She explained rapidly, wide-eyed, her five-foot-four-inch frame stretched toward Lyft.

He had halted in midair at her dialogue. "Humph," Lyft muttered. "Can't have something like that interfering with the project, not to mention having my two favorite people hurt."

"Why, Lyft," I gushed. "I didn't know you cared."

"Well, now you know I do, so no more foolish chances."

Upon obtaining assurances that Barb and I would not be alone at night on foot, Lyft agreed to give the colonels accolades for their gallantry at breakfast rather than a scolding.

Stating how famished he was, we were ready to go. Lyft settled himself on my shoulder, a presence I frankly missed. As Barb opened the door to go down two floors, Lyft morphed into invisibility.

As we entered the suite to find the waiters finishing up setting the last of the condiments on the table, Bashirin boomed, "Welcome to little Moscow on the Pacific."

Salvo guffawed, as did we all. Lyft remained invisible, keeping mum until the waiters asked us if we had all we needed and then gently closed the door upon our approval of their labors.

Lyft became visible on my shoulder, and Salvo and Bashirin chortled how happy they were to see him.

"This calls for a celebratory libation," Lyft said seriously.

I walked over to the pitcher of Bloody Mary on the table, pouring five glasses quickly. I handed one to each.

"To warriors all. I salute you on your performance last evening. Mrs. Wood has told me of your gallantry. I commend you on your course of action and subsequent lecture to those who made a feeble attempt at the practice of malfeasance. A toast to your valor and prowess in battle."

I wondered if Lyft had been drinking prior to the brunch. I didn't smell any alcohol on him, but thought better of it to ask.

"Here, here," we all said in unison.

With that finally out of the way, we all sat down to heaps of scrambled eggs, sausage, bacon, muffins, fresh fish, roasted potatoes mixed with peppers and onions, freshly baked breads, and an assortment of cakes with three different types of flan for dessert. The waiters had made six pitchers each of Bloody Mary and Mimosa. I asked Bashirin if anyone else was coming, and he said laughingly that, knowing Lyft's appetite, he had taken the liberty of ordering a little extra.

Lyft, however, was quite well mannered, more so than I have ever seen him. I predicated it was due to female company in the room, but then as I thought about it, perhaps there was another underlying psychological reason for his subdued mannerism. I surmised that his gluttony had more to do with those food offerings that were off limits, the old "I want what I can't have" dilemma rearing its ugly head, while constantly feigning a continual state of hunger as a ruse. Then I came to the conclusion that it probably was a little of both.

"So," Lyft queried, "what's this magnificent plan you've all concocted to turn dear General Estavez into dust?"

Bashirin piped up, "Lyft, perhaps you could use a little alchemy to facilitate such an action?"

He guffawed.

"Actually," I said, "it's not so much Estavez I'm concerned about. Rather, it's Barb and his wife—at least I'm assuming that she's his wife. I believe I'm correct in that assumption, I might add. It's only a matter of time until Estavez finds out she's alive and where's she's located. We will have to set up a residence, whether it's her own or another for them to stay while she recuperates. No doubt there'll be a substantial amount of rehab for her prior to being able to live on her own again, so I'm assuming in that amount of time we can bring down the general from his current lofty perch. But I feel we need to act soon before he finds out she's alive. It wouldn't be beyond him to try to finish her off in the hospital. So I guess my point is that although we have the appearance of time, we really don't. And it would be convenient for her to go back to her own house at some point, preferably without Estavez in it."

"Well put," said Lyft. "I agree. So what do you propose?"

With the image in my head of a tightly stretched pustule ready to explode, I eagerly laid out my plan for the obese general. I concluded with, "So what do you think?"

"I like it," said Lyft. "This will be a funfest for all. Pass the Bloody Mary, please. Time for another celebratory drink."

CHAPTER TWENTY-SEVEN

The next several days were busy with activity, not so much for Barb and me, but for Alvarez and company. He had much to orchestrate.

The press had gone wild with rumors, discovering Maria was missing via one of her supposed girlfriends, so it was only a matter of time before someone in the hospital engaged in a verbal slip. Time was running short, and we knew it.

But things happen when they are meant to happen, and eventually, all the pieces of the puzzle were placed in a semblance of order. Estavez would have been there sooner, but he begged off, pleading the excuse of military maneuvers, which we had no cause to doubt.

When Alvarez had placed the phone call, he told him an "item of interest" had been found on the island. We envisioned him verbally snapping at his men, cutting exercises short, and in general, being derelict in his duties in order to slip away to assuage the ugly monster of cupidity that continually gnawed at his soul.

We decided in case of a mishap that Barbara should stay with Maria, who was beginning to be conscious of her surroundings, although still heavily medicated for pain. We took the Sastroamidjojo jet to the island out of Valparaiso, parking the plane surreptitiously in the one hanger available, which fortunately was usually empty. Estavez was never there long enough to use it, even though the

Chilean Army had built it specifically for his exclusive use. Lyft, of course, had come ahead, insisting that he remain within hovering range of Estavez as the invisible cover in case something went amiss. I felt he wanted to be in attendance due to his disdain for despots.

Although Alvarez knew of Lyft's existence via Bashirin, he had never seen him. Alvarez, being a true professional, refused to let his curiosity interfere with the implementation of the mission, yet Lyft evidently sensed his slight agitation over his invisibility, so I heard him say in Alvarez's ear, "Don't worry. You'll see plenty of me before this is all through, and then you'll probably wish you hadn't, like Jeff over there who, most days, can't wait to be rid of me."

Alvarez chuckled, as did Salvo and Bashirin. Lyft truly was a master in human psychology, easing the tension and promulgating the focus.

We heard the sound of a small jet approaching the island. Sure enough, it was the same plane from which Maria had fallen several weeks ago, now transporting a corpulent pig to the roast. Bashirin, Salvo, and I slipped into Alvarez's Quonset hut. About fifteen minutes later, the Jeep came over the ridge, almost flying though the air with lust and greed. I swore I smelled the brimstone. Estavez braked hard, skidding the Jeep in the clearing, jumping out hardly before it stopped. He moved fast for his bulk, something to note.

Alvarez had strategically placed a deuce and a half near the open "grave" that showed the lidless cement sarcophagus at the bottom. Alvarez pleasantly greeted the general, giving nothing away.

A touchy general replied, "Fine, fine. What do you have to show me?"

"What, General, no time for a cup of coffee, some genial banter before we get down to it? We really haven't socialized much. Soldiers of rank should really get to know each other, especially from different countries, no?"

Alvarez had put an edge on his voice that went completely unrecognized by Estavez whose avarice now had bubbled to the surface, completely ruling his personality.

"Maybe another time. What did you find? What do you have

to show me? I have no time for chitchat. I am a general with great responsibilities."

"I've no doubt. It's just that every time you arrive here, you're rude and demanding. You are never particularly pleasant, you basically think you own the island, and you expect me to call you if we have found something. But you don't deserve to know what we have found, as you are nothing more than a greedy hog, rummaging around the barnyard in search of riches that you can snarf down and steal from others. You are a disgusting pig. You deserved to be stripped of your commission and imprisoned for crimes against the Chilean people."

Estavez's smile disappeared. He unsheathed his sidearm from his holster and pointed it at Alvarez.

"The last time someone spoke to me in such a manner, they became food for the fishes. I should do the same to you."

Then Alvarez let him have the blockbuster.

"Would that be your wife you're talking about, because we found her floating in the ocean several weeks ago. She's alive and in a hospital in Valparaiso. I thought you'd like to know that information."

Estavez rocked back on his heels.

"You're lying. That can't be."

Estavez was beginning to become unhinged now.

"Oh? And for what reason would I have to lie to you about it, or even make it up? Why can't that be, General? Tell me why you are so incredulous?"

"Because I pushed that bitch out of the plane from a half mile up. No one could have survived a fall like that."

"Ah, so you admit it. I'm sure the court will be appreciative of your confession. Save the Chilean taxpayers a lot of money on a short trial."

"What makes you think it'll ever come to that? You're a dead man, and you're the only one who's heard it."

Just then, all three of us walked out of the hut. I chimed in, "I don't think so, fat boy. There're some other witnesses here."

"Ah, how inconvenient. Well, one body, four bodies, it matters little to me. I've got twenty shots in the magazine, so bring out some more, and I'll have a little target practice. Now let's see what you've found. Then we can conclude this business."

"Certainly, General. Anything you say, since you've got the firepower," said Alvarez. "Come this way."

"That's more like it," growled Estavez.

We all walked over to the truck, where Alvarez pulled back the tarp. There on the back floor rested some of the treasure. Estavez's eyes glowed as he took in the ingots, the jewels, the coin.

"My God, you've found it."

"Yes, General, and there's a lot more. Come over here, we'll show you."

We all walked over to the edge of the open hole in the ground. Estavez peeked over the side, still keeping his sidearm trained on us.

"What's this? It's empty."

"Right," yelled Estavez. "But it's just the right size for you."

All of a sudden, a thunder from over Estavez's head.

"And I'm just the one to put you there."

Estavez was totally confused, looking all around, not able to find the speaker. Just then, his arm jerked, and the gun floated into the air, leaving him empty-handed as he gazed at his vacant right palm. Lyft threw the gun aside and then lifted Estavez up by his belt, floating him gently down into the sarcophagus as he began to scream, finally realizing that a power greater than himself was in control of his immediate destiny. Lyft flipped him in the air between the two sides of the tomb, settling him down into the cement structure face up, thundering for him to remain in place or he'd be killed as he zipped to get the lid in order to secure it in place over the now doubly soiled general. The lid floated down into the abyss, was placed over the screaming Estavez and then secured in place. The muffled screams could be heard at ground level.

Lyft yelled through the cement, "Save your breath or you won't have any left. We want you to know how real terror feels, how your wife would have felt had she known what was coming, how all the people you've murdered felt in their final moments, how all the families you've ruined felt when you made them destitute. We're going to bury you alive and leave you here for eternity, you fat wallowing pig of a human being."

"No. Noooo," came the muffled scream from inside the cement.

Lyft then zipped up to the front-end loader, which, by design, was near the hole with a full bucket of dirt and stone ready to dump. He manipulated the controls, moved the vehicle forward, and dumped about half the mixture onto the top of the cement sarcophagus. The dirt was just the right mix of stone and rock, so it rattled on top of the lid, scaring Estavez almost literally to death, he thinking that we were really going to complete the mission, like any good army unit would.

Then Lyft whispered to Alvarez, "How long? Four minutes?"

"Better make it three. He's shouting like a madman in there, using up all the oxygen."

"OK, three it is. We've already used up one of them, so let's give it another two. Maybe a few more stones and dirt for the proper measured effect."

We saw the bucket tip forward a little more, enough to let out another third, followed by more muted screaming from the hole. The screams began to get fainter.

"Perhaps it's time for him to play Lazarus. Let's get him out of there," said Lyft.

The lid was lifted, with the dirt on top, sprinkling down on a badly frightened and badly soiled General Estavez. Lyft placed the lid near the hole and then went back down and lifted a blubbering Estavez by the belt, placing him on level ground, where he sank to his knees.

"Lord deliver us, who are you people? What evil presence is among us to do these things?"

"No evil presence, General," said Alvarez. "It's our secret weapon. New technology, that's all. Let's get you cleaned up so we can go and see your wife. I know you'd like that. We heard you missed her. What did you say her name was?"

"Maria."

"Yes, a lovely name. Well, she's waiting to see you. You will take a shower in the open, under armed guard. Then you will have a change of clothes, not your own, but ours."

"But where are all your men?"

"At the airstrip, General, guarding your plane and making sure no reinforcements show up. Enough questions. Colonels, please take over and make sure this whale is squeaky clean for the ride to the hospital. I would not want him fouling the plane anymore than necessary."

Bashirin and Salvo oversaw the washing of the white-fleshed leviathan in the outdoor shower next to Alvarez's hut. They then Cloroxed and Lysoled the shower floor while he toweled off. Realizing he would not fit into any standard issue, they had to borrow some clothes from Private Johnson who, at six foot three, owned clothes of an approximate fit. They then handcuffed him behind his back. Lyft suggested ball and chain around the neck, through the hands, and around the ankles, but we thought that slightly excessive, although in thinking about it, the method of restraint definitely fit the crime. Having no ball and chain, we stuck to the handcuffs.

Bashirin and Salvo called the Santiago and Valparaiso police forces, respectively, to have them waiting at the hospital. They were only too happy to accommodate us. Bashirin had a short conversation with the Santiago police chief, surmising that Estavez's activities had been under watch for some time. The chief was delighted to have caught him, although extremely concerned for Maria. He knew her well and was physically ill that something of this severity could have occurred to her. Bashirin let the pregnant question go, which begged to be delivered. There was corruption everywhere, with both sides having their spies. A little payola here, a little threat to a family there, and both sides remained in check. With Maria, however, things would be different. Our team would ensure justice.

Before we left, we off-loaded the small bit of treasure still exhibited in the back of the truck into Alvarez's hut, making sure it passed under the nose of Estavez. We also let him have a peek at the full sarcophagus load on the hut floor before we closed the door. Like using a feather on itchy ivy blisters, he began to twitch and jerk, involuntary movements fueled by the poison of avarice boiling up to the surface, until we thought he literally might explode from the exertion of having viewed so much wealth in so short a time. Then Lyft poured a little more on the flames.

"Hey, General, if you think that's something, that's only about a third of it. You should see the rest. And you'll never be able to spend a cent of it. Ha ha."

He put his head down, the sweat rolling off him now, the stench of his crimes permeating the air around our heads.

Bashirin croaked, "Let's get this bastard on the plane. The sooner we're rid of this lard bucket, the better. He makes me sick."

We couldn't have agreed more. We led him to the truck, seating him in the back on the troop bench, fitting that he be seated in the same location where, moments ago, there was arrayed an empire's fortune.

We arrived at the airport, Alvarez telling his troops to go back to the site, to place a guard on the hut, and continue with their daily activities until he returned. He told Johnson that he had to borrow some of his clothes, but that he would be reimbursed. We climbed aboard, Salvo fired up the engines in the Sastroamidjojo jet, and we were off. We did not use Estavez's jet for two reasons. No one could stand to get into it after what he did to Maria, and we did not want to compromise what could turn into a valuable piece of evidence during what we hoped would be a thorough forensic investigation. We would have to ensure it.

The chiefs of police from both forces met us in the parking lot, along with numerous personnel and with the press, of course. By then, the press was welcome in our eyes. Perfect timing, we thought.

We led Estavez upstairs to Maria's room. She had been untethered from the breathing apparatus and was conscious, but still sedated for pain, although somewhat cogent. Estavez was avoiding her eyes as she was trying to speak to him.

Lyft could not help himself. He gave Estavez a resounding whack on the side of his head, whispering in his ear so only he could hear, "Look at her when she's trying to speak to you. If you don't, I'll throw you out the window into the traffic."

That seemed to have an effect.

Maria looked up through squinted, swollen eyes, her voice like dry, cracked parchment. "Oh, Emillio, what have you done? What have you done? I never thought it could come to this. Look at what you've done to your Maria. How could you?"

There's an ancient adage, saying that people will become afflicted where they have most sinned. Realizing it had all come to an end, he began to cry, tears streaming down his cheeks, clear to me and I assumed to the others, not of remorse, but for himself. His epicenter was shattered, his private universe of terror, greed, and corruption at a screeching halt; his life over. I would not be surprised if he were making plans to kill himself if he got the chance. We could only hope he had the fortitude to carry it through.

The doctors, realizing that the scene needed completion, asked that all now leave so that the patient would not be strained and could rest, a legitimate request, as Maria was extremely pale and weak. Barb pulled up a chair near the bed and took Maria's hand as Alvarez bent over the hospital bed and kissed Maria on the forehead. She smiled up at him as he smiled back. He said he'd be back to check on her, and her smile brightened for a moment. Then she fell asleep. Estavez was led back downstairs and placed into a waiting sedan, still handcuffed, with two burly escorts on either side. Bashirin, never one to mince words, had a conversation with the Santiago magistrate, making it clear that the weight of the entire U.S. and Russian Armies were behind what all hoped would be a clear, concrete, forceful prosecution of Estavez. If there were any aberrations in that regard, both armies would consider prosecuting the general under various terrorist acts, as the crime was committed in their view within the twelve-mile limit of their respective sovereign territories, namely, the plant on Selkirk's being built for humanity.

Although insulted, the chief made it emphatically clear that there would be no compromise on his watch. Bashirin said he could care less about insults at this stage of the game and that the world would be watching. They all drove off to the comedy of the press, following and snapping pictures of the motorcade all the way to Santiago.

I went back upstairs to see how Barb was doing. She was still at Maria's bedside, holding her hand, whispering that all was going to be all right, that she'd be there to take care of her and she need not worry, as one would coo to a child who was afraid of the dark. Maria was sleeping soundly, breathing regularly on her own, a major sign of progress. I gestured to Barb that perhaps we should go, that she could come back later, that Maria should be allowed to sleep. I gathered her up in my arms, realizing, not for the first time, what a kind, loving person she was, and she began to cry into my shirt.

"I just can't believe what happened to this woman. What a beast. How could someone do such a terrible thing?"

"I know, I know. But she's going to make it. I told you she would, and she's going to. A higher power has a purpose in all this. Did you see her strength when she confronted that lout of a husband? Just wait until she's healthy. It'll be like Mount Toba going off all over again."

Barb laughed through her tears, as did I, the dark clouds of Maria's heartache parting to reveal a shaft of bright light reflective of a hopeful, shining future.

We made our way downstairs, where Bashirin and Salvo were conversing in the parking lot. Lyft suddenly alighted on my shoulder, so the band of happy warriors was now complete, including Alvarez.

Bashirin chortled, "Well, it seems a celebration is in order."

"Here, here," chimed Lyft.

We picked out a wonderful seafood restaurant in the central harbor, with the celebration not stopping until midnight. All having had too much to drink and eat, we regaled in the day, popped champagne until well into the evening, with a final toast to now get back to the project that so desperately needed attention. Lyft even revealed himself to Alvarez as we made our way to the car after dinner in the restaurant's parking lot. We all delighted in that, noting the typical reaction, although it was more muted with

Alvarez, as he at least had had verbal dealings with Lyft prior to the enigmatic revelation. Of course, Alvarez was then full of questions, which Lyft waylaid, saying it was time to call it a night and that there'd be plenty of time later with many more food functions to follow. I hoped so. I really couldn't imagine life without this little creature in it.

CHAPTER TWENTY-EIGHT

The Village of San Juan Bautista on Selkirk's has a population of seven hundred souls, most of whom are families of simple fisherman pursuing the spiny lobsters endemic to that area of the Pacific. Those plying the waters fish from double-ended dories relatively close to the island and then ship their catches to the mainland by air, pooling their resources to be timed with the air couriers arriving three times weekly.

We were huddled around a conference table in Bashirin's suite, deciding what to do about the treasure and how best to allocate it. The tenet of the conversation centered on what we thought would be the right course for the villagers, admittedly on our part an exhibition of a slightly imperialist, paternalistic mindset. We figured that they might become corrupted by their sudden wealth, never having to make a living again, leaving their old ways forever. Lyft said so what, that was their problem, that the treasure was rightfully theirs, and they could do what they wanted with it. He was a true communist at heart. I asked what the ramifications were once the government found out about the villagers' newfound wealth. I figured there'd be lawsuits galore, so the only ones who would ever profit from the booty would be the gangs of lawyers hired on both sides. Salvo piped up that Mexico and France probably had a claim, and that they too would be in the mix. Then there would be the regional dispute. Valparaiso had administrative jurisdiction over the archipelago, but the central government in Chile was responsible for the designation of the island as a natural habitat protectorate. So we figured that dispute would be the worst of all. We could see no way out of it.

"Well," said Lyft, "there is one way out of this. I frankly thought this was going to be easier, but I can see you humans would have the greatest propensity to muddle it up so that the treasure would disappear into the ether. So I propose we tell no one about it."

"How's that going to work?" I interrupted.

"If you'd give me chance to explain, then you'd hear the whole story."

"Sorry."

"That's better. Now, what I propose is this." With that, he related to me what he had told Bashirin earlier pertaining to the disposition of the treasure.

"I can't see why this won't work," I chirped.

"Of course it'll work, 'cause you're the one who's going to oversee it. Ha ha," chortled Lyft.

Bashirin, Salvo, and Alvarez guffawed and bellowed at that one.

Bashirin said, "We like this plan. It would seem to be the only course. Are we all in agreement?"

All said, "Aye."

"Now to get the loot out of here and to New York. I'll let you gentlemen plot your flight plan, as you will need to make several stops en route. You may have to think of security, depending on where you stop to refuel. Obviously, the plane will have to be serviced in Valparaiso before the initial leg of the journey. So on that note, I'll leave you to it. I must go now and check on our various projects, which have recently been neglected."

With that, Lyft flew out through the window and then almost immediately returned again. He morphed into visibility, hovering over the conference table, looking directly at me.

"I've been meaning to ask you," he queried, "just how did you leave your message at the Sastroamidjojo enclave?"

"Ah, I thought you'd never ask. I embedded it in the software, which was date sensitive, appearing every fifteen or twenty seconds across the security screens in the guard shack."

Alvarez asked, "And what did it say?"

"That Killroy was there, of course. I spelled it with two Ls, however, taking a liberty with the original spelling, just for fun, mind you."

Lyft quipped, "I really wonder what the American authorities reviewing the tapes are thinking as they see that scroll across the screen endlessly. Oh, I do like it. Kudos to you, m'boy."

"You mean boyo."

"Indeed. Well, I'm off. See you all soon."

And he disappeared again.

Alvarez said, "I'll handle the village council. They'll be ecstatic that someone has finally taken an interest in them. How much per month into a common account?"

I said, "How about fifty thousand dollars?"

Salvo, being a quick study, said, "If my calculations are correct, it would take 1,666.66 years for them to use up the money, provided there was no interest generated on it. With interest, they would never use it up."

"Isn't that the point? In perpetuity?"

"I think we can do better than that. How about one hundred thousand dollars. That would give them one million two hundred thousand dollars per year to utilize for the community of seven hundred individuals."

Alvarez piped up, "That's still not a lot of money. One clinic could cost that, for God's sake. What are we talking about here? Look, guys, one billion dollars, and that's conservative relative to what we have here, invested at 5 percent interest is fifty million dollars per year, and 10 percent is one hundred million dollars per year. I have to tell you, I think we're being a little skimpy. I'd say bump it up to five hundred thousand dollars per month and see how it goes."

Bashirin broke in, somewhat frustrated, "My God, are you guys cheap. Go for a million a month and be done with it. After all, there are seven hundred people on the island."

I said, "I'm OK with it; I just don't want them to become jaded."

Salvo said, "We appreciate your New England sense of frugality, but it is *their* money, and they really deserve a break after what the government has done to them. I have a feeling the council, made up as it is of the type of elders I've seen around the island, will hold the community's feet to the fire. I'm not particularly worried about values and ethics here. I think the best of those traits are ingrained into this small society."

Once we were all in agreement, we decided that I'd accompany Alvarez on his pleasurable task of approaching the council. And so we did.

Epilogue

The council was elated to have Estavez off their backs and also to have the opportunity to be independent of the central governments. The money seemed to be the added bonus, confirming Salvo's appraisal of their society. They eventually would secede from the mainland and become an independent entity, known affectionately to the world as the Republic of Selkirk. Further confirming their values, they even appointed a committee to ensure Maria's care as she gradually recovered.

The trial was a sensation, with Ernesto testifying that there was no doubt as to the perpetrator of Maria's injuries. His testimony set in motion an investigation that shook the Chilean government to the highest levels, forcing a new election ushering in a new government. Estavez received a sentence of life in prison with the initial ten years being at hard labor. The defense persuaded the prosecution not to kill him by imposing life at hard labor, although there certainly was talk of it amongst the prosecuting entities. They finally came around to thinking that they wanted him to live out his full life in incarceration and not kill him in the first ten years, so they relented, although they still felt the sentence too lenient relative to the misery he had caused not only to his wife, but also to countless other families as well.

Maria eventually divorced Estavez with the tacit approval of the Church and moved into their old house. As with many people who have come to grips with their own mortality, she emerged from her trauma a changed person. She insisted that all their accumulated wealth be given to charity. Barb asked her how she was to survive, but Maria said she'd figure out a way. She could not bear to live on the proceeds of her ex-husband's illicit activities. Once around was enough, she told Barb.

Barb mentioned to me what had transpired, and of course, I broached the subject to Lyft, who was always a fan of human reinvention. He assured me Maria would not want for anything, especially since she had now changed her ways. She soon found that an account of five hundred thousand U.S. dollars had been established in her name in the Central Bank. She was told discreetly that this was an initial sum deposited by a benevolent benefactor, that more would be on the way, provided that she did something useful for Chilean society. She eventually established an orphanage along with a home for battered women in downtown Santiago, exhibiting social services the envy of South America. Most of the money deposited monthly in the account went to her organizations, with only a small percentage utilized for her own expenses to run the house along with her now modest lifestyle.

The Sastroamidjojo jet, in the subsequent months of Maria's recovery, seemed to be getting a workout. Alvarez somehow could not get Maria out of his mind, and he decided on occasion to visit her in the hospital and then more often during her convalescence. When she finally moved back into her home, she invited him to come for luncheon, but with the thought in mind of nothing other than thanks for his attentiveness to her over the past months. What was initiated as a simple thank you blossomed into a passionate romance, eventually resulting in a very quiet wedding on Selkirk's in a fitting testament to her rebirth. At the reception in the village, it was later noted that twenty-five complete spiny lobsters in the space of fifteen minutes were missing from the buffet.

As to the culprits who had so frustrated Lyft in his quest to save Mother, he had accomplished his mission, rendering the

Sastroamidjojos into *"sodai gomi."* They were incarcerated with the dregs of Indonesian society in the notorious Gaperta Prison in Medan, known for its abuses by its controller, the regional military command. Ali Junior was tried with his parents, and as Lyft had promised Licia, eventually reunited with them in the same cellblock. His sentence was fifteen years, his parents, life. Arthurio too joined them in the cellblock for a five-year stint, having continuously pleaded no guilt, trying to justify that position by stating that he was only doing what he was told. So much for loyalty to the emperor.

I often thought to myself how the never-ending days must be for them now, at the mercy of the people they were attempting to overthrow. Not something I cared to contemplate in great detail.

Regarding Lyft's philosophy of hiring local dissidents, the waywards in the Wakhan we had assisted proved to be loyal workers, allying themselves with others in the "village" as it was becoming known, trained in the operation of various machinery, being fed three times daily, finally becoming educated, useful citizens of their country. A small school was established for the children, and as word got around about the facility and the benefits attached to it, people straggled in daily to inquire about opportunities. Lyft had been correct in that all these people needed was a chance. I was afraid, however, that the burgeoning social welfare program being established would soon backfire if the inquiring populace outstripped the plant's capacity for employment.

Lyft said, "Bah," it wasn't going to happen. At the very least, he'd send out security patrols on the hour to keep everyone busy. After all, it wasn't like he couldn't afford to spread a little largesse around to a loyal populace. Besides, he told me, the plant needed trained workers now, as the other plants had siphoned our trained personnel off to other locations, so who was to say these people weren't up to the task?

Once again, he was proven correct. For each worker who left, a local took his place. Lyft was no fool, however. Eventually, through Bashirin and Salvo, a consortium of multigovernment agencies took over the payroll and administrative responsibilities of the plant. However, Bashirin and Salvo ensured the bureaucracy was kept to a minimum and that, above all, the workers were taken care of first.

As for Hazelit, well, he left us alone and never did try to impose on us with his interview. He won the Pulitzer Prize for investigative journalism and was on to bigger things in his career than interviewing a bunch of construction workers in the Wakhan Corridor. By the time he got around to it, it was handed off to others at the network who were able to get the story from the various governmental agencies involved with the project.

───────────────

And as for Mother? Did Abzu do the trick? Time was our only hope for a real answer. But for now, all looked well. The martinis Minsky and Jackman discussed never did materialize. The giant berg grounded itself, banging into its neighbors, never moving much from its original location. Although it remained a threat, global warming for once was having a positive effect, the shrinkage evident monthly on satellite photos.

Within the following year, the plants were ready, the giant tunnel built, and all systems were supposedly operational. There was so much that could have gone wrong but didn't. All the plants came online at once, run out of the Wakhan by the central facility. The tunnel was more than ample for the volume pumped into it, and everything seemed to be working as Lyft had so often advertised. What we would not know, for perhaps several years, is whether we were having any success in cooling off Mother. An army of scientists around the globe had been mobilized to monitor the effects of the operation. Earth had given us a break and had ceased its rumblings for the short term, perhaps sensing that the doctor was trying to help the patient with the best medical practices available. It was frustrating to have no sense of immediate gratification from the excessively hard work over the past three years, but there was little that could be done about our ongoing angst.

═══════════════

As for Barb and me, well, I took up a new administrative post on Selkirk's, relatively close to Barb who also helped with Maria's convalescence. Over the course of several surprise trips, the Sastroamidjojo plane delivered the bulk of Ali's library to me on the island, ensuring my reading along with my delight for the next decade. Lyft, it turned out, could not bear to see those wondrous volumes put to the open market. Eventually Barb and I made our way back to New York to resume some aspect of a normal life, to the delight of the children who had been forced to spend several intercessions in their dorm rooms.

Alvarez and Maria, a perfectly matched couple, very much in love, would take us up on a standing invitation to come and visit on several occasions. Barb and I often ruminated on what fate had brought Maria. Although she would never completely recover from her massive injuries, she was a more complete person due to them. Barb and she communicated more than once a week, becoming best of friends.

═══════════════

It was a late summer day early in the morning. Barb and I had settled in after being away so long, and I was out on the back deck, this time reading an article in the recent *Science Times*, outlining the miracle of the Abzu Project.

Barb was still sleeping, so I had made the coffee in anticipation of her arrival into the kitchen. I was having a sip when I felt the familiar flutter around my head as His Excellency settled himself into the chair at the end of the table, appearing at the same moment.

"Well," I said cheerily. "Good morning. And how are we this fine day?"

"We are fine, thank you. And yourselves?"

"Fine as well."

"Then all's right with the world."

"You're in a chipper mood this morning. What gives?"

"Oh, you offend me so. You mean, I'm not normally in a good mood?"

"Not like this."

"Well, I've good reason. Not even *you* can throw a barb to puncture the aura of goodwill that surrounds me today."

"Oh, do wax poetic. And do go on."

"Oh, I say, I've missed your cheekiness as of late. Just to quell it a bit, I am here to inform you that we have some positive results from Abzu that should warm the cold cockles of that heart of yours. Mother's spin looks slower, admittedly only to a small degree, but we believe it has slowed. And because of it, we are beginning to see less seismic and volcanic activity. Borders on infinitesimal, but it's a start."

"Well, that is good news. Would you like a cup of coffee to celebrate? It's a little early for anything stronger."

"Yes, thank you. I would appreciate that."

I went into the kitchen, prepared it the way he liked it, lots of sugar and light cream, and then came back out onto the deck.

I said, "Any other news to report on that score, or is that all you know?"

"That's about it there. We are still working on the data, but it's not in the negative, so that's the good news. Even if we hold the spin at its current level, I would deem the project a success. But I do have some other news. I have hired Bashirin and Salvo to join the team. I am mightily impressed with their capabilities."

"As am I. That *is* good news. I think we all make a wonderful team."

"Couldn't agree more."

"My, you're in a good mood today. This is a real change for me."

"Well, Mother looks like she might be around for a while, so if you think in those terms, you know, of not being blown out into the stratosphere, of actually having the thought that things might go as they normally would, then why not be in a good mood? I am hoping against hope that this project could change the natural inclination of mankind's propensity to annihilate itself through a common bond, although, trust me, I'm not naive in that regard."

"Me either, being somewhat of an ultimate cynic. Say, how did you utilize the talents of the Sastroamidjojo chef?"

Lyft's eyes gleamed as he sipped his coffee. I went over to the chaise lounge to put my feet up. "I rotate him around all the projects to keep morale up. The workers love it and cheer him upon each arrival and weep upon his departures. He loves the travel, the challenge of orchestrating meals out of local cuisine, and it's done wonders for his ego. He is, as you would surmise, highly paid, but he's worth every cent. He's very happy, and we've become great friends. He can also keep his mouth shut, which perhaps is his greatest attribute. And ..." he paused for another sip, "I've some other news. I'll bet, if you think back, you can't find the one link with the potential to be weakest, where lack of discretion could have delayed the entire project and would have been a disaster for us all."

I raised my mug, the one I had ordered over the Internet with my supposed family crest on it. "Hmm. I would say all along the chain, but obviously there's something more here."

"Correct. The one area of most concern was when the treasure was found. Do you realize how difficult it must have been for Alvarez's troops to keep that find to themselves? They were in constant communication with their families and friends in the outside world via satellite e-mail, and any one of them could have proverbially spilled the beans. But there was not a peep out of any of them. We are talking about over one hundred individuals who showed unswerving loyalty and devotion to their commander, thusly to the cause, who kept this quiet." Lyft paused, taking another sip as he balanced on the back of the chair, facing me. I looked out over the backyard, realizing how much I had missed this wonderful setting and how lucky we were to live here, as the large white pines rocked in the gentle breeze overhead. He continued, "Therefore, I placed five million dollars in each individual's account, tax free, with the stipulation that they remain in the employ of the U.S. Army until their retirement, which, of course, they can do if they want at a relatively early age, as some have been in since their teens. I gave Alvarez ten million dollars with the same stipulation, guaranteeing him employment with us when he finishes out his term."

I choked on my coffee. "He'd be a great addition to the team, no doubt. Seems like a lot of money though. You sure they won't become jaded?"

"Bah," Lyft fairly spat. "Stop being so frugal. I have something special for you though. For you, I have the offer of continued employment."

"Magnanimous, at best," I intoned, sarcastically playful.

"Check your account. I'm sure you won't be disappointed."

I huffed, "You know very well I don't do this for the money. It's not where I come from."

Lyft raised his mug in salute to me. "Oh, do I know that. That's why I like to take care of you, since you probably wouldn't do it for yourself. By the way, I took the liberty of inviting Bashirin and Salvo over for dinner this evening. They'll be flying into Westchester County Airport later on in the day. I thought it would be nice to have a small celebration in view of the turn of events. Make sure you've got plenty of vodka on hand."

"We're out. I'll have to get some."

"Gallons."

"Got it."

"Tell Barb sorry about the last-minute notice, but I know she likes spur-of-the-moment events better than planning things months ahead of time, so I'm sure you two can whip something up. Now I'm off. See you all later tonight."

As he made to leave, I assured him we were up to the task and would be glad to see the dynamic duo.

"Before you go, how about Brihamm? How did that all work out?"

"Well, I visit him every so often; you know, voices in the head routine, et cetera, just to keep his train of thought headed in one direction. Once he implores the staff to listen in the hopes they can hear me as well, which, of course, they can't, then he's good for several more years of incarceration in, where else, the Jakarta Mental Hospital."

"Don't you ever feel guilty keeping him in his iron mask?"

"Not at all. He deserves it. He was the head of a major terrorist organization, and we need to ensure that he's unemployable upon his release."

He flitted into invisibility, humming one of his favorite tunes, and slowly floated out toward the wall, probably going home for a short respite before the evening's activities commenced.

I stared at the spot where he'd vanished and wondered how we were able to maintain such a unique, beneficial relationship with what was essentially an alien race, when the various human entities on Earth could not manage the same. I figured it had something to do with a common purpose, maybe more than I imagined. Yet there was more to it than that. Each had become a reciprocal protectorate. Each genuinely cared about the other and, if necessary, would make the ultimate sacrifice for the other.

And I thought of myself as highly educated. My education had just begun, promulgated by an entity that had entered my life that I could not have imagined five years ago. It was Robert Frost who said in the last stanza of his poem, "The Road Not Taken,"

> I shall be telling this with a sigh
> Somewhere ages and ages hence:
> Two roads diverged in a wood, and I—
> I took the one less traveled by,
> And that has made all the difference.

My road showed no return and, currently, no end, nor did I want it to. Lyft was an integral part of our lives now, all bound together by a common purpose about which humanity was mainly ignorant. Perhaps it was better that way, an ethereal benevolent dictatorship guarding humanity against its own irrational exigencies. I looked forward to many philosophical discussions in this regard, especially now that two other highly intelligent individuals had joined the fray.

But for now, we had a party to attend to. I went into the house to make a shopping list, content in the fact that, for now, at least, Mother Earth was to remain beneath our feet.

LaVergne, TN USA
31 August 2009
156517LV00002B/14/P